FINDING IMOGENE

A NOVEL

FINDING IMOGENE

A NOVEL

TERI CASE

BZCE PUBLISHING

WASHINGTON, D.C.

Finding Imogene is a work of fiction and the characters, places, and incidents are products of my imagination or are used fictitiously. Any similarities or resemblances to actual events, locales, or persons, living or dead, are coincidental.

BZCE Publishing, Washington, D.C.

Publication Date: January 2024

Library of Congress Control Number: 2023921422

Hardcover ISBN: 978-1-7341782-5-8

Paperback ISBN: 978-1-7341782-4-1

ebook ISBN: 978-1-7341782-6-5

Large Print ISBN: 978-1-7341782-7-2

Cover Design by Teri Case. Artwork by Canva Contributors.

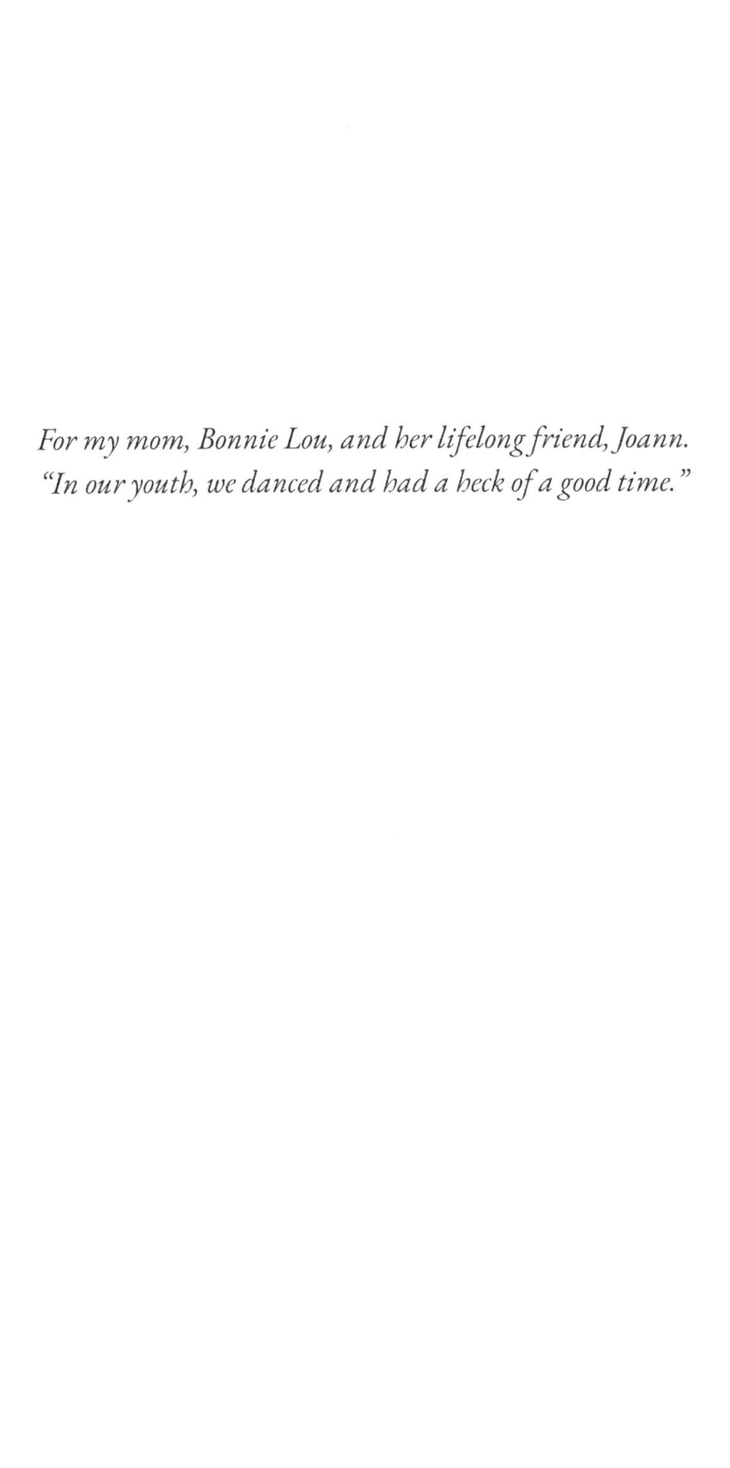

For my mom, Bonnie Lou, and her lifelong friend, Joann.
"In our youth, we danced and had a heck of a good time."

"The most powerful stories may be the ones we tell ourselves."

–Brené Brown

1

FRANCES

SPRING 2022

Frances Jerome dashed out of her tidy accounting office at five o'clock on the dot. Her family was coming over for dinner for the first time in weeks, and if the gray skies forming outside her office window were any indication, the brined chicken she planned to roast would be served later than promised. Nothing bothered her more than outside forces monkeying with her commitments.

Speaking of which . . .

"I'll be late tomorrow," she said as she passed her assistant.

"You? I'll believe it when I see it."

"I'll be here by ten at the latest." The sooner she could get tomorrow morning over with, the better.

The Bay Area skies opened, unleashing feral cats and dogs just as she slipped into her silver Audi. Her hydrangeas could use the rain, and the earthy scent the moisture produced had always been one of her favorite smells. Unfortunately, it seemed that any change in San Francisco's weather affected rush-hour traffic. The warm roads would be slick due to a dangerous combination of water and built-up residue of oils, rubber, and dirt.

Thank goodness for all-wheel drive.

Once she settled her belongings on the pristine passenger-side floor, she grabbed her phone to group text the twins:

Drive carefully.

Jean and Art might be twenty-seven going on twenty-eight, but keeping them safe was one mom-hat she'd never take off, no matter how many times they asked her to burn it.

She turned on the car and blasted the defroster to clear the windshield. Then she inserted her seat belt, gratified by the resounding click.

Art responded first:

Sorry. Working late. Raincheck? Pun intended.

No, no, no. Surely, he'd known earlier that he'd have to work late.

She responded:

When were you going to tell me?
Come for dessert. We'll wait for you.

Except within two seconds, the other part of *we*, her daughter, jumped ship too:

> Better for us as well. Let's reschedule.
> No worries.

No worries? Which was more offensive: the last-minute cancellations or that they were trying to manage her reaction with a joke and platitude? As if they'd been the ones wronged. She'd be eating chicken alone for a week!

She took a deep breath and smoothed a fingertip over the two worry lines between her brows. That pesky feeling that the older her children grew, the more they avoided her wormed its way through her gut. They probably never canceled on their funny and outgoing father.

The windshield wipers switched into high gear against the deluge of rain, and she tapped her left foot to the rhythm.

She *had* raised Art to work hard, and Jean *did* have a three-year-old. Of course, now Jean would have to cook dinner and clean up after her family tonight rather than relax and enjoy the one Frances would make.

Well, she couldn't sit here all night feeling sorry for herself. Her rescue parrot, Bonnie Bell, still expected her.

Once she pulled into rush-hour traffic, it didn't take long for someone in a zippy MINI to start riding her bumper.

Her speedometer confirmed she was going the speed limit.

"Back off, buster, before you hurt someone." She gently tapped her brake to warn him. She was doing him—and everyone—a favor. "If you don't like my driving, take a different way to whatever it is that's so, so, so important."

Mr. Impatient was still up to no good as she neared an area in her neighborhood with heavy pedestrian traffic. A woman waited in the downpour to cross the street with her little girl, who was wearing a yellow rain jacket and red galoshes. Jean and Art had red galoshes when they were young. *"Red stands out in the dark,"* she'd said when they complained about their matching gear.

Frances flashed her lights at the woman and her child. "Go ahead. I'll protect you from the bozo behind me."

In her rearview mirror, she saw the jerk throw up his hands.

A couple reached the street before she could inch forward, so she kept her foot on the brake. If necessary, she'd protect pedestrians from this driver all night. What else did she have to do except talk to her bird? She cracked her window a smidge and inhaled the petrichor.

The male pedestrian carried a shared umbrella at an angle, protecting them both from the showery headwind. Now, there was a considerate man.

The short blonde laughed and tilted her rosy-cheeked head to smile at him. The gentleman's hand cupped and squeezed her shoulder affectionately. As they passed before Frances's car, he dipped for a kiss, and his curly brown hair and round face came into view.

Frances's eyes just about popped from her head, and she gasped with indignation. Her hands involuntarily squeezed the wheel as she leaned forward to stare through the windshield.

Art!

He'd lied. Worse, he had broken one of her cardinal rules: Always be where you say you'll be. What if something had happened to him? What if he'd disappeared, or an earthquake struck? Everyone would have looked in the wrong place, if at all. And who was the woman?

Decades of motherhood and the urge to teach her son to own his actions had her reaching for her horn with unconscious volition.

Yet, she hesitated. Her fingers curled, the cold tips turning into her sweaty palm.

Why had he lied to her?

Her heart hurt and tears pooled in her eyes.

It was obvious, wasn't it? Her son didn't want to see her. Didn't want to spend time with her. She was one of those moms whose kids had a life that didn't include her anymore, and if she embarrassed him in front of this woman, well, she could forget seeing him anytime soon.

After swiping at the damp shadows under her eyes, her hand settled on the steering wheel, determined to turn the other cheek.

Unfortunately, her impatient tailgater had reached his limit and let it be known.

HONK!

Her son's head swiveled to glare, and that was when he saw her.

If she were him, she'd call her immediately to explain

and apologize, or maybe use body language to show how crappy she felt for the deception, but he did neither.

Other than a single-word expletive that Frances could only imagine, her son faced forward, and with a strong hand spread protectively against the woman's back, rushed away.

DARKNESS GREETED Frances as she punched in the keyless code and opened the door of her house on Sea Cliff Avenue. Even her idol Martha Stewart's coconut and lemongrass scents she infused her home with didn't work their usual calming magic.

She couldn't shake the image of her son rushing his companion away as if Frances would hop from the car in the pouring rain and chase them with a machete. What had she ever done to deserve such a reaction to *his* lie?

Door locked? Check.

"Uh-oh," Bonnie Bell said, squawking from the living room. "Uh-oh."

"It's okay, Bonnie Bell. It's me, Frances," she said loud enough for the bird to hear but not enough to scare her.

"Fr-AN-siss. Fr-AN-siss."

"I'll be there in a minute."

Bonnie Bell whistled.

The bright lights reflected off the polished sheen of the entryway's dark mahogany floors as she exchanged her

Aerosoles for the house slippers waiting on the shoe mat. Hers were the only pair with the inner lining flattened due to wear. At this rate, her guest sets would last for an eternity.

Using the toe of one shearling moccasin, she lined the others up against the wall. Once again, her cleaning service hadn't put things back the way she left them, but her cleaner had an eye for dust bunnies, a way with Bonnie Bell, and was a single mother. So, Frances was loath to replace her. Marching through the house, she arranged the layered sofa pillows so that the largest were in the back, the medium-sized ones in front.

There. Much better.

The family photos were next. Her actions slowed as she reached her favorite picture of Jean and Art when they were five.

Back then, they couldn't get enough of her. She could barely go to the bathroom alone.

They'd smiled wide for the photographer. It was hard to imagine that only a handful of years later, they'd grown to hate having their pictures taken, especially Jean. *"You take one almost every day,"* Jean had complained. Frances had explained, again, *"It's important to always have a recent shot. Just in case. Someday, when you're a mother, you'll understand."*

The voice mail indicator flashed. She hit *Play*, knowing full well the only people who called her home line were George and telemarketers. She scrolled through the pitches and scams, waiting to hear George's voice.

"Hi Frances, just your old dad here calling to say hello and that I miss you."

Her hand caressed the cradle, wishing the reality of their relationship was anything other than what it was and that she could call and invite him to dinner.

Shoving her disappointment aside so the bird wouldn't react to her mood, she said, "Hello, Bonnie Bell."

"Hello."

When Frances reached the cage, she unlatched the door, stepping back as always to let the parrot decide if and when she'd leave her haven. "The bad news is dinner's been canceled, but the good news is you can come out if you want, pretty bird."

"Ugly bird," Bonnie Bell said.

"Pretty bird," Frances reiterated despite Bonnie Bell's featherless torso. The vet had explained that feather-picking was a sign of stress and poor nutrition. If, by some miracle, Frances ever crossed paths with the conure's first owners, she'd blast them for their cruelty.

"Guess what time it is?" Opening the drawer of the living room credenza, Frances pulled out the remote. The six o'clock news kicked off, filling the quiet space with the raucous beat of typewriters, telegraphs, and brass horns that Bonnie Bell enjoyed humming along with while bobbing her head. The first time the bird had reacted to the cinematic tune, Frances had laughed with relief. Other than learning Frances's name, the intro music was the first sound Bonnie Bell had added to her repertoire since she and Frances found each other six months ago. Or, she should say, when Bonnie Bell found her.

Frances had been pruning in her small backyard when the scraggly-looking green and red conure landed on her shoulder. Startled and convinced the parrot was diseased and from San Francisco's feral pandemonium, Frances had ducked and flicked away the bird.

But it had promptly returned to her shoulder.

One more shoo and the parrot weakly landed atop a bonsai and said, "Peekaboo."

"Hm. You're a pet." Arms hanging limply at her sides, she asked, "Now, what am I supposed to do with you? I don't like birds."

One overwhelmed bird shelter and a vet visit later, Frances found herself leaving a pet store with a birdcage and bags brimming with bird books, food, and toys.

"You're only staying until the rescue shelter finds you a new home. Got it? But until then, I'll call you"—she stroked her chin, recalling the bright green and red wrapper of watermelon Bonne Bell Lip Smackers from her youth—"Bonne Bell. But I'll spell it with an I and E. I don't want your future owner to mispronounce your name and confuse you."

With Bonnie Bell now climbing atop the cage happily, Frances walked across the open-plan home. Knocking out the walls and reconfiguring the ground floor had been the first project she and her ex-husband had tackled when they bought the house more than twenty-six years before. It had suited her to see her children from the kitchen, and the large bay windows brought the outdoors in. Even now, she could see her hydrangeas and small bonsai garden brighten in the rain and hear the waves hit Baker Beach.

With the oven on preheat, she took a deep breath before pouring her daily allowance of five ounces of Cabernet Sauvignon and taking a sip. She frowned at the dining table she'd set for five that morning to save time.

"Woo hoo," the meteorologist cheered as he danced onto the screen. "We've had more rain today than we have in eleven months. And what can you expect for the rest of the night?"

"Lots of rain and chicken," Frances mumbled as she cleared all but one of the table settings.

"And now," the anchor said, "let's look at today's—"

An alarming tempo startled her as *BREAKING NEWS* flashed across the screen, replacing her familiar hosts.

"Uh-oh," Bonnie Bell said.

"You're safe." Frances made kissing sounds to further soothe the bird.

Foghorns from the bay wailed, adding to the ominous alert as Frances moved to the sofa and placed her wineglass on a coaster.

Anchor David Muir from *ABC World News Tonight* filled the room. "Now, an update that you won't believe. Twelve years after Emily Ann Garcia disappeared while walking home from school in Sparks, Nevada, she's been found alive. She wasn't alone. With her was Veronica Johansson, missing since 2010."

Frances gasped and covered her mouth with her fingertips. "Alive? This entire time?"

Emily Ann's and Veronica's last high school portraits appeared on the screen. The nation must have seen the photos a thousand times over the past decade.

Jumping up from the sofa, Frances grabbed her phone to text Jean:

ABC News. Now.

The cell phone bounced against her couch cushion as she exchanged it for her remote to increase the volume.

"Dozens of people have gathered outside the Vista neighborhood house where they were held hostage. News source, Allison Bales, is live at the scene. Allison, what can you tell us?"

Frances leaned forward, resting her elbows on her knees and her cheeks in her shaking hands.

Allison motioned over her shoulder to a two-story house, heavily guarded by police and surrounded by neighbors and strangers holding hands and hugging. Medics and cops ran in and out of the front doorway. A black steel security door and a faded red door had been torn from their hinges and were leaning against a porch railing.

"Less than two hours ago, Sparks Police responded to Emily Ann's call for help as she escaped and ran to a neighbor's house. When they arrived, officers also found Veronica Johansson. Emily Ann and Veronica were held hostage in this house in conditions that one officer has described as barbaric."

As the camera zoomed in on two policemen standing to the side of the house clutching one another and crying, Frances trembled, remembering long ago when an officer had sat beside her to take her statement.

"The police are looking for Michael Fenn, the long-term employee of Vista Hasty Stop convenience station, as a person of interest. Anyone with information should call 9-1-1 immediately."

Frances scowled when a photo appeared of a middle-aged, clean-cut man with dark brown hair, brown eyes, and a friendly smile. After leaving it enlarged for enough time to allow viewers to memorize his face, the headshot shrank and slid to the edge of the screen, overlapping a map of Sparks. Pinpoints identified five critical locations within walking distance from each other: the store, high school, the last location each girl had been seen, and the house of horrors where they'd been held.

With an unsteady breath, Frances took a gulp of her wine, hoping she wouldn't regret it later. She'd been glued to the television when both girls went missing and had warned Jean and Art, who were teens at the time, "It's someone they know. It's someone they shouldn't have trusted, but no one taught them better, not the way I've taught you."

With an eye roll, Jean had said, "How would you know? *Gah.* Why do you make us watch this depressing stuff? It freaks me out. Our friends' parents don't do this."

But Frances never said it was because of Imogene.

A memory of her childhood friend and Imogene's toothless grin made her heart ache.

The reporter held up her mic. "Officer, I'm told you and your partner were the first on the scene. What do you think has kept them hanging on?"

Seemingly pulling from his years of hard-earned experience to appear stoic, the officer spoke with strength and clarity. "They were allowed to watch the news, so, now and then, they saw for themselves that their families were still looking for them. They said as long as their families didn't give up, they couldn't either."

Deflated, Frances's shoulders dropped, and she leaned against the gray upholstered sofa arm for support. The past couldn't be changed. She'd been a child when Imogene disappeared. What more could she have done?

Not forgotten her. Not given up hope.

The reporter touched her ear and straightened. "They're coming out."

The crowd silenced as four police officers filed out of the gloomy doorway as if they were sentinels. Next, medics rolled out two gurneys, guiding them down the porch stairs as if they were handling fragile crystal.

The crowd's silence seemed reverent. Unable to resist the pull, Frances stood and walked toward the television as if she were on the street with them.

One of the blankets shifted as the gurneys neared the ambulances, and a pale, skinny hand slowly poked free to wave.

People erupted with cries of love and encouragement.

Frances's breath shuddered and tears ran down her face.

David Muir said, "Have we heard anything from the families?"

Frances hugged herself, unable to back away.

Nodding, the reporter lifted a note. "We can't wait to hold our baby, Emily Ann. For too long, we've been haunted by the *what ifs*, carrying guilt for what we might have done differently to avoid her disappearance or to find her sooner. As a family, we will now turn the page, begin a new chapter, and move on together."

What if . . .

What if Frances could find Imogene now? What if she could finally forgive herself and fulfill her promise to her childhood friend? What if the past stopped haunting her?

What would it feel like to finally turn the page?

CHIRP, CHIRP, CHIRP.

After giving Bonnie Bell a treat, Frances climbed the stairs to the guest room and kneeled to look beneath the bed. It was illogical to worry the box may have disappeared, yet she sighed with relief when she recognized her youthful writing in the shadows. *"Confidential. BEWARE!"* A spatter of Smurf stickers undermined the threat.

The box was the only one she stored in her home. Clutter was simply that, clutter, no matter how much Jean liked to pretend it was homey. If something needed boxing up, it didn't serve a purpose and should be tossed or given away.

But this box had a purpose and had been waiting forty-three years for the right time.

What if the right time was now?

Goose bumps rose along her arms and neck as the cardboard slid easily into the light. Resting back on her heels, she took a deep breath to calm her rioting nerves. The last time she'd lifted the lid, her hopes had been dashed, and the depression that had followed lasted until her children were born.

She set the dusty lid aside and sorted through the contents until she found the diary with the heart-shaped brass lock she'd written in when Imogene first went missing.

Despite its age, the clasp opened easily, and she thumbed through the pages. Her chest tightened as she recognized her young handwriting and the frightening details that were never meant for a little girl's diary.

2

JEAN

SPRING 2022

Shane rushed into their house. "Sorry I'm late. New customer. I'll change in a jiffy, and we can head to your mother's."

Jean's eyes were glued to the hell-evision. *Gah.* Her mother had been right.

Loosening his tie and unbuttoning the cuffs of his shirt, her husband squeezed between her and the TV and raised one brow. "Is that what you're wearing? We both know sweats won't go over well with Frances."

Activewear, not sweats.

"And you never watch the news, much less in front of Lexi. Your rule, by the way." He pointed to their daughter playing five feet away, as if Jean didn't know where to find her own child.

Why did he think she was standing close to the screen with the volume as low as possible? "I know," she said, stepping around him, remote in hand. "But this is different."

"Apparently. What's going on?"

In a hushed tone, she said, "They found Emily Ann Garcia and Veronica Johansson. Together. A man who runs a store near the high school has been holding them hostage this entire time."

Shane grimaced. "Lexi." He turned, kneeled next to his daughter, and kissed her head. "Why don't you take your toys to your room now? We need to get ready for dinner."

"Okay!"

As soon as she was gone, Shane said, "Wow."

"Right? My mother will want to say, 'I told you so.'"

"Maybe she isn't watching."

Jean snorted. "Please. She texted me to turn it on."

"And you did exactly what she said." He closed his eyes and groaned. "You're not supposed to feed the bad-news bear. Doctor's orders."

Her brows rose, and her shoulders shrugged. "You know what they say—old habits shoved down your throat die hard."

Shane took a deep breath. "Dinner should be *fun*. On a positive note, Dr. Pfeiffer would say this is a good opportunity to establish a boundary with your mom and say you don't want to discuss the kidnappings with her."

Yes, their marriage counselor had a lot to say, especially when it came to Jean.

"We're in luck. Dinner's been called off. And before you ask, it was Art's doing." *Thank you, Art.*

"Why?" His eyes narrowed.

"He said he had to work late, but twenty bucks says

he's met someone." He'd called to warn her he was going to ax dinner. Not one to ignore a get-out-of-jail-free card, Jean didn't pry. She hit power on the remote. "I can't watch anymore. I won't be able to sleep. I feel like a kid again, dreading danger around every corner."

"You know what I meant. Why does it matter if Art can't go? Why aren't we still going?"

If Guilty Red were a color, she imagined her cheeks were turning the hue now. "I can't handle her without Art. You know that."

"What the flamingo, Jean? I'd be there. I can help."

No, he couldn't. "It's done. And, 'what the flamingo'? Please swear properly. Only I can hear you." When she'd met him, he'd been edgy and fun. She was all for not filling Lexi's head with bad words, but now his vocabulary was church-ready 24/7.

"Will it be rescheduled? Or will you invite her here?" He looked skeptical as he surveyed the room. They'd moved into the house three months ago, but Jean's unpacking method was more of a let's-open-boxes-until-we-find-what-we're-looking-for approach.

"No way! She'd be critical and start organizing everything. Do you want our cupboards alphabetized?"

He scratched his head. "Maybe. It would be better than this, right?"

"No."

"What about Dr. Pfeiffer's suggestion that you find a project with Frances that will help you spend time getting to know each other at a different level?"

"My mother telling me how I should live is the only

level when it comes to her." *Gah*. She wished Art were here. No one else, except maybe her father, understood how overbearing and suffocating her mother could be. She would take one look at her house and say, "*Your slovenliness is a sign of poor self-worth, a lack of confidence, and it's an invitation for someone to take advantage of you.*" No matter how much she had wanted to, she could never please her mom, and her never-ending negativity wasn't welcome in Jean's Sunset District home. Privacy and distance were the reasons they had moved to the opposite side of the Golden Gate Park from her mother.

The doorbell emphasized the end of the conversation. "That's pizza."

"Pizza? Again?" Shane moaned as he trudged behind her.

Once upon a time, they'd lived on pizza and red wine, and they had loved every moment of it. Back in the kitchen, she tried to pretend she didn't hear his disappointed tone. "I'll tackle the kitchen this week." She'd promise anything if it meant she wouldn't have to discuss this third-to-worst issue of theirs ever again.

"But it's been months. *How* will you get it done *this* week?" Shane said.

"Thanks, *Mom*."

"That's not fair, honey."

"My priority is Lexi, and she's a handful some days. I'm raising a human being."

He nodded. "That's why I said we should have the movers unpack for us, but you insisted you wanted to do it yourself so you could find everything later."

Jean *had* insisted, and she knew she wasn't being entirely fair, but dammit, he went off to work every morning and had no idea how much time and energy went into motherhood. Every day felt new, full of unexpected lessons. And mistakes. Lots and lots of mistakes. Sometimes, she felt like the only thing she was getting right was how she cuddled with Lexi and told her ten things she loved about her. Every morning, she squeezed her baby tight and put her heart and soul into her words.

Shane turned to retrieve their daughter but paused. "Maybe it's time to talk about preschool again."

Crap! She'd handed him an excuse to bring up their second-to-worst issue. She was the one who had sworn she wanted to be a stay-at-home mom, and preschool felt like a forfeiture.

She had wanted to be good at something and to do right by her family. Something better than her mom had. And motherhood should have been the sure thing.

LIKE CLOCKWORK, Shane's warm body turned to spoon Jean the following morning. She slipped out of bed before he shed his sleep-induced brain fog and wanted to do more than snuggle.

Tiptoeing to the kitchen, she inhaled the scent of the coffee brewing thanks to a timer. The next twenty minutes of the morning were usually the only ones she had to herself, and she relished them. During this time, she could look around the house and believe she could put her life into some semblance of order and conquer the day.

Keeping the lights dim, she poured a cup and sat down at the kitchen table to do abso- frigging-lutely nothing.

Too bad her vibrating phone on the kitchen counter intruded on her tranquility like an earthquake. She grabbed it before it reverberated the entire household awake. The texting transgressor was Art.

Kumquat.

When they were younger, their mother had made them pick a safe word. "It's a word you'll use, a code, to let me know if you're in danger but need to be sneaky about it. But don't pick a food or animal." Fortunately, *piccolo* was never necessary.

However, *kumquat* was their mama-drama-Mayday alert and had been used more times than Jean could count.

She dialed his number and began to whisper once he answered. "What did you do besides cancel dinner?"

"She saw me on her drive home. I was on my way to eat."

"So? You still need to eat when you work late."

"I wasn't alone."

"Coworkers eat too." She slurped her coffee. If he was dating someone, it was up to him when he'd tell her. Unlike their mother, she respected her brother's privacy.

"It was someone I've been seeing. Someone I want to keep seeing."

There was no need to say more or ask why he hadn't invited this person to dinner instead. Their mother would have produced a confidentiality agreement and run a background check. The first time Shane had met her mom, he'd said, "That was intense. Do I need my lawyer?"

"Mom's going to ice you out for sure," Jean told her brother.

"You need to test the waters for me."

Gah. She let her head tilt back. "I have enough problems of my own right now, bro."

"Pretty please."

"If I call her, she'll bug me about seeing the house. Again."

"You *still* aren't unpacked?"

"What's with you and Shane? You don't have kids; what would you know? Give me a break. Not to mention, I'll have to hear all about the kidnappings."

"Oh no. Which ones?"

"They found Emily Ann Garcia and Veronica Johansson. Same perp, and he worked at the convenience store by the school."

"No shit? Oh . . . shit."

Finally, an adult who swore.

"That's wonderful they were found. But, yeah, Mom's going to want a medal."

"I know," Jean said. "She texted me last night, just like the good old days, well, except for the text. Can you imagine if she could have texted us then too?"

"Thank technology for small favors," Art said.

"What's in it for me if I do this? BTW, go big or go home."

"Tell you what," Art began his negotiation, "if you make contact today, I don't care how, chip away the edges, manage her . . . I'll come over after work tonight and unpack for you. I'll even bring pizza."

Yes! He wouldn't talk the entire time, and they'd use their twin telepathy to put stuff away that she'd easily find later. "This sounds too good to be true. Kitchen is first. Shane will be ecstatic. What about your girlfriend, though?"

"She's out of town for a few days."

"I'll call Mother this morning. And bring anything except pizza."

Ten minutes later, Jean crawled into Lexi's bed and curled her body around her daughter's tiny one, inhaling against her sleepy head as if Lexi were oxygen itself. "Good morning, sweetie. Rise and shine."

Once awake, Lexi rested her tiny palm against Jean's hand as Jean began to count with her fingers. "One. I love your kind heart and brave spirit. Two. I love how you laugh with your entire body. Three . . ."

3

FRANCES

SPRING 2022

Frances stirred her coffee—the first of many cups to come, she was certain. Thanks to her sleepless night and, therefore, early morning, she'd be moving slower than a sloth by this afternoon.

The foghorns sounded from behind. Her back faced the bay window as she sat at the table, hoping not to disturb Bonnie Bell before sunrise. To date, the most controversial choice Frances had made for Bonnie Bell was to leave the birdcage uncovered at night. The internet was flooded with fierce opinions from parrot owners about routines and whether to cover or not to cover the cage. However, the most helpful post had been one that suggested to opt for whichever way caused the parrot the least stress. Covered up, Bonnie Bell had made her discontent clear by repeating, "Uh-oh."

If only someone or something could communicate or send a clear sign on whether Frances should uncover the past.

Dazed, she stared at her diary on the table before her. The painful details were inside, masked by a vinyl cover embellished with rainbows and clouds. All the information she would need to try to find Imogene, if she dared, was in there.

Last night, she crawled into bed and read some of her entries. Some pages were skipped—after all these years, the pain in her words was still too fresh, the guilt overwhelming.

Would her failings as a friend ever stop?

Maybe with the truth and closure.

But the truth could have a cost. She'd always known this, and it had stood in her way. Except she wasn't nine and afraid to be torn away from her parents anymore. She wasn't twenty-five and pregnant. Was now the time to face the facts, damn the risk to George or the heartache the truth might cause her children? There was always the minuscule hope that Frances was wrong. Either way, the truth would set her free, allow her to forgive herself, and help find justice for Imogene.

What was the harm in a preliminary search on her own? As she looked about her empty home, it was clear that no one in her life would even know she was searching unless she told them. Whatever she first discovered would be for her eyes, her ears, her heart, and her curiosity alone. One step or answer at a time.

But where to begin?

Like the detectives in the unsolved crime shows she watched, she could set up a crime board. Smack dab in the middle of her living room if she wanted. With a whiteboard or corkboard, she could use the diary to outline the timeline of Imogene's disappearance. Yes, that would be a harmless start.

WHEN FRANCES's cell phone rang three hours later, she jerked and turned her crime board shopping list face down on the table as if caught doing something naughty.

"Jean," she said after she hit the speaker button.

"Hi, Mom. How about Lexi and I drop off lunch for you today?"

Drop off, not join.

Her daughter had chosen her words carefully, as always. Once Jean had hit puberty, she had started adding emphasis to word choice, especially when it came to discussions with her mother. They'd been dissecting or arguing over semantics *ad nauseam* ever since. Whenever Jean had earned a C on a class assignment that she should have easily aced and Frances accused her of failing or of not doing her best, Jean had always fired back, "An F is a fail. Maybe I wanted a C."

More than once, Jean had gotten detention at school for nitpicking a teacher's word choice too. Her daughter should have been a lawyer.

"Unfortunately, I'm packing a *chicken* sandwich. And I have an appointment this morning before I head to the office. However, if you'd like to come over for dinner tonight for leftover chicken that would be wonderful. Six-thirty?"

"Um . . . can't. We have, um, plans tonight."

"Ones you intend to keep, apparently. What do I have to do to get you to come over?" *Especially since the divorce.* "Pay you? Die?"

"Mother! Don't say things like that. We're adults. We have lives. Things come up."

Frances rolled her eyes. "Why didn't Art trust me enough to ask if he could bring his lady friend?"

Jean sighed and said, "Ask Art, but probably because you would have bagged her fork for DNA."

"That's an exaggeration."

"Is it?"

It had never been enough of a reason for her children when she explained she was protective of them because she loved them. Maybe they'd understand if they knew about Imogene.

What if she told them?

No. She couldn't. Not yet. They wouldn't understand why she hadn't before, and Frances wasn't prepared to explain.

She smoothed her hand over the diary before her.

"When do I get to see your new place?"

"It's not ready. My cozy clutter would drive you bananas."

Hmph. Frances had invested in enough property over the years to appreciate what cozy clutter implied: *unorganized, messy, needs work*. Maybe Jean should have been a realtor. "I could help you at night, you know."

"We'd end up arguing. You know that."

"Since you won't even give me the address, I guess I'll have to wait until you want to invite your poor mother over. Has your dad seen it?"

"Mom . . ."

But Frances didn't truly want to know so she changed the subject. The divorce had been her decision, after all. "Did you watch the news?"

There was a long pause, and her daughter may have mumbled something about Art. "Yes. You mentioned an appointment. What kind of appointment? It's not like you to go into the office late."

Jean didn't want to discuss the rescued girls, obviously. And ironically, Frances didn't want to discuss her appointment. "It's nothing, Jean. I've got to go now." She hung up, cutting off Jean's protest.

Before heading upstairs to shower, she spoke to Bonnie Bell while the bird pecked at her breakfast and couldn't reject Frances's praise. "Good morning, pretty bird."

Let's get this over with.

With her purse in the crook of her arm, Frances took a deep breath and pushed open the glass door of the laboratory, her clear-polished nails clattering against the pane.

Several people were spread about the waiting area,

some watching an overhead monitor listing the patients who were next. Others stared at their phones, despite the signs in the room asking patrons not to use them. The only person who noticed Frances's arrival was a darling girl around five with braided brown hair who waved at her with her baby doll's rubber hand.

Instead of responding, Frances shook her head and glared about the room, wondering which irresponsible adult the child belonged to.

Don't you people watch the news? A stranger could snatch the girl in a heartbeat.

After checking in at the digital kiosk, she walked briskly to the chair nearest the exit where the child played.

She held her purse tight against her chest; one corner of her diary jabbed at her left breast through the canvas. The seven-by-five-inch journal weighed less than a pound, yet she felt like she'd been hauling around an extra lifetime all morning. Was it irrational that she was afraid to let it out of her sight now that she'd cracked it open?

"I'm Mandy. What's your name?" The girl climbed into the chair next to Frances.

Frances looked fixedly forward.

Instead of taking the hint, Mandy climbed to her knees in the chair and leaned toward Frances. "Are you afraid of needles?"

Truth was, Frances hated needles. She'd had enough draws and infusions during her childhood to last her a lifetime, but instead, she said, "I'm a stranger. Not your friend."

"It's okay. It won't hurt long."

"Which of these adults is yours?"

Mandy pointed toward a woman slumped in a chair, about Jean and Art's age, bent over her phone, oblivious to the fact that her child could be absconded at any second.

"Mama's findin' friends on Facebook."

Hmph. Finding friends? More like asking for identity theft; Facebook was a privacy forfeiture nightmare.

But there was that *what if* again.

What if she used Facebook briefly to see if Imogene's name came up? It was an optimistic and easy start, wasn't it? If the careless mother could figure out how to find someone, Frances could too.

An inner door opened, and when Mandy's name was called, she ran across the lobby toward the technician. She turned to wave goodbye to Frances and smiled. A missing tooth reminded her of Imogene's innocent grin.

Five minutes later, it was Frances's turn. She took a deep breath and followed the lab tech into a room, taking a seat in the phlebotomy chair.

"You can put your purse over here." The technician pointed.

"No, I'll leave it right here where I can see it."

"Afraid it's going to walk away?"

"Precious cargo," Frances said.

"Please confirm this is your name and date of birth on the blood collection tubes."

"Five tubes?" Frances shook her head. "That seems

excessive. Are you sure that's correct?" With her medical history, she hadn't been surprised when Dr. Cochran wanted to play it safe and check her blood work after she'd complained of unusual body aches and lethargy. But, when she expected her symptoms had more to do with the extended tax season or possibly the beginning of menopause, the number of multicolored tubes was unsettling.

Straight-faced, the woman said, "Would you like to read the doctor's orders?"

"Yes, I would." Phlebotomists weren't inhuman.

"Then first, confirm this is your name and date of birth, please."

With a sharp nod, Frances extended her hand for the orders.

Seconds later, she handed them back, her palms growing sweatier than a chilled bottle of water on a hot summer day. "You're right. Sorry." Next time she had a headache, she'd think twice about calling her doctor.

As the phlebotomist gave her instructions to extend her right arm and pump her fist, Frances looked in the opposite direction. "I've probably been poked more in my life than you've ever poked. Sadly, I've had my share of missed veins too."

Patting her vein, the lab tech said, "My boss always says that women will forget the pain of childbirth time and again but never a bad blood draw. Sweetie, don't hold on to your past experiences. Let go, let be, and let me. I'm going to take good care of you."

God, how she'd love to let go of the past where the

pain began. Her fears for Imogene. Her fears of the truth about George. Her shame. Her regrets.

Was this the sign she'd been waiting for? This innocuous message delivered by a phlebotomist?

She flinched as the needle missed the vein.

4

FRANNIE

LATE FALL 1975

Frannie's dad had told her he wished he could take the chemo for her, but she wouldn't wish her crying stomach on anyone, not even the bully who lived down the street from her South San Francisco home and made fun of her for being six years old and using training wheels. The first time he'd teased her, her dad had said, "He's teasing you because he thinks you're cute, mark my words."

"That makes no sense." When she got better, she would practice riding her bike without training wheels and run the boy over.

Her first room at the children's hospital was at the end of a long hall, next to the nurses' station—to "calm her mother's nerves." Her dad was the hospital administrator, and he'd said, "I pulled some strings to get this room." Through droopy eyelids that she squeezed closed whenever a ball of sick rolled through her tummy,

Frannie spotted the skinny girl walking down the hall toward her room.

Now's my chance.

Even though moving made her stomach pitch like Mom and Dad's fishing boat on the bay, she pushed herself up and scooted over on her hospital bed, one inch at a time, to make room for the girl to sit, just in case she made it all the way. Mom was in the bathroom—for once, not standing guard.

She might make her first friend.

Except, she didn't know how to make a friend because instead of letting her go to a school like other kids, Mom taught her at home.

When her mom and the nurse had pushed her wheelchair past rooms over the last three days, she'd seen kids sitting on each other's beds, playing together. In homeschool, Mom made her imagine a picture and add it to her memory jar for new words or ideas. Frannie didn't hesitate to add the image of kids piled onto her bed to her memory jar: *share your bed to make friends.*

As the girl reached her doorway, Frannie patted the empty spot beside her.

Please don't give up, little girl, when Mom comes back.

Mom worried about everyone's germs regardless of Dad's reassurance. One look from her and the other children scattered, like the Munchkins in Munchkinland did when the Wicked Witch of the West appeared. Whenever another kid got close enough to say hello, Mom turned them away. "Her immune system is too weak to play, sweetie."

When Frannie had complained to her dad, he'd said, "Mother knows best. She's the boss of me too." Then he winked, which always made Frannie laugh. Dad was a big man who ran the entire hospital, but he always said Mom could boss him around like "the best nurse in town."

Frannie self-consciously brushed her bangs off her sweaty forehead. She'd been too sick from the chemo to let Mom comb her hair and add her favorite gold barrettes. But when she pulled her hand away, some of her bangs came with it.

Uh-oh. My hair.

Mom always said it would be okay when it fell out and that it would grow back. But today was too soon.

Don't cry, Frannie. She curled her fist on top of her warm blanket to hide the loose hairs. After all, the other girl had already lost her hair—Frannie knew what that pink crochet hat meant. She licked the top of her mouth where her front tooth used to be then smiled at the girl.

Don't lisp.

The girl was now inside her room, and Mom was nowhere in sight.

"Hi, I'm Imogene," she said as she sat on the bed—*it worked!*—and removed her pink hat with a purple flower stitched into the side. Ginger fuzz and freckles covered her pale head.

Over Imogene's shoulder, Frannie saw her mom step out of the bathroom down the hall. She frowned and raced toward them.

Nurse Penny appeared and blocked Mom at the door,

resting her plump hand on Mom's shoulder, which seemed to grow thinner every day "from stress."

"Oh, honey. Wait," Nurse Penny said. Sometimes, her mom let Nurse Penny be the boss, and this was one of those times.

"Oh, honey," Imogene said, mimicking Nurse Penny's Southern accent. She took Frannie's hand and swept the hairs away. They floated in the air like the dandelions Frannie liked to blow in her backyard.

"It will grow back," Imogene said. "When mine comes back, I'm going to wear it like Ginger from *Gilligan's Island*."

Frannie covered her mouth and giggled. "But she's grown up."

"Here." Imogene handed her the crochet hat. "It will look pretty on you."

Frannie looked to her mom for approval. It was one thing to sit close to another kid's germs, but she'd get in big trouble if she put the hat on without permission.

Nurse Penny squeezed Mom's shoulder again. "It will be okay."

Her mom frowned and bit her lip as if she was ready to say *no,* but she nodded.

As soon as Frannie got the nod, she smiled and took the hat. "I'm Frannie. Thank you. It's pretty."

"The flower goes on the left side for luck." Imogene moved closer and helped Frannie adjust the hat. Her blue eyes sparkled.

"Why is the left side for luck?"

Imogene shrugged. "Lucky Left. That's what Pops says about rolling dice."

Something else for her memory jar.

"What kind do you have?" Imogene asked.

Frannie touched the flower on her hat, wishing she had something to give Imogene in return. "Leukemia," she whispered, hoping her mom wouldn't hear her. Whenever someone said the L-word, Mom started crying.

"Me too," Imogene said. "How old are you?"

"I turned six in September."

"No kidding? I turned six in October. Hey, do you want to be my best friend?"

"Yes, please."

"Do you want to go to *Oliver!* with me Tuesday?"

Frannie wrinkled her nose. "What's *Oliver!*?"

Imogene's jaw dropped. "What's *Oliver!*? Only the best musical ever." She slid off the bed, and Frannie reached for her, afraid she'd lost her chance to keep a friend.

Stupid mistake.

But Imogene didn't leave. She danced and sang the song "Consider Yourself" from the musical about making a home together and becoming best friends forever.

Frannie laughed so hard she got dizzy and fell back on the pillow. But she wasn't feeling sick anymore; her new friend was magical.

Imogene's warm breath brushed Frannie's face like sunshine as she sat next to her again, even closer this time. "That's Artful Dodger's song. He's my favorite. I've seen it three times. Tuesday is movie night here. They have a film projector and popcorn."

"Frannie, who's your friend?" her mom asked, escaping Nurse Penny's hold.

"Imogene, this is my mother, Sally Jerome." Her mom would be proud of her for using the manners she'd been taught.

"Hi, Mrs. Jerome." Imogene turned her freckled head and smiled.

Imogene was missing a tooth too.

"Look, Mom." She smiled widely. "Imogene and I have the same teeth."

Her mom covered her mouth and chuckled. The first time since Frannie got sick. "Yes, you do."

Nurse Penny came in and rested her hand on Imogene's head. "Artful Dodger, it's time to go back to your room and let Frannie rest."

"Do I have to?" Imogene asked.

Frannie's stomach hurt again. "But she helps me forget I'm sick."

Her mom touched her forehead and then looked at Nurse Penny. "No, we're okay. If it's okay with you. If it's okay with Imogene's parents."

Nurse Penny grimaced like Mom had said something silly. "No problem there."

Mom sat on the other side of the bed. "Where are your parents, sweetie?"

"Pops is at work, and Mama is over the rainbow."

Her mom's face softened like it did whenever she looked at Frannie when she hurt.

"What about aunts and uncles?"

Imogene shook her head. "Pops and my mama left them in Maryland before I was born. Have you been to Ocean City, Maryland?"

"We haven't," Mom said.

"Mama's sister sent me a postcard. There's a beach boardwalk with a Ferris wheel and everything. Someday, I'm going there, and I'll eat saltwater taffy and French fries made with peanut oil. Can you believe that people fly kites right on the beach?! I'm going to jump in the Atlantic Ocean once I learn to swim. And Pops told me there are wild horses on a nearby island called Assateague. And guess what? There are horseshoe crabs on the beach. Isn't that funny? A beach with horses and horseshoe crabs? It's going to be amazing."

"You can send us a postcard when you go," Mom said, but Frannie was thinking bigger.

"I want to go there too," Frannie said.

Her mother looked away. "Someday you'll go. When you're better."

Imogene smiled, and her tiny hand reached for Frannie's. "We can go together. Do you have brothers or sisters?" Imogene asked.

Frannie hated that question because, like *leukemia*, it was the kind of talk that made her mom cry. She shook her head. But Mom didn't have time to get sad this time.

Imogene's jaw dropped, and her eyes widened. "Me either! Hey, let's play thumb war."

Frannie had never played the game before and snorted

when she lost the first round, but she laughed when she won the second.

Mom gently patted Imogene's fuzzy head. "What's your favorite color? I'll bring you a new hat tomorrow."

5

FRANCES

SPRING 2022

Two days later, still weighing the life-changing risks she'd be taking if she looked for Imogene and after enough back-and-forth that left Frances exhausted by her inability to act, she called Rhonda into her office.

"What's up, Ms. Jerome?" All six-feet-five-inches of her assistant bounded into the room.

"Do you use Facebook?"

"Never at the office. I follow your rules."

"But you do use it?"

"You bet I do! I have over one thousand friends. I'm more popular now than I was in high school. One of my posts almost went viral and—"

"Have you ever found someone you haven't seen for years?"

"Every day. Why? You looking for someone? Who are you looking for? High school sweetheart? Ex-lover? I've wondered how long it would take you to start dating. Five years is plenty long."

This was a mistake. "No, a woman. A friend."

"If you want help, I'm your girl. I owe you big time for how you helped me get over my ex and back to work."

Now was not the time—actually, there was never a time—to let Rhonda go down that rabbit hole of man trouble.

"If you open an account, be sure to send me a friend request."

"I won't keep the account long enough," Frances said as her cell phone buzzed. Recognizing the number, she asked Rhonda to leave and to close the door behind her.

"Hello? This is Frances Jerome."

"Ms. Jerome, this is Nurse Hart calling from Dr. Cochran's office. We have the lab results, and the doctor would like to see you in his office."

Frances froze. "Can't we handle it over the phone? It's tax season. I'm working on extensions."

There was an agonizingly long pause.

Her pulse increased in tandem with the minutes she waited. One hand unwittingly went to her head to brush her hair, as if her childhood memories could make it fall out.

"He'd like to see you in his office as soon as possible." The nurse suggested she not come alone, implying that she would need comfort.

You have cancer again—that's what the nurse may as well have said.

"My children and I don't handle stress well." Frances leaned back in her chair in a stupor.

"Then a close friend could accompany you."

Not when one didn't exist, not since Imogene.

She shoved her free hand between her knees to stop it from shaking. After coordinating an appointment for the next day, she rang off, intending to dig her heels in and bear the news alone. Emotional supporters were better suited for sensitive or touchy-feely people, not her.

With each passing decade, she'd let herself forget the odds stacked against a childhood cancer survivor having cancer as an adult. She'd believed she had nothing to fear, that she had suffered enough pain as a child and was a permanent survivor; she'd die of old age with well-used organs and bones, not from disease. And she'd done everything a normal and healthy person was supposed to do. She never missed a checkup, exercised, ate a well-balanced diet, and slept eight hours almost every night, at least until lately.

Her adult life had been good, but she wasn't ready to say, *That's a wrap.* She'd beat cancer before, but back then, Imogene had been fighting and surviving right beside her.

Time had seemed insignificant and irrelevant when she was a child. When you're six years old, a day feels like forever.

But, at her age, the days would fly by.

Why now, when she was finally gaining the guts to find Imogene? Would she have time to redeem herself in honor of Imogene's friendship?

She thought of the rescued women, Emily Ann and Veronica. A sense of urgency coursed through Frances's blood as if she, too, were in danger of being held hostage if she didn't escape. A monster stronger than her would grab her from behind.

She had to do something.

As her idol, Martha Stewart, would say, "So the pie isn't perfect? Cut it into wedges. Stay in control and don't panic."

Without checking her afternoon schedule, she jumped from her chair and grabbed her bags.

"Where are you off to, Ms. Frances?" Rhonda looked at her as if she'd lost her mind.

Right now, she felt like she might have.

"I've got to go. Reschedule my appointments for the rest of today and tomorrow."

She needed order, control. Organizing her thoughts around Imogene might help. Quivering, she drove to the nearest Target.

She pushed her cart down the office supplies aisle, grabbing colorful Post-its, dry-erase markers, and magnets. When she couldn't manage the magnetic whiteboard herself, she marched around the store until she found the first person in a red vest who could.

"Are you okay?" the cashier asked as Frances fanned her face.

"Yes." *No.*

In the parking lot, she stood aside as two employees pivoted the board until it was wedged in her back seat.

Once home, she realized she'd never get the whiteboard inside the house.

Overwhelmed, she dropped her shopping bags in her foyer. Her toes were cold in the house slippers as she walked into the living room. She reached for a sofa pillow to straighten it but almost threw it instead. Bonnie Bell's concerned *uh-ohs* stopped her outburst.

"You're okay, Bonnie Bell. It's me who's not."

Cancer. *Why her? Why now?*

6

FRANCES

SPRING 2022

"Acute myeloid leukemia," Dr. Cochran had said with his practice's oncologist beside him.

He'd said plenty else:

"Advanced . . ."

"Terminal . . ."

"Second opinions, but . . ."

"Chance a stem cell transplant . . ."

"If not months, maybe weeks . . ."

"Quality over quantity . . ."

"Affairs in order . . ."

Frances lost track of how long she'd been sitting at her dining table with her phone, diary, and blank Post-its.

"The mind is powerful. Set goals or milestones . . ." the oncologist had also said.

Live to find Imogene.

Her body had betrayed her spirit. Now, she knew that she couldn't rest in peace without learning the truth about Imogene, but her body had gone on strike, told her to *F-off* and *it's not happening*. Time was everything, but she didn't have any time to barter with. Time couldn't be bought. The only way to create time was to borrow it from someone else's bank.

She could ask for help. She couldn't find Imogene alone, not while fighting for her life, going through chemotherapy, and praying that a stem cell transplant might save her life again.

She needed help.

Jean and Art were the only people she had that might care. It was horrific enough that she'd have to tell them about her cancer. But Imogene? And their grandfather?

Did she have a choice?

There was no one else. She'd wanted to spend more time with her children, but not like this. She should never have teased Jean that she'd need to be on her deathbed to get their attention.

She dialed Art first. Then Jean.

FRANCES STARED at her children's heads from the back seat of the car, her feet surrounded by crusted fast-food wrappers and her granddaughter's discarded sippy cups. Based on the state of her car, Frances now knew that Jean's teenage messiness (or desire to aggravate her mother) had seeped into her mid-twenties and motherhood. No wonder she wasn't welcome at Jean's new home.

Years ago, Jean's father had said her sloppy habits were a cry for attention, not rebellion.

"Perhaps she only gets your attention when she's doing something wrong or if you think she's in danger," Douglas had said.

At the time, Frances had scoffed at her husband. "Slovenliness implies she lacks awareness. She can cry all she wants, but at least she won't get the wrong type of attention from the wrong kind of person as long as I'm her mother."

Frances pushed her motherly failings and the trash aside with her heels and cracked the window to let in some fresh air.

Jean's shoulders were hiked up to her ears, making her look as if she didn't have a neck. Frances deplored poor posture too—it made criminals think you were an easy target.

She caught Art's eye for the umpteenth time in the mirror and frowned when he didn't look away, as if she might die then and there. "The road, Art."

They'd fuss over her from now on rather than focus on what she needed them to do.

Granted, they were in shock. It wasn't every day they learned she might have mere months, or weeks, to live. Could they find Imogene without her holding their hands through the process? They must. She tried subliminally to plant her mettle in their minds and backbones.

Art parked Jean's car in Frances's driveway. Jean had been too emotional to drive after Frances told them she was walking to Baker Beach and that it was urgent they meet her there. She'd used their emergency word, piccolo, to avoid rejection.

"Why are you stopping here?" Frances asked Art. He hadn't pulled to the end of the roundabout driveway as Frances preferred but had stopped in the center, in front of her door. She supposed it was sweet of him, but already they were treating her with kid gloves.

"Never mind. Come inside. There's more to discuss." She didn't wait for him to switch the engine off before she pushed her door open, swung her long legs out, and raised her chin high as she walked up the stairs and unlocked the front door.

"Uh-oh," said Bonnie Bell.

Frances headed straight to her living room, ignoring the house slippers.

She crossed to the birdcage and made smooching noises. "Hello, Bonnie Bell. We have company."

"Mom." Jean spoke behind her as she and Art entered and took a seat.

Frances had named Jean after Imogene, though her daughter had no clue. Art's name had been selected with Imogene in mind too. They'd never asked about the origin of their names, and she'd never offered the information. At most, before Jean married Shane, she'd asked, "Why did you decide to hyphenate your name, Mom, rather than take McGee or stick with Jerome?"

At the time, Frances hadn't known how to explain that her choice had been a practical one: if by some miracle Imogene were alive, or if someone found her,

Frances's maiden name would be remembered, and it was noted on the 1979 police report.

"Mom," Jean started again, "we don't know what to do or say. It's not right. Fifty-two is too young, and your birthday is in September."

"I agree. None of this is right or fair, but it doesn't change the facts."

Feeling numb inside, she tightened her arms across her chest in a self-hug. "After the nurse's call, I'd prepared myself to learn about the cancer, but I had hoped for more time. I need more time." Keeping her back to the twins, she started a sentence and stopped.

"Mom?" her son asked.

Again, Frances opened her mouth, but the words wouldn't come. Sometimes she had a nightmare where she wanted to shout out, but no matter how hard she tried to scream for help, her dream-self couldn't make a peep. That's how she felt now.

Hem. Hem. She tried to express herself again. But nothing happened. It was as if every fiber of her being willed her to remain silent about the past.

Bonnie Bell sat on her perch, her head tilting from side to side, staring at Frances. "Fr-AN-siss. Fr-AN-siss."

"Mom?" Jean this time.

With a deep breath, Frances imagined Imogene's freckles and smiling eyes and willed herself to let go of her fear and say, "I need you to find out what happened to someone for me—a childhood friend, Imogene."

"What?" Jean asked. "Our priority should be caring for your health. Arranging your treatment."

It was a fair point. Her daughter couldn't appreciate how hard it had been to ask for help or that this was the first time she'd spoken Imogene's name aloud since 1994. "We'll find a way to do both. Finding Imogene is a priority." To her own ears, Frances sounded like a petulant child. Vulnerability surged through her body, tightening her throat again.

"Imogene?" Art asked. "How come we've never heard about her before?"

Frances bet he really wanted to ask, *"You had a friend?"*

This was her last chance to remain silent about her past. But, without their help, there'd be no chance of closure for Imogene. And resting in peace would be a miracle for Frances at this rate.

"Because she disappeared the summer we were nine."

Art and Jean's silent twin language hung in the air behind her. Frances imagined them staring at each other, trying to make sense of her announcement. She used to spy on them when they were small, always worried something would happen to them, that she could lose them like she'd lost Imogene.

Jean spoke first. "Holy shit. Disappeared?"

"Don't swear," Frances said, turning to them at last. "The police believed she ran away, but Imogene wouldn't have run from anything."

"As if cancer isn't enough bad news for today," Art said in his deadpan voice that always left the listener waiting for a punchline he would never deliver.

Her daughter pushed her overdue-for-a-trim hair

behind her ear and grimaced when the strands caught on a hangnail. She glanced at a photo of Lexi on the console table. "What about Grandma and Grandpa?"

Frances's spine stiffened. "I'm sorry to tell you this, but your grandfather was the last person to see her alive."

7

JEAN

SPRING 2022

Sitting in her mother's living room, Jean brought a shaky hand to her forehead and tried to still her chattering teeth. "Why haven't you told us about Imogene and Grandpa before?"

"Once you were born, I tried to put Imogene behind me. And you love your grandfather."

"Why now, then?" Jean's breaths quickened.

The obvious answer was because her mother could die, but she still needed to ask. *"Ask more. Assume less,"* her marriage counselor had recently encouraged.

"Because I can't rest in peace until Imogene can too. If a stem cell transplant doesn't work, I don't want my legacy to include how I've forsaken her."

Her mom's legacy.

Jean's chest hitched, making breathing painful. Her grief would have to wait; her mother needed Jean to be strong and confident.

She caught her brother's eyes and lifted her palms, pantomiming. *What should we do?*

What would she and Art be able to accomplish in searching for a missing child from, what, 1979? Most of the time, she didn't know how to locate her daughter's missing shoes or favorite blanket.

Art pursed his lips and sliced his finger across his throat as if to convey: *Grandpa? Missing girl? Count me out.*

But her mother had never asked them for help, and now she might die. This could be their last chance to be close. To be anything except what they'd been. Dr. Pfeiffer had said to pick a bonding project with her mother, but perhaps the project had picked them instead.

Sitting tall, Jean reached for Art's hand in solidarity.

He tried to evade her grasp by leaning away and swatting at her hand, but she won, as usual.

Taking a deep breath, Jean braced herself. "What do you mean, Grandpa was the last person to see her alive?" Her false confidence lasted seconds. She should be used to it, but her mother's look of disappointment still took her aback as she turned to face them. It was the look that made her feel stupid and inept, as if she didn't understand a thing. The look that said, *You can do better than that, Jean.*

Her therapist's voice interrupted her thoughts. "*Have you ever asked your mother what that look means?*"

"She was left in his care one night. He was the last person to see Imogene alive."

For as long as Jean could remember, her mother had

called Grandpa *your grandfather* or *George.* Not Dad. Not Father. Once, in her teen years, and in a spurt of rebellion, Jean had tried calling her mother *Frances,* but her attempt was short-lived—the name didn't roll off the tongue during an argument as easily as *Mother* or *Mom.*

"It's why . . ." Her mother's words trailed off.

"It's why your relationship with Grandpa is so weird," Art said.

"This explains a lot," Jean said.

"Speak for yourself," Art said under his breath.

When they were children, her mother had insisted she and Art never be left *alone* with their grandfather. Once Lexi was born, it went without saying that her mom expected Jean to never leave Lexi unsupervised around him. But Jean had ignored her mother's wishes. She remembered telling her husband, "I'm not taking on whatever problem my mom has with Grandpa. That's between them. He's a giant teddy bear."

Jean had left Lexi with him countless times. If her grandpa had something to do with Imogene's disappearance, Shane would divorce her for sure when he found out.

"Does our dad know about this?" Art asked.

"Yes, Douglas has always known. But, like I said, once you were born, I tried to put Imogene behind me, and by then, he wanted me to as well."

Jean shook her head. None of this made sense. Her dad never openly discouraged their mother from clobbering them over the head with a fear of imminent danger. Maybe if she had known about her mom's past, she might have understood, been more patient, hell, even more diligent about her own safety so her mother wouldn't have been so anxious. And how sad that her family had asked her mother to keep Imogene to herself. The mother in her kicked into gear. As parents, it had been Jean's and Shane's priority to teach Lexi to express herself; it pained her that no one had done the same for her mother.

But what if Jean could? Her mom needed her help. And Jean needed to help her.

Resolution forced Jean to her feet, and she moved to stand behind her brother.

He leaned back so she could rest her hands on his shoulders.

Jean encouraged her mom. "Tell us what happened. We want to know."

Her mom moved to sit beside Art and then patted the seat on the other side. "Come here."

Once they were seated, her mom awkwardly reached out and took each of their hands into her freezing ones. "I'm the only one who cares about Imogene. The only one who hasn't forgotten her."

Jean's empty womb spasmed. If anything ever happened to Lexi, Jean would never forget her.

Her brother rubbed his free hand down his jean-covered leg, shedding his sense of calm.

Knowing their mother, she had a specific way she wanted them to proceed. Jean turned her hand to grip her mother's. "What should we do next?"

8

FRANCES

SPRING 2022

Frances bowed her head and let the relief sink in. Jean was in, so Art would be too. This was the way they had always been; Jean was more apt to rush in without a plan (and often give up), and Art would finish what was started. Which was why Frances did have instructions for them.

"Two things. First, hire a private investigator. I don't expect you to do this on your own or to navigate old police records. Hire the finest. Cost is not an issue, but my first request is that you avoid one detective, Peter Whittaker. I hired him in 1994 while I was pregnant with you. He failed, even though he was supposedly the best."

"Then this won't be *our* first time dealing with a private eye?" Art asked.

Her daughter narrowed her eyes. "What exactly do you mean by 'failed'?"

Ah-ha. Her daughter was listening.

Art's voice rose. "Can we focus on what happened and not word choice?"

Jean's brows slammed together. "I *am* focused."

If Frances was reading Jean's eyes correctly, they were accusing Art: *We're supposed to be a team.*

"He *gave up*," Frances said, capitulating to the word war. "After two weeks."

"But he must have done or found something," Art said.

Frances had asked Peter Whittaker the same thing: "You found nothing? Nothing at all about Imogene's vanishing?"

Peter Whittaker had looked away and then back at her. "Nothing conclusive."

"Mr. Whittaker, take a seat and tell me what you know." Her legs were so shaky she had sat on the couch, waving toward the empty chair across from her.

"Nothing," he said again, as he remained standing. Then he took out his wallet and extended her check and the picture of her with Imogene in the hospital taken the summer before they started second grade. "I know nothing."

She'd been unable to reach for the check scrawled with her handwriting, hanging in the air between them, as if taking the check meant she was giving up too. "But did you find and talk to her father? Did you go to the police station? Did you do anything? There was a police report. You must have found something." Decades-old frustration burst from her, and she placed her palms on her growing belly, her twins kicking inside as if agitated on her behalf.

His eyes followed her motions, settling on her extended abdomen. Shaking his head, he put her payment and photo on a side table. "I'm sorry." And then he left.

Jean slapped her palms on her knees, bringing Frances's thoughts back to the present. "Okay. Shane has a good friend at the police station—"

No, the police were part of the problem, Frances thought. She was ready to interrupt and say they shouldn't raise the alarm before the search began.

"Actually, scratch that. I don't want to involve Shane. Not until I understand more."

Frances nodded, relieved. Okay, her daughter was thinking this through and recognized the need for discretion. "That's good. Very good, Jean."

Eyes wide and chin lifted, Jean looked more confident than she had mere seconds ago. Startled by the transformation, Frances paused. Had her ex-husband been right? Had she so rarely acknowledged her daughter's better choices that an attagirl was so obvious?

Jean continued. "We'll set up appointments with investigators and interview them. We'll keep the information to a minimum and say it's someone who went missing in 1979. Once we hire someone, we can share whatever information we have."

"Not that we have any information to share," Art said.

Ignoring Art, Frances tested her theory about praise and nodded. "Yes, Jean. Less is more, at first."

Her daughter sat up straighter in response.

Fascinating.

Frances clapped her hands together once. "You must find an investigator who has experience with missing persons. Can I trust you both to do this?" She stared hard at each of them.

Art froze, as if someone had sprung a marriage proposal on him. The thought reminded her of his mystery woman.

True to form, her daughter didn't hesitate. "Yes, you can trust us."

Frances tapped her lips with her index finger. What was the best way to say what she needed to next without deflating what little confidence she had given her daughter? "You must work together and see this through to the end. Even when you don't want to, even if you don't like the results. Even if I'm no longer here."

Jean paled, but nodded.

"Because, as incredible as it sounds, you think Grandpa is involved," Art said.

Frances grimaced. "He made Imogene nervous, but I dismissed her fears." How was she to understand then about the power of remorse and how it could grow, layer upon layer, year over year? How not knowing the truth could be the most damaging?

She pinched the bridge of her nose. "It's not fair to ask this of you. You can still walk away, but I can't. Not as long as I'm alive. But if you go down this road for me and find the person responsible, can you do what needs to be done?"

"Kill him?" Art stood and paced the room.

"Unnecessarily dramatic, Art," Frances said and then thought, *Yet impeccable comedic timing.*

Art ran his hand through his curly hair. "I don't understand what has happened. I need more information before—"

"Art, stop it!" Jean yelled. "She—we—might not have enough time."

The harsh reality crashed into them like a rogue wave on Baker Beach, threatening to carry them into the dark, cold depths of the Pacific.

"Mom," Jean said, her voice shaking, "we will find Imogene for you. No matter what it takes. We can do this for you."

Art threw his hands up in surrender.

Her children were acting as expected. Jean was ready to jump in. Art was anticipating there'd be broken pieces he'd need to pick up. Together, they'd be her heroes, hopefully.

Frances couldn't recall a time she'd ever cried in front of her family, but she blinked away tears now. "Thank you."

"You said there were two things," Jean said. "What's the second?"

Art sounded more resigned than curious. "Right. There's more."

Frances stared hard at her children. "You can't tell your grandfather we are doing this. No one can interview him."

9

FRANNIE

LATE FALL 1975

Her mom never let her go to Imogene's room.

"Other kids play in each other's rooms," Frannie pouted.

"Until we meet Imogene's dad, it's not right."

That didn't make much sense to Frannie. "But what if he comes to Imogene's room and she isn't there? Won't he be worried?"

Nurse Penny checked her blood pressure, and Imogene rested on the end of Frannie's bed, looking at her sticker collection.

"It's okay, Frannie. Pops will find me when he comes."

"Mm-hmm, when he's capable." Nurse Penny shook her head as she loosened a valve and deflated the blood pressure cuff. "Brrr, this place is cold today." She fluffed up Frannie's blanket and grabbed an extra one from a dresser to rest across Imogene's shoulders. "That darn coat closet ate another one of my sweaters."

"Closets don't eat stuff." But Imogene sounded skeptical.

"Second one this month. One minute it's there, next it's not. Either it's the closet or someone is taking my things, and my coworkers wouldn't do that."

"Penny, I have an extra sweater in my car. Would you like to borrow it?" Mom asked.

When Mom and the nurse stepped out of the room, Frannie asked, "What did Nurse Penny mean about your dad?"

Imogene shrugged her shoulders and looked away. "I don't think Pops is like other pops."

"How come?"

Imogene shrugged again and lifted a Scratch n Sniff Cherry Sticker to her nose. "Once upon a time, Pops got in trouble, and the judge said I had to live in an orphanage, like Oliver. For a whole month. It wasn't as bad as *Oliver!*, but it was still scary. I didn't know if I'd get to see him again."

Frannie's eyes widened. "Judges can take children away from their parents?" The idea of living without her mom and dad made her heart slam against her chest, but never, ever would her parents do anything that might make this happen.

Imogene nodded. "It's my fault because I was sick, and Pops was sad, got drunk, and started talking to Mama like she was still alive. The judge told something called CPS to take me away until Pops got better. Don't tell anyone, okay?"

The girls shook their pinkies.

"What's drunk mean?"

"Drinking too much beer and whiskey."

Frannie's mom and dad got sad too—sometimes her mom's worrying "stretched her nerves thin" and gave her migraines. That's why she took medicine to help her sleep for a long time. But as far as she knew, they never got drunk.

Her dad was always somewhere in the hospital doing boss-doctor things. He used to have patients, but now he ran the hospital like President Ford ran the country. On his lunch break, he came to check on her and her mom.

Mom picked up her purse. "Honey, I'm going to get some fresh air while you're here. I told the girls that Frannie can't go to Imogene's room until we meet Imogene's father."

"What's your father's name, Imogene?" Dad asked.

"Benjamin Dryker."

"I'll ask Rodney Schultz to look him up, and maybe you can play together then." Dad's friend was a cop and married to Nurse Penny. Imogene knew this, too, because Nurse Penny's husband had dropped by a few times.

Imogene wrinkled her nose and looked at Frannie.

"No, George." Mom wagged her finger. "My point is, *we* need to *meet* him. I'll be back in a while."

But Frannie's dad didn't have time to ask Rodney to look up Imogene's pop because Mr. Dryker came looking for Imogene later, as Imogene had sworn he would.

He came stumbling down the hall toward Frannie's room, like Frannie might walk if she felt like throwing up. At first, she didn't know who he was, just that he was yelling for Imogene in a slurred voice. Was this how being drunk sounded and looked?

Imogene's face lit up.

Frannie's dad jumped up, his big shoulders blocking the door. "She's in here, but you can stop right there." Dad tapped the name tag affixed to the lapel on his white jacket. "Who are you and have you been drinking?"

Mr. Dryker burped and shook his head at the same time. "Her fodder."

Imogene slid from the bed and squeezed between Dad's leg and the doorframe.

Frannie's dad stepped aside, his face tight and his voice concerned. "This true, Imogene?"

Imogene's smile disappeared. She hung her head and took Pops's waving hand. "Yes, sir. This is Pops, Benjamin Dryker."

Frannie didn't like the way Imogene's dad smelled, and she could tell her dad didn't either.

Dad was acting strange. He didn't practice his manners like he normally would. "You need to be sober to stay here. Think of the children."

Frannie's friend frowned and pulled on her father's hand. "Let's go, Pops."

"If you want help, *Mr.* Dryker, I will call a social worker."

Imogene flinched as if Frannie's dad had slapped her and Pops.

"Dad?" Frannie asked. Even she knew he was being bossy and mean. Mom would be as angry as her when she found out.

Imogene's lower lip tremored. "Let's go." She tugged on her dad's hand with both of hers.

Frannie worried that Imogene wouldn't want to be her friend after this.

"Dad, come here now." Frannie's voice shook with anger.

Imogene gave her father a strong hug. "Let's go to my room, Pops." She stopped for a second and made eye contact with Frannie. "See you at *Oliver!*, Frannie." Imogene turned and hung her head as they walked away, making Frannie's stomach ache.

Once they disappeared from view, Frannie said, "You were mean."

Her dad raked his hand through his hair and came to sit beside her. "The hospital has rules, and it's my job to enforce them. But, you're right, I should have talked to him privately. Don't tell your mother. It will break her heart. She'll want to take him under her wing."

True. It's what she loved about her mom. She was a helper, like Mr. Rogers liked. He always said, "Find the helpers."

"Okay. Let's not tell anybody," Frannie agreed, not wanting Imogene to be taken to an orphanage again because her dad was drunk.

Imogene didn't return for the rest of the day, but Nurse Penny told Frannie, "You'll see her at the movie."

When Mom came back, Dad believed Frannie was sleeping, but she wasn't. She heard everything. He broke their promise not to tell.

"I checked the hospital files. Dryker's an alcoholic.

He's been in the emergency room more than once for alcohol poisoning and injuries from falls and fights. I bet he's even worse than my dad used to be when I was a kid. I don't think it's a good idea for Frannie and Imogene to keep playing together or to grow closer. He's trouble and will lead to pain."

"George." Her mom's voice sounded surprised. "They're little girls fighting cancer. Surely, you wouldn't hold Imogene responsible for her father's—and your father's—actions." Her last words were a whisper, but more like a shouted whisper.

Dad said, "Apples don't fall far from the tree."

Frannie wasn't sure what he meant, but she could tell her mom didn't agree. "George Jerome, that's not true, and you know it. You're nothing like your dad. Imogene's an innocent child, like you were an innocent child, and she is Frannie's first friend. And that is that."

But when Frannie woke up, her mom and dad told her that she and Imogene could only play in Frannie's room—no ifs, ands, or buts about it.

10

GRIFFIN

SPRING 2022

Griffin Whittaker set his backpack, stuffed with his case files, laptop, and high-zoom camera, by the front door before joining his wife in the kitchen. He had time for breakfast before his meeting with a potential client, Jean Wallace. The woman's email address hadn't included a business name, which meant she probably had a personal job for him.

Please, not another extramarital affair.

"Morning, love." He kissed Annie's temple and poured a cup of coffee.

"I'm making us an egg white omelet," she said, smiling as if proud of herself.

Oh, joy.

"You know, the yolk is the best part of the egg," he said as a loud thump from above startled him, causing him to splash his hand with scalding coffee. "Dammit." Griffin grabbed a spare dish towel.

The creaky old house in inner Richmond shared

every annoying movement and noise—something he should be used to by now, having grown up in it. He and Annie should have sold the house years ago and moved into a new cookie-cutter home like they'd planned. When they'd gotten married and bought it from his parents—who had wanted to work less and downscale to an apartment—Griffin swore to himself and Annie, "We'll fix it up and sell it after two years. We're only taking my parents' offer to get ahead." Otherwise, he would have ditched his childhood house and never looked back. He had wanted something of his own, something he could earn outside of his dad's pressurized good intentions. But that was almost twenty years ago; he and Annie had grown complacent after their son was born. Rather, Annie had pointed out that she was the new mom who'd have to manage the house hunting, packing, and moving. She was right. He had always worked at a constant pace—at a job he'd never wanted, one he'd taken on during a stupid, weak moment to make his father, Peter, happy.

Griffin set his coffee down on the table before dropping into a chair. The familiar soul-crushing acceptance that he was too old to do anything about his purpose in life settled on his shoulders, creeping across his chest.

If he could go back in time, he'd be a musician or a music teacher, or anything other than what his father had wanted his only child to become: a private investigator in the "family business."

"It was your choice, and it's your business," Griffin

had said as a teen. "Stop calling it Whittaker & Son. I want nothing to do with it."

"Then take off your clothes and run around naked because *our* business pays for the shirt on your back," his dad had said. "Sleep on the street since it pays for the roof over your head and the bed beneath it."

Another house-rattling noise ruined his first swallow of coffee. Normally, the only racket from upstairs at this time of day was his son's alarm clock blaring between snoozes.

"What's up with Tony? He's louder than a mosh pit at a Smashing Pumpkins concert. Makes me glad we only had one kid."

"Field trip," Annie said as she sat across from him. She leaned over, tugged his tie, and asked, "New client?"

"Any other reason to wear a tie?" He winked. There were two other occasions he'd slip on the noose: his wedding anniversary and Mother's Day brunch. "I don't know what the case is about yet. It's either personal or for a small business. If it's the second, I don't relish another workman's comp investigation." Unfortunately, fraudulent comp claims were the bread and butter of his work. Those and extramarital affairs, but he avoided talking to Annie about the latter; they seldom made for good conversation. "Got any bread and butter or flavor to go with this white stuff?"

"No yolks. No butter," Annie said. "Doctor's orders."

Fine, he'd pick up something with flavor on his way

to work. He nodded toward the rooms above. "What kind of field trip?"

"Prison," Annie said and looked at him.

Griffin choked on the slimy egg white. "What?!"

"It's for his AP U.S. Government class. Students have an option to attend the men's prison for extra credit."

"Last time I checked, Tony had an A, and even if he had an F, I still wouldn't agree to this"—he did air quotes—"'field trip.' No son of mine is ever stepping foot in a prison. There are twenty million better ways and places to spend his time. What in the hell has happened to our education system?"

"You don't have to agree." Annie sipped her hot water with lemon, ginger, and turmeric. "It reduces inflammation," she always said. So far, he'd ignored her subtle hints that it would reduce *his* inflammation too. Eventually, she'd demand he drink it, and when that day came, he would. One thing about Annie: he never questioned how much she loved him or that she wanted him to outlast her in this world. But stuff like this from his son would trigger that heart attack the doctors warned Griffin about, and sooner rather than later.

She lifted her eyebrows and gave him one of her *you-may-not-like-it-but* looks. "He may still be in high school, but he's eighteen. He doesn't need our permission to participate."

"He's been eighteen for one week. He has a year of high school left."

Griffin's father, Peter—if he hadn't had a massive heart attack and were still alive—would say, "Not while he eats, sleeps, and showers under my roof." But Griffin was not his father, no matter how the trappings appeared.

"Annie, you and I both know what this is about. Tony!" Griffin yelled through the plaster ceiling. "Get down here! Now!"

Too many minutes later, Tony trotted downstairs wearing a stubborn expression and a "Sherlock Holmes: Crimes and Punishments" T-shirt.

There. Right there. That's the problem.

His son thought private detective work—damn, any work dealing with lowlifes—was like some stupid video game. If he wasn't pissed and didn't think Tony would turn an inch into a mile, he'd take Tony to work with him and show him how uneventful the job was in real life, or I-R-L, as his son would say. How had he raised such a naïve, romantic kid inspired by a PlayStation 4, or whatever number they were on these days?

Griffin leaned back in his chair and crossed his arms. "What's this about you going to prison voluntarily?"

The obstinate teen reclined against the kitchen counter and crossed his arms too.

How, why, and when had his son gotten it into his thick skull that following in Griffin's footsteps was a good idea? Why didn't his kid see how lucky he had it? Griffin would have given anything for his dad to encourage him to be anything but a private investigator dealing with cheats and liars day in and day out.

Who and where would Griffin be today if his dad had said, "Son, you're a gifted musician. I'll support you any way I can." Instead, he'd said, "Every musician

I've been hired to find is an addict living on the streets."

"It's the Scared Straight Program," Tony said. "We get to meet prisoners, hear their stories, and see what prison life is like."

Griffin turned to his wife, looking for shared disgust, but instead, he found saint-like patience. For him, or their son? "We should have put him in a private school."

Turning back to Tony, he said, "When I went to school, they took us on tours of colleges, not prisons. No, the answer is no. You're skipping it. Go to the band room instead. Practice your clarinet."

Tony snorted. "Clarinet is all about you."

Griffin punched the air with his index finger. "It's not about me. It's about you having choices. About you looking beyond your small world and doing something bigger. You're not going to prison."

"Let's discuss this calmly," Annie said. "Besides, the chaperones are expecting him."

"You're okay with this?" he asked her. "Look at him. He wants to go to a prison wearing a detective T-shirt. No way in hell is our son skipping a day of education to go tour some dead-end jail cell."

"I'm going," Tony said.

Griffin slammed his hand down on the table and glared at his son. "Why? Will you be a prisoner when you grow up?"

Tony smirked. "Someday, I will work at Whittaker & Son. I want to know what criminals are like."

Shit. Griffin had walked right into his son's trap. "I've

told you no a million times. I'll tell you again. No. End of story. When I'm done, the business closes with me." Griff's skin turned hot above his tie.

"Fine. I'll open my own business."

"Oh yeah?" Griffin pointed at the offensive T-shirt. "Any of your PlayStation games show you how to open a business without money?"

"Griffin," Annie said. "Focus on one thing at a time."

Right, first the prison trip, not their son's future happiness. "You want to be scared straight? Do you know what prisoners will do to cops and detectives, given a chance? And before you try to tell me that being a PI isn't the same as being a cop, let me tell you something—prisoners consider them one and the same."

His son glared.

And was that a friggin' eye roll?

"If Grandpa were still alive, he'd be supportive."

Griffin shoved his chair back and stood. "I'm not your grandfather." He stormed out of the house and past the bus stop. He'd walk to the office and burn off his coronary conniption before meeting his new client.

Dammit. Tony would go on the field trip anyway. His heart constricted, scared to death that he was running out of time to convince his son to give his life a chance. To discover a career path more meaningful than digging up dirt on scummy losers.

When Griffin thought about the number of days he'd thrown away to please his father, it hurt to breathe.

He'd given Tony the world—a world full of opportunities to pursue anything he wanted and to live a better life. And what did Griffin get for it? What did his son want to do?

Be like him.

He'd be flattered if he actually felt like he'd taught his son a damn thing. Somehow, he'd failed as a father. Life was a sneaky son of a gun, and if his kid wasn't careful, he'd end up resentful and floundering for a purpose like Griffin. Being a PI did that to a guy.

There was a gyro with his name written all over it at the Greek food truck parked across the street. If emotional eating was the way to survive the next several years before retirement then he'd eat his way through them.

By the time he reached his office on Clement Street, Griffin had walked off his frustration and felt more rational on a full stomach. Maybe the prison visit wasn't such a bad idea. Maybe his son would see who he'd be dealing with and would be scared straight the hell away from investigative work.

11

JEAN

SPRING 2022

Parked outside her mother's house, Jean glanced in the rearview mirror at Lexi. She moved the cell phone closer to her lips. "Shane, let's discuss this tonight."

"Tonight. Really?" her husband said in disbelief. "We should be discussing *this* at home this morning. *This* is the third morning in a row this week that you have grabbed Lexi and were out the door while I showered. What is going on with you?"

"I can't tell you." She had told him about her mother's cancer but nothing about Imogene yet.

"Why not?"

Because he'd tell her they needed to focus on their marriage, not on finding Imogene.

And telling him prematurely about the grandpa bit was a bad idea.

"I'm at Mother's now. She'll watch Lexi while Art

and I go to an appointment." Jean released her seat belt in a private show of dismissal.

"But we're supposed to talk to Dr. Pfeiffer about Lexi and her little friend some more today." Jean could imagine him tapping his watch as he said, "In thirty minutes."

"How do you know she's little, Shane? She's imaginary."

"Don't dissect my words now. Listen, it's a big deal to me that you're ditching our therapy."

"I'm sorry, but Art and I must take care of something for Mom. Consider this that project with my mom that Dr. Pfeiffer suggested. You should keep the appointment and talk about you." She'd been going to one-on-one sessions for weeks now—Dr. Pfeiffer's idea—and they helped her more than the joint sessions. Except, maybe she was kidding herself, because she and Shane were bickering more than ever, and their areas for improvement hadn't improved. Jean was still a people pleaser. Plus, she was still beating herself up for being a terrible mother and wife, always lacking compared to her friends' perfect family Instagram accounts.

For months now, Shane had pressed her to get out more often with her girlfriends, but she had nothing in common with her friends, who'd turned into ideal daughters, mothers, partners, or power women. Somewhere along the line, Jean had fallen behind on doing things right—even humor and venting.

Social media was her enemy. Once, after a taboo glass of wine—Jean was nursing Lexi—her dark humor had risen to the top. She'd created a meme with a mother nursing and the words, "Being a mother sucks sometimes."

Most of her so-called friends had sent her private messages or texts saying she was out of line. Then they unfollowed her.

She'd become a hashtag-outcast.

"Oh, I'll go," he said. "I'll tell Dr. Pfeiffer how you're doing cartwheels for your mom, except you still won't invite her over."

It was a super analogy—cartwheels. A point for Shane even if he didn't know how clever he'd been. She couldn't do cartwheels. She feared letting go, positive her lack of balance would have her fall backward or land on her head.

"I'm not saying you shouldn't help Frances, but if she passes, Lexi and I will be who you have left."

Dies, not passes.

"I'd have Art and Dad too," Jean said.

"You know what I mean."

She did. She didn't.

"Tonight, I promise," she said.

He didn't answer.

Her chest tightened. Was this the moment he'd tell her he was leaving her, even though he'd said she'd always have him and Lexi?

"Shane?"

"Fine. But definitely tonight, Jean. I'm talking to Dr. Pfeiffer about Lexi today, regardless of your absence. Being around more kids would be a good thing for Lexi.

You joining a club or working part-time would be a good thing too."

Jean rolled her eyes. Give the man a few therapy sessions and he thought he was a psychologist. Worse was the way he implied that she had made the wrong choice for Lexi by wanting to stay home with her for the first five years. Dedicated full-time for three years, and she still was an inadequate mother. But if she wasn't a stay-at-home mom, what was she? Shane was such a hypocrite—if he was annoyed that she wanted to help her mother, did he truly support her carving out a life for herself as they'd discussed in therapy?

"Lexi is excited to see my mom."

"What if Lexi brings up—"

"She won't," Jean interrupted. She peeked at Lexi, who was talking up a storm in the back seat. "I'll tell her not to."

"Great. Now, we're asking our daughter to keep secrets."

#momfail.

"I don't want your mother involved, not at Lexi's expense."

"My mom might not be a super mother, but she's been a surprisingly amazing grandmother." Not to mention, she was learning more about her mother and what made her tick.

"I want to see G-Ma and Bonnie Bell," Lexi said from the back seat, making it clear they no longer had privacy.

Shane sighed. "I know. You're right. I may not always

like how your mom treats you or raised you, but I can't fault her as a grandmother."

"Thank you, Shane."

"Do what you've got to do today, and we will talk later. Okay?"

"You've got it." She hung up and turned to her daughter. "Ready to spend the day with G-Ma?"

"We sure are." Lexi grinned and kicked her feet.

Uh-oh. "Just you today, cutie. Remember how I told you G-Ma is going to be more tired than usual? I'm not sure she can handle Booby too."

Lexi frowned, grabbed her tattered blanket close, and stuck her thumb in her mouth.

"But you can take your blanket. Maybe G-Ma will cuddle with Blanket." This made Lexi laugh.

Jean let go of Lexi's hand once they reached the front door. Her girl loved to hit the doorbell—though even her doting grandmother had put her foot down at "one ring is sufficient."

In the fun voice that her mom reserved for her granddaughter and that Jean faintly remembered from childhood, her mom spoke through the door. "Who's there? Is there a ghost at my door? I don't see anyone."

Judging by the exuberant tone, no one would have guessed her mom was ill.

Jean lifted Lexi until she was even with the peephole.

"It's me. Lexi the Great."

When Jean was Lexi's age, her mother had said, "If you're not tall enough to look out the peephole, you're not old enough to answer the door."

The door opened, and Lexi wrapped Blanket and her arms around her grandmother's legs.

When was the last time Jean had hugged her mother with that type of abandon? Fourth or fifth grade?

Dr. Pfeiffer had told her that children identify with egos around nine and ten years old, and parent-child relationships naturally change then. An image of her mom and Imogene as nine-year-old girls came to mind. Her mother had lost more than Imogene; she'd lost her innocence and, possibly, a sense of security with her father. The idea that her grandfather may have had something to do with Imogene's disappearance made her want to vomit. Picturing his cheerful face, she couldn't believe him possible of harming anyone, much less a child. She'd get to the bottom of this as soon as possible.

"Are you coming in?" her mother asked.

"No. Art and I have an interview at nine. I'm meeting him there. Then he'll head back to work, and I'll come here after."

"Good. Lexi and I will have lunch waiting."

Lexi skipped down the hall and called over her shoulder, "We want peanut butter 'n jelly."

Darn you, Lexi.

Her mom looked to her. "Since when do you eat peanuts?"

Jean had seconds to choose between telling her mother about marriage counseling and Lexi's newfound imaginary world or her digestive problems.

According to Dr. Pfeiffer, Booby was Jean and Shane's responsibility.

"Booby is due to a healthy imagination or a temporary coping mechanism," the counselor had said. "Children pick up on conflict between their parents more often than the parents do themselves."

Hives, cramping, and diarrhea, it would be. Jean shrugged and waved off her mother's curiosity. "My intolerance has changed with age."

Her mom didn't seem skeptical and let it go. "Who are you meeting today?"

After five days of calls and three days of interviews, Peter Whittaker's son had come up over and over. But telling her mom that she was meeting Griffin Whittaker wasn't an option.

Griffin was the best. Everyone said so.

She was still shocked that the other private investigators had been so forthcoming, especially when it meant they were turning down a paycheck. A few detectives, both male and female, had point-blank said, "Griffin Whittaker is the person you want, not me."

A retired cop had been most specific. "Missing person, you say? If Peter Whittaker couldn't finish the job, the only person who might is his son. And I find it hard to believe Peter couldn't."

"Well, it's the truth. He couldn't. Why should I take your word that his son is the best?"

"You shouldn't. But ask around. Everyone will agree."

So she did, and they had.

It was hard to say how much time they had to find Imogene, or rather, how much time her mom had, and eliminating someone because of his last name wasn't prudent.

Art had agreed. "We should at least interview him. If he doesn't stand up to the hype, we'll ask for a referral."

"Jean?" her mom repeated. "Who are you meeting today?"

Defensive about betraying her mother, Jean huffed and crossed her arms. In the strictest sense, she wasn't *betraying* her. Her mother had said not to hire Peter Whittaker. And Griffin Whittaker wasn't hired yet. It was just an interview. "Mom, you asked us for help. Trust us. This won't work if I have to tell you about everything we're doing and everyone we're meeting. You're on a need-to-know basis, okay?"

Darn it. She'd done it again. Dr. Pfeiffer would say, "End on a statement, not by asking permission."

Jean tried again. "Focus on your health and on Lexi. We're focused on the rest."

Her mother peered at her as if she had something on her nose. Maybe it was growing like Pinocchio's.

Gratefully, her mom smiled. "Good. I want to trust you."

12

GRIFFIN

SPRING 2022

For all his twenty-seven years of investigating and his ability to jump to accurate conclusions, Griffin didn't have a frigging clue what the twenty-something brother-and-sister duo wanted from him. The guy, Art—every nuance of his body language shouted, *Get me out of here*. And he was lying about or withholding something. Griffin could spot a liar within seconds. The dude was a typical prevaricator: he rolled his lips between his teeth, looked everywhere but at Griffin, and fidgeted worse than a man about to get married for the fifth time.

The sister, Jean, watched Griffin with soul-starved earnestness, and Griffin struggled to maintain eye contact. He was used to having people desperate for his help, looking at him like he was their last hope, but without knowing what the two wanted or what they were hiding, he wasn't sure he could deliver, or if he wanted to.

Griffin raised one brow. "Let me get this straight. You

want me to investigate a forty-three-year-old disappearance, but I can't run the investigation?"

He wasn't a magician, and he was the only Whittaker in Whittaker & Son. Griffin leaned forward to emphasize his point that this request was ludicrous. Crowding people who weren't straightforward was an effective way to gain answers. But, as he parked his elbows on the desk, fervor flashed across Jean's face, so instead, Griffin reclined in his desk chair. It was the same one his dad had used. *They don't make things like they used to.* The long-lasting chair was the one thing he was glad his dad had left him.

"Exactly," Jean said.

"Still not following."

The sister looked to her brother. They'd introduced themselves as twins. Mum's-the-word Art sat up straight.

Ah-ha, so he would contribute to the meeting after all.

Art cleared his throat. "My mother, Frances Jerome, has cancer. She asked my sister and me to help her find closure about her friend who went missing in 1979. Our mother is very particular, and she has two deal breakers."

Gotta love a mother who has stipulations when asking for help. How badly does this Frances woman want to find her friend? Everyone had baggage, though. Maybe this was hers.

Art continued. "She hired a private detective in 1994 and refuses to use the same guy because he gave up."

When Art said *gave up*, he emphasized the words and looked pointedly at his sister.

Griffin wouldn't hire someone who gave up either.

Art met Griffin's eyes again. "We interviewed other detectives, and every one pointed us to your firm as"—Art made air quotes—"'number one.'"

They were right. The fact was one of life's great ironies. Much to his chagrin, and his father's satisfaction before he died, Griffin was *numero uno* in northern California.

"But I can't be the investigator? Still confused here, folks."

Now Jean hopped in. "The firm my mom first used was"—she looked around his office—"yours."

Nope. His dad never *gave up*. He had never quit a case. Never. His dad's record was stellar. Except . . . There was one case his dad had never *solved*, and that case—that night—had changed everything. When Griffin was seventeen years old, his dad had come home from work despondent. He headed straight to his room when he was normally eager to drill the day's work into Griffin's brain. That night, Griffin walked by his parents' bedroom and heard something he'd never heard before—his dad crying. Griffin placed his cheek and ear against the door.

"That poor girl," Dad said, and his voice cracked.

His mom said, "You did what you could."

"People will go down for this. What if I'm wrong? What if I missed something?"

"Like what?"

"I wish I knew. Maybe I'm losing my edge."

His dad changed after that. He withdrew from talking about work and, therefore, from Griffin too.

Griffin's heart rate increased. He tugged at his tie. Stupid thing was coming off as soon as the meeting ended.

Jean pulled a yellowed, tattered card from her purse and handed it to him.

His father's card. He'd recognize the blue W&S logo anywhere. Dad had named the firm Whittaker & Son before said son had agreed to join. "Do you know what this says, Griff?" his dad had asked him when he was in first grade and learning to read.

Griffin shook away the cobwebs and asked Jean and Art, "What year did you say she hired my firm?"

"1994," Jean said. "She would have gone by Frances Jerome-McGee at that time."

The same year as his dad's withdrawal. Griffin willed his heart rate to slow the hell down.

"Excuse me for a moment." He walked into the office next to his, where his father had boxed up old cases before he died.

Griffin never cracked open his father's files. His dad had always said, "Never reopen a closed case unless a client or a judge asks you to." His dad had never had to reopen a case, and as a result, Griffin never had either. Especially not *that* file.

Griffin pulled down the box marked 1994 in his father's chicken scratch. "From years of writing fast notes and observations," his dad had said.

Setting the dusty box on his father's vacant desk, Griffin worried his dad's ghost might appear and howl, "Don't open that, Son."

With shaking fingers, Griffin lifted the cardboard lid and thumbed through the file tabs. They were organized by last name and filed in alphabetical order as expected. All except one.

13

FRANCES

SPRING 2022

As Lexi took a break from peekaboo with Bonnie Bell and colored at the kitchen table, Frances called Rhonda and asked her to clear her schedule. "It will be okay. I'll make sure you get a severance package once we transition our customers." If Frances played her cards right, she'd land Rhonda a job too.

"Oh Frances."

Sobs flooded the line. While Rhonda collected herself, Frances scooped up a crayon that had rolled away. "Lexi, mind your crayons, please. We don't want one to get lost and mark up my floor."

Her floor. When she died—if not now then later—Jean and Art would decide whether to keep the house or sell it. It was the house they'd grown up in, but she was hard-pressed to understand if they felt any attachment to it. She looked around the well-ordered space peppered with Martha Stewart's practical yet beautiful solutions. Her new whiteboard rested against a wall.

Lexi corralled the crayons. "Okey dokey, pokey."

Frances smiled as her granddaughter swung her legs back and forth in the chair. Gray scribbles were the art *du jour*. Every crayon pulled from the box was in the gray family. A lump formed in her throat. Gray shades were Frances's favorite colors. One look around her house and it was obvious.

"It's not about a paycheck," Rhonda said and hiccupped. "You're the best boss I've ever had."

Frances may not have been the best friend to Imogene, the best mother, the best wife, or even the best daughter to her mother, but Frances knew she was an exceptional business owner, boss, and accountant. Rhonda had spent more time with her in the past several years than anyone else, including her family.

Lexi looked up at her and blew a kiss.

And the best grandma too. Frances blew one back.

A niggling fear wormed its way into her heart that she would be forgotten, just like Imogene. How long would Rhonda remember her? And how long would Lexi?

Rhonda blew her nose. "And you just got that Martha Stewart croc-embossed leather tote you've been waiting for too."

"True. I shouldn't have waited to get the tote." One would think that after surviving cancer as a child, she would have lived life with a don't-wait-until-it's-too-late mentality. Instead, she'd been daring about time. She imagined Rhonda holding the croc-embossed bag against her abdomen like the model on QVC had been when

Frances had caved and ordered the bag. She added the image to her memory jar: *give tote to Rhonda.*

Thank goodness she didn't have many people to tell she might have a shelf life. Other than her employees and clients, she needed to tell her ex-husband, and George. But she wouldn't tell George until she could also tell him they'd found Imogene. Her pulse sped up. After all these years of not knowing what had happened, if Imogene was alive or dead, she wanted and deserved to see his reaction once he knew that she knew. Would he be relieved? Surprised? Or afraid?

"Rhonda, thank you. I've got to go. Once you've collected yourself, please set up the virtual meeting with my COO. We can redistribute my clients and responsibilities. Do not mention my health. Can you handle this? Can I count on your continued professionalism?"

Frances bet Rhonda rolled her shoulders back. "I've got this, Frances."

"Thank you, Rhonda. Goodbye for now."

The rest of today, she could focus on her precious granddaughter and dig out materials that would help the investigation while adding notes to the whiteboard. Though Peter Whittaker's efforts had been unfruitful back in '94, Frances knew from experience that an investigator would need more details than Jean or Art could provide. To start with, she could create that timeline of her diary, and photos would be required.

"Lexi the Great, please come upstairs with me. I need to get my box of memories."

Lexi screwed up her face and set her gray crayon down, making sure it didn't roll away. "Like the memory jar?" she asked as she slid from her chair to the floor with a plop, her orange Crocs making a sucking sound.

"Your mother taught you about the memory jar, did she?" This pleased Frances more than she would have expected, that her mother's trick lived on. The memory jar would survive them all.

"Yup. Mine's got lots of stuff in it." Lexi spread her arms wide.

"Good. A memory box is different. The memory box contains keepsakes from when I was little."

"Little like us?" Lexi asked, reaching for her blanket.

Us? "I was a few years older than you." Frances extended her hand. "Please, leave your blanket here because it's not practical to take it upstairs. You might trip on it. We'll be right back."

Lexi's eyes widened as she set down Blanket. She murmured out the side of her mouth, "Come on, Booby."

Frances's brows lifted. "Who is Booby?"

Lexi wrinkled her nose. "Mom said not to tell no one."

"Not to tell *anyone*. Why doesn't she want you to tell me?"

Lexi shrugged.

Frances recalled Jean's discussion at the front door. "Does Booby like peanut butter 'n jelly?"

Lexi smiled wide and bobbed her head.

Ah-ha. Her daughter would rather suffer than expose Lexi and Booby. What did Jean think she'd do? Frances liked to think she and the kids had had fun together when they were little. *Doesn't Jean remember?* Sure, she'd taught them to be practical and aware—some days all Frances could do was make sure they stayed alive and in one piece—but she'd also taught them how to play and how to pretend.

"I have a secret too. Would you like to hear it?" Frances asked.

Lexi nodded.

"I had a friend like Booby when I was your age."

Lexi's eyes widened. "You did?"

"Yes, I did."

"Was her name Booby too?"

"Her name was Dandelion."

Lexi covered her mouth and giggled. The action reminded Frances of Jean when she was little, and her heart clenched. Something she'd never been able to explain to anyone was how sometimes she felt as if she had four children: Jean and Art before they were ten and Jean and Art after they were ten. She missed little Jean and Art.

"Dandelion lived in my backyard with the other flowers. What does Booby look like?"

"Like me. What does Dandelion look like?"

"She had yellow flower petals for hair, and she liked to run through the sprinklers on hot days."

Lexi's eyes widened again, and she looked around the room. "Is she here?"

"No, she was with me when I was three. Then, she left."

"Oh no. Will Booby go bye-bye too?"

Frances brushed the top of Lexi's head with the palm of her hand. She wouldn't lie to her granddaughter, but she hoped Jean would appreciate her answer if she ever heard it. "Only when you want her to, honey."

"When did Dandelion go bye-bye?"

Frances hesitated. "You know, I can't remember." And she had no one to ask. "Where is Booby now?"

Lexi pointed to the space beside her.

"Booby," Frances said, "if I let you come upstairs, will you do as I say?"

"Booby only talks to me."

Frances encircled her granddaughter's chubby fingers with her lean ones.

"Okay, let's all go upstairs."

Her granddaughter's awkward gait was ideal for Frances's lower-than-usual energy levels. How long before she wouldn't be able to visit the second floor? She'd have to move her things downstairs and hire a caregiver while she received treatment—Jean and Art needed to focus on Imogene. Besides, she didn't want to be remembered as dealing with the side effects of chemo, bent over the toilet or a bucket. She'd make the arrangements sooner rather than later. She wanted to spend as little time as possible in the hospital—she'd spent too much time there as a child. To this day, the smell of cleaning supplies and plastic—everything was plastic at the hospital—reminded her of her sickly early years. She wanted to be in the home she'd made for herself, surrounded by natural light, the sound of waves and fog horns, and the scent of the ocean breeze and her favorite candles.

She steered Lexi into the bedroom and pointed to the bed. "You and Booby can sit there. No bouncing." Frances got down on her knees to reach beneath the bed. Her movements were clumsier than usual and her fingers tingled, a sensation she'd written off as being chilled prior to her diagnosis.

The doctor had said, "The numbness and tingling are due to neuropathy. It's to be expected. I'll prescribe you pain medications when it becomes unbearable."

Not *if* it became unbearable. *When.*

Funny how the box had gone untouched for decades, and now, this was the second time she was opening it within days. Last time, she'd been intent on finding the diary, but now she could take her time. Stored within was a fabric photo album her mother had made. The puffy cover included a photo of Imogene and Frances—their first photo together. Their crochet hat-covered heads touched at the temples, and their smiles spread across the photo. Frances brushed her thumb over the image. Imogene's new hat had matched her blue eyes.

Oh, Imogene. I love you so much. I will not let you down again.

"Who's that?" Lexi asked.

"This is me with my best friend, Imogene, when we were six."

"What's your name again?"

"Frances, but back then, I went by Frannie."

Frances had gone by Frannie until the summer Imogene vanished, until she'd told her parents to stop treating her like a baby, as if calling her Frances had drawn the line.

"Frannie is bestest, G-Ma." Lexi sang the name again and again.

The memory of Imogene's voice when she said Frannie's name caused a tsunami of feelings, rushing an aching, tender warmth from her head to her toes and back again. Every hair follicle on her body rose. She didn't have to hide her feelings about Imogene anymore. She didn't have to keep secrets or protect anyone. She didn't need to be strong. *You can be Frannie again*, she thought.

"Lexi the Great, you're right. Frannie is better. From now on, I'll use Frannie."

"I'll call you G-Ma Frannie."

Frannie paused to kiss Lexi's cheek. "I love you, Lexi the Great."

"Love you, G-Ma Frannie."

Frannie set the photo album atop the bed. The detective would need a picture. Peter Whittaker had had one even though it hadn't helped. She'd given him a picture of her and Imogene hugging the summer before they turned eight and started second grade. Sadly, it was the latest one she had of Imogene. The last pictures her mother had snapped of them together, just before Imogene's disappearance, were lost by the photo lab.

Perhaps with twenty-first-century technology, the new detective could do one of those age-progression images. She smiled, setting her notebook of chicken jokes on the bed. Imogene was the only one who had known about her chicken jokes and comedic aspirations, and Frannie stopped making them up after Imogene was gone.

In high school, Jean had gone through a phase of secreting what she wanted. "Put it out in the universe, and you shall receive," her daughter had said. Now, Frannie would ask the universe for Imogene. She'd find Imogene any way she could, and the right place to start was to think about her, feel for her, not stuff away the pain anymore.

Ironically, the next item was a thick file with a copy of her hospital medical records. Maybe by keeping the file, she'd accidentally given the universe permission to return the cancer these many years later. She set it aside in case the doctor wanted it. Were her childhood and adult cancers linked? Could anyone be so unlucky twice?

Lexi leaned forward, almost tipping over. "What else is in there?"

A clear bag full of Smurf toys was next. Lexi and Booby could have them now because toys were for playing with, not for burying.

14

FRANNIE

SPRING 1976

"Glass-half-full news," Mom said. That's what Mom had started saying whenever good news also meant bad news. "Mr. Dryker said Imogene will be there."

Frannie hated chemo, but she'd get to see Imogene in the hospital. She was tired of feeling sick and sick of being tired. She wanted to practice riding her bike and run through the sprinkler with Imogene at home in South San Francisco. Mom had said that when she and Imogene were both better, they could have playdates at Frannie's house—that would be loads more fun than phone dates.

Dad didn't like that Mom had become Mr. Dryker's phone friend. "This will come to no good," Dad kept saying. "I checked with Rodney. Do you know how many times the police have been called out to the storage sheds that Dryker manages? Did you know that she and her dad live on site in a trailer behind the office? I don't want

Frannie ever going over there. Too many people coming and going."

Once, Frannie overheard her mom say, "You're turning into an elitist. People probably call the cops every time they skip out on their rent and their storage gets sold off to cover the bill. Have you thought of that?"

"You're taking the wrong people under your wing," Dad said. "And you're forcing them on me too. What happens next time he comes here under the influence? You'll put me in an awkward position. And your nerves, Sally. Have you thought about the additional stress that helping him might cause?"

"George." Mom used Dad's name whenever she wanted to make him listen carefully, which was often. "He's going through the same thing we are, and he has no one to share the worries with."

At the children's hospital, Mom placed Frannie's clothes in the dresser in her usual room at the end of the hall. That meant she'd be here longer than she wanted. If not for Imogene, she'd get homesick at night. Having her things around was what made home, home, but knowing Imogene was down the hall helped. This time, Mom packed her pillow because it smelled like her bedroom.

She sat on the hospital bed watching her dad set Papa Smurf, Smurfette, Brainy, Doc, Grouchy, Bashful, and Gargamel on top of the dresser. This was the first time the Smurfs had gone to the cancer center with her.

Her collection had grown slowly at first because she had to save her tooth fairy and chores money for each toy.

Then she'd gotten sick. When the oncologist told them she had leukemia, Dad said, "I may be a doctor, but I'm a father first. I need some space and time to collect my thoughts." When he came home, he brought the entire Smurf village with him. Mom didn't even get mad—she wiped her nose and eyes and said, "So much for making her earn them with chores like a normal kid."

Her dad said, "Life is sh—"

"Don't say it," her mom said. "You did good."

Her dad spread out the village on the floor beneath Frannie, where she was lying down, feeling sick, on the couch. It was funny to see Dad in his work clothes playing with her new Smurfs and mushroom houses.

Frannie giggled. "You're too big for Smurfs."

"Are you laughing at me?" he asked. "Check this out. You see these blue guys?" He placed the plastic Smurfs on the shag carpet below her. "They are your good cells. And this jerk"—he lifted up Gargamel—"is leukemia. What does Gargamel say at the beginning of the Smurfs?" He didn't wait for a response. He continued in his best Gargamel voice, "I'll get you. I'll get all of you if that's the last thing I ever do."

Frannie giggled more, even though laughing made her head hurt.

"And what is most important to Papa Smurf?" Her dad handed her the red-hatted blue figure.

Moving made her dizzy, but she got up to one elbow and said, "To protect his Smurfs."

"That's right. Papa Smurf always protects his Smurfs,

and no matter how hard this rascal Gargamel tries, the Smurfs always win, right? And you're going to win too, Frannie."

Back in the hospital, Imogene entered as Dad said, "Oops, almost forgot Jokey." He set him on the dresser with the rest of the village.

Frannie sat up in bed for the first time in hours and opened her arms to her friend.

Frannie liked how Imogene rested her head on Frannie's shoulder and purred like one of Ms. Cornelius's cats next door. "I missed you, Imogene."

"I need to get in on this," her mom said, leaning over and embracing them both.

Dad chuckled. "You act like you're not on the phone every day, all day long."

Imogene turned her cheek to look at Frannie's dad, and that's when she saw the display. "Smurfs! Oh boy!"

Dad grimaced. "There are plenty of other toys in this wing for you. These are a special gift for Frannie. I'd rather you leave them be."

In spite of Dad's warning, Imogene leaned as close as she could to look at each Smurf without touching one. "Nurse Penny would be Papa Smurf. Frannie, you'd be Jokey."

Dad shook his head and grumbled. "I'm Papa Smurf."

"Really, George?" Mom rolled her eyes.

Imogene looked up at him patiently, as if he didn't understand The Smurfs. "You're Grouchy, Mr. Jerome."

Dad snorted. Frannie wasn't sure, but she didn't think he realized he glared like Grouchy might.

"Why is Frannie Jokey?" Mom asked.

"Because of her chicken jokes," Imogene said with confidence, almost touching the mushroom house with her nose.

"Chicken jokes?" Dad asked. "I haven't heard about any chicken jokes."

Uh-oh. Imogene didn't know it was a secret that Frannie wanted to be a famous comedienne when she grew up.

"Frannie tells the funniest chicken jokes in the world."

"What chicken jokes? You've never told me any jokes." Dad frowned.

Frannie tried to change the subject. "No, *you'd* be Jokey, Imogene, like Artful Dodger." Frannie had seen *Oliver!* twice now. "*Two times too many,*" her mom had complained. "*You could get sick at the group events due to your compromised immune system. I worry overtime, every time you attend.*" It didn't matter how many times her dad assured her mom that the hospital took extreme precautions sanitizing the common areas used by the children.

Imogene pinched Bashful's white hat and bounced him across the surface to Smurfette.

"I asked you not to touch them," Dad said, reaching for her.

Imogene jerked away and then set the Smurf down softly. "Sorry."

Frannie knew he'd snapped for her, but it wasn't okay for him to scare her friend. Just as Frannie had never told her dad about her jokes, she'd also never told Imogene that the Smurfs were her cancer fighters.

"George, toys are for playing with. They are for *children*."

"Imogene's my best friend, Dad. It's okay. She has cancer and needs cancer fighters too."

Imogene's eyes widened as she connected the dots. "Smurfs are cancer fighters?"

Dad ignored Imogene and looked at Frannie strangely. She didn't know what his eyes were saying, but he looked sad—the same as she would look like if she were homesick or if she'd lost something important to her.

He rubbed his head. "I should go back to work." He pointed at the Smurfs. "They don't leave this room."

"Bye, Dad."

"Bye, Mr. Jerome."

"I'll walk you out, Grouchy," Mom said. "I can use a cup of coffee."

Just then, a police officer walking down the hall said her dad's name. "Jerome, that you?"

When Dad turned, he smiled and strode toward his friend, hand outstretched. "Rodney, what brings you here? Nothing serious, I hope."

The cop looked over her dad's shoulder at Frannie and waved. "No, it's Penny." He lifted a sweatshirt in his hand. "She lost another jacket."

Mom stepped around Dad. "Ah, the infamous

clothes-eating closet is at it again, hey? I'm glad you take such care of Nurse Penny. I don't know what we'd do without her."

"Hiya, Sally. You two walking out?"

Her dad nodded. "I have a meeting. Sally is cafeteria bound. Care to join her? I think it would do her good to hear your opinion about that person we discussed."

"George Jerome . . ." Mom said in her you-are-in-big-trouble voice.

Rodney patted Dad's shoulder. "I'll get this to Penny and walk out with you."

As soon as the trio disappeared, Imogene picked up Jokey Smurf, put him in her pocket, and winked at Frannie. In her Artful Dodger British accent, she sang the chorus for "You've Got to Pick a Pocket or Two."

Frannie giggled and then bent forward with excitement. "I have something to show you when my parents leave. At bedtime."

"A surprise? What is it?"

"A secret fort for you, me, and the Smurfs."

LATE THAT NIGHT, after the nurses changed shifts, Frannie grabbed the flashlight she'd asked her parents for, saying, "In case I get scared at night when I'm alone."

Keeping an eye on her door, she fluffed her pillow under her blanket and turned out the lights. Hopefully, the night nurse would believe she was asleep.

Imogene was waiting in the hallway as planned.

Grabbing her hand and pointing the flashlight, Frannie giggled and said, "Come on."

Several more steps and they reached the closet. Her mom and dad had taken turns reading *The Lion, the Witch, and the Wardrobe* to her. When Nurse Penny swore never to use the *thieving* closet again, Frannie's imagination had taken flight. What if the closet was another portal to the magical land of Narnia?

She'd posed the question to her dad, and he'd laughed his pants off. "Narnia isn't a real place, Frannie."

But she wasn't so sure, so the next time she was alone and none of the nurses were about, she snuck to the closet down the hall, halfway between her room and Imogene's. Poking her head between the coats hanging there, she found a recessed area not large enough for adults but just right for kids. On the floor in piles, as if they'd fallen off hangers and had been accidentally kicked backward, were several sweaters, sweatshirts, and jackets.

And it was perfect. She and Imogene could use all the clothes as a rug and make it super cozy. Over the next few days, Frannie snuck in pillows. It would be their very own place with their very own rules.

"Oh, honey. Where have your pillows gone?" Nurse Penny had asked. "It's a good thing I don't believe in ghosts or I'd be spooked to the next county."

Maybe it wasn't really another world, but it felt like a new world made just for Frannie and Imogene whenever they wanted privacy, or when her dad was extra grouchy about their friendship or Mr. Dryker, or when Mom was stressed out.

Now, flashlight on, Frannie said to Imogene, "Welcome to Narnia." And she pulled Imogene through the jackets.

15

GRIFFIN

SPRING 2022

Griffin tore off his tie. Screw it. Breathing was more important than keeping up a professional appearance right now. He pulled out the last file in the box. Not only was it out of order, as if it were its own category, but it was also stapled closed. And instead of being labeled in his dad's usual style—with the client's name, such as, *Frances Jerome-McGee*—it read, "Imogene Dryker."

Using his fingernails, he pulled out the staples. Damn it if he couldn't stop his hand from shaking.

"Never open this one," his dad had instructed, patting the box when they moved to their new office. Now, Griffin knew his dad's warning wasn't about the box; it was about *this* file.

Everything has always been about this file.

There was no way in hell he would open it in front of Jean and Art without knowing what he might find inside. Over the years, he'd perfected his poker face, but today had already been trying, starting with his son, and now with this unexpected connection to his dad.

Dropping the staples on the desk, he said aloud, "Dad, I'm opening the damn file."

But, except for three items (Imogene's birth certificate, a note written on the inside of the file saying *4/1957,* and a picture of a young girl), the file was empty.

What the hell?

He looked at the files preceding *Imogene Dryker.* Normally, they were bursting with yellow legal pages full of notes. *"Crimes are in the details, Son. Write down and keep everything."*

Why was this file empty? Why had his dad kept a file with only the cryptic numbers and a single photo of a girl? Had his dad emptied the file? Destroyed his notes? No way. His dad had kept every case. "Just in case, pun intended," he'd said every time he finished a job.

Griffin turned the photo of the blonde girl over. On the back, someone had written, *August 1979.*

"That poor girl," his dad had cried. "People will go down for this."

This girl? Some other girl? Who was in this picture? What had his dad gotten involved in? What did this photo stand for?

Griffin dropped into the chair behind the desk and connected the dots as best as he could remember them.

After *Imogene Dryker,* his dad hadn't been the same.

When Griffin was young, his dad would come home at night for dinner with the family. Sometimes, he would need to go back to work after dinner because of *"the criminals who don't sleep."* On the nights he could wrap things up early, his dad would settle in for an evening with the family. Before dinner, his dad would go into his office, pour a splash of whiskey, and call Griffin to join him. Every night, as Griffin did now, his dad wrote a report on lined yellow paper about his daily activities on each case, adding it to the appropriate file. His dad would often give him the highlights of a case he was working on and would share the steps he'd taken and the resources he'd used, trying to engage Griffin in his future career at Whittaker & Son. But Griffin had hated it all. He had always watched the clock hanging on the wall behind his dad, knowing his mother would call them for dinner promptly at seven. Griffin would practice his guitar or clarinet in his head, counting the seconds until he could be free to be himself.

No, those moments had not endeared him to his father or the profession; they had tortured Griffin. But one night, everything changed.

Griffin was seventeen in 1994. He heard his father come through the front door, expecting another boring half-hour in the study. Instead, he stepped into the foyer and kept walking straight to the second floor without taking off his coat or calling out hello.

His mother came to greet her husband, as usual. She looked to Griffin and asked, "Where is your father?"

Griffin pointed upstairs, equally relieved and confused.

She asked, "Did he look sick?"

"No."

The two of them stood side by side until his mom finally called, "Peter, are you ill?"

His father didn't respond, but Griffin could hear movement above. A minute later, his dad appeared at the top of the stairs, still in his coat. Then he trudged downstairs as if he were carrying an immense burden. At the foot of the stairs, his dad patted Griffin's shoulder, kissed his wife's cheek, and silently proceeded toward the den.

"Peter," Griffin's mom said, turning to watch her husband walk away. "Your coat?"

"I'll take care of it in a minute," he said.

Griffin's mom looked down at her son expectantly and gently nudged him forward. Griffin sighed and followed her bidding, but when he stepped into the study, his dad stood silently before his file cabinet, looking down at an open file, seemingly oblivious to Griffin's arrival.

"Dad," Griffin said.

When his dad glanced over his shoulder, Griffin took a step back. His dad's eyes, his face—Griffin had never seen such a heartbroken and defeated look from his father before. His dad closed the file and put it in the back of the cabinet. Shutting the drawer with a resounding thud, he locked it. He didn't sit down behind his desk like he usually did. Instead, he walked toward Griffin, kissed his crown—something he hadn't done since Griffin was small—and walked heavily to the den's door.

Confused, Griffin asked, "Aren't you going to tell me about work?"

His father paused. "Not tonight. You know your music?"

"Yeah, what about it?"

"Go for it."

Griffin wasn't dumb. He raced upstairs and grabbed his clarinet. After years of arguing over his music, Griffin expected his dad to change his mind and come marching up the stairs to pull him back to his study to talk business, but he didn't. Griffin didn't put his instrument down until his mother called him to dinner.

His mom tried to diffuse whatever bothered her husband by telling him about her day. For all of her comments and offerings of more of this dish or that dish, his dad only stared down at his full plate. Finally, he set his fork down. "I'm sure this is delicious, but I'm not feeling great." He went upstairs alone. Later, Griffin overheard his parents' conversation.

"That poor girl."

Ironically, his dad's withdrawal was the very thing that made Griffin want to follow in his father's footsteps. Several solemn weeks later, Griffin thought he would do anything to revive his dad's spirits and alleviate his mother's worry. That's why he pretended to discover a newfound interest in his father's work, convincing his father he wanted to join the family business, that music was a hobby he'd grown bored with.

His father had looked relieved. "I could use the help. I'm getting rusty, and we need to keep this roof over our heads."

If Griffin could travel in time and change his decision,

appreciate the magnitude and consequences to his own life, he would not have made that promise to his dad, and he would not have made the promise to himself that he'd become the best. Yet, he'd done both.

He grabbed some blank paper sitting next to the printer and placed it in the empty folder to bulk it up before heading next door to Jean and Art. He was going to solve this case once and for all.

16

JEAN

SPRING 2022

"What if this guy, Griffin, says yes?" Art asked. "What will we tell Mother? She asked us to do two things. Two! And we're already backpedaling." He rubbed his unshaven jaw.

For once in her life, Jean wished someone would believe she was capable of making the right choice. Earlier, he'd agreed they should make an informed decision and at least meet the man the others had recommended. "Try to show some confidence that we can hire the right person. We've done our due diligence. We aren't backpedaling. Mom said not to hire Peter Whittaker."

Art nodded. "Strictly speaking, you're right, but she'll be pissed we went behind her back."

"We haven't gone *behind* her back; we *have* her back. And we won't tell her yet." Jean held up a finger. "Let me finish. We have no choice. She needs to trust that we can do this for her, help her find closure. We can't do that with anything less than the most capable help. This is the guy everyone else forfeited a paycheck to, out of respect for his success. When the time is right, we'll tell her, but it's not now."

"Then when is the right time?" he asked.

"When we find Imogene." If she hadn't realized it before, Jean felt it in her gut now. Finding Imogene had become as important, if not more so, to her as it was to her mother. The urge to prove to her mom, to everyone, that she was able to accomplish the seemingly impossible was making her feel . . . something. Something worthwhile. And she needed the right person to help keep this . . . whatever the feeling was . . . alive. After months, maybe years, of feeling like a failure, she wanted to succeed.

Art rubbed his eyes. "I hate this idea, but in the end—"

"Don't say 'in the end,'" she interrupted, but then finished what she knew he was trying to say since it supported her decision. "It's more important to get answers for Mom."

"This could be a no go anyway. Wait until you tell him he can't talk to Grandpa. He might laugh us out of his office." He closed his eyes, wrinkled his nose, and whimpered. "Is it wrong to hope he says no?"

The detective marched back in; his tie now loosened. He looked more determined and interested than he had a mere five minutes ago. As soon as he sat down, he pushed a picture across the desk. "Recognize this girl?"

They huddled over the picture. Their mom wore a

light blue polo shirt and a gigantic smile while relaxing on a purple beanbag chair, one arm spread wide as she smiled into the camera. She sported a chin-length blonde bob with strands of her hair tucked behind her ears. Jean's heart melted. This was her mom when she was young and on the verge of becoming a teenager. Jean had never seen her look so happy and carefree.

"It's our mom," Jean said.

"Flip it over," Griffin said.

With shaking hands, she turned the photo over to read, *August 1979*. "That's when Imogene disappeared."

"I hardly recognize her," Art said.

"Do you recognize the writing?"

"No," Jean said.

"Me neither," Art confirmed.

Griffin turned the picture over again. "Snap a picture of this, show it to your mother, and see what she can tell you about it and the writing. We need to find out why this photo is relevant."

Jean eyed the file bulging with paper. "Aren't there notes about the picture?"

"No."

Her mom was right; Peter Whittaker had been lazy.

"We can't ask her. What if *she* gave it to your dad? She'll know we're talking to Whittaker & Son."

"Right. Sorry. In that case, I'll compare it to others. Bring me every picture your mother owns. Leave it to me to decide what's relevant. Got it?"

"Does this mean you'll take the case?" Jean asked.

"Anything else I need to know before we sign a contract?"

She turned and looked at her brother. *Art?*

Art elbowed her softly and said, "Last chance to walk away."

But there was nowhere else to go. Convinced, Jean turned and stared hard at the private eye.

"There's one more thing. You can't talk to our grandfather."

Griffin raised his brows. "Does he know pertinent information?"

How much should she tell him? It was his job to discover the truth. But if her mother wanted a resolution, this investigator needed to know what she and Art knew.

Right, Art? she asked him with her eyes.

Art gave her two thumbs-up.

Jean cleared her throat. "Our grandfather was the last one to see Imogene alive, supposedly."

Griffin shot back in his seat. "You're joking. I must talk to him."

"You can't."

"Listen," Griffin said. "Some of the most important leads come from, one:"—he ticked off his fingers—"the interview with the client, which is your mother, who you don't want me to talk to, and two: the last people or person to have been in contact with the missing person, which is your grandfather. You can't expect me *not* to talk to the last person who saw her alive."

"*Supposedly* the last person who saw her," Jean said.

"All we know is what a woman—my mother—remembers as a nine-year-old."

She pointed to the thick file on the desk, itching to sort through it. "That's your father's work on the case, right? It looks as if you have a lot of groundwork laid out already. Start there, can't you? If that's not good enough for you," Jean said, bluffing, "I'll take that file and the case elsewhere."

Art groaned and gripped the arms of his chair as if he might jump up and run away.

The detective placed his hand on the file as if worried she might grab it. She didn't have the guts, though.

"I'll take the case. But if everything points to your grandfather, he and I will be talking. If you want to know what happened to Imogene Dryker, you need to trust me."

Trust. No one had it, but they all wanted it.

Channeling her mother's don't-cross-me look, Jean said, "Fine. If it gets to that point, we will go with you."

The detective rubbed his palms together. "Shall we get started then? I'll need some information from you up front. And you'll have to figure out how to get several questions answered by your mother. If you insist on hiding my involvement, I'll give you a list. If you can record her, it's a start. I'm the detective, not you. You might miss something."

A shiver ran up Jean's spine. "Yes. Let's begin. Time is of the essence."

17

GRIFFIN

SPRING 2022

As soon as Jean and Art left, Griffin opened a drawer, grabbed a file folder, and wrote *Frances Jerome* on the tab.

A new yellow legal pad followed to capture his case notes. His silly son probably thought he could do everything on an iPhone, but even with today's technology, hard copy was the best copy—a pen and paper didn't need charging, and Griffin never forgot anything he wrote down first.

Griffin had been opening cases for so long, he could do it with his eyes closed. No matter the purpose—workman's comp, fraud, infidelity, missing person—he worked a case through the same process, using the three phases his dad had taught him.

Phase 1: Gather information.

Phase 2: Review the gathered information, and see if it produces evidence that will conclude the case. If not . . .

Phase 3: See what leads or clues the unsatisfactory

evidence creates, and then run those new leads through the wringer again, starting with phase one.

But Imogene's story was far from the norm. Other than her name, the date of her disappearance, and the last place Frances Jerome had seen her, he had scraps to go on until he received the woman's answers.

Nope, this case wasn't same old, same old. Griffin opened his dad's file, removed the stack of blank pages, and added his dad's old file to the new file.

How about that, Dad? You're part of the mystery, which means you are part of the problem.

The first lead in this case was his dad's almost empty file with the single photo of Frances and that damn cryptic number: *4/1957*. The birth certificate was typical to include in a search file, so there were no alarm bells there. It confirmed her parents were Benjamin and Darlene Dryker; the latter having died during childbirth.

April 1957? *Assume nothing*—that was Private Investigation 101. He couldn't assume that the numbers meant a date. But, if it was a date, what was its significance?

On the top of the first yellow page, he wrote *4/1957*. And on the first line, he added *April 1957?*

On the top of the second page, he wrote *Dad, Peter Whittaker—that poor girl.*

On the first line, he wrote *Imogene*. His dad wouldn't have referred to his client, Frances, as a girl—she was a grown woman in 1994 when she'd hired him. Dad must have found out something about the missing girl. Next, he wrote *Photo of young Frances—what's the significance?*

Regardless, without Frances's answers, the next step in gathering intel was to get online and dig around.

Where are you on the internet, Imogene?

Maybe he'd solve this case before it got going. Internet and social media sites wouldn't have been a resource for his dad in '94, but today, Griffin could solve most cases with a few mouse clicks.

First things first. Was Imogene Dryker's grave listed on Find A Grave or Ancestry? *Nope.* If she was dead, she hadn't been buried legally.

Next, he pulled up the national archives of vital records to search for a death certificate, but after entering Imogene's full name, the year she disappeared, and the state, California, there were zero results. He pushed the date of death out by one year at a time for eleven years until 1990, because it was all too true that a kid could go missing, but it didn't mean they died right away, if at all. Look at Emily Ann Garcia and Veronica Johansson, for crying out loud.

But nada. He changed the search filters to include the USA and an exact match to the name. The broadened search added zippo. He played around with the year some more, but by the year 1995, he moved on.

The missing person cases he had covered in the past had never involved a young girl or someone taken against her will. Normally, the person he was hired to find wanted to stay lost, such as a deadbeat parent who didn't want to pay child support. An addict who didn't want intervention. Someone who didn't want court orders or divorce papers served. Sometimes, it was a person who'd left a violent partner. But whenever Griffin suspected an abusive relationship, he turned the case down—just as his father had always done.

Wait. Abuse. Maybe his dad did solve it.

What if Imogene had been abused by her father or someone else? Left with no alternative, had she run away for her own safety? Jean had told him her mother said the police thought Imogene was a runaway, only Frances never believed it. If his dad had located an adult Imogene and had confirmed abuse, he would have let Imogene decide if she wanted Frances to know she was alive and how to reunite. And if his dad had learned she was dead as a result, he would have involved the police. "*That poor girl.*"

"People are going to go down for this," his dad had said that fateful night.

His dad might have discovered the truth. *But no . . .* His dad would have kept the notes on this case. *Why the empty file, Dad? Why the picture? Why 4/1957?*

Focus, Griffin. Next step.

If Imogene were alive, he would only find her on social media if she wanted to be found.

His heart rate escalated at work for the first time in probably . . . well, ever. A search on Facebook turned up four instances of *Imogene Dryker*—five if he counted *Mary Imogene Dryker*. But age and ethnicity eliminated them all.

If she was married, she might not use her maiden name. He typed *Imogene*. Facebook turned up hundreds of profiles.

Crapola.

He switched over to Spokeo, a site that most citizens didn't have a clue about, and if they did, they'd freak out about how much of their info was legitimately available to strangers online for a few bucks. He mentally crossed his fingers for luck and a worthwhile list of potential phone numbers and addresses.

Searching *Imogene Dryker* turned up close to four hundred hits across thirty-eight states. Too many. He'd never get through this list on his own and not in a timely manner. Frances was unhealthy. Time was a luxury he didn't have.

His son Tony would think this part of the job was tedious and time-consuming; it was as far from an action-packed video game as possible.

Maybe he should give Tony what he thinks he wants, hire him as an intern, and make him comb through the list and call all four hundred Imogene Drykers. Could be a win-win: Griffin would have help narrowing down the list, and Tony would be bored the hell away from the (more often than not) butt-in-chair career. And no way would he pay Tony. When Griffin was in high school, he would have loved any job—except private investigation—that paid him money.

Right now, Griffin couldn't assume Imogene was alive. Time to get the worst part over with. Griffin pulled up Search for Missing Children, a site started by John Walsh after a monster had killed his son. No way could Griffin have found the courage to make a positive out of such a tragedy. The resilient dude repeatedly said, "It's my mission that no child be forgotten."

Hats off to this Frances woman, too, for not forgetting her friend when everyone else had.

He scrolled past the two dozen images of innocent little ones to find the digital form.

Who was he looking for? The child or the abductor: CHILD
Female or male: FEMALE
Name: IMOGENE DRYKER
Missing from: SOUTH SAN FRANCISCO
Missing date: . . .

The date caused a dead-end. The system's drop-down menu offered 2022 dates only.

This is a bust.

He clicked on *Help Identify These Children.*

The page filled with children, unfound and unclaimed.

The world was screwed up.

Disappointment in humanity was another thing Griffin would like to protect Tony from if he could, and avoiding this career was a start.

Damn. There were six hundred and fifty-two Jane and John Does. But it wasn't enough that the unidentified body's name was Jane Doe. Nope; more clarity was required, therefore, they grouped them by year, such as *Jane Doe 2020.* Or when there was more than one Jane Doe from the same year, they added a middle name, such as the city they were found in: *Jane Mount Shasta Doe 2020.*

He exported the six-hundred-plus names to an Excel file and filtered out the info he needed, starting with a sort by *date body found* and then *gender*.

Thinking about the rescued girls, Emily and Veronica, again, he kept the years through 1995.

He included *females* and *unknown gender*; that additional filter brought him down to a hundred twenty-five unidentified children. *Down to? Holy hell.*

He deleted twenty-eight African American girls and five Hispanic children, leaving ninety-one missing.

Five hundred and sixty-one kids dismissed with a delete button. *Heartbreaking.*

"Imogene," he spoke aloud. "I'm going to find you. That's a promise." Whatever his dad had gotten involved with, Griffin wanted to know. And what was up with Frances Jerome's father? Why was she protecting him if she was suspicious?

Griffin typed *George Jerome, Bay Area* in Google's search bar, yielding several pages of links and references to Dr. George Jerome's accomplishments and contributions to the community and the children's hospital.

> *Since joining the hospital's board of directors, Dr. Jerome has helped raise $168 million in philanthropic gifts, exceeding the hospital's five-year goal . . .*

Dr. George Jerome receives the Bay Area's Humanitarian Award . . .

"The children's hospital saved my daughter's life, and I'm committed to paying this forward the rest of my life . . ."

Whatever the reason the family didn't want Griffin to interview Jerome about Imogene, the retired doctor appeared to be a model citizen online.

Clicking on images, Griffin sized up the man who was often surrounded by young children, obviously fighting for their lives. It wasn't hard to find a birthdate. The man looked exceptionally well for someone in his eighties.

Having a clear purpose in life obviously keeps a man in good health, Griffin thought. He may not be able to interview the people who saw Imogene the week before her disappearance, but he knew someone he could interview ASAP about his dad and *"that poor girl."*

His mom.

18

FRANNIE

FALL 1977

"Run, Tammy!" the girl, Becky, screamed to her friend hiding in the bushes as Becky broke free from the evil man in the forest. Becky's yellow blouse glowed like a lantern as the man thundered after her. The dim room and the clicking sound of the film projector had once been one of Frannie's favorite sounds, thanks to *Oliver!*, but after watching *Dangerous Strangers* with Imogene, the rest of the school, and a police officer in the auditorium, Frannie never wanted to watch another movie in the dark again. Yesterday, she'd heard a sixth-grade boy bragging that he'd seen the documentary last year and had nightmares for a month. Who cared if she'd turn eight in one month? Never again would her bedside lamp be off at bedtime. She wanted Mom and Dad. Right now.

Her teeth chattered. Why did the child molester—that's what the movie called the stranger—take Becky and Tammy from the park to the forest? Why didn't he give them candy and take them home like he'd promised to do?

The music turned to a deep *duh, duh, duh.*

Frannie could barely spare Imogene a glance as her friend groaned, covered her ears, and stared at the floor.

Whatever a child molester man was, Frannie never wanted to meet someone like him.

The auditorium echoed with every kid's gasp as the angry man reached for Becky, but just in time, Becky darted to the left. Frannie tried to squeeze her eyes closed and stop watching, but she was afraid to miss what happened next. Would the man catch Becky? And what had happened to Tammy? She watched the whole thing, all the way to the end, until the two girls were lying face down in a dark cave; Becky's yellow blouse was gone.

Her classmates and Imogene sniffled. Frannie was too scared to cry. Why was Becky naked up top? The only time her parents allowed Frannie to run shirtless was through the sprinkler in her private backyard. At the end, Becky's and Tammy's parents were dressed in all black, and they cried next to two tombstones in a cemetery. Goose bumps rose along Frannie's arms. She tried to show Imogene, but Imogene stared at the floor in a trance, as if she was pretending to be somewhere else.

"Oh, honey. We'll be okay," she whispered to Imogene, though she wasn't feeling too confident herself.

She would never take candy or a ride from a stranger. She would never talk to strangers for any reason.

"Be quiet, weirdo."

That meanie, Danny Sutter, poked her from behind.

She swung her elbow back in case he tried to tease her again. She'd told Mom about him once, and she'd said, "Sometimes boys pick on cute girls. Ignore him." But that was the same puzzling advice Dad had given her about the bully in her neighborhood.

The narrator said the third girl, Cathey, was safe because Cathey's parents had taught her to avoid strangers.

When the lights came on, Father Kelly said, "Children, remember to be a Cathey, not a Becky or a Tammy."

A fifth-grade girl started crying. "But my name is Becky."

"And my name is Tammy," a girl from third grade said.

Mine too echoed throughout the room.

Nurse Bowman put her palms together as if she were about to pray. "Girls and boys, what the movie and Father Kelly mean is that you always want to be the smart, cautious child who never talks to strangers without your parents."

Nurse Bowman's tone made Frannie feel better about being smart, but not much.

Before the bell rang, Father Kelly led them in prayer, and after *amen* said, "Everyone back to your classroom to get your things and then head straight home as usual."

That night at home, Dad said unkind things about Mr. Dryker again.

"That film has it right. Not only should you never go near a stranger, but sometimes people you know can be a threat too." He pointed a finger at Frannie. "Exactly why I never let you go to the Dryker's place."

Wait, this was the worst lesson ever. "A child molester isn't always a stranger?"

"George Jerome," Mom said. "How dare you insinuate such a thing about Ben? I know you don't like him, but come on. I wish I hadn't signed the permission slip for Frannie to see the film. She isn't old enough to understand."

Dad hated it when Mom called Mr. Dryker by his first name. It always made the vein on his forehead bulge. "He's not your friend, Sally. We don't truly know him."

Feeling brave after surviving the movie, Frannie asked, "Is Mr. Dryker bad?" Imogene had told Frannie that the courts had taken her away from her dad because he was drunk, but was there a worse reason? Her palms sweated and her lips trembled.

Frannie would never have thought she and Imogene would keep secrets from each other, but maybe Imogene knew her dad was a child molester. Whatever one was . . . She still didn't understand. The more questions she asked adults, the more they confused her.

Mom pushed away her plate. "See what you've done, George?"

"Imogene stared at the floor during the movie, and she was quiet after school. Is she in danger? Should we take her away?"

Sighing heavily, Dad put down his fork and reached across the dining table for Frannie's hand. "Mr. Dryker drinks a lot, and alcohol clouds his judgment, which means that I can't trust him to make smart choices about men who might come around his place. Customers—strangers—are in and out all day at storage facilities. It's his addiction and poor decisions that are questionable."

"But that means Imogene *is* in danger. Mom, we have to let her live with us."

Mom stood to wrap Frannie in her arms and kiss her crown. "I promise that Imogene is safe where she is, isn't she, George?"

"But Dad said—"

Her dad ran his hand through his hair. "Listen, the big lesson here is to never talk to or go with anyone without our permission. During the day, when you walk home from school, never take a different route. And never walk alone at night, no matter how old you are, got it?"

Drying her cheeks on her napkin, she nodded.

"May I be excused for the bathroom?" Once she stepped outside the dining room, she snuck to the phone. Since they spent their school days, and most afternoons and weekends together, Frannie never called Imogene, but she still knew her number by heart.

All would be better once she heard Imogene's sunny voice. Except the phone rang and rang, giving Frannie no assurance that Imogene was okay. She returned to the dining room and hugged herself in her seat.

"What do child molesters look like? The film never showed the molester's face."

Her dad answered. "There isn't one look. Anyone can be a bad man underneath his skin. He can look like our grocer, one of our neighbors, and even like me. Don't trust anyone."

That night, Frannie had her first nightmare. Imogene was playing jacks, like Becky and Tammy, when a man in a plaid jacket and tan slacks bent over her with a handful of candy. The man's back was to Frannie. Over and over, she tried to scream, "Run, Imogene. Run!" But no sound escaped her lips except a tiny moan, and she watched helplessly as Imogene took the man's hand. As they walked away, the man's stride reminded Frannie of her dad's.

19

FRANCES

SPRING 2022

No wonder people complained about social media; how many times had Frannie logged into Facebook today?

Two new friend requests.

Please let one be Imogene.

Her finger shook as it tapped the digital bust.

No, not an alive Imogene. Of course not. Too easy, too forgiving, especially after Frannie's years of neglect.

Not Art or Jean either. In a weak moment, she'd invited them to be her friends. Neither had accepted yet. What did it mean if they never did?

One request was from a creepy-looking man whom she didn't recognize by appearance or name.

No thank you. Declined.

And the other was a man as well—Daniel Sutter. The name rang a bell, but why?

"Alexa," Frannie spoke to her digital pal, partly in jest. "Who is Daniel Sutter?"

But once Alexa began citing Wikipedia and referenced a season of *Dancing with the Stars*, Frannie asked her to stop.

"Is Alexa a Booby and Dandelion, G-Ma Frannie?"

Pausing to look across the open kitchen at Lexi surrounded by Smurfs on the living room floor, she said, "No. She's like a computer. Everyone can talk to and hear Alexa."

Her phone rang, and dread clamped her chest when she recognized the number.

"Hello?" She hated how her voice shook.

"Frances, this is Nurse Hart. We'd like to schedule a follow-up MRI and the growth factor injections in preparation for your peripheral stem cell collection.

"But I just had an MRI." God, she hated that claustrophobic tube.

"The doctor would like to make sure it's not spreading aggressively as that could impact decisions around chemotherapy and a transplant."

And so the difficult journey begins. Mere days ago, the phlebotomist had quipped that a woman never forgets a bad blood draw. Frannie would add chemotherapy to the list. Especially the extreme dose administered before the transplant. The chemo killed not only the cancer cells but the healthy stem cells, too, hence the need for a transplant of good ones. She hoped most people would never experience their bodies turning on them. Even once the transplant occurs, one doesn't recover immediately. There is the debilitating exhaustion and inability to focus or distinguish between being awake and asleep. It had been a long time since she thought about the experience, preferring to block it out of her mind. But now, it came flooding back to her.

To explain the procedure when she was small, George had called upon the Smurfs once again.

Her dad had sat beside her and spread the toys across her blanket-covered lap.

"When we found out you had cancer, we signed you up for an autologous bone marrow transplant trial. We took some of your bone marrow where stem cells are born. Then we froze the healthy cells just in case you'd ever need to replace yours. Now, you need them."

"I remember," she said. "Imogene and some of the other kids did too."

"That's right. Now, we know Gargamel is a bad cell, and we know the Smurfs are good cells. But let's imagine you have several Gargamels." He tapped her blanket, creating dimples where more bad cells would be.

Lifting a mushroom house, he said, "This is chemotherapy." He knocked Gargamel and the Smurfs over. "Chemo doesn't know the difference between the good and bad guys, so it destroys them all." He brushed the toys from her lap with his fingertips.

Turning at his waist, he grabbed Papa Smurf, Smurfette, and Bashful from the nightstand and stood them on her lap. "But we have frozen healthy cells that we can thaw out and return to your system. In no time, they will encourage more healthy blood cells to grow and join them."

Frannie laughed as he swooped up the discarded

Smurfs and added them back to her lap. "No Gargamel," she said.

"No more cancer." Her dad kissed her forehead. "That's the goal."

Frannie shook away the memory. "Nurse Hart, I had a bone marrow transplant in 1977. In fact, I found a copy of my medical file. I'll have my daughter drop it off."

"Frances, I'm sorry that you're facing this again. We will be here for you every step of the way."

Frannie glanced around her beloved home. "Is it possible to use a service to give me the growth factor shots at home? My insurance isn't an issue. I'll pay if necessary. I've had enough of hospitals in my lifetime."

After agreeing to help her arrange a mobile service, the nurse ended the call.

"It's me," Jean called from the foyer after entering the front door code.

"Uh-oh," Bonnie Bell said.

"You're okay, pretty bird."

"Ugly bird."

"Mommy's back," Lexi said without abandoning her Smurf village.

Sitting at the table, Frannie pushed the diary aside and positioned the photo of her with Imogene squarely before her on the table. It was the same one Peter Whittaker had returned decades before. Jean could make a copy for the new detective once she hired one. Life ahead might be a short path, and she wanted to frame the picture with her and Imogene for her bedside table rather than risk never seeing it again. Going through her album, she'd been saddened by how few pictures she and Imogene had together—had she taken enough pictures with Jean, Art, and Lexi? If she died, would they be hard-pressed to find pictures of her? Goodness, did people even print pictures anymore? They kept them on phones and on the cloud, thousands upon thousands until they ran out of storage and started deleting them, making room for new photos. Frannie might be deleted over time. Out with the old, in with the new. Forgotten. Obsolete.

She brushed her thumb across the picture. She and Imogene had both been seven years old the summer of 1977. Their eyes sparkled, their smiles were so wide, and their lips connected at the corners, despite their chemo-swollen cheeks that normally made the simple expression of happiness painful. The picture had captured a special moment, indeed.

It was the day they had found out that both of them would attend St. Agnes Elementary School.

Frannie remembered the day well, photo or not, but the picture certainly helped jog her joy. She'd been coloring with Imogene in her hospital room when her mom entered with Mr. Dryker behind her. It was the first time she'd seen them together.

Mom and Imogene's Pops had big news for them.

Her mother handed her a large bag, like the ones from department stores. Frannie opened it and pulled out two blue and green pleated skirts and white polo shirts.

"Clothes? Boring."

Her mother clapped her hands and jumped in place. "You're both going to St. Agnes for second grade."

And Mr. Dryker said in a scratchy voice, "Imogene, baby, you got financial aid."

"I'm goin' to school? With Frannie?!" Imogene screamed, jumped off the bed, and hugged her pops, her new uniform smashed between her chest and his legs.

Frannie sorted through the pictures until she found one that Nurse Penny had taken that same day with all four of them. Her dad was conspicuously absent. He'd probably hated the entire idea of the girls going to school together and her mom spending time with Mr. Dryker to arrange it.

Jean came into the room and kneeled beside Lexi to kiss her. "Hi, sweetie. Having fun?"

"Yup."

"Are those Smurfs?"

"G-Ma Frannie gave them to us."

Frannie supposed Jean's back stiffened at the mention of *us,* a.k.a. Booby. A brief flash of panic crossed her face.

Probably intent on distracting Frannie, her daughter said, "My mom? Saving toys?"

"Oh, Jean, I'm not an ogre. *We* used to have fun when you were little. Don't you remember?"

"I don't remember playing with Smurfs together." Jean joined her at the kitchen table. "G-Ma Frannie, is it now? I like it."

If they'd been alone, Frannie would have flat out asked when Booby had joined the family. But despite Jean's poor opinion of her mothering skills, she had no intention of dissecting the reasons for Booby's existence in front of her granddaughter.

"I stored the Smurfs with my diary and photos." Her mother's words from decades before came back to her. "As my mother once said, 'Toys are for playing with.'"

Jean sat up straight. "You kept a diary?"

"When Imogene and I started school, we had to watch this horrible awareness movie. I started having nightmares, and the school nurse, Nurse Bowman, recommended I keep a diary to get the nightmares out of my system. Then, when Imogene . . . well, I blamed myself. Though I had left St. Agnes, my parents asked Nurse Bowman to talk to me. I'd always trusted her. She suggested I write down all the details. It was meant to be cathartic."

Her daughter glanced toward Lexi, probably to make sure she wasn't soaking up their discussion. It gave Frannie pause to recognize her daughter as a mother. She had never protected Art's and Jean's young ears, and she couldn't help but consider the consequences of her actions now. What was the true definition of protecting your children?

"Mom, I'm sorry for all the times I got mad at you for preaching about safety and awareness. I thought you were over-the-top for no reason. I didn't understand, but I'm beginning to."

"I should have explained my fears long ago. I see that now. But I didn't know how to, not with your grandfather and all."

"Tell me about the diary. Was it as therapeutic for you as the nurse had hoped?"

"No, not then." She remembered the last time she had held the diary as a child and the wretched guilt that came with it. "But it should help now. There are dates and times in here that I'd forgotten. When you find a detective, it will be of use. Here, I've written out a timeline of events."

"Whoa." Jean finally noticed the whiteboard covered with precise lines and multicolored Post-its covered in neat printing. "Is that the timeline?"

"Yes, I transferred it to paper. Each person involved has been assigned a color, naturally."

"Naturally." Jean smiled at her. "Mom, this is fantastic. And just in time. We found someone to help us."

Relief almost overwhelmed Frannie. "The *best*?" she asked.

"According to everyone Art and I talked to, yes, *the best*. Even other investigators pointed us in his direction."

"What's his name?" Frannie asked, her interest piqued as Jean stood and retrieved her purse from the floor next to Lexi.

"He gave me a list of questions for you to answer."

"Did you hire Peter Whittaker again?"

"Peter Whittaker is dead."

Another person was gone who might have known something about Imogene. "How do you know?"

Jean lifted her eyes to Frannie's. "Does it matter? Art

and I are handling everything. You need to save your energy so you can be here when we find her."

Though Frannie appreciated her daughter's tone of confidence, she sensed Jean was withholding something important.

"I need to write the person a check," Frannie fished.

Jean rolled her eyes as if to say, *Who writes checks anymore?*

"I should add him to the crime board," Frannie said.

Lexi chastised one of the Smurfs from the living room. "Papa Smurf said no!"

Her daughter glanced at Lexi. "He prefers payment once finished."

Frannie shook her head, and her voice rose. "That's a sign he lacks commitment and dedication."

"No, Hefty Smurf," Lexi scolded.

"You're wrong," Jean said, lifting her chin.

"It's like Peter Whittaker, not cashing my check to begin with. Find someone else."

Jean's face turned red, but Frannie wasn't sure if it was from embarrassment or anger. If she pushed her daughter too hard, she'd lose her help, and for a moment, Frannie didn't know what to do next. She couldn't afford to lose Jean's assistance, but she couldn't jeopardize finding Imogene because of another mediocre detective.

"Jean, I don't like this—"

"Of course you don't like it, Mother. You're not in control. I am."

"Uh-oh," Bonnie Bell said.

"You're hurting our ears, Mommy."

Jean tilted her head back, closed her eyes, and took a deep breath. "Sorry, sweetie pie."

For the first time, Frannie noticed the circles under Jean's eyes. "You look tired." Too much pressure and stress and Jean would walk away as she'd always done.

"Tired is an understatement, but I don't want to talk about it. You have enough to deal with."

Pushing aside the dread of face-to-face rejection and criticism, Frannie asked, "Did I hurt you by not telling you more as a child? By not explaining my reasons? Is that why it's hard for you to talk to me now?"

Jean bit her lip, but then said, "Mom, you've got cancer. I don't want . . ."

"I asked."

Jean reached across the table to rest her hand atop Frannie's. "Your paranoia about strangers and the horrible things that could happen to us came at a price. It was hard to talk to you about my dreams and the things I wanted to try or do without you dissecting them with hypothetical outcomes and worst-case scenarios. I didn't have a mother when I started dating, or when I was excited about going away for college. I had a security guard, a warden. And now with L-E-X-I, I can't tell you everything we are doing or invite you along, because I'm afraid you'll judge me and Shane and tell us we're not keeping her safe." Tears filled her eyes. "I don't want her to be afraid all the time, like I used to be."

Frannie clenched her jaw to will her tears away as her heart dropped to her stomach.

All her life, she'd been afraid of what had happened

to Imogene and what George had and hadn't explained. With no understanding or the truth, Frannie had felt she couldn't rely on anyone to protect her. And when her children were born, teaching them to be safe had been her way, she supposed, of proving she was their protector. That she was looking out for them always. Only, something had gone wrong. Something had gotten lost in translation from mother to child.

Jean continued. "You've never trusted me and Art to use common sense, and we have, in turn, learned not to trust you with the things going on in our lives."

Just as Frannie had never fully trusted her father again. Though for different reasons, that same loss of confidence—the loss of faith—had been passed down to her children. Frannie had over-corrected. Yes, that's exactly what she had done, over-corrected, like a driver hitting black ice, gripping the wheel, and forgetting to turn into the direction the vehicle slid. She'd never realized before that, by teaching them to staunchly keep their guard up, she'd robbed them of the very innocence she had lost when Imogene vanished.

Oh my, what have I done?

Turning her hand underneath her daughter's, Frannie gripped Jean's. "I'm sorry." There was probably more she should say, but she was at a loss for words for now.

Squeezing her hand back, Jean let out a slow breath. "I shouldn't have spoken for Art, though."

Despite the weight of regret that had settled on her shoulders, Frannie chuckled and tried to lighten the mood. "The two of you have always spoken for each other."

"That's true."

If Frannie wanted to find Imogene and gain her children's trust, she'd need to extend her own. And the best time and place to start was obvious. But it would take practice. It had been a long, long time since she'd trusted anyone. She cleared her throat. "You're right about the detective. I said I'd trust you, and I have to give you a chance. Please give me one as well."

Jean tilted her head. "So, no more questions about the investigator unless Art and I think it's important?"

"Yes. I'm going to try. But never lie to me. Are you hungry? I made you a tuna sandwich."

Frannie would have to be blind to miss the relief that washed over Jean's face.

"What happened to peanut butter and jelly?"

She slid the plate before Jean and sat down across from her. "Booby ate yours."

"Um . . ." Jean took a large bite that prevented a response.

If Jean wanted to talk more about Booby, she would. Earned trust was more valuable than forced confessions. So, Frannie changed the subject.

"Can I see the questions?"

Jean retrieved the questions between bites. "The detective said he learns most of what he needs to begin the investigation in the initial interview. He asked me to record your answers since he might have additional questions based on your answers. Or I can show you how to record the answers if you'd prefer to answer them alone."

"I'd like for you to know."

Lexi skipped to the table with Hefty and held it far too close to Jean's eyes, so she leaned away to see better.

"Who's this?" Jean asked.

"This is Hefty. He's strong."

Frannie said, "He sounded more like a troublemaker a few seconds ago."

"That's G-Ma Frannie's friend." Lexi pointed to the photo between Frannie's hands on the table.

Jean took a closer look, and her eyes grew moist. "I've never seen pictures of you with leukemia." She traced their smiles and tiny heads with the tip of her finger. "You were both so resilient."

"Youth." Frannie nodded. "We didn't believe we could die. We never thought about death, even then."

With more eagerness than Frannie thought necessary, Jean asked, "Which picture did you show to Peter Whittaker?"

Frannie couldn't remember saying she had, but it was a logical assumption. "This same one."

"And which other ones?"

"Only this one. It was the summer before second grade. We'd found out we would go to school together, and we posed in our matching uniforms." She smiled fondly.

"Do you have later ones? Closer to her disappearance?"

"We took others. Unfortunately, the film was lost by

the photo lab . . ." Frannie stilled. *Unless that was a lie too.* Was it one more piece of evidence her parents had held back to protect themselves?

Jean scrunched up her nose and frowned. "You didn't give him a different picture? One of just you?"

"No. I wasn't the one missing. Why?"

Ignoring her question, her daughter curiously inspected the album's contents as if searching for something specific.

"What are you looking for? I can help," Frannie said, growing frustrated by her lack of understanding.

"A photo of you, at least, close to the time Imogene would have disappeared in 1979."

"Why? How will that help, to know how I looked?"

"Because the detective will need as many photos as possible to help jog peoples' memories." Turning to Lexi, Jean said, "I need to talk to G-Ma alone. Can you please go to the other room?"

"No. We want to stay with G-Ma Frannie," Lexi whined.

"Lexi," Frannie said. "Go play in the next room while I talk to your mother."

"Okay." She danced off.

Lexi always did as Frannie told her to, and she knew it irked Jean sometimes. Like now. Frustration was written all over her daughter's face.

Frannie patted Jean's hand. "If you didn't *ask* her to do things, Lexi couldn't say *no*."

Jean rolled her eyes. "So I've heard. Not now, okay?" She groaned. "I mean, not now." Jean slid the questions across the table and took Frannie's phone. She downloaded a recording app and showed her mother how to use it. "Some questions might be difficult to answer."

"Let's start with one of the hardest," Frannie said, her fingertip sliding down the list. "Was Imogene afraid of anyone?"

20

FRANNIE

SUMMER 1979

As the two girls left the corner drugstore, the bells jingled on the door, signaling their status as bona fide shoppers. Neither had ever gone shopping at the South San Francisco neighborhood store without Frannie's mom before.

"Please. It's one block away. I'm almost ten and will be a fourth grader," Frannie had argued with her mom. "My new school is farther away than the store." Frannie added the *new school* bit with a pouting lower lip.

A few weeks before, when her parents had broken the news that she'd be leaving St. Agnes for fourth grade, she asked, "Why do I have to change schools? What about Imogene? Who will she walk home with?"

Her mom reached over and patted her hand. "You can meet her after school at our house and see her on the weekends. Aren't you excited to make new friends?"

Her parents were confusing sometimes. Her mom and dad did everything together. She didn't see them going out of their way to make new friends. Why should *she*?

"But you've always said that if I can count my friends on one hand, I'm a lucky person."

Her mom nodded. "You're right, I have said that. And it's true, but it's time to change schools."

"No, thank you. I'll stay at St. Agnes with Imogene."

"Not an option," her dad said.

"But why?"

Her mom slid a school brochure across the table. "Whitney Prep is a better school."

"How is it better? I like my teachers now. And what about Nurse Bowman?" The idea of not being able to talk to the nurse whenever she wanted made her sad. She'd seen Nurse Bowman every week while at St. Agnes to check her temperature, throat, and weight (to make Mom feel better about the cancer being gone), and they always got to talking about school, Imogene, and home. Frannie liked how she could ask Nurse Bowman things that upset her parents, like why the area beneath her nipples was sore but Imogene's wasn't, and who did she think would get their period first (hello . . . she'd read, *Are You There God? It's Me, Margaret*). And after the first nightmare about Imogene leaving with a molester who walked like Frannie's dad, it was Nurse Bowman who'd told her what molesters did. She explained the dream didn't mean anything. Nurse Bowman gave her a diary—with a lock and everything—to record her fears and get stuff off her chest.

"It's a private school with excellent teachers and a nurse," her mom explained.

"St. Agnes is private too." Frannie lifted her chin stubbornly.

Mom looked helplessly at Dad.

"It's not up for discussion. You're going to Whitney," he said.

"But I don't get why Imogene can't go too."

Dad tapped the table with his finger. "Sweetheart, Whitney Prep is expensive. We've saved for it for the past few years, and—don't interrupt me because I know what you're going to say—Imogene can't get a scholarship as she did for St. Agnes."

"How do you know?"

Her dad gave her a look of finality. "Enough. What's done is done. My daughter deserves the best. It's why I work hard."

It was a done deal; Frannie would be a Whitney Prep Wild Horse while Imogene remained a St. Agnes Saint.

Now, Frannie waited for her mom to give her and Imogene the A-OK to walk to the store.

"It's hard to let you grow up. I'll always think of you as my little girl, but you're right." She nodded and pulled out her wallet. "I'll stand in the front yard until I can see you heading home."

After waving to her mom from outside the store, Frannie rooted through her shopping bag for her most daring purchase to date. Well, maybe not too daring since Mom had given her permission. The red and white KINGS cigarette-shaped box opened easily.

Frannie sniffed the pink bubblegum wrapped in white and yellow paper. She lifted one to her lips and blew. A billow of powdered sugar filled the air.

Walking home beside Imogene now, Frannie said, "Guess who I am." Then she pursed her lips and puffed again. Lifting the candy cigarette to the side with a flourish, she walked forward as if in high heels. Pretending to toss a feathered boa over her shoulder, she said, "I'm going out with Peter. Hey. Hey. Hey."

Imogene covered her belly with her hands as she laughed. "Carol Burnett. 'A Swiped Life.'"

"You got it."

Imogene said, "I'm going to miss seeing you at school and walking home with you."

"Just remember . . ." Frannie said.

"I know. No strangers, stick to the same route, and never walk after dark."

Frannie and Imogene hadn't had a single close call for the past two school years. "But you can still walk straight to my house after school, and I'll meet you at home every day."

Frannie paused before tossing the candy package into her bag. "Want one?"

"Nah, save 'em for yourself. Pops says no candy."

"Don't you think it's strange what things your dad decides to care about?"

Imogene flinched. "Now you sound like your dad."

"I'm sorry. I guess I'm just nervous. What if no one likes me at the new school?"

"Oh, honey. Everyone will like you."

"You know what I mean. I want to be normal. Not the 'girl with cancer.' I want to fit in. And I want to make more friends."

"You'll always have me for a friend."

As they neared her house, Frannie said, "I wrote a new joke."

"A chicken one?"

"It's the funniest one yet."

Imogene stopped in the middle of the sidewalk. "Tell me now, in case your dad's home and makes me leave."

Lately, Imogene had insisted Frannie's dad didn't like her, and she wouldn't let it rest.

"Give it up, Imogene. My dad likes everyone."

"No, he doesn't. He has never liked Pops."

"So what?! He likes you, I swear. You mumble, and he can't understand what you're saying. That's all."

"He thinks Pops and I aren't good enough for you. Like I'm a bad influence."

Frannie twirled the candy cig in her fingers like a baton. "You're wrong."

"Forget it. It doesn't matter right now. Tell me the joke."

Grateful for the change of subject, Frannie stepped back and lifted her chin, standing tall like Ms. Burnett would do on stage. "Why did the chicken cross the road?"

"I don't know. Why did the chicken cross the road? Again. For the billionth time."

"No comments from the peanut gallery, please. I'll start again. Why did the chicken cross the road?"

"I don't know. Why did the chicken cross the road?"

Frannie's fingers tingled with anticipation. She counted to three before she delivered the punch line. "To visit her chick *kin*."

Imogene snorted and swatted at Frannie.

"Come on," Frannie said before running the rest of the way home, up the steps, and through the door.

"We're in the kitchen." It was her father.

Imogene cringed. "I'll wait outside. Or I can go to your bedroom."

"Come on. It's rude not to say hi. Then Dad won't like you for sure." Frannie beckoned her to follow. Her parents were sitting at the small kitchen table, which they used more often than the one in the dining room.

Frannie's mom turned her head and tapped her cheek, begging for a kiss. Frannie didn't hesitate.

"Hi, Mr. and Mrs. Jerome," Imogene said, shyly hanging back at the threshold to the room.

"I heard you laughing when you came in," her dad said. "You going to let us in on the fun?"

Frannie hiked her thumb over her shoulder toward Imogene. "Imogene likes my latest joke."

Her dad looked toward the doorway and glared. His anger caught Frannie off guard, and when she looked again, he still frowned in Imogene's direction.

Imogene self-consciously smoothed her faded skirt and old, stretched-out sweater. She crossed her arms over her chest and boobs, even though only Frannie and Imogene knew they existed under her shirt, and then moved one ankle behind the other to hide at least one scuffed Mary Jane shoe. "Her joke is super funny," Imogene said, her gaze fixated on the floor.

Frannie had never noticed her dad scowl at Imogene like that before. What if Imogene was right? What if her dad didn't like her? But he liked almost everyone. How could two of her favorite people not be each other's favorites too? Still, she stepped closer to Imogene to lend comfort.

Her mom came to the rescue and smiled. "The true mark of a best friend is one who laughs at all your jokes."

Imogene blushed and ducked her head. "Thank you, Mrs. Jerome."

Dad shoved his chair back from the table and stomped to the kitchen door, heading to the backyard. The screen door slammed behind him.

Maybe Imogene's right.

Too afraid to learn the truth by asking her mom, Frannie asked instead, "Can we go to my room?"

"For a bit, sure," her mom said, nibbling her lip like she did whenever she was worried or thinking hard about something.

21

GRIFFIN

SPRING 2022

Grabbing his cell, Griffin called Annie. "Love, I'm stopping by Mom's to ask her a few things. I'll need to go back to the office and wrap up a background check. I'll be later tonight than I expected."

His wife never minced words. "Must be important questions if you don't want me or Tony to go with you. Everything okay?"

Annie was right. His first choice was to have her with him to diffuse the heebie-jeebies the senior living center gave him. Not that the place was doing anything wrong—his mom liked the home. But it wasn't anywhere he wanted to end up. He'd rather die first. And it wasn't just the place and his own future fears; it hurt to see Father Time having his way with his mom.

Yet, the conversation was necessary and best conducted alone since it involved his father. He'd never told Annie about *"that poor girl."* When he'd first met her, she'd thought that being an investigator made him hunky and cool.

"Like Tom Selleck in *Magnum P.I.*?" she'd asked him when they met for coffee.

"Yeah, except for the sports car, mustache, and short shorts, just like him," he'd said.

Her awe and laugh had stolen his heart right then and there—salve to his bored soul, so he hadn't fessed up for years that he'd never wanted to follow in his dad's steps. At first, she didn't question why he joined the firm; maybe she'd assumed it was natural. After all, her mom had been a teacher and Annie was a preschool teacher. Her brother was a long-haul driver like their father. Griffin hadn't admitted that he'd joined to boost his dad's spirits until Tony had decided to become an investigator and Annie couldn't understand why Griffin was being a pain in the butt about it.

Now he assured her, "I'm good to see Mom on my own today."

"Don't eat before dinner—I know your tricks."

She was guessing . . . unless she'd hired a competitor to follow him and take pictures of him at the food trucks where he shoved fatty foods from the naughty list down his throat for a temporary high.

"You having me tailed?" he asked, half-joking.

"I don't need to. You're still gaining weight despite the healthy food I'm feeding you."

"I'm gaining weight because I can't turn down anything you make me." It wasn't a lie.

"I'm making pasta-free vegetable lasagna tonight."

"Sounds delish." He'd stop by the bakery and pick up hot croissants for him and Mom. "By the way, have you heard from Tony? Did they let him out of prison?"

"Is it so horrible that he wants to follow in your footsteps?"

"Somewhere, Dad's cheering, hearing you argue for him," Griffin said.

He and his dad had had the same argument, over and over.

"I've laid down a good future for you, Son. Music isn't going to put food on your family's table. You need a viable career to do that."

"I'm seventeen. I don't want a family."

"But you will."

Dad had been right. Griffin had a family to provide for. But who was to say a music career wouldn't have earned enough for them? If his dad had supported his pursuit of music, maybe Griffin would be a happy musician now, or maybe he would have changed his mind on his own after being broke and working from gig to gig. It would have been *his* choice, and that choice might have made all the difference.

"I'll talk to you later, sweets," he said.

On his walk over to his mom's, he blasted "Santa Monica" by Everclear in his earbuds. When he arrived, a bag of croissants in hand, the center was in the middle of a rousing game of bingo.

It never mattered if the residents were being entertained, though, because when Griffin came through the door, as always, the players looked up with hope.

They all wondered, *Is the visitor for me?*

Everyone deflated when he came into their clear line of sight, except his mom—she waved like a bingo winner. He hurried to her and kissed her cheek.

"Hey, Kiddo. Want to play bingo?" she asked.

"Not now, Mom." *Not ever.* "Can we go to your room and talk?"

"Sounds serious. You sounded like your father then."

Great.

It took a while to reach her room. His mom kept pausing to introduce him to other residents and staff members. He'd met most of them before, but he was happy to humor her motherly pride. While she got settled into her electric recliner, Griffin looked around. It was as cozy as cozy could be in places like this. She had her bed, a television, and a computer for accessing social media—against his advice. He had repeatedly warned his mother about Facebook and screening so-called friends. Scammers were everywhere.

"Okay, sweetie," his mom said to him as if he was a youngster and not almost forty-five years old. "What's on your mind? You look like your father did whenever he had a troublesome case."

Oh, the irony.

He dangled the white pastry bag before her. "Priorities, Mom." He sat on the foot of her bed and passed out the croissants.

"Does Annie know you went to the bakery?"

"What she doesn't know won't hurt her."

"A croissant could hurt you as it hurt your father."

Yeah, yeah. He'd probably die like Dad too.

"Can you take him some flowers for me?"

He nodded, not relishing a visit to the cemetery. "Speaking of Dad, do you remember when he came home after he closed that case he couldn't solve?"

"Hard to forget the one and only case. Why?"

"What do you know about it?"

She sipped cold coffee left on her side table. "Not enough for me to understand what happened."

"Anything you remember might help."

She perked up, her eyes widening. "Why?"

"Someone has contacted me to solve it."

She set down her croissant, the flakes sprinkling her lap, and rested her palm against her chest. "Well, I'll be. I don't know. If your dad didn't solve it, there was a reason."

Didn't solve, not couldn't solve.

"'The only unsolved case is the one with unfound evidence,'" he recited his dad's work playbook.

A faraway look entered her eyes. "My dear Peter. That case made him doubt himself."

Griffin wanted another croissant, but he hadn't bought more than two. "I might understand Dad more if I solve this case." That last line was planted to ply his mother. If anything encouraged her to cave in rather than remain stubborn, it was the idea that something might help his opinion of her husband.

"I remember he cried. The only other times I saw him cry were when you were born, when his father died, and when you said you would join the firm. But that night, he kept saying, 'that poor girl.' Except for the interviews, he never spoke of it again."

Boom. Griffin's heartbeat kicked up. "What interviews?"

"In 1994, he had to speak to police administrators about the initial investigation in 1979 and something he found in '94. He couldn't tell me more. Can you tell me about the case now?"

"A nine-year-old girl went missing in 1979, and she was never found. Someone asked Dad to find her in 1994."

She quoted his dad again. "'That poor girl.' Now it makes sense."

Did it? Far from it.

"Mom, if you think of anything at all, please let me know."

"Son, solve this for us all, okay? Your dad was right. You were meant for this job."

She meant it as a compliment, but he knew his dad had wanted someone to carry on his legacy. It had never had anything to do with Griffin's competence. "I'll do what I can."

So, his dad had been interviewed by administrators. By whom, exactly? On his walk back to his office, Griffin called records. "Darla, Griffin Whittaker here. Fancy some company tomorrow morning?"

Darla laughed; the sound hoarse due to decades of smoking. "At least you ask. Your dad always showed up unannounced. What's on your agenda? I always like to see you, but when I do, it means you're up to no good, or looking up the no-good."

"A missing girl from 1979. Imogene Dryker."

"Doesn't sound familiar. If we have anything, it will be in microfiche. We switched from hard copy to software in '92. I'll check the books to see if we have an evidence box. If we do, it'll be in the basement warehouse. But, to quote Mr. Jagger, you know what they say about evidence inventory from the late seventies and early eighties . . ."

Unfortunately, he did. "'You can't always get what you want.'"

"Mick knew things," she said. "Most records prior to the nineties were purged or destroyed, but if it was marked as a cold case, we might be in luck. When will you be here?"

"Bright and early. Eight."

"Bring me an iced caramel macchiato, will you?"

22

FRANNIE

SUMMER 1979

Following a light tap on the door, Frannie's mom's voice carried through. "Can I come in? I have jam sandwiches."

"Yes, please," Frannie said.

Mom had stacked one sandwich atop the other, both cut into triangles with the crusts removed.

In her Artful Dodger voice, Imogene said, "I like the triangles. They're like afternoon tea. But I'm not hungry, thank you."

"More for me and Mom then." Frannie licked her lips.

Mom joined them on the floor next to the beanbag where they'd been looking at JCPenney's newest catalog.

"Mom, why did Dad glare at Imogene like that?"

Her mom set the plate on the shag carpet. "I didn't notice. I'm sure you mistook his expression." She turned to grab the photo of Frannie and Imogene off the dresser. It was Frannie's favorite picture because it was from two years before, when they were told they'd be going to second grade together. "But it was five years ago today that we found out you had leukemia. It's a hard anniversary for your dad."

Frannie wrinkled her nose. "But that's a stupid anniversary. Shouldn't we celebrate my remission anniversary? I'm cured. Imogene is too. Dad owes her an apology. Right, Imogene?"

"Stop right there. You're speaking disrespectfully about your father, Frannie. Like you, he has a right to his feelings."

"Thank you." Imogene nodded at Frannie encouragingly. "But she's right."

Frannie dropped her eyes to her sandwich. "I'm sorry."

"He wants you to stay healthy, be happy, and live a normal life. We almost lost you. We'll each recover and move on when we are ready and in our own way."

Frannie sure hoped so. Her mom looked sad now, too, but Frannie didn't know how to fix things.

Imogene, as always, knew what was needed. "I know what to do. How about you take a new picture to replace this old one?"

Frannie smiled. "Super idea. Mom, can we take a picture together? I'll wear my new uniform like last time."

"No, not with me," Imogene said. "Just you."

"I'm only taking a new picture if you're in it. I can hang up a copy in my school locker."

"Can you?" Mom asked, biting her lip. "I guess that

will be okay. I'm not sure if we have film for the camera. I'll be right back."

While Mom retrieved the camera, Frannie changed into her baby blue polo shirt and navy blue skirt. Next, they pinched color into their cheeks and fixed their hair.

There was a commotion outside her room. Frannie put her finger to her lips to keep Imogene quiet. She crept to the door and put her ear against it.

"You might not like Imogene, but she's Frannie's best friend." It was her mom, followed by her dad's deep sigh.

Her mom had known all along! Frannie glanced back at Imogene; glad she couldn't hear.

"Frannie said it's for her school locker."

"But—" he started.

"It's the first time she has been okay with the new school."

"I guess that's a good sign. How are you going to do this?"

Her witty mom said, "Same as I always do. Aim the camera and hit a button."

"That's not what I mean, and you know it," he said.

"I'll figure it out later," her mom said.

Figure what out later? Frannie wondered. But she didn't have time to wonder long. She tiptoed back to Imogene. She'd settled in the beanbag with Imogene when her mom swung the door open.

Mom had the camera ready to go. "Ready to be models?"

The girls giggled. Frannie rested an arm on the

cushion behind Imogene's shoulder, and the girls tilted their heads together.

"Gorgeous. One, two, three. Say cheese."

"Cheese."

Dad pushed open the door and stared at them.

Imogene cringed and burrowed into the beanbag. Mom might pretend Dad liked Imogene, but Frannie knew now that Imogene was right.

Frannie waved her mom over. "Take a picture with us, Mom. Dad can take it."

"I don't want any more pictures." Imogene crossed her arms over her chest and stared hard at Frannie.

"Oh, honey. A few more," Frannie insisted. But their term of endearment, which usually made each other smile, didn't work this time.

Her mom spun the camera track to move the film forward while taking a step away from her husband's outreached hand. "But I'm the photographer," she said.

Dad said, "Not anymore."

Frannie and Imogene moved over to make room for Frannie's mom. Then her dad took several shots.

"Try to smile," Frannie whispered in Imogene's ear.

"Now one of Imogene alone," Dad said.

"No, thank you," Imogene said. "I want to go home now."

"Smile, Imogene," he said.

Frannie was glad that for once Dad was being friendly. But Imogene flinched as if she was afraid when he moved closer to her with the camera.

"Frannie." Imogene looked at her with big, scared eyes. "Why won't you help me?"

This had been a mistake. "Dad, stop. She doesn't want her picture taken."

"George, that's enough," Mom said.

But he ignored all three of them and took a picture of Imogene staring at her lap. Frannie recalled how Imogene had looked watching *Dangerous Strangers*.

"You're scaring her." Frannie moved in front of Imogene.

"That should do it," he said and left the room, her mother on his heels.

For some reason, his words sounded like a threat.

23

JEAN

SPRING 2022

"You're still awake." Jean forced a pleased tone as she set down her purse and took off her sweater. "I thought you'd be sound asleep, like Lexi."

She'd taken the long way home to guarantee Shane would be dead to the world by the time she got back, ergo, she could avoid answering his questions about her mom. And sex. She was avoiding sex too. The given outcome of an appointment with their counselor, even if Shane went alone, was that he intended to get her naked in bed in order to *save* their marriage.

Earlier, when he'd picked up Lexi from her mom's after work, he'd asked, "What's up? Why are we doing this?" He pointed first to Lexi buckled in the back seat of his car and then to her mom's front door. "This morning, you promised we'd talk tonight. Why aren't you coming home? We have a lot to 'discuss.'"

He used air quotes around *discuss*. She wasn't sure

which she hated more: the air quotes or the use of *discuss* to imply *sex*.

She looked away. "Art and I are talking to Mom about a few things. It can't wait."

"Like a will?" Shane asked. "Because I know she is sick, Jean, but—"

Jean interrupted, offended by how he sugarcoated the truth. There was plenty she didn't want to talk to him about, but seriously—*sick*? "She's more than sick, Shane. She will die unless a stem cell transplant works."

He had the decency to blush. "Okay. I appreciate your mom's condition, but it doesn't explain your transformation in the past seventy-two hours, or why you're suddenly able to spend more than two hours at a time with her. Especially when it impedes saving our marriage."

Doesn't it? Doesn't the threat of death change everything?

"I will explain when I get home."

"That's what you promised this morning." He climbed into his car and drove off.

Now, she plopped down on the couch next to him and in front of the paused TV show. He'd been binge-watching their date-night show, *Parks and Recreation*. "Choose something light and funny," their counselor had suggested.

"Bad boy, Shane. You watched new episodes without me. Isn't that like cheating?"

He shrugged. "Amy Poehler was here—you weren't."

"It's one of our things that we agreed to do together,

for our counseling homework." Why she was trying to sound like the injured party and deflecting blame, she wasn't sure. He had every right to be annoyed. She'd deliberately stalled coming home, and now she was the one raising their problems.

Maybe she was in shock from recording her mom's history.

"Yes," he said, hitting the power on the remote. "And you also committed to counseling, which you ditched today. Besides, watching TV isn't really doing something together. At most, we sit next to each other, maybe laugh or cringe at the same time."

She reached for levity. "We share a bowl of popcorn."

"This isn't funny," Shane said, resting his elbows on his knees. "We're barely hanging on here, Jean. Do you get that? Your idea of a relationship is watching a series and snacking together until we fall asleep. That's not enough for me. We haven't had sex . . ."

Gah. Their worst topic.

Not this. Not now. Not after hearing her mother's answers and coming to appreciate how much her mom had lost when her friend had disappeared. Even now, her mother's girlhood diary haunted Jean from her purse. She had planned to read it and compare it to the recorded answers tonight while Shane slept.

The loss of her mother's childhood innocence added perspective to, you know, a husband complaining about the poor frequency of his sex life.

Still, she did miss intimacy. Just not with Shane. She missed it with before-parenthood Shane, the guy she'd met over a shared love of wine and who wouldn't have wanted more than one child. Or perhaps she missed herself pre-parenthood.

And that's why she held back in her conversations with Shane and during her one-on-one sessions with Dr. Pfeiffer. What kind of woman regretted becoming a mother because she missed her freedom and independence? What kind of woman missed what she had with her husband before he was the father of her precious child? She kept pushing away the answer, but its tentacles often found her in the middle of the night when she should be asleep: someone who didn't deserve to be a mother.

Jean didn't want to have sex because Shane wanted more kids. And she didn't want to lie to him about contraceptives or timing. She wished she understood why, but she feared having another child would mean she'd lose herself completely, killing anything she and Shane might have left. How could she explain herself in a way he could understand, in a way that wouldn't make him question the fact she loved Lexi with all her being? Because that was the other irony. She regretted having Lexi, but she also couldn't imagine living without her. If something happened to her daughter—she shook her head. She couldn't bear the thought.

After a few moments of silence, Shane turned to face her on the couch. "At least tell me what's going on with your mother, beyond the cancer? Give me a chance."

Jean sighed. "When she was nine years old, her best friend disappeared. They never found her."

His jaw dropped, and his heavy brows collided. "Son of a nutcracker. That's horrible."

"You sound like an overgrown elf."

"Who, what, when?" he asked.

"Her name was—maybe *is*—Imogene. They met in the children's hospital when they were six."

"Oh man. You know how thinking about suffering kids makes me worry about Lexi."

How would he take the news that her mother believed Grandfather knew more than he'd admitted about the disappearance? Should she tell him yet? Wasn't it too soon? Once he knew, he'd never let Lexi visit her great-grandpa, who pulled quarters and hard candy from behind her ears. Wasn't he innocent until proven guilty? When she was young, her mom had once told her, "Don't hand out trust for free. People should earn it first."

Hadn't Grandpa earned her trust?

"What does this all mean?" Shane asked. "Did you know about this?"

"Not until the day of her diagnosis. She asked Art and me to hire a detective to find out what happened to Imogene."

"Oh. Wow. Wow," he said. "What about your grandfather? What does he say?"

Grandpa is a suspect. No—innocent until proven guilty. "I haven't talked to Grandpa yet. We don't want to stress him out." She wasn't *lying* to Shane. "We hired a detective today, but he needs some answers from Mom. We recorded them."

"Was the detective with you?"

"No. I'll be the one dealing with him, not Mother. More than Art, too, since he has to work."

Shane squinted. "Wait, how old is this guy? Good looking?" Shane expanded his chest and squared his jaw. It was the first time she'd seen this vulnerability in him. "How much time are we talking about?" he asked.

She wouldn't tell him that Griffin looked like his favorite character and actor, Star-Lord, a.k.a. Chris Pratt, but with a thicker waist. No, that wouldn't go over well.

"Shane, it's not like that." She took a deep breath. "Here's the problem—my mom hired a detective before, in 1994. Art and I promised not to hire the same guy. But we also promised to hire the best PI for this case."

"So, who is the best PI?"

"The son. From the same firm."

Shane let out a breath. "But you're not telling Frances."

"That's right. We don't have time to walk away from someone that everyone else suggests we work with."

They were silent as he weighed the limited details.

"Do you want to help her? Is it important to you?" he asked. "Because, you know, I've always worried if you left work and didn't have your own thing . . ."

Her heart warmed toward him. It was true. When she'd said she wanted to be a stay-at-home mom, his only reservation was how much she'd enjoyed managing the Trois Vignes Wine Shop. He'd said, "I don't want you to feel like you're only a mother."

At the time, she had bristled at his word choice—*only*

a mother. Now, irony with a capital I came at her in spades.

She squinted, thinking how she'd been afraid he'd try to discourage her. "I do. I want to help her. I think it's tragic, and it's a puzzle I want to solve. I want to give that last piece, and peace, to my mom. And Dr. Pfeiffer did suggest a project—not that I'd call a missing child a project."

He nodded. "Then you should, and you will. The only person I know who is more stubborn than your mother is you. Anything else I need to know?"

Last chance to tell him about Grandpa. She shook her head. "Not yet."

"One more question, and we can save the rest for tomorrow," he said.

She tensed, expecting something that would keep her up all night, such as, *Should you go back to work?* or *Can we enroll Lexi in preschool now?*

Instead, he asked, "Have you heard about Dandelion?"

"Dandelion?" she repeated. "What are you talking about?"

Shane pointed his finger toward Lexi's room. "Lexi is now talking to Booby *and* Dandelion. And Alexa, too, but I figured out Alexa on my own."

Oh, jeez. Failed Mom of the Year right here. Perhaps her scattered emotions had created yet another imaginary nurturer and confidant for her daughter. "Did you ask her about Dandelion?"

"Apparently, Dandelion is, or was, Frances's imaginary friend, and your mother gave her to Lexi."

"What? Can someone *give away* imaginary friends?" Jean asked.

"Semantics aren't the point, babe."

"My mom would never have an imaginary friend named Dandelion." Except, her mom had been quite understanding and jokey, rather than judgy, about Booby.

"Still not the point," Shane said. "Did your mom say anything? Lexi must have told her about Booby." He grimaced.

Jean wrinkled her nose. "Now that you mention it, yes. Booby ate my peanut butter 'n jelly sandwich."

He nodded and said in a deadpan voice, "That explains why Lexi wasn't hungry at dinner."

That made them both laugh. She admired the sparkle in his eyes. She saw a glimmer of the fun-loving guy she'd known before they were parents, when he was a wholesale wine rep and she was his favorite customer. For the first time in a long time, she felt a hint of a flutter in her stomach.

24

GRIFFIN

SPRING 2022

Griffin brushed off the nagging sense that he'd made a mistake by inviting his son into his work world. Annie had thought it was a good idea, after all.

"But no pay, Tony. Consider yourself a desperate intern for a few weeks. Your schoolwork comes first for the next"—Griffin looked at his phone calendar—"four-ish weeks until summer break. And you do what I say and how I say to do it."

His son wagged his head like a treat-hungry puppy. "Awesome sauce! What's our first crime?"

Crap. This was a mistake. "Private Investigation 101: never assume there is a crime. There's a case."

Beside him, Annie smoothed her palm over Griffin's back as if he were a dog desperate for encouragement to keep doing what he was doing. A greasy, salty piece of bacon would work better right now.

"Got it," Tony said.

Griffin scooted his chair forward and slid the list of

*Imogene Dryker*s that he'd compiled the day before toward Tony. "Here." Griffin handed him a file folder, a yellow legal pad, and a prepaid flip phone, and he almost laughed when his son looked at the products as if they were foreign objects.

"What do I do with these?"

After Griffin gave him the spiel about documenting everything and always opening a file—even if this one was technically a sub-file—he said, "Only use this phone. Never use a personal phone because people will call you back. I want you to call each of these numbers —pay attention to time zones—and ask for Imogene Dryker. Ask whether she is the same Imogene Dryker who lived in South San Francisco from 1969 to 1979. Verbatim. If someone says no, cross them off. If they say yes, transfer them to the yellow pad for me to call back."

"That's all? I'm making calls?" Tony scanned the list. It was a dozen pages long.

Griffin almost pumped his fist with success at his son's look of dismay.

"You're gathering information. That's what PIs do—gather information to find leads," Griffin said, eager for his son to throw in the towel.

Except, Tony the Tiger didn't.

Tony gave him a thumbs up. "Outstanding. I'll start anywhere, and if this is where a beginner starts, fine."

Crud. He's tenacious, like Annie.

"Remember, just confirm the name and if and when they were in South San Fran. Nothing more. If they ask you questions, rather than say yes or no, hang up and put a mark next to it. I'll follow up."

While it might seem normal for people to ask who was calling, answering a question with a question was typically a sign of defense. But Tenacious Tony didn't need that tip yet.

"Will do," Tony said. "Who is Imogene Dryker, though, boss?"

Boss. Had to give him credit for humor. "If I think you need to know something, I'll tell you. Just focus on the list. Right now"—he looked at his watch—"I've got an appointment."

Annie followed him to the front door and kissed him. "Good job, boss."

"You like a man with direct reports, do you?" He kissed Annie back. "Maybe I should have hired our son sooner."

They both knew he didn't mean it, but Annie rewarded him with a second kiss anyway.

ON HIS WAY TO RECORDS, Griffin stopped at the front desk of the police department to say hello to Officer Leah Seville. During college, she'd done a three-month special studies course with him: *Private Investigation Ins & Outs.* Griffin had enjoyed teaching the course for one semester, but being a professor hadn't suited the schedule of a private investigator—the people he needed to follow didn't work around his commitments.

Leah had been a sharp student with plans to become a police detective. Unlike some, she understood how private investigators and police might work together when needed. Unfortunately, after graduating from college and the police academy, during her first month on the job, things had gotten nasty when she pulled over a man with a warrant; now, she had an injured foot and wore an ankle boot to prove it.

"Hello, professor."

"How's your recuperation going?" Back in his day, a person would have had to walk around with armpit-torture crutches, but now they had knee scooters. Go figure.

Leah grimaced and eyed his white bag from Emile's Bakery. "Stationary. Anything exciting in the bag?"

Griffin juggled the paper sack and cardboard tray with two caramel macchiatos, handing the bag to her. "Help yourself. They're cronuts."

Jules from Emile's had said, "You've got to try the croissant-slash-donut, Griffin." Not that he ever needed encouragement to try something that included flour and sugar. He'd bought more than his fair share.

Leah dug one out. "Thank you." She eyed the two drinks in the carrier. "One of those for sale?"

Griffin knew from experience that the coffee at the station sucked. "One for Darla. One for you. My treat." He didn't need more caffeine, or the whipped cream.

"What brings you to our shop today?" Her eyes lit

up. Griffin would feel fine giving her his business if she ever wanted to cross over, but that was because he trusted she knew what she wanted and had made a well-informed decision about her career. Didn't hurt that her lifelong happiness wasn't his responsibility, either.

"Records. Missing girl from 1979."

"Runaway or cold case?"

"Not sure."

"Anything I can help with?" she asked. "I'd be more than happy to scoot around with you on a day off or whenever. I'm stuck behind the desk these days. I'm sure the Lieutenant wouldn't mind if I assist, especially if it's for a good cause and one that will take pressure off our cold case team—if it ends up being one."

Griffin gave her a thumbs up. "I'm heading downstairs to see what I can learn. I'll keep your offer in mind."

AFTER ELBOWING THE INTERCOM, Griffin said, "Darla, Queen of Records, your caramel macchiato has arrived."

They kept the location locked twenty-four-seven for obvious reasons, so he waited for the veteran assistant to buzz him in.

She tested the drink and smiled before leading him to the microfiche machine. "It's locked and loaded."

"That's a start," he said, unzipping his backpack.

Most decades-old reports were purged or destroyed. So far, so good.

"There's not much to see."

"What does that mean?" he asked.

"You'll see. I've never seen anything like it before. You won't have either. I'm shocked the evidence locator is there. I'll go downstairs and check it out now."

"My, oh my, Darla. Aren't you being the mysterious one today?"

"I'll be back with the evidence, hopefully."

He half expected her to sing the Rolling Stones again, but she headed downstairs, sucking her drink instead.

In the seventies, there had been minimal understanding and police training about evidence preservation. Any gathered evidence had, more than likely, ended up in an old warehouse without temperature control, allowing it to become ruined or contaminated. A few years ago, the city and county had consolidated inventory to a single location. Fingers crossed, Darla would return with untainted evidence. He'd find out soon enough.

He pulled out his case file, yellow pad, and pen. The microfiche machine whirred as he flipped it on. True to her word, Darla had found the police report. He first compared the location number to *4/1957*—dead-end.

Page one covered the standard protocol and information:

Police Case Number: 79-63133-MP
Date Reported: August 10, 1979

Time Reported: 3:04 p.m.
Last Seen: August 4, 1979
Missing Person: Imogene Dryker
Age: 9
Officer: Sergeant Rodney Schultz

Rodney Schultz. Now, there was a name Griffin hadn't seen or heard in a long time. Rodney had been a friend, of sorts, of Griffin's dad. When was the last time he'd seen the officer?

His dad's funeral, probably. Not that he could remember any of the hundreds who had paid respect to his father—he'd been in shock and the funeral had been standing room only.

The printer beeped and spit out the case stats when Griffin hit print. Then he turned the knob to the second page.

What the hell is this?

A series of bold black lines covered the page.

25

JEAN

SPRING 2022

"What are your plans today?" Shane asked as he helped Lexi with her shoes.

Putting her palms against her cheeks, Jean exhaled. "*Gah.* Too much. For starters, my mother asked me to deliver a gift to her assistant. Then I need to drop off a jump drive with Mother's recorded interview."

"To the detective? I can take it to him if it helps."

The only thing *that* would help was Shane's curiosity. Stopping everything, she frowned at him. "No thanks. I'll do it. We don't need too many sous-chefs in the kitchen."

"Then what?"

Then she wanted to visit her grandpa, but she wasn't ready to broadcast that plan. "We'll spend the rest of our day at Mom's. Do whatever comes up."

"Rest of the day? What about dinner?" he asked, reaching for his keys and wallet.

"What about it?" Didn't he get that everything was

uncertain in her life right now? Frazzled, she shoved everything within reach into her purse.

"Well, we are a family. Are we having dinner together?"

"Yes, but I don't know what time and where. Maybe at Mom's, if you're up for it. If she's up for it."

It was confusing how her mom's diagnosis and the revelation of Imogene had compelled her to spend more time with her mom. Maybe it was expected. Could cancer and a missing person cure *them*?

"Can I call you later and tell you?"

Shane jingled his keys as if agitated. "Lexi, go use the bathroom."

"Okay!"

As soon as Lexi was out of earshot, her husband dropped the bomb, telling her that Dr. Pfeiffer had referred them to a child psychologist. Worse, he'd made the appointment without talking to her first.

"Why didn't you mention this last night?" she asked.

"When? Before or after you told me about Imogene? It would have been too much last night."

"It's too much now." She looked at him, dumbfounded. "You had no right to make that decision without me, Shane."

"Listen, it's a consultation to see what might be best for Lexi."

"And as her mother, you don't think I know what my daughter needs? You think our marriage counselor does?"

He snorted, tapping his chest and then pointing at her. "*We* don't know what *we* need."

Her face grew hot, and she was about to blow her top. “She’ll outgrow Booby.”

“And Dandelion,” Shane added, pushing her buttons and losing any points he’d gained the night before.

“And Dandelion,” she impersonated his snotty tone.

“Real mature, Jean.”

She wanted to copy him again, but she decided to be an adult.

“Hon,” he said. “She might not get over us if *we* get over us.”

He might as well have punched the biggest buttons she had. First, she hated these slogans and wordplays he came up with. If he were one of her former friends obsessed with Instagram, he’d probably spend his day making memes. The second was his implication that he might leave her.

“You mean if I fail, and our marriage doesn’t last, Lexi will be harmed irrevocably.”

He shoved his keys deep into his pocket. “It’s not what I want, and it’s not a matter of you or me failing. It’s an us-thing. We need to prepare Lexi, give her the right tools, just in case.”

An us-thing. She should never have suggested he see Dr. Pfeiffer alone.

“When is this appointment?” She huffed and put her hands on her hips.

“In two weeks.”

“We can talk about it later, Shane. When I’m calmer.”

“Except, you don’t know when,” he complained.

What a jerk. Why did he have to do this to her now?

"I will call you once I know." Desperate for him to leave and to end this conversation, she walked away. "I need to check on *our* daughter. Have a good day at work."

JEAN HAD ALWAYS BEEN uncomfortable walking into her mom's firm, as if she shouldn't be there, shouldn't see or know this side of her mom. For as long as she could remember, the annual office holiday party had been for employees only, and there had never been a company picnic or family day like many other companies hosted, as if her mom hadn't wanted the lines blurred and preferred her life compartmentalized.

It was the reason she was shocked when her mom had asked her to drop off a gift for Rhonda.

"Won't it mean more if you give it to her yourself?" Jean had asked. "I've never met her before."

"I belong here, preserving my energy and preparing for my transplant."

The idea that her mom might never step inside this particular compartment again was unsettling too. Jean stopped before the front desk with the gift bag swinging from one hand and Lexi swinging the other. Feeling confident she'd found the right person, thanks to a nameplate, she said, "Hi Rhonda. I'm Frances's daughter, Jean." She set the bag on the counter. "And this is for you."

The woman jumped to her feet and clasped her hands in front of her. She towered over the desk and Jean.

Jean's jaw dropped before she could hide her reaction.

"Whoa," Lexi said on an exhale, her head leaned back as far as it would go.

"I am over the moon to meet you, Jean. I love her. And you must be Lexi the Great. I've heard all about you."

The recognition surprised the hell out of Jean. Maybe her mother wasn't as compartmentalized as she'd assumed.

A troubling thought seeped its way through Jean's being. First, Imogene. Now, this. Had she ever known her mother? Was it too late to try? Tears filled her eyes.

"Don't you cry, or I'll cry too." The large woman barreled around the desk and pulled Jean into a hug, lifting her off the ground. Rhonda's hug was tighter than Jean's father's, and his embrace was hard to beat.

"Open your present," Lexi said as Jean's feet touched the floor.

Widening her eyes and opening her mouth in an *O*, Rhonda looked to Jean. "May I?"

"I wish you would," Jean said. More than ever, she was curious about what her mom had chosen.

Lexi happily took the tissue paper Rhonda handed over.

"Oh my gosh!" Rhonda reached into the bag and pulled out Frannie's Martha Stewart croc-embossed tote.

Not what Jean expected.

"Squeeeee!" Rhonda hugged the tote to her chest.

Jean had no idea what to make of the unfolding scene. "Is there a story behind the, um, used purse?"

"Your mother bought it as a pact."

"A pact?"

"I was a wreck, you see. My husband left me for another woman. I couldn't sleep in our bed. Couldn't stop crying. I made a few mistakes at the office. Then, one Friday afternoon, Frances said to grab my things. I thought I was fired. But do you know what she did?"

"Ah . . . no."

"She made me take her to my apartment. I was beyond nervous for her to see it. It was a mess, and I had a habit of collecting things—you never know when you might need something. And then . . . you know Marie Kondo, the Spark Joy lady? Your mother helped me spark joy in my apartment to make it mine."

"My mother?"

"She took me on a Martha Stewart Home Collection shopping spree and changed the look and feel of my entire bedroom on her dime. She changed my life. Slept like a baby after that. My room had nothing to do with my ex anymore. We sparked him out of there."

"I'm flabbergasted."

Rhonda wasn't done. She held the croc-embossed bag in her hands as if it were a trophy. "We had the home shopping network on the TV while we cleaned and purged. Frances kept pausing to watch when Martha displayed her tote. I challenged her right then and there to buy the purse or I would buy it for her. I wanted to spark her some joy too."

"Mommy, we're hungry."

Baffled, Jean shook her head. "I've never known this side of her," she admitted.

"You still have time. Don't be wasting it. I bet she has worked magic in your home too."

After another hug, Jean and Lexi left. Jean was too embarrassed to admit she hadn't let her mom step foot in her new house. Maybe it wasn't her mother who had compartmentalized her life but Jean who had compartmentalized her own.

26

FRANNIE

AUGUST 4, 1979

"No," Frannie's dad told her for the second time. "You're going to the open house alone."

"But—" Frannie said, shocked when her mom interrupted.

"Your dad's right. The open house is for students, and as much as we all wish it were different, Imogene will not be a student at Whitney Prep."

"Can't she be my guest? You're both going with me, and you're not students."

Her dad tilted his chin down and looked sternly at her. "That's enough with the smart mouth. Loyal friends don't care if they go to different schools. Starting now, you will not hide behind Imogene and avoid making new friends, and that's final."

"You can't make me find new friends."

"You're right, I can't. But your stubborn hide will prove to be poor company at recess."

She rested her elbow on the table and her cheek against her fist. "What if no one likes me?"

That took the strain right out of her dad's mulish jaw. He reached across the table to squeeze her arm. "Frannie Jerome, you were strong enough to beat cancer, and you'll be brave enough to adapt to a new school and make friends."

Her mom tried a different angle, but it was a good point too. "Just think. You can start this school fresh. You can be anyone you want to be. Remember how you didn't like it at first at St. Agnes because everyone referred to you as the girl with cancer?"

"Most still do," Frannie admitted.

"Well, that won't happen at Whitney. No one will know that you once had leukemia unless you tell them. You can be whoever you want to be."

She kind of liked that idea, but it shouldn't mean that Imogene couldn't go to an open house as a supportive friend.

"Can Imogene at least wait here while we go? I can tell her about it when I get home." Frannie knew Imogene wouldn't like this idea because she hated being alone and would probably rather go home, where she was used to being on her own, but it was worth a try.

Her mom shook her head. "No, not alone. Tomorrow will be soon enough for you to tell her about tonight's event."

But her dad removed his hand from hers and placed it on the table in front of him with a resounding clap. "I'll tell you what, if it will make it easier for you, you and your mother can go, and I'll stay here with Imogene."

"Really?" Frannie sat up straight and smiled.

"George." Her mother frowned. "You should go with us."

"Nope. The two of you go. It's settled. Happy with that, Fran? It's that or Imogene can leave now. But she can't go with you."

Frannie wished Imogene was next to her and not waiting in the bedroom. Imogene wouldn't like the plan because she was afraid of Dad lately. "Can she stay in my room, or does she have to come out here with you?"

"Staying in your room is fine," he said.

It surprised Frannie that he agreed, but she didn't want to change his mind.

"Go get ready. I need to talk to your dad."

Frannie raced to her room. Imogene was staring absentmindedly out the bedroom window when she came in. "Imogene, you can't go with me, but my dad said you could wait here, and he'll wait with you. You can stay in my room until I get back."

"No way." She could almost feel Imogene shrinking from the inside out.

"Please? Come on. I begged them to let me bring you as a guest."

Imogene crossed her arms. "No. I'm going home while it's still light out. I told you he doesn't like me. He scares me."

Nibbling her lip, Frannie asked, "Are you mad at me for going to a new school? Is that the real problem?" As their summer had inched toward the new school year, Imogene stayed home more and more, forgoing their precious summer days together. "You'll always be my best friend. Please don't be mad."

"I'm not mad. I'm scared. Will you forget about me when you have new friends?"

"No way, José. We will *both* make new friends, but we're best friends for life. Please, please, please wait so I can tell you about it. Dad won't bother you. He promised."

Imogene's eyes filled with tears and her lips trembled. "Okay, but you don't see your dad the way I do. He doesn't like me the way you want him to."

27

GRIFFIN

SPRING 2022

Griffin scrolled back to the first page with stats then forward through five pages; the entire report had been redacted. Every single frigging line. The only legible notes were Rodney Schultz's signature and the evidence locator, which didn't match *4/1957* either.

Holy shit. A censored police report sure as hell meant something. What was he getting involved in? Reaching for the greasy bag, he chewed on a second cronut for fortitude. He clapped his hands to shake off the glaze flakes and started a new page in his yellow pad. After scribbling *Police Report # 79-63133-MP* up top, he added the officer's name and *redacted report* on the first two lines. Now he knew what Darla had been hinting at—a fully redacted report was something he'd never seen. And before this case, he would have sworn his dad hadn't seen one either, because why wouldn't he have told Griffin?

There it was again—that awful feeling that he hadn't

known his dad. Time didn't lie; his dad would have seen this in '94 when Frances Jerome hired him.

He retrieved a copy from the printer and was placing the blacked-out report in his file when Darla returned with a sealed black plastic nine-by-twelve-inch envelope. It was as flat as the bland pancakes Annie made without milk and eggs each Sunday morning.

Doesn't look promising.

He followed Darla to her counter where she scanned the envelope's barcode. He digitally signed for the evidence and agreed to the terms of opening the file.

An evidence technician had stamped the portfolio *No gloves needed*.

Crap—a solid indication there was a lack of evidence to test for DNA.

Prior to the mid-eighties, no one thought tying DNA to a crime would be possible, but it was now. With proper evidence, they could solve old cases, thanks to modern technology. Too bad no one had anticipated using it someday. Investigators back then didn't gather what they didn't know their successors would need.

"I want to see this too," Darla said as she trailed after him back to his table.

Griffin pulled away the tape, untwisted the string looped in a lazy eight between two circular tabs, and lifted the flap. He pulled out a three-hole-punch folder that was less than a quarter inch thick. On top, as usual, was a list of people who had checked out the evidence in the past. The last two signatures were dated 1994. The first signature was Peter Whittaker's. The second, dated a few days later, was Internal Affairs.

Griffin's heart thumped in that odd pattern. His cardiologist said it wasn't supposed to do that. For a second, he hesitated to look any further. He could still turn away. He could avoid what was inside, avoid whatever had changed his father. Or he could solve this case for himself, Frances, and Imogene. His hands shook. And he waited. *What are you going to do, Griffin?*

"You okay?" Darla leaned forward.

Griffin stared at his dad's large signature. A graphologist would say the larger the signature, the greater the writer's self-esteem, and his dad's signature confirmed his bold and confident personality. But Peter had scribbled the return time—as if he had been in a hurry.

"What are you waiting for? The anticipation is killing me," Darla said.

This case had changed Griffin's life, too, though he hadn't known it at the time. He needed to understand what the redacted report was about and what his dad had to do with this case. Griffin took out a phone and took a picture of the sign-out sheet adhered to the cover. He opened the folder, looked at the first page, and then thumbed through the remaining fifty or so pages. He did it twice to make sure he hadn't missed anything. He lifted it up by its binding to see if anything slid out.

The entire file was blank paper.

"That's another first," Darla said.

He made a video of the blank pages and then shook

his head. He put the contents back in the evidence folder as the process required, blank pages or not.

Darla applied pressure to her temples. "After all my years . . . It can't be a coincidence IA reviewed this immediately after Peter."

"Someone replaced them," Griffin said, his heart fluttering. He shouldn't have eaten the cronuts. Someone or several *someones* had covered up Imogene's disappearance. He knew it. His dad must have known it too. Question was, had his dad been an insider or an outsider? Had he been part of the problem? Or the solution? "*People will go down for this.*"

On his way out, he stopped by Officer Leah's counter.

"Leah, do you know Officer Rodney Schultz?"

"Doesn't ring any bells."

"Retired by now, perhaps. Can you see if you can find his contact info?" He could go through his own tricks of tracking someone down, but he and his dad had always had a personal credo to avoid violating an officer's privacy. There was no doubt about it—Griffin needed to talk to Rodney ASAP.

"Run it by your supervisor first. A phone number is good enough for me," Griffin said.

"You have the same number?" Leah asked, and he nodded. "I'll text you what I can find out."

28

FRANCES

SPRING 2022

After Jean and Art left last night, Frannie had trouble falling asleep. The questions about Imogene had stirred up several fearful and confusing moments when she'd been lied to, misled, or asked to do things she didn't understand.

Such as the time her mother asked her to bury a piece of Imogene.

She'd fallen asleep once she decided to remedy this first thing in the morning. Despite her restless night, she'd woken up with more energy than she'd had for a few months—probably since her cancer had returned.

She stirred her coffee as she eyed her gardening tools on her back patio. Would a hand trowel be enough, or would she need the heavy-duty straight shovel for deeper digging? Thinking back, it felt as if she'd dug for hours to make a hole several feet deep. But, surely, as a child she'd only been able to make a shallow grave, less than a foot below ground. Had her mother helped her? She couldn't remember. She recalled the sense of dread about doing something wrong, betraying Imogene further.

What would cemetery-goers think of a skinny, middle-aged woman showing up with Martha Stewart's gardening tools—*bright green for easy location*, Martha said—to a graveyard? They'd assume she was planting or tidying up, not exhuming something, right? Or did most people bring cut flowers, like George did once a month for her mother? She only knew about that because he'd once told her during one of their awkward visits, after they'd ran out of safe, superficial topics to discuss such as family, work, and golf tournaments.

Perhaps the cemetery had rules against people poking about with shovels. How could she know? She hadn't been back since her mother's funeral. Most likely, she'd start her excavation and be stopped by a groundskeeper, but she'd rather beg for forgiveness than ask for permission only to be told no.

Frannie had never been a fan of cemeteries. That first time had been too much for her, the piece of Imogene burning her hand inside her pocket.

She remembered how her heart had raced, and she'd shouted, "This isn't right! It's not fair!" Her mom had rested her hand between Frannie's small shoulder blades, prodding her along.

Her father tried to joke around. "Have you heard about this cemetery? Everyone's dying to get in here."

They didn't laugh. "Go back to the car, George."

Frannie was in the process of putting her devices,

wrapped in plastic bags, next to her car keys when her doorbell rang.

She hesitated, waiting for Bonnie Bell to express her concern. But the bird continued tweeting, unfazed. Her heart clutched. Bonnie Bell finally felt safe under Frannie's watch. But what would happen to Bonnie Bell now? Frannie had expected to meet the new family once one was found. She'd planned to screen them closely, watching for any unrest in Bonnie Bell. But what if she ran out of time?

A second ring of the doorbell was a welcome distraction.

Having her son and ex-husband on her doorstep when she was ready to undo a terrible memory wasn't ideal. From the look on Douglas's face, Art or Jean—or both of them—had told their father her days might be numbered. She hoped they hadn't told him about the search for Imogene, but for the life of her, she couldn't remember if she'd asked them not to. Normally, her memory never failed her, but she knew from her childhood how cancer expended typical energy and abilities while it worked behind the scenes to consume her.

Douglas stepped inside and wrapped his arms around her in a bear hug. She'd never been sure if she liked these for their comfort or disliked them due to the all-consuming pressure to return the same level of devotion and gregariousness.

"Frank, my love, I can't believe it. I can't imagine this world without you."

Since they'd met, Douglas had nicknamed her Frank. "Frances sounds dorky, and you're cool," he'd said when they were young, but she'd shunned the use of Frannie by then, even with her parents. Her face squished against his thick shoulder, she mumbled, "The transplant should buy me time. Besides, we've survived apart fine the past five years, and I'm sure your latest girlfriend will help."

Douglas's chest rumbled with laughter as he released her. He stared into her eyes. "No, Frank. You're irreplaceable."

He spoke the last word with such sincerity that she recalled the moment they had exchanged wedding vows. Though she'd never regretted their divorce, a warm pressure rose in her chest.

Douglas won't forget me.

"Are you going somewhere?" Art asked, probably desperate to avoid hearing about his father's younger lady friend or the topic of girlfriends in general. His eyes, and hand, settled on the green shovel. He lifted it as he lifted his brows.

Hopefully, the truth would spare her any more sentimentality with her ex-husband. He was the one person, other than Rhonda, who was immune to her direct nature. He had a way of glossing over her sternness with his convivial attitude while taking her fears and feelings seriously. His outgoing and optimistic personality —traits she needed after losing Imogene—had attracted her when they'd first met. Funnily enough, the same qualities that had drawn her to him in her youth had pushed them apart the older they got. "I'm going to visit my mother's grave."

Both men's eyes widened.

"That's a first, ain't it?" Douglas asked.

He'd always used *ain't* to rile her up. Even Jean was apt to correct her beloved father for his ain'ts.

"You hate cemeteries," Art said aloud, as if to invoke memories of every time she'd ever driven by a cemetery and pointed, saying, "Never put me in one of those."

She nodded. "That's correct, Art. Glad you remembered."

"We'll join you for support and to pay respect," Douglas said.

Art shook his head. "Dad . . ."

Frannie sighed. The more she resisted, the more her ex would insist on going, the well-intended goof. And she needed to accomplish her goal so she could sleep tonight. If they wanted to be accessories, so be it. She stepped past them both, taking the tools from Art. "Fine. But no questions allowed."

Douglas chuckled and rubbed his palms together. "Sounds like a challenge."

Art whined. "Jean would be better at this than me."

Poor Art. Jean had called earlier to say good morning and that she would stop by later.

"I assume she's with Lexi," Frannie said, marching toward the car.

"She's with the detective," Art said.

Douglas halted. "Detective?"

In a very un-Art-like moment, her son squared his jaw

and put his foot down with his father. "You heard the lady, no questions allowed."

THE SCENT of freshly mowed grass soothed Frannie's nerves as she walked through the cemetery. She was grateful that Art and his father followed her from a distance, especially since her ex-husband seemed intent on reading aloud every epitaph along the way.

"He lived. He laughed. He loved."

Two seconds later, he read, "A lover of animals, flowers, and music."

Then, he chuckled before reciting, "She made us laugh too hard and eat too much."

Art moaned. "You don't have to shout every word you read. You're going to wake the dead."

"Last one suits me too," Douglas said. "Make note of that one, Art."

"Cut me some slack, Dad. One parent at a time, okay?"

Frannie stopped next to her mother's grave, cautiously stepping to the left and onto the plot reserved for George. In movies and shows, people talked to their long-gone loved ones for comfort, yet it seemed too strange to greet her mother as if she, her essence, were connected to Frannie merely by some dirt, a coffin, remains, and a headstone. She much preferred speaking to her mother whenever she thought of her or imagined she could feel her presence when most needed. This wasn't her mother; it was a grave. And yet, facing her mortality, a twinge of guilt stabbed Frannie for not coming sooner and now coming only to undo a wrong.

Her mom had never outright admitted she thought Imogene was dead, but after they'd buried a piece of her, her mother had kneeled before her on this very land. "Imogene will always be with you in here"—she'd tapped Frannie's heart—"and here"—then she'd tapped Frannie's temple.

And when her mother had suffered a stroke when Frannie was twenty-six years old and was a new mother herself, she had held her mother's non-paralyzed hand, crying, "Please, Mom. Don't leave me too. We need you."

Her mom, who couldn't speak, had withdrawn her good hand from Frannie's to raise her finger to tap Frannie's heart and then pointed to her temple as if to say, *I'll always be with you in your heart and on your mind.*

If her worst fears were confirmed and Imogene had died, and if there was an afterlife of any kind, Frannie hoped her mother and Imogene had found one another. She eyed the turf on the other side of her mom's plot, mentally measuring where the digging had begun many years before.

Art caught up to her and stood where she'd been eyeing but otherwise didn't interrupt her reflections.

Douglas, on the other hand, didn't hesitate to break the silence. "A devoted, loving mother and wife," Douglas read her mother's headstone. A few seconds later, he pointed at the cut flowers resting before the headstone. "Beautiful tiger lilies."

"I assume they're from George. They were her favorite." In fact, her mom and Imogene had both favored the flower.

"Pops says they grow wild in Maryland," Imogene had once said.

Douglas pointed to her feet. "Is that reserved for George?"

The question was understandable, so she didn't blame him for breaking his promise. "Yes. Switch sides with me please."

Art frowned and looked down at his feet. "Then whose spot is this?" he asked, looking around the otherwise full cemetery.

"Mine," Frannie said.

Art paled and hurried to the other side. "What? Why? You won't be buried here."

If she wasn't so fixated on what she needed to do, she'd hug him for his confidence. Her wishes to be cremated would not be dismissed when she was not here to defend them.

"Art?"

"Yes?"

"Thank you. I know you'll do the right thing for me when it's time."

Her son batted his eyelashes, swallowed, and nodded. "Yep."

For once, Douglas was silent, probably imagining what her epitaph might have read if she had wanted one.

Frannie shivered as she stepped onto the grass where she'd stood long ago.

"I didn't know at the time, of course, but when I was diagnosed with leukemia, a priest suggested my parents buy the interment rights so the three of us could be together again someday if I didn't make it. Fortunately, I made it."

Art spoke with wonder, his voice tinged with respect. "You've always had to be strong, Mom."

She swallowed hard. *Always strong*. That's what her epitaph might have said if she were buried and had a grave marker.

It had been a long time, but Frannie focused on the area about two feet to the right of her mother's headstone.

"Art, hand me the trowel."

29

FRANNIE

AUGUST 4, 1979

Frannie couldn't wait to tell Imogene about the boys and girls she'd met, especially the cute and friendly boy, Douglas. Her mom took pictures of her with him. Best yet, it finished off the roll with the photos for her locker they'd taken with Imogene.

"When can we get them developed?" Frannie asked during the car ride home. "I can't wait to show Imogene."

"I'll drop the roll off tomorrow."

She hugged the Whitney Prep welcome bag to her chest. Her mom had let her take two of everything: pencils, rulers, notebooks, and flags with the school's logo. "Imogene is going to love these. St. Agnes doesn't have cool stuff with its name."

Her mom looked away from the dark road and smiled. "You made friends easily. That one boy smiled at you a lot. Wait until I tell your dad about him."

"Mom!"

Thanks to nightfall, her mom couldn't see her rosy

cheeks. Mom was right—she had made several friends. She hoped the truth wouldn't hurt Imogene's feelings, but she was now excited about attending her new school. "Wait until I tell Imogene they have a theater club. I can practice my jokes with an audience."

As soon as her mom turned off the car, Frannie grabbed her bag and raced inside. "Imogene! Imogene!"

She was partway to her bedroom when her dad stopped her.

"You can yell all you want, but she can't hear you if she isn't here."

Her mom caught up to her, stopping dead in her tracks hearing his last words. "George, you promised to wait with Imogene."

Deflated and confused, Frannie asked, "Where is she? I want to tell her about the open house."

"Tell me about the open house instead," he said. "You were gone longer than I thought you'd be, and you're glowing. Must've been a success." He gave her two thumbs up.

"I want to tell Imogene first." As if she would ever tell her dad about a cute boy.

"Sorry." He shrugged his shoulders. "Imogene is gone." He spoke with a finality that raised the hairs on her arms.

"What do you mean she's gone?"

"George." Her mother set her purse down with a resounding thud. "I would never have agreed to let you stay behind had I known you'd do something like this."

"Do something like what?" Frannie asked.

He put his hands up defensively. "After you left, Imogene's dad called. She walked home."

"In the dark? All by herself?" Frannie knew better. Imogene wouldn't, and Mr. Dryker never called their house. He liked not worrying about Imogene. Frannie got a weird tightness in her chest and she shook her head.

"No way. She wouldn't have left at night," Frannie said, her voice quivering as she squinted at him. "She and I have a pact. You told us not to walk alone, no matter how old we get."

"George, what have you done?"

What did her mom mean?

Dad paled and stuttered, "I offered her a ride home, but she said no."

"Because she's afraid of you. She warned me you didn't like having her around." There, Frannie had said it, the thing that made her feel guilty about leaving her friend behind.

Her mom rested a trembling hand on Frannie's shoulder.

"You promised she could hang out in my room alone," Frannie accused. "Why did you let her leave? In the dark?"

Her dad gritted his teeth. "This is ridiculous. She's fine."

"How do you know?" Frannie asked, biting her lower lip. "A child molester might have taken her."

"No, no. I'm sure one didn't. Let's have ice cream, shall we?" her mom asked abruptly.

Frannie wasn't one to turn down ice cream, but she

couldn't wait until tomorrow to make sure Imogene was okay—her gut told her something was super wrong. It would take a lot to make Imogene walk alone at night—something that scared her more than perverts and kidnappers. Had her dad been that scary? Or what if Imogene had lied and was mad at Frannie for leaving her out? Would hurt feelings be enough to make her brave the night alone? Frannie should call and say sorry, tell her that she'd thought about her so much she'd brought her school supplies. Then everything would be fixed for tomorrow. It would cheer Imogene up. Everyone would be okay.

"I'll call her now," she said louder than usual, dropping her bag on the kitchen floor.

"No, you won't," her dad said. "You know the rules. No calls after five o'clock. It's almost eight."

"It's a rule not to walk in the dark too," Frannie said.

Empty bowls and spoons clattered together as her mom sat them on the table next to a carton of her favorite ice cream. "No, honey, it's rude to call after five. Who wants rocky road?"

"It's rude not to see if she's okay." Frannie stomped her foot.

"That's it," her dad said. "You don't speak to your mother that way. No call and no ice cream for you. Go to your room."

That night, while Frannie lay restless in bed, she overheard her parents arguing, but she couldn't hear what they were saying. The next morning, when she went to the living room, her dad was asleep on the couch.

Something weird was happening. Her parents always slept together.

She looked at the clock. It was seven a.m. Her mom was usually up by now. Another phone rule was that she couldn't call anyone before nine a.m., but that seemed like a stupid rule this morning when Imogene might need her. She tiptoed to the phone. No one answered the first time, so she hung up and redialed Imogene's number. This time, Mr. Dryker responded with a slur. "Lo?"

"Hi, Mr. Dryker. It's me, Frannie. Can I talk to Imogene?"

"Frannie?" There was a long pause. "But . . . she's not here," he said and hung up.

Three days later, Frannie still hadn't heard from Imogene. She was worried sick. Something terrible must have happened. Even if she'd been upset at first, Imogene would have wanted to hear about her party by now. She wouldn't have ignored Frannie unless she was sick or in big trouble. Frannie had called Imogene's house every day to no avail, and Imogene's dad had stopped answering. Finally, on the fourth morning, she lucked out.

She didn't bother with being polite. "I must talk to Imogene."

"Don't call here no more," Mr. Dryker snapped and hung up on her.

No appeals to her mom could convince her to drive her to Imogene's home.

"If she wants to be in touch, Frannie, she will," her dad said while he read his newspaper, as if he didn't care at all.

"Why don't you care if she got home safely, Dad?"

On the fifth morning since Frannie had last seen Imogene, she squeezed her eyes closed to hold her tears at bay. She couldn't bear to wake up and face another day worrying about Imogene when no one else was upset. Imogene always said no one loved her like Frannie, and Frannie had always laughed her off. She wasn't laughing now.

Her mom tapped on her door and pushed it open. "Frannie, baby. It's time to get up."

Frannie's whole body hurt. "I can't. I'm scared, and no one will help."

"Darling, I'm sure Imogene is fine. Everything will be okay."

"If she's fine then that means she hates me. Why else wouldn't she call me, if she was fine?"

On the sixth day, Frannie's dad yelled her name when he walked in the door after work. "Frannie, you got mail!"

Frannie jumped up from her beanbag, shoving Jokey Smurf into her pocket, and ran out.

Her dad extended a stamped envelope toward her.

Frannie thought her mom looked more curious than her and asked, "Who from?"

"Imogene." Her dad smiled.

But her mom frowned.

Frannie ripped it from his hands. On the upper left-hand corner it said *Imogene Dryker*, and the return address listed Ocean City, MD.

"I need privacy," she said. She ran into her room and

dropped into her and Imogene's favorite spot on the beanbag chair. Her fingers shook as she opened the letter. *Please let us be friends. Please let Imogene be okay.*

Except, Imogene wasn't okay, because it wasn't Imogene's handwriting and sounded nothing like her bestie.

> *Frannie,*
>
> *Sorry I didn't say bye. Dad thought it was best that I move to Ocean City, Maryland, to live with my aunt while he tries to get sober and stop stirring up trouble. My aunt doesn't have a phone.*
>
> *Good luck at Whitney Prep. I'll write when I can.*
>
> *Bye,*
>
> *Imogene*

Something wasn't right, but Frannie wanted it to be right. She wanted those to be Imogene's words. She wanted to be excited about the idea of Imogene running on a boardwalk or seeing horses on a beach.

But Imogene would have shared more about Ocean City. Imogene never called her pops *Dad*. And the only person who thought Mr. Dryker stirred up trouble was Frannie's dad.

Frannie's breath grew shallow and fast. She turned the envelope over. The stamp was postmarked from San Francisco.

Tears of frustration raced down her cheeks, and her nostrils flared as the truth ate at her belly.

Her dad made up this letter. She was sure of it. He was lying to her, and he knew what happened to Imogene. Now, he was hiding something bad with this letter.

The last time Frannie saw her, Imogene had told her, "You don't see your dad the way I do. He doesn't like me the way you want him to." But Frannie had ignored her concerns. An image of Imogene looking afraid during *Dangerous Strangers* and again when her father had taken pictures of her almost made Frannie throw up.

She stormed to the kitchen where her dad was reading his stupid paper and her mom was making dinner. In the past week, her mom and dad seemed to have switched places on the happiness scale, and Frannie's gut told her it had to do with her friend.

"This letter isn't from Imogene." Frannie slapped it down on the table. "Something bad has happened, and I want to call the police."

"Oh, George, I told you this could happen," her mom said, wringing her hands.

"What does that mean?" Frannie asked her mom, brows furrowed.

Her dad shook his head. "Fine. You want the truth? Imogene ran away because her dad can't take care of himself, let alone her. That's why she is now in Ocean City with her aunt. Believe me, you're both better off."

Frannie pursed her lips and shook her head. She hadn't let him read the letter yet, so how did he know about Imogene's aunt? Why was he trying to trick her?

"Dad, tell me right now. What happened to Imogene? Did a child molester get her?"

Her dad winced and looked away.

"Look at me, Dad," she said. "Please, tell me."

But he couldn't.

"Are . . . are you a child molester?"

A sick feeling came over Frannie. He'd warned her to never trust anyone. He'd said a child molester could look like him. Those had been his own words years ago.

Her mom inhaled deeply and placed her hand over her heart. Her dad looked like he'd been hit over the head with a frying pan.

Finally, she had his full attention. "Absolutely not."

Too afraid to say it loudly, she whispered, "But you know what happened to Imogene, and it's all your fault. You let her walk home. You're lying about something."

His skin turned a shade of green.

"But the letter says—" her mom said, tears running down her face.

"No, Mom. He's a liar. It's not her writing, and the letter says she's in Maryland, but it's postmarked in California. Dad *knows* something about Imogene, and you know it too. That's why you won't take me to see her. You're on his side."

Her dad got angry and slammed his hand on the table. "You want to go to Imogene's? Get in the car."

"No," Mom said. "This is not the way to handle this."

"You too," he said, grabbing his keys. "She wants to know what happened? Fine."

Dad does know. Terror overtook Frannie, like when

she'd watched the scary movie at school. She was equally afraid to know and not know.

"Stop it, George," her mom said as Dad wrapped his big hand around the back of Frannie's neck and steered her outside.

Dad drove them in silence over to the storage units where Imogene lived. "Wait here," he said as he parked the car and marched up the steps to the trailer parked behind the business.

That's where Imogene lives? Frannie was glad she didn't live there; it looked sad and lonely. It didn't have grass or bright yellow dandelions like Frannie's home. More than ever—seeing this dirty place that wasn't a home—she couldn't wait to see that her sweet friend was okay.

Imogene's dad opened the door and looked surprised. "What are you doing here?" she heard him ask. Dad's back was to her, but he said enough of something bad to make Mr. Dryker's eyes widen. He gazed over her dad's shoulder and straight at their car.

Mr. Dryker looked back to her father with a frown, shook his head violently, and began to close the door. Her dad stuck his hand out to keep the door ajar and pulled something out of his pocket, handing it to Mr. Dryker.

"What's he giving him?" Frannie threw open the car door and ran toward the trailer, screaming, "Imogene, I'm here to help!" She tripped when she saw the money in her father's hand.

"Why are you giving him money?!" she screeched.

Her dad turned and scooped her up in his thick arms,

ignoring her kicking and crying, aside from a grunt when her foot landed against his stomach.

After many days of frustration, helplessness took over. "I want to see Imogene," she bawled. She reached over her dad's shoulders toward Mr. Dryker like a baby might have done when reaching for their mother. "Please! Help me find Imogene!"

"Frannie." Mr. Dryker raised his rough voice over her sobbing, "Imogene ran away to my sister's. Don't come here ever again." And he slammed the door.

"You paid him to say that. I used to love you, but now I know . . . you're a bad man. It's not fair." Frannie glared through her tears at her dad as he set her down by the car.

In the front seat, her mom cried and avoided Frannie's eyes.

"And you let him," she said to her mom's profile. "I hate you both."

Over the next three days, her parents argued nonstop. "What aren't you telling me?" her mom asked over and over.

Her dad started sleeping in the spare room, and her mother wouldn't look at him when he spoke. Frannie wouldn't either. Her mom and dad weren't best friends like they used to be, and that was proof enough to Frannie that her dad knew something he shouldn't about Imogene's disappearance.

That afternoon, while her parents were arguing in the backyard, she went to the kitchen and dialed zero. When the operator answered, Frannie said, "I need to report a missing girl."

30

JEAN

SPRING 2022

Jean pulled up next to Griffin on the curb, where he'd told her to meet him in response to her text. He had a backpack slung over one shoulder and a Joe's Burgers bag in one hand. He took the jump drive that held her mom's interview and put it in his pocket.

"You've got to see this too," she said. The diary wobbled in her hand as she gave it to him. It had kept her up all night. "The folded paper is a timeline based on notes in the diary, and I included one photo, the one she said she gave to Whittaker Sr. I'm working on getting more."

"Similar photo to the one I have?"

Jean shook her head. "No such luck. I couldn't find any similar."

Griffin looked determined, more so than when she'd met him the day before. "I'll go through this now for more leads. I've just come from records. I'm on to something."

Goose bumps rose along her arms. "Sounds ominous."

"It is."

"My mother doesn't know, but I'm going to see my grandfather. I'm keeping the visit as light as possible for now."

Griffin looked down at the diary and raised his hand an inch as if to test the weight of the information inside. "Must be good reading if I don't have to beg you to see him. Don't push too hard—it will be tempting. If he starts avoiding your eyes, let it go."

She shouldn't have brought Lexi with her. *What if Grandpa* did *have something to do with the missing girl?*

Jean squeezed Lexi's hand. Her stomach turned as she guided her girl down his walkway, feeling guilty about putting her in his orbit, even though Jean had been safe and happy around him her entire life.

Last night, she'd asked her mom, "For Lexi's sake, I need to know. Do you think Grandpa hurt Imogene? Do you think he could harm a child?"

Her mom said, "It has never made sense to me why he let her leave at night and later refused to help find her."

"Do you think he would make the same choices again?"

"I don't know. To be safe, I never left you alone with him."

Jean had a desperate urge to reconcile the man she'd grown up loving with the man she couldn't blame her mother for suspecting of something.

"Remember, sweetie, while I talk to your great-grandpa, you should color with Booby." *Not to mention, never tell your grandma we came here.*

"And Dandelion," Lexi said, skipping beside Jean.

As usual, Grandpa welcomed her with outstretched arms as soon as he opened the door. "Belly Jeans," he said with glee when he saw her, the old nickname tugging at her heart. *A killer-slash-kidnapper would never come up with Belly Jeans.*

"Grandpa," she said as he kissed her on her cheek.

Once inside, he bent over Lexi and stared into her eyes. "And how is my favorite girl?" He cupped his palms over her cherub cheeks with reverence.

"Lexi." Jean scooted her daughter to the coffee table several feet away. "Let's get your crayons and paper out."

"Didn't expect to see you today," Grandpa said as Jean sat next to him at a small table in the corner of the room where he appeared to be reading hospital board minutes.

"We were in the neighborhood."

"How's Shane?"

"Busy, as usual."

"Your mom? She's well and healthy?" It was the same question he always asked. He'd once confided in Jean,

"When your child survives cancer, you're always afraid the monster will come back."

"Same, same," she lied. No matter what had happened, and no matter how strained their relationship, Jean believed her grandfather loved her mother; learning she had cancer again would kill him.

"And Artsy Fartsy?"

Well, he recently found out his mom has aggressive cancer and that you were the last person to see her childhood friend alive, so . . . "He's well. I've spent a lot of time with him lately."

"The two of you were always inseparable. I wish Sally and I could have given your mom a brother or sister to play with."

She paused as she set her purse down, a corner of her mother's medical file poking out. Once she finished at Grandpa's, she needed to take it to the doctor's office, where she hoped they'd be more forthcoming about her mother's treatment plan than her mother had been.

"Why didn't you and Grandma have more children?"

His deep breath puffed up his cheeks before he exhaled heavily. Shaking his head, he said, "Not from a lack of trying. Frannie was, is, our miracle baby. Over the first five years of our marriage, we suffered three miscarriages. It was a difficult time, but"—he nodded toward Jean and then Lexi—"you can imagine how it affected Sally. Gosh, we wanted children. We wanted a big family. We'd all but given up the dream when we got pregnant with Frannie."

His eyes sparkled, and his smile was gentle. "She was a

fighter from day one. Sally could hardly eat because her morning sickness was horrible, but she never minded. Sally would say, 'The baby's reminding me that it's alive and kicking every day.'"

Jean rested her chin on her fist. "Did you keep trying after Mom was born?"

He shook his head. "When Frannie was two, we had another miscarriage. We decided it was time to be grateful for the family we had."

"And then mom got leukemia."

He looked down at his hands covered with sunspots. "We were terrified we'd lose her. It turned out to be a double-edged sword that we couldn't have more children. On the one hand, another child could have leukemia, too, and we couldn't have managed mentally, emotionally, or physically. On the other hand, Frances got terribly sick, and she needed a . . ." He stilled and then shook his head. "You don't need to hear this. The past is a place to learn from, not live in."

Jean tried not to look too eager as she encouraged him to continue. "But I do." She reached for the file in her purse. She couldn't tell him about the cancer returning—she didn't have the heart, and it was up to her mother to do so. Therefore, she had to play this off well. "Mom went through a box of old things yesterday and found a copy of her hospital file. She let me take it because I'm curious about her experience."

Her grandpa blanched and reached for the file reflexively. "How did she get this? The hospital should have shredded it decades ago."

"Once a hospital administrator, always a hospital administrator," Jean said, letting him take it. "Maybe Grandma kept a copy."

His hands shook as he set it on the table before him, staring at the green pressboard file as if opening it would release demons. Finally, he cracked it open and thumbed through the pages. When he reached a certain point, he stopped and ran his index finger across the upper left-hand corner before flipping to the next page. He released a weighty breath, as if calmed by what he'd found.

What was he looking for? Jean wondered.

"Grandpa," Jean said, reaching for the file to break the spell. "I'm sorry. I didn't think about how this would make you feel."

He placed one large hand firmly atop it as if he intended to keep it and looked at her with sad eyes that cut to the fiber of her being. "We were close to losing her. I would have done anything and everything to help her."

"Oh, Grandpa." She rested her hand atop his large one.

"Today, we know donors don't need to be a perfect match and that a match of several of the markers is sufficient. But, back then, donors had to be spot-on. Sally and I weren't a perfect match for Frannie's bone marrow transplant. Parents seldom are. But a sibling"—his breath caught—"often is perfect. The one thing we couldn't give her."

"Oh, Grandpa. I can't imagine."

Smiling gently through his tears, he said, "I pray you never can."

31

FRANNIE

MAY 1977

Confusion swamped Frannie as her parents' expressions changed from hopeful to frightened. Her mother fell against her dad, hiding her face in his chest while she cried.

They'd stepped into the hallway with her oncologist, but she could hear their conversation, even if she didn't understand it. The higher dose of chemotherapy had done what it was supposed to—wiped out all her cells. When she wasn't throwing up, she slept deeply. But today was transplant day. She would start getting better.

"I'm sorry, George and Sally. Some cells were damaged during the freezing and/or thawing process. I'm afraid we don't have enough," her doctor said helplessly.

Her dad looked dumbstruck as he stared at the doctor. He wrapped his arms around her mom to keep her upright. Her dad's head jerked frantically around as if searching for something.

Frannie wished she could find the strength to call to them or, better yet, join them in a family hug and ask questions.

Her dad's eyes finally settled on the doctor. "A donor. Another patient. Or a staff member. Someone in this hospital will be an acceptable match. We have HLA tissue and blood records. Yes, we'll find a donor," her dad said. But his voice was higher than usual, as if he was begging rather than giving an order.

Her oncologist set a hand on her dad's shoulder as he shook his head. "You know it's difficult to find a perfect tissue match. If it were easy to find one, you'd have done so from the beginning. You wouldn't have had Frannie enrolled in the self-donor trial. There aren't donor registries. And even if we found a perfect match and willing donor, we'd need a week to follow protocol, obtain permission, and extract bone marrow."

Her mother turned to look at the doctor and then her husband. "But Frannie's numbers. If we don't move forward . . ."

Her dad glanced toward her room; his eyes wild. When he saw her watching them, he smiled as if to reassure her. Turning to the doctor, her dad said, "Move forward with the viable supply you have. It's our only choice."

Frannie's head hurt too badly to remember how her father had explained the procedure with her Smurfs, but she did remember this: getting better started with only Papa Smurf, Smurfette, and Bashful.

Soon, her room was swarming with people, including a nurse giving her mom a shot while saying, "This will calm your nerves."

"It's time to receive your healthy cells, baby," her dad said, his voice rough and lower than usual.

"Will I be okay?"

"I won't let anything happen to you. I promise." He pulled her into his arms and almost squeezed her breath out of her.

"Will you stay with me?"

"I'll be right here. Always right here."

THAT NIGHT, Frannie dreamed that a man cloaked in darkness came to her bedside. At first, as he loomed over her, she couldn't understand him, but then, she recognized Gargamel's words as he finished his promise. ". . . if that's the last thing I'll ever do."

Frannie drifted in and out. She no longer had a sense of time or knew if she was feeling better. When she woke up, her doctor and Nurse Penny stood by her side.

Nurse Penny's smile was wide. "Oh, honey. It's about time you woke up." An extra pillow placed behind her back propped her up enough to sip water.

"Am I okay?" Frannie told them about the visit from Gargamel.

Her doctor said, "Sometimes sedation causes nightmares. Remember, if you have that dream again, Gargamel isn't real."

"Dad says that Gargamel is cancer."

"In that case"—the doctor winked—"Gargamel should be afraid of you."

32

JEAN

SPRING 2022

"As I've said, the past is in the past." Jean's grandpa pulled his hand free of hers, taking the file with it. Waving it in the air, he said, "My girl was resilient. Our miracle baby became a miracle girl and beat the odds and her cancer."

Jean cringed, knowing what he didn't about her mother's health. How would her grandfather handle the news once he learned? At eighty-four, he was still a healthy and active man. He had retired in his early seventies as the hospital administrator but continued to dedicate his time and energy to the hospital that saved his daughter.

How could this man have anything to do with a girl's disappearance? There must be a logical explanation, yet she couldn't ask him outright. Not without her mom's permission.

"And I'll tell you one more thing about your mother, although Douglas likes to take the credit." Her grandpa chuckled. "She had you and Art. A possible long-term effect of chemotherapy is infertility. And did that stop my girl from becoming a mother? No siree."

"I had no idea." Jean placed her hand above her heart. "Her pregnancy must have been worrisome for you all."

His lips thinned, and he nodded. "We did what we had to do to avoid creating stress for your mother."

Perhaps her grandfather and Peter Whittaker most of all. Had senior Whittaker learned about the odds of her mother's pregnancy? Did this have anything to do with his decision to withdraw from the search after two weeks? It would mean Griffin's dad had spoken to her grandfather. Would Griffin draw the same conclusion once he listened to the recording she'd begun on her phone before climbing out of the car?

"Grandpa?"

He looked at her as if ready to soak up her every word. This was something she'd always loved about her grandpa: he was interested in every word she uttered.

Lexi jumped out of her chair and ran toward him with a drawing. "For you, Great-grandpa."

Jean resisted the urge to send Lexi back to her spot, anxious to finish this conversation.

"Why, thank you, young lady." He laid the picture flat before him as she waited for his praise.

Jean, who was well-schooled in interpreting Lexi's scribbles, was at a loss on the blue-and-red work of art.

"I don't have my glasses on," her diplomatic grandpa said. "You'll have to tell me what I'm looking at."

"Papa Smurf."

He picked up the picture, and the paper trembled in his hands. When he turned back to Lexi, his eyes had a sheen of tears. "How did you know how much I like Papa Smurf? He's an old friend."

Lexi shrugged her shoulders and ran back to her seat.

"I bought your mother a Smurf village when she was diagnosed."

"That explains why she unpacked an ancient mushroom-capped village and gave it to Lexi yesterday."

He looked up, his eyes glowing. "She kept it? All these years?" Though he was a strong, barrel-chested man, the wrinkles showed every year of his life, and the sight of his tears weaving their way through each and every lifeline unsettled Jean.

Grandpa will die someday too.

He wiped his cheeks. "I've gotten sappy in my old age. No one warned me this would happen, or else I would have invested in Kleenex stock." He chuckled the warm chuckle she'd heard her entire life.

Oh, sweet Grandpa, what happened forty-three years ago?

Channeling Griffin, she chose her words wisely. "Speaking of Smurfs, Mom told us about a friend she met when she was in the hospital. Do you remember her?"

Grandpa turned his face to the right and peered at her with his left eye, as if he looked through an eyepiece. "Sure. She made lots of friends."

She gasped internally. Not only was he prevaricating, he was fibbing—her mom had never made friends easily, and she'd never had *lots* of them.

"Don't push too hard." Griffin's warning played through her mind.

But Grandpa maintained eye contact, so she kept going.

"This friend was special; another girl who had leukemia. You and Grandma helped her get a scholarship to attend St. Agnes with Mom."

He looked down at Papa Smurf and smoothed his hand over the paper. "Imogene."

Good, he'd said the name for her.

"What else did your mother tell you about her?"

Technically, she'd told the video camera a lot and, ultimately, Griffin not Jean. "Not much."

"I don't want to talk about her." His jaw was set, but he didn't look away. He drummed his fingers against his table between the drawing and the medical file.

"Why not?"

"Brings up too many bad memories. We've revisited enough sad ones already today, and I'm too old to deal with them or do anything about them. I decided long ago to move forward by paying forward."

But your daughter has dealt with them her entire life, she wanted to say. *Your daughter couldn't move forward.*

"Mom hinted that you hadn't liked Imogene because she was from the wrong side of the tracks or something. Is that true?" It was a risk making him defensive, but asking was justified, especially if he thought this was the worst her mom had shared about him and Imogene.

He picked at a spot of peeling plastic on the tabletop. "That last part, that was Imogene's dad's fault. But, to answer your question, no, I didn't appreciate Imogene's friendship with Frannie. Something about it brought out the worst in me." He pulled away a strip of plastic, marring the tabletop. "Your grandma used to tell me I was jealous of Imogene."

Griffin was right: it was hard to stop while she was ahead. She ducked her head to try to see his eyes. "Jealous of a little girl with cancer?"

"Now you sound like your grandmother." He looked up and around the room. "She was stronger than all of us."

"Who? Grandma or Imogene?"

He stared at Lexi across the room. "I loved Imogene as much as I hated how she made me feel."

Jean recoiled at his unfamiliar bitter tone. This was what Griffin had meant by not pushing.

Screw it.

"What do you mean, 'made you feel'? She was a child." She grabbed her mom's file and shoved it into her purse.

He stood and looked at the file poking from her bag and then down at her. "Thanks for coming, Belly Jeans, but don't ask me about Imogene again. I don't want to lose you too." Clapping his hands, he said, "Lexi, can Great-grandpa draw with you?"

33

GRIFFIN

SPRING 2022

Griffin watched Frances's video three times.

He should've insisted on interviewing her himself—now, he'd never get her to answer the questions as freely again.

Such as how she had answered, *Do you have any photos of the missing person?*

Frances had said, "The last one I have of us together is from 1977. Later, in 1979, we took pictures before she disappeared, but I was told the film was lost by the developer."

Bullshit.

Griffin compared the picture of Imogene and Frannie that Jean had given him to the one from his dad's file. The differences were clear. Frannie had aged a few years and was vibrantly healthy in the latter photo where she was alone. In the former, both girls had puffy faces and appeared to be in a hospital, though in matching uniforms and crocheted hats.

He'd bet his next three meals that the photo his dad had saved was a picture from the supposedly lost roll. If his hunch was right, there wouldn't be any more like this one, and Frannie had never seen it. But how did his dad get it? What did it mean? On the yellow pad, Griffin wrote, *Who had access to the film?*

He texted Jean:

> Need all family photos from 1975–1979.

He flipped through his notes. Rodney's name had popped up more than once. He'd interviewed Frannie when she'd reported Imogene missing. According to the diary, nine-year-old Frannie had called the police on her own father—now that had taken gumption. Not that he could verify it on the stupid redacted police report.

So much for exercising patience; he called the police station and asked for Leah.

"Hi, Leah. Griffin Whittaker here. Sorry to trouble you, but do you have contact information for Rodney Schultz yet?"

"Can I call you back in one second? I want to step outside."

That doesn't sound good. "Sounds good."

While he waited for her to call back, he filled out new pages in his yellow tablet:

Benjamin Dryker

George Jerome

Nurse Bowman—St. Agnes School

The last one should be an interesting discussion and

was another nugget from the diary. The young girl had written that, despite switching schools, her parents had arranged for her to see her former school nurse after Imogene vanished.

> *Nurse Bowman said it will make me feel better if I use the diary she gave me after that molester movie to keep my facts straight about Imogene's disappearance and how I feel. She is the only adult I trust, but she didn't offer to help find Imogene either.*

Yeah, Griffin wanted to talk to this nurse if he could, see what she thought about the entire debacle.

But nothing in Frances's video or diary added clarity to the mysterious *4/1957*. He'd get Tony working on the numbers if he persevered and finished his first assignment. If the calls didn't turn his son off, perhaps a second ambiguous list would do the trick.

"Hi, Leah," Griffin answered his phone.

"Off the record?" she asked, traffic in the background.

"Off the record."

"Rodney Schultz's file has been sealed by personnel. I asked around and was told that he was 'encouraged' to take an early retirement in 1994."

Damn. X marked the spot. That was the same year his dad had looked for Imogene and Internal Affairs checked out the evidence folder. "*People will go down for this.*"

Sounded as if Rodney might have gone down.

"My contact told me that, from what she

remembered, Schultz got sacked for something he did in '79. Isn't that the year you mentioned on your way to records?"

"Good listeners make good detectives, Leah. Keep it up."

"I have a last known address for you."

"Excellent." Once he hung up, he checked his watch. There was time.

Closing his backpack, he first drove by Rodney's place. It was early evening. All the lights were out. Griffin had never been a fan of knocking on a police officer's door unannounced, retired or not. He'd call first and drop by tomorrow morning. Next, he drove over to the area where Benjamin Dryker had managed storage units decades before. Frances hadn't remembered the exact location. There were multiple storage facilities, and he struck out at the first two. Hopefully, this would be a case of third time's a charm and not three strikes, you're out.

The office was open, and a young, twenty-something man sat behind the counter.

"How can I help you?"

"Hey there," Griffin said. "Stab in the dark, but do you know how long ago a Benjamin Dryker last worked here and where I might find him?"

"Benji." The guy nodded. "He doesn't work anymore, but he still lives out back. The owners let him stay."

That was easy.

"But he's in rehab right now."

Not so easy.

"Do you know when he checks out?" After reading about Dryker from young Frannie's perspective, Griffin felt sorry for the old man. And other than stating his full name the first time in her recordings, Frances referred to him as Mr. Dryker, as if her relationship to him had reverted her to being the small, uncertain child trying to piece together a messed-up situation on her own.

She'd written, *Dad said Mr. Dryker was a no-good drunk.*

Sounded like Dryker still struggled with his alcoholism. Or was he battling demons and a guilty conscience? Griffin concealed the shiver that worked its way up his spine. This man had lost his child. Had he been involved? Empathy for his alcoholism aside, right now, everyone was a suspect.

The clerk shrugged his shoulders. "Hard to say."

Griffin pulled out his card. "Can you give him this when he's back? Or call me yourself?"

After the guy put the card in a drawer, he asked, "What's up?"

"Has Benji"—Griffin applied one of the oldest tricks in the PI book of gaining someone's trust by borrowing nicknames and familiarity—"ever mentioned his daughter or a family?"

"He doesn't like to talk about them."

"Do you know what happened to them?"

"Nope. Not sure I want to know either."

"Thanks," Griffin said. "Mind if I look around his place? I won't go inside."

"Should be okay."

There wasn't much to see except dirt and a small run-down trailer. He climbed the stairs to peek in a side window, but the curtains were pulled. He lifted the lid to a small trash bin; it was full of old McDonald's bags and empty Filet-O-Fish boxes.

BY THE TIME Griffin arrived home, he was exhausted but ecstatic to hear the sound of a clarinet floating downstairs. This was the first time in a long time he hadn't had to encourage Tony to practice. The fact gave Griffin a much-needed boost of energy and confidence.

He all but danced the rest of the way into the house to greet Annie.

"Someone's happy," his wife said.

"Because *someone's* playing his clarinet. I knew he'd get bored of making calls. Success."

"You're getting ahead of yourself," Annie said.

He paused mid fist-pump. "What's that supposed to mean?"

She pointed to a pile of paper sitting on the table.

Frowning, Griffin sifted through the sheets.

Damn.

Tony was almost done. He had made notes precisely as he'd been asked to. None were in the affirmative so far.

Still, Griffin thought, *he's playing his clarinet*. "Bet he won't want to do this again, especially since there are no hits yet."

Annie raised her brows. "You always say not to make assumptions."

Feeling smug, Griffin walked upstairs. "Hey, kiddo. Thanks for making the calls. Dead-ends are ninety percent of my day. Tough luck."

His son rested his clarinet across his knees. "No problem. It was good practice. I'll have better luck tomorrow."

Uh-oh.

"What's next once I finish the calls?"

Crap.

Avoiding the unexpected question, Griffin nodded toward the instrument and said, "You're sounding good."

"Wouldn't you know, Dad, that the clarinet comes naturally to me after work? It relaxes me and helps me switch gears."

After work . . . As if his kid had a day job—not this bogus internship.

"You should try it sometime. You know, playing again," his son said.

Victory slipped from Griffin's clutches.

"Hey, Dad," Tony said, "how come you stopped playing?"

He really didn't feel up to this conversation. "Some other time," he said and turned away.

"Mom said you used to love it, and that you wanted to be a musician."

Thanks, Annie.

Tony smiled. "I was thinking, maybe we could start playing together at night, when we are done working."

When we *are done working . . . Jesus.*

"My clarinet is buried up in the attic and hasn't been played in decades."

His son shrugged. "Well? What have you been waiting for?"

For once, Griffin couldn't think of an explanation, at least not one that made sense.

That was the one thing that Griffin could never get used to about being a father: how his kid made him second-guess his decisions.

34

FRANCES

SPRING 2022

Frannie hid her yawn behind her cup as Art and Douglas chortled like mischievous boys from across the table, and Jean listened, slack-jawed, with Lexi beside her.

Her adventure to unbury a piece of Imogene had brought the people she loved the most to her table tonight. Imogene had always done that—created intimacy and magic in Frannie's life. In the past, they'd had many family dinners together, but Frannie had always felt like an onlooker, observing the humor shared between her ex and her growing children rather than understanding it. Once, in a rare philosophical moment, Douglas had explained, "It's a choice you make, Frank. Every year, you grow more reserved and distant, as if you've lost a piece of yourself."

In hindsight, she accepted he had been right. Imogene had been a huge part of her, and the gaping hole her absence and lack of answers left in Frannie's life had accumulated over the years, like a cancer, until the hole crowded out the whole of Frannie. But in telling her children about Imogene and allowing Douglas and Art to visit the cemetery with her, she had chosen to be included, an insider. Now, as a result, she and Imogene were at the center of their good spirits, and it was liberating to embrace thoughts of Imogene rather than to shove them aside, too afraid to hurt.

If she could change the past, she would've told her children about Imogene sooner.

Frannie swallowed some of her strong coffee. Her body was turning on her, wearing out too soon, not caring that she never wanted this evening to end. As her doctor had warned, she had numbness in her feet, and her ankles were swollen after her eventful day. She didn't want to give up, but at the same time, she could tell her body was deteriorating. The stem cell treatment was her only hope.

"What happened next?" Jean asked. "Wait. Should I cover Lexi's ears?"

"Did you see his face?" Douglas asked Art for the tenth time, jumping ahead in the story.

After the trio had escaped the cemetery, the two men couldn't be bothered to leave her side the rest of the day. She'd briefly wondered what Douglas's girlfriend would think, or if Art's boss was curious about his whereabouts. Once, she would have asked, but she'd been loath to ruin the mood and lose their company, even though a significant portion involved her son and ex sitting on her couch and binge-watching a series about hillbilly mobsters, as if their stint of crime as "grave vandals"—a name called out by the groundskeeper as he'd four-wheeled toward her—had turned them into money-laundering, murderous drug dealers in the Appalachians.

Art impersonated the groundskeeper's deep, stern voice: "'What have you taken? Hand it over.'"

Lexi *tee-hee*'d on Jean's lap over her uncle's strange tone.

"And?" Jean demanded. "I'm dying to know what *it* is. I can't believe you took tools to a grave and dug something up. Scandalous, Mother."

Douglas roared theatrically, "Free Imogene!"

He was married to Frannie when she'd hired Peter Whittaker, and while he'd been supportive, he hadn't liked to see her hurt when it fell apart. Hurt was an understatement. For two weeks, she'd sunk into a depression. Beside himself with concern, he'd said, "Maybe your parents are right. It's best to let Imogene go. Think of the twins we're going to have."

It wasn't that her parents had wanted Frannie to let go of Imogene for her own happiness—they had wanted her grief and obsession with finding Imogene to stop disrupting their lives and family life. Her parents had asked her to forget her dearest childhood friend simply to make *them* feel better. Therefore, the unfulfilled hole had continued to grow year after year.

Over time, Douglas had become another person who thought she should move on rather than hang on, but where her true pain thrived was in the incessant need of other people to pretend Imogene had been insignificant. Her shame was due to how she'd capitulated.

When she'd given birth to the twins—and for several years later, when the munchkins loved her presence so much that they would crawl to the bathroom and sit outside the doorway, waiting for her to come out with an empty bladder so she could shower their cheeks and round bellies with kisses—she forgot the void left by Imogene. Jean and Art had brought much-needed and unconditional love to her life, and they'd also taught her she could love someone else more than herself, more than Imogene. Yet, her children had only needed her for so long. Soon, they'd grown into young people who wanted to be with their friends, not their needy mommy. The loss of Imogene returned, and the hole expanded. Frannie threw herself into an accounting career to fill herself up.

"And"—Art composed himself—"Mom handed him Jokey Smurf."

"Jokey Smurf," Douglas repeated. His gut-busting laughter almost overturned his chair.

"You should have seen her, Sis. Classic Mom."

Frannie wrinkled her nose. *Classic* would make a strange epitaph. Good thing she'd be cremated someday.

"Classic? Hardly. She dug up a Smurf from a cemetery," Jean said.

"Yeah, classic," Douglas said. "So straight-faced when she handed it to him, the guy was speechless. He asked, 'What in the hell is this?'" More of Douglas's wheezing ensued.

Straight-faced. Another epitaph potential that made Frannie glad she wouldn't be buried.

"Then," Art said, pausing to wipe the tears of mirth from his eyes, "Mom gave him her deadpan look and said, 'Jokey Smurf, obviously.'"

Frannie remained quiet, soaking up how they were talking about her in the third person, because maybe this was how they'd share this memory together once she was gone.

Lexi giggled away at life and reached over to touch Frannie's arm. "Silly, G-Ma Frannie."

Frannie smiled at Lexi and patted her small fingers.

"Mom took Jokey Smurf back and asked, 'Any more questions?'"

Douglas had to catch his breath before saying, "The guy stared at us like we were aliens. He didn't say another word as we walked away. When I looked back, he was still standing there, his hand outstretched as if we'd wiped his memory like Tommy Lee Jones in *Men in Black*."

Jean's smile was about to split her face in two. She looked at Frannie and saluted her.

Frannie wasn't sure what came over her, but she winked at Jean. She was inspired by the sensation that Imogene had joined her in spirit. From time to time, after her mother died, Frannie had sensed her mother's presence. But in all these years, she'd never been able to feel Imogene.

Douglas said, "I've always told you there was a sassy troublemaker in your mother. Wicked sense of humor deep inside this one."

Frannie set down her empty but heavy cup. *Sassy troublemaker.* A more memorable tribute.

Shane's arrival with Chinese food interrupted their musings and the group turned introspective as they ate.

After a while, Jean asked, "What was Imogene like?"

Something in Frannie's chest cracked open. No one had ever asked her to talk about Imogene after she vanished. Other than the investigative questions, everyone had encouraged her to avoid the subject of Imogene for years, as if talking about a loved one was more painful than forgetting.

She told them about *Oliver!* and how Imogene would dance around, pretending to be Artful Dodger. She told how Imogene laughed when she listened to Frannie's chicken jokes. And she talked about the time Imogene borrowed craft scissors from the hospital library to cut off Frannie's hair. "So it can't fall out," Imogene had said.

"And our first trip together was going to be Ocean City, Maryland, for kite-flying, Ferris wheels, and taffy."

"Chicken jokes?" Art asked. "Wow. Who knew?"

Jean caressed Frannie's hand. "I wish you could have gone together."

Lexi picked the cashews out of her dinner and handed them to Shane to eat. She laughed when he pretended to gobble her fingers.

"Artful Dodger, like Uncle Art?" Lexi asked.

Art set his fork down. "Whoa. Mom?"

Shane leaned forward. "And Jean, like Imogene?"

Jean rested her palm over her heart. "Omigosh. Seriously, Mom? You named us after her?"

"She would have loved you both," Frannie said, tears forming.

"Wait a minute." Douglas spoiled the moment. "You told me we named them after Art Garfunkel and Neil Diamond."

Jean choked on her drink, and Art laughed while wiping his eyes. "Neil Diamond?" he asked.

Douglas frowned. "Yeah. 'Forever in Blue Jeans.' It was our first dance together in sixth grade."

"Oh boy," Shane said while Art rolled his eyes.

Frannie laughed. "No. You assumed that's why I suggested the names. And we all know how you are once you get an idea stuck in your brain."

"Well, I'll be," Douglas said, shaking his head.

Frannie watched as their children shared a silent exchange. Finally, as if in agreement that Jean should speak on their behalf, her daughter turned to her and said, "We're honored."

Later, while the three men played *Chutes and Ladders* with Lexi, Jean cleared their dishes. "Mom, take a seat and rest."

"Thank you. It's been a tiring day."

"But a good one?"

"Yes. One of the best in a long time. You're all here. I love this. It's mostly all I ever wanted."

Jean dried her hands and sat next to Frannie again. "I'm sorry Grandma had you do that before you were ready."

"Me too. In hindsight, I think she had good intentions, and she wanted me to say goodbye."

"Don't we all have good intentions?" Jean asked, looking across the open room at Lexi and her husband.

"Are you okay?" Frannie asked.

Jean's eyebrows lifted and her chest expanded in a synchronized expression of hopelessness. "All my friends seem to be happier about motherhood and marriage than me. I feel awful even admitting it. It's like I'm losing myself, and that no matter what I try to do—and I do try—I'll never be a good wife or mom. I mean, every day I make choices for Lexi, and I won't know if they were good ones or bad ones until years from now."

History proved that Frannie was apt to say the wrong thing during fragile moments such as this one. What would an adult Imogene say, she wondered?

Nothing. She'd listen. Be there.

Frannie reached over and set her hand atop Jean's.

She wasn't sure how long they sat there, quiet and touching, but apparently it wasn't enough since it wasn't the norm.

"No words of advice, Mom? No tough love such as 'self-pity won't get you anywhere' or agreement that I'm a bad mom?"

Tough love, another avoided epitaph. Truly, Frannie was too tired to dish out platitudes or remind Jean that she'd always had a bad habit of comparing herself to her friends.

But Jean's confession did remind her of something she'd once read about Martha Stewart. It was a long story, but maybe long would work better with Jean.

"When you were little, we'd go to neighborhood

barbecues. Or everyone would get together for a picnic after tee-ball. The families always put their best appearance and attitudes forward. The host and hostess were always the mostest.

"Whenever I hosted, someone always complained about something, even though I might have borrowed the recipe or table settings from someone who previously did the same and was applauded. I felt like it reflected on my inability to connect with people, and I couldn't anticipate their needs like a normal person.

"I grew to hate the gatherings, always comparing *us* to *them*. Why weren't they tired after working all day or week? How did they keep their kids happy? How did they please everyone? I liked order, predictability, and control."

Jean nodded. "You still do, though I understand why now."

"Your father had bought me a subscription to Martha Stewart's new magazine, *Living*, to help me better prepare for said events."

"Ah-ha. Your idol," Jean said.

"Martha was practical about everything and prepared for every outcome."

"Where is this going, Mom?"

She cut to the chase. "Martha says, 'Bake the cake people most want to eat.'"

Jean raised her brows. "Some more context please."

"Who cares if a cake looks good? It only matters if it tastes good."

Jean nodded slowly at first and then more vigorously. "Make the cake that we want to eat."

"Yes," Frannie validated. "It may not look perfect, but it will be one you'll want to experience again and again, like a happy memory."

"You couldn't have told me anything better, Mom."

Finally—she'd said the right thing to Jean.

Thank you, Martha Stewart.

Jean sat back in her chair and tilted her head. "It must have been terrifying for you to go to a cemetery when you were a child after surviving cancer."

"Yes. I had spent my childhood fighting death, not moving toward it."

"Mom, if the transplant doesn't work, are you afraid to die?"

"I'm more afraid of being forgotten. Like Imogene." Frannie surprised herself with her confession.

"You won't be. I promise." Jean pressed her fingertips against her eyelids and then reached for a tissue.

"But I also don't want to be remembered for the wrong reasons, like being an overbearing mother."

"Then make the cake you want to eat while you're here." Jean returned her advice.

Frannie nodded. "Yes, I have some time to add ingredients, don't I?"

"What was it like to have cancer as a child? You've never talked about those years."

"Believe it or not, the hospital could be fun. At the children's hospital, we felt normal, because many of us were experiencing the same feelings. There were days I felt like I was dying, but I knew I wasn't—it was the chemotherapy doing its job, such as the time Gargamel haunted me after the transplant and promised to get me 'if that's the last thing I ever do.'"

Jean smiled at Frannie's impersonation.

Frannie grew reflective. "But there was one night I wouldn't have survived if not for Imogene."

35

FRANNIE

MAY 1977

Mom and Dad had barely left her side since her transplant almost a week ago, even though her doctor explained a trillion times that, despite the risk they'd faced, Frannie's health was improving.

Nurse Penny called her Miracle Frannie, but every time Frannie asked to see Imogene, her dad said, "You're getting better, and your numbers look better than ever, but your immune system is immature and needs to strengthen. We will not sabotage this win or the incredible efforts people have taken to save you. Right? Especially with the horrible flu that has hit the hospital over the last few days. We can't take any chances, sweetie. Not with your health or anyone else's. This isn't only about you. Imogene has a slight fever, and we want her to get better too."

As soon as her parents said goodnight, Frannie called Imogene's room.

Cradling the large receiver between her shoulder and

cheek, she opened the bedside drawer to withdraw the present she couldn't wait to give Imogene.

"Hello?"

Whispering so Nurse Penny wouldn't hear, Frannie said, "You okay, Imogene? Dad said you have a fever."

"Frannie! I miss you."

Frannie said, "Meet me in Narnia, ASAP."

"But Nurse Penny will pull out her hair. I'm not supposed to leave my room 'cuz of my temperature."

"We'll be fast. I have a surprise for you, and I can't wait forever. If I catch the bug, or you get worse, it could be a million days before we see each other."

"Oh, honey. That's too long."

The phone felt heavier in her palm than usual. "Leave now. Before it's too late."

Imogene coughed. "Ready, set, go."

Frannie's knees knocked against each other when her feet hit the floor. When she reached the doorway, she peeked around the corner. Nurse Penny was on the phone. At this rate, Imogene would beat Frannie to Narnia.

"Rodney, I've got to go. I'm busier than ants at a picnic." Nurse Penny took off in the opposite direction carrying a stack of puke buckets.

Whew.

As Frannie turned to her left, a wave of dizziness made her stomach turn.

Real fast.

She rested her palm against the wall as she walked down the hall, clutching the gift against her chest.

Just a few more steps.

Except, when she reached for the doorknob, her world turned upside down.

FRANNIE'S EYELIDS were too heavy to open. She was more tired than she'd ever felt in her entire short life and her head hurt. She tried to open her lips and say, "*Don't cry, Mom. I'll be okay,*" but Frannie wasn't sure it was the truth.

She couldn't hear Dad, could only feel his silence; it was sad, and angry, and took up most of the room.

She was burning up. *Take these blankets off.*

But no words came out. Now and then, she felt her dad's cool, large hand on her forehead, and she wanted it to stay there. Except, she'd never known his strong hands could shake so much.

"You need sleep," someone said.

Nurse Penny? Can you hear me?

"No. I'm not leaving her again," her mom said.

"We set up a cot for you in the next room."

"She needs us." *Dad.*

What she needed was for someone to remove her blankets.

"We shouldn't have left her," her dad said. "I knew her immune system was compromised."

"The doctor said to hope for the best. And she's beat the odds before." Her mother sounded unsure.

Nurse Penny said, "Please, use the cot. You need to stay strong. We're doing everything we can." But Nurse Penny sounded like she might be crying too.

"No," Mom said, but her voice sounded farther away now. "I'm not forfeiting one second with her."

"Nothing you do now will help her fever break," Nurse Penny said. "But you do need to be here when it does."

Mom, crawl into bed with me. Even though Frannie was hot, she didn't want to be alone.

Her mom choked. "Right. Right. Okay. You're right."

"I'll stay with her," Dad said.

"We'll take turns," Mom said. "Wake me up if . . ."

If what, Mom?

"I'll tuck you in and come right back to Frannie," Dad said.

"This was my fault. I should have watched them more closely."

Oh, honey. What's your fault, Nurse Penny?

Her dad's voice was strong. "No more of that, Penny. This flu isn't yours or the hospital's fault." And then the room grew silent.

Later, her shivers woke her.

Frannie's arms and legs felt like icicles. *Is anyone there?*

Just when she thought she might freeze to death, a small hand took hers.

"I'm here," Imogene said, lying down next to her.

Imogene. Frannie tried to smile.

"In Ocean City," Imogene spoke in her ear, "we'll fly kites in the shape of dragons together. There are fudge stores and taffy that tastes like peanut butter. We'll feed the birds. And we'll eat until we are sick, and we'll splash in the ocean."

And we'll go to the pony beach where there are horseshoe crabs.

"Hey, Frannie, why did the chicken cross the road?" Imogene's voice grew more distant with each word.

Frannie fell asleep before she could say, *"Hey, that's my line."*

FRANNIE OPENED ONE EYE, stunned by the brightness. *Daytime.*

Her mom's face was red and puffy as she stared at the ceiling while stroking Frannie's hand.

"Mom?" she asked, even though her throat hurt when she talked.

Her mom's eyes darted to her, and she exhaled on a sob. "Hi, sweetie. Welcome back."

"Why are you crying?"

Her dad all but ran into the room. "Frannie?" He bent over, resting his hands on his knees, and took a deep breath. "Thank God."

"They're happy tears. You scared us," her mom said.

She reached behind her for Imogene, but she was gone. "Imogene kept me warm. Where is she?"

Her dad and mom frowned.

"In her room," Mom said.

Her dad looked super tired, more tired than Mom. He closed his eyes, turned his back to her, and reorganized the Smurfs. When he was done, he clenched Gargamel and threw him in the trash.

"Dad?"

He didn't face her. "That's what I want to do to cancer. Throw it in the trash for all the pain it causes."

"I WANT TO SEE IMOGENE," Frannie said for the millionth time later that morning.

"You can't," her mom said. "We need you back in fighting shape so we can go home."

"This stinks." Frannie reached for the phone to call Imogene's room, but there was no answer. "What time is she going home, again?"

"I'm not sure," her mom said, stroking Frannie's cheek.

Just then, Imogene poked her head around the corner.

"Imogene, you read my mind!" Frannie's yell startled her mother.

"Frannie," her mom gasped.

But Frannie was too excited to see Imogene to feel sorry about breaking the hospital's no-shouting rule. She patted her bedside like always until Imogene sat down. "I was afraid I wouldn't get to see you before you went home."

Imogene smiled. "Oh, honey, no way."

Her mom reached over and touched Frannie's head. "You don't feel warm."

"Thanks for cuddling with me last night."

"You're welcome," Imogene said.

"I'll get Nurse Penny to take your temperature," her mom said, pushing the call button.

"I can't wait to go to second grade together, and someday, Ocean City," Frannie said.

"And another nap would be a good idea," her mom said.

The girls knew what that meant: it was time for Imogene to go.

Imogene stepped around Frannie's mom and waved. "See ya."

"Wouldn't want to be ya," Frannie said.

As the nurse joined them, her mom sighed with relief. "I think I need a nap too."

36

GRIFFIN

SPRING 2022

"Can I come to work with you today?" Tony asked.

"It's Saturday. Don't you have better things to do? Friends to hang out with?"

"Sure, but they're driving to Santa Cruz to hang out at the beach. I'd rather go to work with you."

"You must be adopted," Griffin said, hoping to end the discussion.

"Come on, Dad. I'm graduating next year. I want to get a head start."

"Yep, definitely adopted." Griffin was relieved Annie liked to sleep in on the weekends. He had a feeling she'd side with Tony.

"Son, you have the rest of your life to be an adult. Go and have fun. Trust me, I wish I had done more of that while I could."

"You still can have fun," Tony said, pushing his bowl of cereal aside.

Griffin shoved the unsolicited teenage advice aside to assess his son's motives.

Another list should kill this stupid obsession.

"I'll tell you what. You can go to the office and do some online research."

Tony jumped up and grabbed his backpack. "Ready when you are."

Enthusiastic cub.

After leaving Tony the Intern at his office with instructions to unpack *4/1957* and to write everything down and not assume anything, Griffin headed over to Rodney Schultz's. He called first and left a message. Fingers crossed, by the time Griffin got back to his office, Tony would be bored stiff, and Griffin would be armed with Rodney's answers.

GRIFFIN KNOCKED three times and picked up a week's worth of newspapers that had piled up outside the door.

Out of town? This trip may have been a waste of time.

At least he'd have an extra breakfast burrito and tater tots to show for it. Neither his intern nor his intern's mother need know about it.

"Who's there?!"

"Griffin Whittaker. I called earlier and left a message."

"Peter Whittaker's son?"

"Yes."

"Come back with a bottle of whiskey or scram."

Griffin rubbed the back of his neck, frowning at the door. He'd known Benjamin Dryker struggled with alcoholism, but he had no recollection of Rodney being a heavy drinker. Regardless, he never bribed anyone with alcohol—a rule his dad had taught him and one he'd taken on as his own. "I won't do that, but I can offer you breakfast. From Belinda's." Nobody, especially a former local cop, could resist the takeaway from Belinda's by the courthouse.

The door opened.

Damn. Rodney had not aged well.

"Sanctimonious, like your goddamn father." He grabbed the bag from Griffin's hand and turned back into the house, leaving the door open for him to follow.

The stench of stale whiskey almost gave Griffin a contact buzz.

He set the pile of newspapers on a cluttered side table. He hated to see cops go down the tubes like this after retirement—missing the rush of a life tethered to a purpose or a good case. He may resent his own career choice, but at least he hadn't turned to alcohol or drugs when his dad had nixed his music career. Unless he counted food as a drug . . .

Rodney pointed at the couch. "Push that stuff aside. Take a seat. But don't get too comfortable. I can guess what this is about, and it's not my favorite topic."

Okay, first things first. Griffin showed him the photo from his dad's file. "Have you ever seen this?"

He teetered forward but shook his head. "I recognize Frannie Jerome but not the picture."

"Does *4/1957* mean anything to you?"

"No."

"Tell me what happened with this case." Griffin skipped the preliminaries, sitting on the edge of his seat.

The old cop sneered. "Had your dad asked me that instead of charging ahead with his holier-than-thou attitude, I might have retired when I was ready."

"People will go down for this."

"You wrongfully redacted the report in 1979," Griffin guessed. "And my dad was the first to find out in 1994."

"I did what I thought I had to do. And I've paid for it."

The drunk man pointed at the half-empty bottle of Jack Daniel's on the coffee table. "Hand that to me."

Griffin picked it up and toggled it between his palms. "Why did you destroy a report that you originally investigated? What did you have to hide?"

"It was for her own good."

The *she* must be Frances Jerome. Griffin had all but memorized young Frances's final diary entry:

> *Officer Schultz came to our house and listened to all my worries. At first, I was scared, because when he got here, he said, "Hi, George," like they were friends because of Nurse Penny, but then he said, "I have a job to do." Dad did what he was told and let Officer Schultz take Mom and me into another room to write a statement. He asked for a description. I told him we had new pictures of Imogene, but Mom interrupted and said the film had been lost by the*

lab. The officer promised me that he would help me and that everything would be okay. Then, Dad left with him, and he's not home yet.

"She shouldn't have asked Peter to start digging around after all those years. And he should have let it go."

"He pretty much did, Rodney."

"Not soon enough."

"Frannie Jerome trusted you. What happened to her friend?" Griffin stood but didn't extend the bottle, and he cringed as the man's eyes followed it like a cat focused on a laser beam.

"Internal Affairs put me through the wringer. Personnel let me retire with pension. That should mean something to you, or do you want to take my pension away too?" He stood to retrieve the booze himself, the burrito falling to the floor with a *thud*.

Griffin held the bottle out of reach and said, "Finding Imogene would mean something to me."

"Well, Daddy knows best," Rodney said.

George Jerome? Or Benjamin Dryker?

"Meaning?" Griffin asked. "Tell me what you know about the girl's disappearance in '79, and I'll leave you with Jack Daniel's."

Like hell he would. The bottle was going with him.

"It was over forty years ago. You all judge me based on resources and knowledge available today and in 1994, not in 1979. I did the right thing at the time. I kept my Oath of Honor to protect and serve. You'll never take that."

His body language said he believed his words.

"Time for you to leave. I've got nothing else to say."

"Frannie's cancer is back."

Rodney fell back in his chair and groaned. "I'm sorry to hear that. She was a sweet kid." He reached for a wedding photo sitting on the table beside him, but he missed it with his first attempt and knocked it over on the second.

Griffin leaned forward and straightened the photo of the young couple. "Where is your wife?" Based on the condition of the man and house, it was safe to guess she wasn't nearby. "Frannie remembers her fondly."

"She's gone. Died in '92. Car accident," he said forlornly. "She loved those kids. Every single one of them. Would have done anything for them. And I would have done anything for her."

"I'm sorry, Rodney."

"And George Jerome would have done anything for his wife and daughter. I respect that."

In most instances, the statement would have been innocuous, but given that a child had disappeared, it wasn't.

"We're talking about a missing girl who was last seen by Jerome. Did you respect that? Enough to sacrifice your career?"

His jaw twitched. "I keep my promises, even for George Jerome."

Even for George Jerome? Bingo. A sure tip that there was a pot to be stirred.

"A promise or pact?"

Rodney glared at him.

"Hats off to you, Rodney. I don't think I could be as forgiving as you."

"What'd ya mean?"

Griffin looked around the room with distaste and pity. "For your promise, or whatever it was, and for whatever reason, you walked the hall of shame, took early pension, and now live in a bottle while George Jerome is applauded as a community hero. Hell, they'll probably name a hospital wing or a park after him soon." Griffin shoved an empty bottle on the floor with the toe of his shoe. "It's obvious who got the better end of the deal."

That hit the spot. Rodney's fist curled and he pounded the arm of the chair once. "I was a good cop, damn it."

Private Investigation 101: A defensive reaction can lead to a positive reaction.

Because if a person being questioned is first defensive, their second reaction will be, how do I prove myself? It was time to give the man some time to ruminate on his existence.

"One last thing, and I'll leave for now," Griffin said. "The evidence folder was empty. What happened to the letter George Jerome forged from Imogene?"

"Told you. I got nothing to say that I haven't said already."

Yup, Rodney definitely needed some time for self-reflection and enlightenment.

Griffin looked around the pathetic space again. "You know what I think? You're afraid. You mentioned your pension. If you trust me, I might be able to help you."

The man's jaws were clenched so tightly, Griffin was surprised his teeth didn't break.

Frannie Jerome was right. She'd been surrounded by people she couldn't rely upon.

Griffin tucked the bottle in the crook of his arm and turned to leave. Opening the front door with more force than necessary, he peered at Rodney. "This crap is coming with me. If you stand by what you did, show yourself and your profession respect by getting out of that chair and getting help. If you ever clean up and are ready to talk, call me."

As Griffin sat in his car out front and updated his notes, he didn't doubt the down-and-out cop was watching him from a slit in the curtains. Once a cop, always a cop. Let the man wonder what Griffin documented.

George Jerome was written across the top of the page and underneath it he wrote *last one to see Imogene; daughter doesn't trust him; has some hold or promise over Rodney Schultz.*

37

FRANNIE

AUGUST 10, 1979

Late that night, no one suspected Frannie was awake when the police car pulled up outside their house. She'd pleaded, but her mom wouldn't let her wait up for her dad's return. She'd been sent to her room to get rest, but Frannie had lain there clutching her diary, imagining her dad in handcuffs being led off to prison.

What had she done? Would her actions be worth the price? Would they bring Imogene back safe and sound?

When she'd called the police, she'd wanted an adult's help to prove Imogene hadn't run away, that she was in trouble, so they could find her. But she'd never expected the officer to ask her father to go to the station with him for being the last person to see her alive.

The cops must know something terrible. He's been gone for hours.

Through a gap in her bedroom curtains, the front porch light cast eerie shadows as her dad climbed out of the front seat of the police car and waved goodbye.

She tiptoed to her bedroom door and opened it far enough to hear.

Too nervous to sleep, her mother had been cleaning the house for hours as she waited for her husband. The sound of dishes clinking and furniture scraping across the floor had carried through the walls to Frannie's bed and now covered the noise of the car pulling away.

Frannie had been angry about her parents' lack of help, but they were probably mad at her now too.

"George," Mom said as the front door opened.

For a long time, Frannie heard nothing. Maybe her parents were hugging like they usually did, or maybe her mom was patting her dad down to make sure he was okay, like she did to Frannie that time she crashed her bike once she had ditched her training wheels.

"Where is she?" her dad asked, sounding funny.

"Have you been drinking, George?"

"It was Rodney's idea. I'm sorry. I need to see she's okay," he said.

"She wanted to stay up, but I sent her to bed. Let's check on her together."

Frannie rushed to her bed, closed her eyes, and tried to breathe evenly.

The creak of the hallway floor echoed as they made their way toward her bedroom.

"See? She's out cold." Her mother spoke in a hushed tone.

As soon as she heard the familiar tap of their steps against the kitchen floor, Frannie pulled her blankets back and crept out of her room to listen at the end of the hall.

"I'll get you some tea."

"I'd rather have bourbon."

"You've already been drinking, and you don't drink."

"I do tonight. You might want a splash too."

"It's that bad?" Glasses rattled against the Formica table. "What happened?"

"It's that bad. They brought in—"

"Don't say it," she said.

"Yes. Ben Dryker. He answered Rodney's questions, but he was drunk. They're keeping him overnight."

"That's not fair to Ben. This isn't his fault," her mom said. "How is it you came home drunk, but he has to stay overnight?"

Frannie could imagine her father's forehead vein swelling with blood. For a second, Frannie felt guilty about Mr. Dryker, but then she remembered he wouldn't help her find Imogene either. The cops were doing their job.

"What else do you want me to do about it?" her dad said, his voice both forceful and hushed.

"I feel a migraine coming on. Did you tell them what really happened?"

Frannie's heart pounded in her ears. Her mom knew something!

"Yeah. Rodney said he'd keep Frannie's report and statement to himself but that we have to make this go away. Sally, we both know Frannie won't give up. She's stubborn. But, unless she does, the truth is going to blow up in my face." Her dad sounded like he choked on a sob. "You should have seen Rodney's face. I could tell he thinks I'm the worst father ever. 'Who does that to a kid?' Rodney asked me. I should have never written that stupid letter."

Frannie almost gasped out loud. *Who does that to a kid?* What had her father done to Imogene?

"Rodney thinks the courts might take Frannie away from us for her well-being until this is straightened out. I need you to stop asking questions and trust me. Support me no matter if what I say makes sense to you or not."

Her mom started to cry. "We're going to lose her. After cancer, all that pain and heartache, we are going to lose her anyway. This will tear our family apart."

"No one's taking my daughter away," her dad swore.

Frannie's gut clenched, and she covered her mouth. How could she forget? Imogene had once warned her about the judge and orphanage—though she'd never thought it could happen to her. Imogene had said she had thought she would never see her pops again.

Frannie could lose more than Imogene.

"Rodney said we need to handle Frannie before others, or the courts, get involved. This has to stop. We have to convince her to let Imogene go. No one is going to understand our actions or Frannie's."

Frannie covered her ears. She couldn't bear to hear more. She tiptoed to her room. Closing her door, she ran to her bed to bury her cries in her pillow. Like Becky and Tammy, Imogene might be face down on a cave floor, all alone and gone forever because of Frannie's dad or because an evil man had taken her while she walked home alone. Frannie's dad could have stopped this from happening if he'd kept his promise.

Imogene was lost to her, and now, Frannie would lose her parents too. She stood and stared down at the diary in her hands. It no longer contained her father's forged letter. Officer Schultz had kept it as evidence; more proof that her dad was covering up the truth of Imogene's disappearance, and now, the officer was too. Wiping her tears and snot on her hand didn't stop more tears from falling. "Imogene, I love you. I'll never forget you." She paced between her bed and the beanbag chair. "But if I keep looking for you, Dad will go to jail, and I won't have a family anymore. I can't live in an orphanage. I can't live without my mother. I'm so sorry. I'm so sorry, Imogene. When I grow up, I promise I'll find you someday."

Her chest racked with silent sobs as she shoved the diary far beneath her mattress and crawled into bed, soaking her pillow with her grief.

THE NEXT MORNING, Frannie sat at the kitchen table and waited for her parents to wake. It took everything she had to look at them, say good morning, and pretend that she didn't know more than she should and that they hadn't broken her heart into a million pieces.

She folded the letters she'd been writing and stuffed them into the envelopes she'd taken from her mother's desk without permission.

Frannie stiffened when her mother rubbed her back.

"I didn't hear you get up. What are you writing?" Her

mom's voice sounded nervous, and Frannie imagined that her mom was looking at her dad as if Frannie was about to cause them more legal problems.

"Letters to Mr. Dryker and Officer Schultz," she said, unable to look at her parents.

"What do they say?" Her mom was the first to ask.

"I told Mr. Dryker that I'm sorry Imogene ran away and that I'm a horrible friend. And I asked Officer Schultz to forgive me for being a troublemaker."

Too bad her mom had always been able to tell when she was being less than honest. It meant it would be hard to pretend her parents hadn't ruined her life.

Her mom's hand stilled on her back. "You aren't a horrible friend, darling."

She clenched her jaw, willing her pain to stay inside, and gave a single sharp shrug of her shoulders.

Her dad reached out to smooth his palm over her crown, but she jerked away.

"But you don't mean any of it, do you, Frannie?" her dad asked.

Frannie's face grew wet with tears. "Don't call me Frannie. I'm not a little girl anymore. My name is Frances. I know you've been lying to me and that you wrote the letter from Imogene. I know something bad happened to her and she's never coming back. But I'm just a kid, and I can't do anything about it."

Except for once, about a month later, when her mom took her to the cemetery to bury a special memento for Imogene, her parents ignored Frances whenever she mentioned Imogene and acted as if she had never existed.

When fourth grade started and she and her new friends were allowed to walk home, Frances always carried a stick or rock and walked against the traffic so she could see what cars were coming her way. She took wide turns around corners—no one would surprise her.

Her parents pretended she was fine without Imogene because the phone at her house rang non-stop as soon as Frances arrived home from school each day.

"You're very popular," her mom said.

"I told you you'd make more friends than you could imagine," her dad bragged.

What they didn't know was that she asked her friends, even the boys, to call her to say they made it home okay. If they forgot to call, she called them. They all cooperated because she'd confided in Douglas about Imogene's tragic disappearance, and he'd spread the word. At Whitney Prep, Frances wasn't known as the girl who survived cancer—she was the girl whose friend vanished.

Seated in the back of her classroom, she focused on one classmate at a time.

Tiffany has braids with green ribbons today.
Beth dropped red jam on her collar at lunch.
Burt has a scratch on his forehead.
Jake has orange shoelaces.

Sandy got her ears pierced with topaz studs.

The list went on, and she updated it daily.

If any more friends went missing on her watch, she'd be able to tell the cops what they were last wearing so the police could update the search party and spread the word on the news.

Bobby was last seen wearing an Ocean Pacific blue rain jacket and black-and-white checkered Vans.

She memorized who walked home with whom. And her eyes shot daggers at any man she saw walking alone or hanging around the schoolyards and parks, never breaking eye contact.

I see you.

Frances's diligence stuck throughout high school and college. She adjusted the parameters as necessary. Friends weren't left alone at movies, restaurants, football games, bars, or the campus library at night. "Worrywart Frances," they called her. She took pride in the nickname.

Douglas—her steadfast companion, then boyfriend, and finally husband—joined in her efforts, which became the norm after years, until the hyperawareness wore out Frances. The idea she could fail another friend was too much, and she found it easier to stop having friends altogether.

38

JEAN

SPRING 2022

A line of disgruntled customers was growing behind Jean at Office Depot's print center, but there wasn't much she could do to expedite her departure. She only had two hands, and her daughter had decided to yank off her shoes and socks while Jean was paying for the flash drive of photos. The day before, she'd felt clever and efficient when she'd come up with the perfect way to hand over the photos to Griffin while still honoring her mom's request. *"Don't lose them—they are all that's left."*

Now, her three-year-old daughter seemed intent on stripping down to her Disney Princess underwear.

"Ahem." The person behind her cleared his throat as Jean stuffed Lexi's socks and shoes into her big purse. Her daughter's feet would have to survive the cool air until they got to the car.

"Hug G-Ma's pictures." She handed Lexi the heavy photo album and scooped them both into her arms. "Why are you taking your clothes off?"

"Booby told me to."

Note to self, your daughter would jump off a bridge if a friend asked her to. #teachablemoment.

"Booby's on a time-out. We don't undress in public," she said, grateful for automatic doors and the cool fresh air against her warm cheeks and neck.

"No."

"Yes."

Jean made a beeline for her Subaru Outback, which was in desperate need of a wash. Every time she opened the back door to put Lexi in her car seat, trash or a long-lost toy fell out. She needed to clean it, but when?

How do mothers do it all? She didn't have a job, and she still couldn't keep up.

"Jean, is that you?" an overly cheerful voice called from behind.

Jean froze in her tracks. Without turning, she recognized the voice of her Instagram-perfect-mom nemesis.

"It's me. Carla-with-a-C Clarke."

Jean tugged at Lexi's blanket to cover her bare feet and turned around. "Carla. Hi. It's great to see you."

"Don't use your fake voice, Mommy."

Dr. Pfeiffer was right; Lexi was a sponge when it came to her and Shane's arguments.

"Imagine running into you here," Jean continued, but then she regretted her words. Carla-with-a-C had probably been at Pottery Barn scouting for perfect photo props, not shopping at an office supply store.

Carla raised a thick paper bag with corded handles

and tilted her head to the side, her blinding white teeth glowing as she smiled. “I popped into Pottery Barn to buy baubles for tonight’s table setting. I’m having a dinner party.”

Lexi turned her face into Jean’s neck as Carla reached over to squeeze her chubby fingers. “I recognize this cutie pie from Instagram.”

“More like a tired pie,” Jean said as Lexi mewled. Perplexed, she continued, “I haven’t posted Lexi in ages.” *Because I’m too busy combing knots out of Lexi’s hair, feeding her, keeping her clothes on, and keeping her alive to remember to take a picture.* Plus, she couldn’t remember Carla liking any of her pics. Not once. And she’d remember because every like from someone had made her feel temporarily better.

Carla’s trill of a laugh made Jean’s ears ring. “Not yours. Shane’s. He’s got a good eye.”

Hmph. Her husband was a closet Instagrammer after all. He wasn’t even Jean’s IG friend. Apparently, he was also a closet Carla-with-a-C compadre.

“How are you?” Carla asked. “What brings you to”—she looked around at the possibilities—“Office Depot on this beautiful day?”

My mom’s missing friend, Jean could have said. Instead, she blurted out, “Work.”

“Work? I didn’t know you were working again. I’m out of touch. What kind of work?”

Mediocre twenty-four-seven motherhood. “Private Investigation.” *Omigosh, what am I doing? What is wrong with me?*

Carla's eyes widened. "Wow."

"Trust me, you're no more shocked than I am." *That bit was at least true.*

"For reals? I had no idea."

"I keep it rather quiet." Jean dished out more untruths. "Super confidential. Word-of-mouth referral clients only."

For once, Carla's face was straight. "What types of cases do you take on? Like affairs? Things like that?"

"Sadly, yes." *Why not go all in?* "Very common."

"I might . . ." Carla paused and looked away. She looked vulnerable for a moment as her left eye twitched and her lower lip puckered. "I might know someone who would like to hire you, given that you're discreet."

Uh-oh.

"Now I understand why you're never on social media. Maintaining a low profile. Speaking of which"—Carla returned to her perky self, set her bag down on the ground, and retrieved her phone from her purse—"did I show you my new car? A surprise from Kenny. It's over there," she said as she scrolled through her pictures. "But the post is too good to be true."

Was it really too good to be true?

Ugh. Yes, it was. Jean's eyes narrowed when she saw the picture of Carla standing next to her immaculate, dust-free Tesla. Her son, Chaz, was dressed flawlessly (Lexi couldn't keep her socks on, but Chaz could wear a bow tie?) and smiling. He stood beside her with a stuffed Velveteen Rabbit cradled in his arms.

"How is Chaz?" Jean asked. Lexi grew heavier in her

arms by the second, but she couldn't set her down since she was shoeless and C-w-a-C would see.

"A little brainiac as always. He's in a gifted junior kindergarten program. Did you know?"

Of course Chaz was. And yes, Jean knew. Carla posted about her wonder kid's accomplishments on Instagram as if Chaz was her trophy child.

Lexi started kicking her feet, causing Blanket to pull away from her pink toes and the photo album to shift in Jean's arms.

"Oops." Naturally coordinated, Carla held her phone and righted the album between Lexi's and Jean's chests. Carla covered Lexi's cool feet with one of her warm hands. "*Brrr.* Someone needs shoes in this weather. Can I help you get to your car? Which one's yours?"

The Subaru of Shame was steps away, but Jean nodded in the opposite direction. "Please, don't let us keep you. I know you have a lot to do."

Carla glanced at her phone. "You're right. I need to pick up Chaz from school and get ready for tonight." She was turning to go, much to Jean's relief, when she paused. "I'll call you. I mean, I'll ask my friend if she can use your help. Oh, by the way, are you joining the high school reunion committee?"

Over my dead body. "So soon? Our ten-year is a few years away." Most days, Jean felt as if she was losing her mind, but she hadn't forgotten math yet.

"It's never too soon to start planning a phenomenal party. Can you believe it's been almost a decade since we graduated? And don't worry, your clandestine career is safe with me. Although, you'd have a shot of winning 'Most Interesting Career' if you wanted. Toodles, I've got to run."

"Toodles." If not for her panic, Jean would never have lowered herself to repeat the goodbye slang.

OMG. What have I done? How will I get out of this mess?

Dr. Pfeiffer's voice started to sneak its way into her head, diagnosing her with a bad case of *comparisonitis,* just as her mom might have labeled it in the past. But her mom's recent advice and voice entered the mental head game instead. "*Make the cake you want to eat.*"

Okay, she wasn't a private eye, but maybe the cake-life she wanted to bake and eat included a job, something of her own, separate from her family, as Shane had hinted at too. She giggled. Out loud.

"What's funny, Mommy?"

Jean waited until Carla and her Tesla disappeared before parking Lexi in her own ratty car. "Life. Life's funny. Let's go say hi to G-Ma."

TWENTY MINUTES LATER, Jean and her shoe-clad daughter let themselves into her mom's place after the doorbell had remained unanswered.

Silence was nothing new when it came to her mom, but the living space seemed devoid of life, even Bonnie

Bell was quiet. She held tight to Lexi's hand. *Was Mom outside? Was she okay?*

Rounding the corner, they found her sound asleep on the couch. Four boxes were marked *Keep*, *Donate*, *Trash*, and *Sell*.

So far, the keep box was empty. Lexi started poking through the boxes—one woman's junk was a little girl's treasure.

Bonnie Bell sat atop her cage silently as if she, too, understood Frannie's need to rest.

Ah, Mom.

Admittedly, Jean had spent more time with her mom in the past week than she had in years, but she knew falling asleep mid-project was unlike her. Her mom had always preached, "Don't start a project you won't finish." Jean eased her mother into a lying position on the couch.

Her eyes fluttered, "Jean?"

"*Shh.* Rest."

"I'm dreaming about Imogene."

Then she was fast asleep again.

Jean put her finger to her lips and reached for Lexi's hand. They slipped off to the kitchen. After she had Lexi situated with a snack, she texted Art.

One of us needs to be with mom today.

Is she okay?

Snoozing on the couch. Mid-project.

That's a first.

Can you come now?

Now's not a good time.

When is a good time? Need to take pics to Griffin.

I'm not alone.

Ah-ha. The mystery girlfriend. Her thumbs flew as she typed:

Bring her with you.

Bad idea.

You're mom's favorite son.

I'm her only son.

Exactly my point.

You win. On the way.

When Art arrived, he was alone.

"Where's your friend? What's her name?"

"Angela. Mom would never want to wake up and meet someone. I didn't want to be disrespectful."

Art was the better child. He was right; her mom would have felt exposed and vulnerable waking up to a stranger, not feeling pulled together enough to present her best self. Jean had tunnel vision and was on a high about her lie-athon to Carla and her epiphany that she did want a job—if she could figure out what job exactly and work past her guilt about putting Lexi in daycare as needed.

She hugged Art. "Thank you for protecting Mom's feelings and not judging me for being a self-absorbed idiot."

His bear hug, much like their father's, spoke volumes, but he said the words anyway, "I've got you."

39

GRIFFIN

SPRING 2022

Griffin licked the flakes of pastry off his index finger and thumb before texting Jean and entering the shop:

> We need to talk today about next steps. Meet at my office in an hour?

> Perfect. Will tell you about my talk with Grandpa, and I have photos for you.

"Is the doctor in?" Griffin asked over the sound of jingling bells as he stepped through the glass door of Nine Lives Thrift Store.

"Doctor. *Pfft.* I was a coroner, thank you very much," Joe Purdy said from his seat behind the glass display filled with ceramic and plastic maneki-neko cat figurines, which waved at every customer who came through the door.

"Those bring you any luck or fortune yet?" Griffin asked, returning their waves. "If so, I'll buy the lot."

Joe removed his glasses and set his book down. "Luck and fortune aren't for sale."

"Too bad."

The retired coroner came around the counter to clap Griffin on the back. "How are you, Griffin?" He pointed to Griffin's growing waistline. "That belly fat can kill a guy, you know?"

"Ha-ha. You've been talking to Annie."

"Wanda and she met for lunch a while back. Afterward, Wanda put me on *your* strict diet. Obviously, I'm the only one following it." He patted his flat stomach. "You've got powdered sugar on your shoulder, by the way."

Griffin snorted. "Saving it for later."

"Your humor reminds me of Peter's. I'd kill to be forty-something again and joking with your dad over a beer. Or two."

Griffin put one hand in his pocket, fingered his clarinet-shaped keychain, and looked around. "What's with the creepy porcelain dolls?" A shelf that ran the length of one wall was packed with unblinking rosy-cheeked dolls posed in various positions, modeling their bloomers, pinafores, and Mary Jane shoes.

"They remind me of the good old days at the morgue."

Griffin chuckled. "Speaking of which, did my dad ever ask you about a missing nine-year-old girl? A case he worked on in the nineties."

"Imogene Dryker. Never forget a name."

"Holy crap. This was more than I hoped for."

"It won't be my brain that makes me kick the bucket. Well, technically, it will. The brain is in charge of everything. My memory won't be a problem."

"Guess not. What else do you remember?"

"Never saw her come through my lab. She didn't match any Jane Does during my day either."

Griffin dropped his head and rubbed the back of his neck. "Yeah. That's what I figured. I'd love to find her alive."

"Same lady hire you? The friend?"

"You should patent that memory of yours," Griffin said. "Her son and daughter reached out. The friend, Frances Jerome, is in her fifties now and has cancer. Again."

"Leukemia, that's right. Both girls had it. Sorry hers came back. No child should have to have it once, much less twice."

Some gut instinct kicked in. Griffin froze. *Wait. No child. Twice.* What if Imogene's cancer had returned in 1979? He bounced the germ of an idea off the retired coroner. "What if Imogene didn't disappear? What if she had cancer again, and Frannie's parents didn't know how to tell her?" Griffin couldn't imagine having a child with cancer. It'd be unnerving as a parent to deliver a message to your child that, if cancer could return for her best friend, it could return for her too.

"Now, that's nothing your dad mentioned, but you could be on to something. There's no layover at a coroner's if and when someone, even a minor, has died of known medical problems."

Griffin's idea felt possible but also like a leap. Like him, his dad wouldn't have immediately thought of the possibility Imogene had grown ill again, but he wouldn't have missed it entirely. Which brought him back to Rodney Schultz and how he would justify his actions and George Jerome's—whatever they may have been—as honorable. But why the redaction if this was about cancer?

"Joe, since HIPAA didn't exist before the nineties, if I call the hospital to see if Imogene returned as a patient or for treatment in 1979, can they tell me?"

Joe gave him a thumbs down. "The state only requires hospitals to keep medical records for a maximum of seven years. Even for a study or the children's hospital, tops would be twenty."

"And I'm looking at a forty-plus-year gap, so that's out."

"What about a record of death?" Joe asked as he turned to straighten an empty picture frame on the wall.

"I searched the national archive of vital records online but didn't find a death certificate from 1979 or onwards. I'll call the public health department. They can double check on Monday. Can't hurt."

Joe gave him a thumbs up. "You know, scientist Paul R. Ehrlich said, 'To err is human, but to really foul things up, you need a computer.'"

"Good one. Hey, does *4/1957* mean anything to you?"

"Sure does. People spotted a UFO over Wigtownshire, Scotland, on April 4, 1957. Can you believe the CIA had an entire file of global sightings spanning decades? They released a 186-page file after forty years. Read the entire thing."

That'd be a no. "I bet you did. Anything else you can think of about my dad's visit?"

Joe's index finger sprang up in the affirmative. "Yes. Your dad said he was off to visit a school nurse."

The diary. "Nurse Bowman."

Joe snapped his fingers and pointed at Griffin. "That's the one."

Griffin dropped a few bucks into the SPCA can on the counter. "She's been on my list. I guess she's my next visit too."

Joe grabbed and shook a maraca on his way back to his seat behind the display case. He slid the glass open, grabbed a small maneki-neko cat, and tossed it to him. "Let me know when you find Imogene. Alive, preferably."

As Griffin slid into his car, he perched the cat on his dashboard before checking the notifications on his phone.

Tony had texted him:

When's lunch?

Ha-ha!

Griffin would work in his car rather than head back to the office. Jean wouldn't be there for another fifty minutes or so, and this way, his intern could learn that life's comforts are never on schedule in the PI world. On countless stakeouts, Griffin had sat in his car with his camera for hours, waiting for the perfect shot while his stomach growled and his bladder threatened to burst. Many peers took to pissing in an empty bottle. Not him. Griffin had opted for dehydration and compromised health instead.

He pulled out his notepad where he'd scribbled down the phone number for St. Agnes. It was the weekend, but he might get lucky, and he'd rather not wait until Monday.

Luck was in his favor. A chipper woman answered on the first ring. "St. Agnes, how can I help you?"

"Hi, my name is Griffin Whittaker. I'm trying to reach Nurse Bowman." His dad had taught him that giving your name makes people comfortable and less is more. The average person would ramble on and say something like, "I'm looking for Nurse Bowman. I'm not sure about her first name. She doesn't know me. She may have retired by now . . ." And then they would share the elaborate details about why they needed to reach Nurse Bowman, *blah blah blah*. By the time they finished, the person with answers would have shut down, catching on that the caller didn't have an adequate reason or relationship.

Ms. Chipper said, "Nurse Bowman retired from the school and is now a voluntary traveling nurse. In Haiti, of all places. She never quits."

"That's inspiring," Griffin said. Maybe he should

have been a nurse. He wouldn't mind helping where needed, putting lives back together instead of dissecting individuals for cheating and fraud.

"I can email her with your contact info," Ms. Chipper offered.

After he reeled off his phone number and email address, she asked. "Can I tell her what this is about?"

Less is more. "Imogene Dryker."

"Ah-ha," she said.

A promising response. "You recognize the name?"

"Of course. The friendship of those two girls is a legend here. We tell the students about them all the time to teach the value of faith and friendship. I've heard time and again that she was a real angel. And there's the scholarship too."

Every hair follicle on his body stood on end. "Scholarship?"

"The Imogene Scholarship."

Years of experience helped him keep his cool, but barely. "What's it for?"

"It's aid for disadvantaged students. It's not a lot, but it helps one or two students at a time with tuition, uniforms, and field trips. Stuff like that."

One thing was for certain—Frances Jerome would have told Jean about this had she known. "Who is the sponsor?"

"He's modest about his help, but George Jerome. The father of the other girl, Frannie."

40

FRANCES

SPRING 2022

"I want this dream to last forever," Frannie said to an adult Imogene, whom she recognized from her ginger hair, round face, dimpled cheeks, and sky-blue eyes. "I never forgot you."

"You had to let me go," Dream-Imogene said as they fed seagulls on a boardwalk. "Tell your dad you're looking for me."

"I'm afraid to tell him."

"Oh, honey. You must."

"I will, but not yet."

The wind picked up, pulling at Imogene's hair. When she turned to Frannie, her eyes flashed with frustration and her lips were pinched. "There's no time. Tell him now!"

Spread out on the couch, Frannie gasped and opened her eyes. She pushed herself to a sitting position despite her trembling arms.

How long had she slept? Her sorting boxes sat before

her. Frannie hadn't gotten far, not that she had extra things lying about or much to sort.

Soon, Jean and Lexi would be here.

"Hello," Bonnie Bell said. She'd left her cage and was perched atop the television.

"How did you get out, Pretty Bird?" Frannie asked.

The bird chirped but didn't reject the compliment.

They were making progress. Frannie worried about the parrot. She needed to find her a safe home sooner rather than later, but the shelter had been overwhelmed. She'd better tell them about her health and ask them to prioritize Bonnie Bell's adoption.

A movement outside her window caught her attention.

Her action had caught theirs too; Art and Lexi waved and came inside.

Lexi squeezed between the boxes and the couch to hug Frannie.

"We didn't want to wake you," her son said, nodding at the boxes. "We knew you'd put us to work."

"Hilarious," Frannie said.

"You were Sleepy Smurf," Lexi said.

Frannie's neck popped when she stretched. "I don't feel like a Smurf. How long was I asleep? And where is Jean?"

"She found you dozing on the job two hours ago. She had a hot date with the detective, so you got Lexi and me." He smiled and wiggled his eyebrows.

"What's a hot date?" Lexi asked.

Her private son was cheerful today. If the secret woman he'd been seeing had anything to do with Art's uplifting mood, Frannie hoped he would trust his mom enough to introduce them before it was too late. If she went into hospice, she wouldn't want a stranger to see her.

"You look happy," she said.

"I am happy," he said and smiled. Then he cringed and shook his head. "I mean, except for your—"

"Oh, honey. I know what you mean."

"'Oh, honey?' Was that a Southern accent?" Art smiled and rocked on his heels.

Frannie chuckled. "Blame it on memories of Imogene."

"You were Southern belles?" he asked. "Wow. Bless your heart."

If there were an afterlife, Frannie would eavesdrop on Art from time to time to hear his deadpan voice. "It was our term of endearment. We borrowed it from our favorite hospital nurse."

"I'm hungry," Lexi said as she tipped over an empty box and climbed beneath it.

Art's phone buzzed. He glanced at it and typed quickly.

"Let's make something to eat," Frannie said before making her way to the kitchen slowly. Lexi ditched the box to follow, but Art was staring at his phone with great intent.

"Is there a problem?" Frannie asked.

Art blew up his cheeks and let out a slow breath. "No

biggie. Everything's good. I had to cancel some other plans."

Perhaps it was now or never. "What's her name? Invite her over."

His eyes widened. "I, well . . . Angela. I was going to tell you about her. But then, your diagnosis . . . I didn't want you to wake up to a stranger."

"Thank you. That's all very considerate but invite her over. If you want. I don't want to pressure you. I know I'm not as easygoing as your father, but I don't bite. And" —she laughed at herself—"I won't give her a lie detector test."

"Who are you, and what have you done with my mother?"

"You know what Martha Stewart says." Frannie snapped her fingers. "'The more you adapt, the more interesting you are.'"

"You're definitely interesting." Her son snickered. "By the way, I'm laughing with you, not at you."

What a bittersweet moment. Who would she have been if she'd never lost Imogene? Happier? Lighter? More fun?

"Hey," Frannie said to Lexi and Art. "Let's bake a cake everyone will want to eat."

ANGELA ARRIVED with hugs for everyone.

As Angela latched on to Frannie, she popped Frannie's upper back.

Oof.

"It's wonderful to meet you, Mrs. McGee. Art and Douglas have told me a lot about you."

"Ang, my mom goes by her maiden name now, Frances Jerome. The hyphen and McGee were dropped after the divorce."

"Oopsy-doopsy. I'm making a bad first impression."

"Of course not. Please, call me Frannie."

Another embrace. Angela was Frannie's height, and her round chin rested snuggly on Frannie's shoulder. This hug was like a cozy cocoon, conveying Angela's earnestness to connect, like Douglas's and Rhonda's embraces.

Art pulled Angela away and looped his arm around his girlfriend's waist to hold her in place. Her son knew his lady well because she took a step forward as if to enfold Frannie in her arms a third time.

Art's hold on Angela tightened. "Twice is enough on a first date," he said.

Angela wrinkled her nose in self-recrimination, relaxed her shoulders, and stared adoringly at his profile. "Thanks, boo." She smiled at Frannie, tilted her head, and shrugged her shoulders. "Sorry, Frannie. Hugging is my thing."

Good. Her family might need more heartfelt hugs. Frannie had been desperate for reassuring hugs when Imogene disappeared and after her mother died.

Art waved toward the small table. "Mother made a

strawberry spinach salad and homemade macaroni and cheese. A chocolate cake is in the oven. Lexi has dibs on frosting it. I get to lick the spatula."

Angela covered her mouth with the tips of her fingers. "Martha Stewart's recipes? Did Art tell you that we share a love for Martha? Her mac and cheese is the best."

"Okay," Art said as he pulled out chairs for her and his mother.

Old Frances would have been honest and told Angela that Art hadn't told her anything about Angela, not even her name, before today. But, instead, Frannie covered for her son. "Yes, he did."

Art released his breath before taking a seat. "Lexi, come eat with us," he said. "Pretty, pretty, pretty please."

It occurred to Frannie that there had been no mention of Booby today.

Angela leaned forward. "It's sad about your friend, Imogene. Art told me all about her."

Art groaned. "Lexi, you're missing all the fun. Come see me. Now."

Frannie smiled. Boundaries and filters weren't Angela's thing, and she was utterly refreshing for the family. "Thank you. If she were here, Imogene would like your openness, Angela."

Angela blushed and swatted Art's shoulder. "See? I told you your mom would like me."

Ouch. Art had been protecting Angela from her.

"Indeed, I do. Iced tea?" Frannie asked before passing

the glass pitcher around. "How did the two of you meet? Online or through friends?"

"Oh boy," Art said. "Lexi!"

"In a cooking class at Williams Sonoma," Angela said. "I melted when he said he wanted to learn to cook with his mother and that Williams Sonoma was the closest he could get to Martha Stewart."

Frannie set a casserole dish down and looked across the table at her son. How little she knew her children. He'd wanted to cook with her? To bond over Martha Stewart? "We should cook together. We can host a dinner party or Sunday brunch together."

His eyes grew glassy. He cleared his throat and nodded. "That would be nice, Mom."

Angela carried on with enthusiasm, unaware of the touching moment. "I thought he was cute in a Seth Rogen kind of way. Once I can convince him he does want children someday then I can propose."

Art choked.

Frannie paused, her salad tongs hanging over an empty plate. Thanks to this woman, she was learning something else about her son. "You don't want children, Art?" Was it because he liked his freedom? Overpopulation concerns? Or maybe he hadn't settled on Angela?

Lexi skipped into the room and climbed onto her uncle's lap.

Sweat beaded on Art's forehead, and he mewled like a caged cat. "Let's talk about something else."

Angela spoke as if Art weren't sitting next to her.

"He's afraid the responsibility will give him a heart attack. You know, worrying he couldn't protect them. He said you taught him to be very careful as a child, and he took it to heart. Being an uncle is enough worry, he says."

Frannie had been holding her breath and now felt a migraine coming on. This was too much, and her conversation with Jean came back to her. "Art? You don't want children because of me?" Her years of resentment toward her parents for short-changing her innocence settled like a brick in her stomach. In her desire to protect her children, had she harmed them irrevocably? Had she short-changed *their* innocence? "Art?"

He mewled again. "Can we talk about cooking again?" His eyes pleaded with her to drop it.

Her best intentions to protect her son had done the exact opposite. Her choices had informed his adult choices, out of fear, not guidance. Now, he needed her, was begging her, for a reprieve. It was the least she could do for him, but she'd find a way to make it up to him before it was too late.

"Who's Seth Rogen?" Frannie asked while she willed herself not to cry and scooped up mac and cheese for Lexi.

Art's entire body relaxed. "Um, yeah, Mother doesn't watch Seth Rogen movies . . . I don't think." Looking at her, he said, "But you've surprised me a few times lately, so maybe you do?"

"But of course she knows who Seth Rogen is," Angela said. "He was on Martha and Snoop Dogg's show. They baked chicken wings rolled in potato chips. My brother says Seth has one of those dry, throaty voices that sounds like a bong would sound if a bong could talk."

"Oh, jeez." Art covered Lexi's ears and closed his eyes.

"You know what a bong is, right, Frannie?" Angela asked.

"I've never used one, but yes. Who is Snoop Dogg?"

Angela's eyes widened and her jaw dropped. "Snoop and Martha are best friends. My goodness, we'll have to watch at least one episode."

A memory of a gobsmacked Imogene introducing Frannie to *Oliver!* flashed before her, and her body filled with bliss and curiosity.

Oliver! had been the start of a beautiful friendship. Maybe she and Angela would have a beautiful friendship too.

There was a knock at the front door before the keyless lock thrummed, and her son-in-law, Shane, strutted inside.

"I am so glad to see you," Art said.

Frannie was having a lovely time but could imagine why Art wanted a distraction. The more the merrier in this case.

"Hey," Shane said, releasing a breath when he saw Lexi. "Jean and Lexi were supposed to meet me this afternoon, and they didn't show. She's not answering her phone. Where the heck is she?"

With her mouth full of cheesy pasta, Lexi shouted, "Mommy had a hot date!"

41

JEAN

SPRING 2022

Jean was early, but she knocked on Whittaker & Son's door and tried the knob.

"What's up?" a startled young man asked as she pushed the door open.

Based on the crease in his cheek, Jean guessed she'd interrupted a nap.

"I'm Jean Wallace. I have an appointment with Griffin Whittaker."

The young Griffin look-alike stood up and walked toward her, holding out his hand. "I'm Tony Whittaker, his son."

"That explains the resemblance."

"Yeah, everyone says I'm a mini-him. Nice to meet you. Which case?"

Just because he was a Whittaker, it didn't mean he was in the know. The company wasn't named Whittaker & Son*s*. Peter had been the Whittaker. Griffin had been the singular Son. She hadn't seen mini-Griffin on the day she and Art first met him. Jean hesitated to alert too many people about why she was working with a PI. And would Griffin tell his teenage son a bunch of details about a client's case? Hopefully not. Most teenagers weren't known for being discreet.

Her skepticism must have shown because he said, "I'm interning. I'm working my way up the ranks."

Okay. That makes sense. Initially, Jean assumed the company had remained Whittaker & Son after Peter Whittaker died due to their well-established reputation, but now she understood; Griffin planned for his son to join him.

For the first time, Jean wondered what it took to become a private investigator. Her conversation (and consequential giddiness) with Carla came to mind. Maybe Jean could intern for W&S and help with her mom's case, and then, technically, she wouldn't be a big fat liar that Carla could call out. Since she didn't know what kind of job she wanted to have, wasn't interning a great way to find out?

"How exciting for you. It's nice to meet you, Tony. Your father is helping us locate a long-lost friend, Imogene Dryker."

"Ah, so that's what it's kind of about. I'm working on the case too."

Kind of about? Not reassuring. If it got back to her mom that a teenager was working on her case, her mom would freak. Art shouldn't even know about this development.

Tony deepened his voice an octave. "My dad will be

back soon. Would you like to see what I've come up with, Ms. Wallace?" he asked, his voice returning to a normal pitch.

Tony was growing on her. So what if he was young? He was enthusiastic, happy to divulge information to her, and treating her like someone of importance. His respect made her fiasco of a morning slip away. "Of course, I'd love to see what you've got."

He grabbed a chair, set it next to his behind a computer desk, and slid a yellow pad covered with notes aside. "Take a seat. Can I get you coffee or tea?" His stomach grumbled, soliciting a response from her own. The last thing she'd eaten was Lexi's leftover cereal hours ago.

"Tony, if I order a pizza, will you share it with me?" she asked.

An *aw-shucks* expression transformed his face and body language. "I wish I could. I'm starving, but my dad didn't mention lunch. I don't have any money. Please, go ahead. Don't worry about me." His stomach growled again.

Jean wouldn't have pegged Griffin as a hard-ass of a dad-boss, but he also didn't seem like he'd want to hold anyone's hand through a day's work.

Look at me, pretending to know Griffin.

What did she know about the guy? Next to nothing. But her lips curved into the beginnings of a smile whenever she thought about training to be an investigator, working for him part-time, having something of her own away from Lexi. Away from Shane.

For starters, via Tony, she could see what type of work Griffin passed off. If she could glean enough experience, she could fudge her way around Carla if she ever saw or heard from her again. She could even work on Carla's friend's case, whom Jean suspected was actually Carla (except that would mean Carla's life was as imperfect as her own—go figure), while interning, depending on what it was about.

"Lunch is on me," Jean said, and she placed the order. "Thirty minutes, plenty of time to get started."

"Can I ask you for advice?" Tony asked. "Do you think I should refer to my dad as Dad, Boss, Griffin, or Mr. Whittaker when dealing with customers?"

In truth, she was flattered he'd asked her, although a small part of her wondered why he didn't ask his dad about his preferences. But she was not one to judge another family's inability to communicate—look at both of hers.

It had been a while since Jean had worked for anyone, but she suggested, "He's your supervisor at work, and the dynamics of your relationship will differ from yours at home, I think. It's important to have regular check-ins with your manager. Normally, I'd say to start with Mr. Whittaker, but Griffin doesn't seem like the mister type. Try Griffin and ask him which he prefers next time you meet about work."

Tony lifted his hand to give her a fist bump. "Yeah, that's the move. I'll do that."

"GRIFFIN," Tony used his deeper voice as if it conveyed his seriousness and intent to help, "entrusted me with discovering the significance of the lead, *4/1957*."

"Four-slash-nineteen-fifty-seven? I haven't heard about this *lead*." She was learning the lingo. Good.

Tony slid his yellow pad before her and tapped the list's header: *4/1957*.

"Oh, like April 1957."

Tony scoffed condescendingly in that way that only teenagers could pull off without sounding aggressive. "It might mean April 1957, but it might not. Never assume anything, Ms. Wallace, that's Private Investigation for Beginners."

Jean hid her smile. The way Tony said it reminded her of his dad, or, um, Griffin. "Duly noted," she said. "And call me Jean, please."

He frowned, as if it made him look more mature and serious. "Let's start with dates, Jean, but we can't assume that four is a month. It could mean April 1957. It could mean the fourth of a month in 1957. Ya feel me?" He pulled up Google and ran a search.

"I *understand* you." Jean gravitated toward the computer screen. "But why are you looking at *4/1957* at all?"

Tony's face fell. "Don't know yet. I wasn't told. My

job is to find all the options and report them back to my manager." He pointed at the yellow pad.

She bit her lip to control her smile. Tony was taking her advice seriously about not calling his dad *Dad* at work.

"But wouldn't it help to know the context?" Jean knew she'd perform better research if she knew more context.

He slipped. "Dad won't tell me much. He doesn't want me to do this work. He's kind of a solo-working guy. Maybe he doesn't know more about *4/1957*. Or maybe he is trying to get me to quit. That's what I think he's doing."

The parental control pushed Jean's buttons. Griffin was being domineering, in her humble opinion—like her mother. Except, her mother would have loved it if Jean had pursued accounting.

Note to self: do not choose Lexi's purpose. But wait . . .

How did an exemplary mother help her child find a purpose? She didn't even know how to find her own. Her armpits began to sweat. At this rate, she'd have wet rings down to her waist in a minute.

Seemingly grateful to have a willing ear by his side, Tony talked on. "My mom told me that if I'm serious about this opportunity, I need to zip my lips and do what I'm asked until I earn his trust."

There was that T-word again. They all wanted trust yet hesitated to give it. Despite her earlier resolve to be nonjudgmental, she was desperate to distract herself from her future parenting failures, and his innocent chatter and worries were welcome. "Have you asked him why he doesn't want you to be a private eye?" Dr. Pfeiffer would be proud of her for paying her advice forward.

"I guess he felt pushed into it by my grandpa. Dad had wanted to be a musician. But I don't care. I know what I want to do. Investigating is in my genes. My grandfather started this business."

Rather than point out that professions aren't genetic or that Griffin might have a good point, Jean said, "Don't let him discourage you. Here, I'll help you do more research until he arrives."

Tony had already begun a robust list, but by the time they'd finished brainstorming about meanings and numeric configurations and had devoured their pizza, they had five yellow pages of notes for boss-man Griffin.

Most were unlikely leads. After all, what would the Soviet Union's launch of Sputnik, an emerging virus in Hong Kong, an issue of *Life* Magazine, a Fender Twin Guitar, or Johnny Logan's Topps #4 baseball card have to do with Imogene's disappearance?

Assumptions may be a no-no, but hello, these were definitely unrelated.

They had several more improbable and impossible explanations for the digits, but they agreed one scenario could make sense, even if the possibility made Jean queasy —Imogene may have been a victim of a hit and run as she walked home in the dark.

In some county police codes that they found online, the number fifty-seven equated to *hit and run*. There was also a police list that signified distinctive marks or peculiarities on a person:

4: Mark left cheek

19: Left side of nose

57: Broken nose

Could her grandfather have hit her? But why would he have been away from the house?

Jean wanted the young man to be prepared, to impress his dad in a way that Jean had never impressed her mother at his age. "Tony, what will you suggest first to Griffin?"

"I'm going to lead with the police codes and the hit and run. Second, I'll suggest a locker or box number four somewhere with a combination lock code of 1-9-5-7, or 19-5-7 since the dials stop at forty on some. Last, an address: 1957 Street Name, Apt. 4."

Jean sat up. "What if it's a section, row, and seat, like a concert hall or auditorium?"

"Good one," Tony said and gave her a high five. "I'll look for matches in local joints."

They both jumped when Griffin spoke from behind them. "What in the heck is going on here?"

42

GRIFFIN

SPRING 2022

The oregano-infused *tête-à-tête* between Jean and his son made Griffin crankier than before. His son should be starved or bored to death by now, not high-fiving a client with more enthusiasm than Griffin had felt in years.

"Hello, Griffin," his son said, jumping up and walking toward him with the yellow pad. "I have potential leads to discuss with you, sir."

Griffin. Leads. Sir. Argh.

Griffin flipped through the five pages of notes. His son was thorough, he'd give him that. If Jean wasn't there, Griffin might tell him to learn to be more discriminating. Though he still wanted Tony to quit, he wasn't cruel enough to embarrass him in front of a client. Instead, he begrudgingly said, "Good work." Keeping the tablet in hand, he motioned toward Jean. "Let's meet in my office."

His eager protégé followed them.

Nope. Not happening. Once Jean was out of earshot, Griffin turned to Tony, blocking him at the door.

"That's it for today. I'll see you tonight at dinner."

"But . . ." His confused kid tried to look around Griffin at Jean and then down at the yellow pad in Griffin's hand. "I'm helping find Imogene, Dad."

That was the worst thing his son could have said. The words made Griffin grind his teeth. He'd intentionally left his son in the dark since he was apt to romanticize everything. Thanks to Jean, Tony believed that finding Imogene would make him a hero.

"You're an intern. That's it. Don't get too big for your britches." Griffin grimaced. It was something his dad would say. Did kids even know what britches meant?

"But Jean and I worked all—"

"I'll see you at home." Griffin shut the door in his face softly.

When he turned around, Jean looked away, but not fast enough for him to miss her glare. After his morning, he welcomed her anger and would have no problem tossing this case.

"You got a problem with how I run my business? Because I have a problem with you telling my employee more than I wanted him to know about this case."

Her jaw dropped, and she gave him the evil eye. "You've got some nerve. He's your intern who was researching some clue you never mentioned before on *my* case and was happy to help." Then she paused, as if her words might have consequences. "Except, don't fire him for that. You're right. I'm sorry. He was upfront about not knowing more than Imogene's name. He told me you asked him to look up all possibilities for four-nineteen-fifty-seven. He didn't ask me anything."

Griffin sat, reclined in his chair, and rubbed his eyes. "I'm rarely told I'm right." And for reasons he'd never be able to explain or even wanted to understand, he confessed, "I don't want the legacy I leave to my son to be this soul-sucking profession and business."

When he looked at her again, Jean was staring at him with wide, understanding eyes. "I worry all the time about what I'm doing to my daughter."

Griffin's chest tightened. For a long time, he'd wished he could say the same thing to Annie and have her understand. Instead, whenever the subject had come up over the past year, she'd said, "That again." As if he was turning a runny nose or small cough into pneumonia.

He cleared his throat. "Everyone says there's no love like that of a parent. No one ever tells us how hard it will be or how easy it is to screw up someone else's life."

Jean shook her head. "It's all-consuming."

Griffin nodded, relieved that she hadn't tried to correct him.

"I lied to someone today about what I do," Jean said. "I'm so bad at mothering that, when she asked me what I was up to, I told her I was a private investigator. As if it gave me an excuse for being a worse or less available mom."

Griffin's eyes bulged as he choked on his laughter. "Wow," he said as he wiped moisture from his eyes. "Awesome sauce, as my son would say."

She laughed at herself. "She can't find out. Therefore, I hope you'll hire me as an intern for this *soul-sucking* business. I promise not to tell Tony anything else about Imogene. This way, if I see my friend again, I won't be lying. And another thing. I told my husband you were unattractive when he asked."

"Another lie, obviously," Griffin said, smiling.

She blinked. "I have no idea why I admitted that to you."

Funny business aside, he had to give her credit for being ballsy. "I'm trying to downsize my business, not grow it."

"I know now. But I'll do anything. I need a place and something of my own. Independence, you know? But it's a stupid idea. Ignore me. I'm embarrassed I brought it up. I could never find a preschool I'd trust anyway. Not to mention the waiting lists."

He looked at her long and hard. Jean didn't need him to sort out life for her, but he wanted to thank her for their refreshing, honest exchange. "How much space and time are you looking for?"

"Anything. Mornings or afternoons. Two or three days a week. I want to spend time with my mom while I can, and I'm not ready to let Lexi go full-time."

"You can only work on your case if I ask you to do something, okay? Don't step on my toes about Tony. You can help me with background checks—process stuff. The state has requirements about doing more than that, but you can learn other things. Interns work for free here."

"Seriously? Yes. I mean, if I find daycare. And that's a

big *if*. I worry everyone is a pedophile. It's one of the hand-me-down lessons from my mom. 'Strangers aren't the only danger,' she always said."

"It's not uplifting advice, but it's not terrible advice either," Griffin said. He pulled a card out of his wallet and handed it to her. "This is my wife's preschool. I run background checks on every employee. Annie's there now, taking care of a few things she can't when the critters are about. Tell her I sent you."

Her eyes glistened. "Omigosh. Thanks for understanding. For helping."

"You got it. Okay, tell me what happened during your meeting with your gramps."

As Jean shared the specifics about her visit with George Jerome, Griffin's skin began to crawl with suspicion.

"Lastly," she said as she set a green file on his desk, "he behaved oddly possessive of my mom's medical file when I showed him her copy, like he meant to keep it. And he seemed preoccupied with the dates in the upper left-hand corner. I made a copy for the doctor and kept this one."

"Good work, Jean. The devil's in the details. I'll fax it to an ex-coroner I know and see if anything jumps out at him. Now, I need you to do something for me, and it involves your mother and grandfather.

43

GRIFFIN

SPRING 2022

Jean had been eager to leave and talk to her mom about the Imogene Scholarship, but when Griffin had pushed her to show her mom the photo from the file and ask her if she'd seen it before, or given it to his father, Jean remained stubborn.

"No," Jean had said. "Until I admit we hired you, it's too risky."

"Don't you see that she might recognize it from the lost roll of film?" He pushed her further. "What's more important to you? Pretending you hired someone else or discovering the truth?"

"I need time to figure out how to tell her about you. When I do, I'll ask her if she remembers taking the picture."

"There's more."

He told her about his visit to Rodney Schultz and his insinuation that her grandfather knew more about Imogene's disappearance. But he still wouldn't tell her about the redacted police report; that detail couldn't be shared yet. Civilians tended to go nuts when they thought the law had cheated them. Not that he blamed them, but he would not say more until he knew more. He didn't tell her he would need to ask George Jerome about the letter or the hunch Griffin had: What if Imogene had relapsed in 1979? Griffin had tried to step into the shoes of a father whose child had survived cancer. If attitude and mindset were a big part of the battle, would he have the heart to tell his kid, "*Hey, that demon, Cancer, came back for your friend for good this time. This means it can come back for you too. Them's the breaks.*"

In this hypothetical scenario and wearing Jerome's shoes, Griffin might have lied to his fictitious daughter and said Imogene ran away too. He might even have forged a letter like the one Frannie wrote about in her diary to make her feel better, but Griffin would like to think he'd give his fictitious daughter a choice. He was big on choice, and being a parent didn't mean he should play God in someone's life. But, if that were the case, why wouldn't Jerome have told Frances when she was older and able to handle the truth? Especially in the nineties, when she was an adult and hired a detective. And again, what about the letter?

But Griffin was unwilling to brainstorm with Jean. Intern or not, she was a client first. So, he said nothing else, except, "I need to talk to George Jerome about the letter he forged from Imogene."

Jean said, "I'll talk to Art. We promised to make this decision together."

He doubted Art knew Jean had already spoken to their grandfather once already.

"Tell me more about your visit with your grandfather yesterday."

"I can do better." She brandished her phone and hit play with proud aplomb.

After listening to the recording in its entirety, Griffin rewound it and hit play, trusting the goose bumps rising on his arms.

George Jerome said it again, "I would have done anything and everything to help her."

Griffin would be adding that quote to his yellow pad.

"Why are you replaying that part?" Jean asked.

Hesitant to explain to Jean that there was something in the way that Jerome said the words that gave Griffin the chills, he answered with a question. "What do you make of what he said?"

She shrugged her shoulders. "Isn't it what every parent would feel and say in his shoes? I'd do anything and everything to keep Lexi safe. What about Tony?"

Fair point. Still, the funny feeling in his gut wouldn't dissipate.

Griffin rubbed the bridge of his nose, thinking about his father.

Unused to his silence, or him really, Jean didn't wait for him to gather his thoughts and takeaways.

"Maybe your father quit my mom's case because he didn't want to jeopardize her pregnancy with the stress of his findings, potential or otherwise."

That's something Dad would've done. And it might

also answer why Jerome still wouldn't have told Frances what he knew, or the truth—whatever it may be—in the nineties. But then, why not after Art and Jean were born safely?

And the tail end of Jerome's reflection on Imogene had been a whopper. He'd loved her as much as he'd hated her for what she made him do? WTF?!? Another addition to the yellow rap sheet. He could not wait to talk to the pillar of the community.

Upon Jean's exit, Griffin half expected to find Tony performing a sit-in protest in the front office. Instead, the lingering aroma of an empty pizza box awaited him.

Fortunately for him, his favorite pizza joint was one block over. Two slices should get him through an afternoon of scouring Frances Jerome's photos, conducting background checks, and returning calls to potential clients without ruining his appetite for whatever bland, heart-happy dinner Annie might cook up. He'd offered to make his own meals, but she'd said, "You'd add salt and fat."

The fresh air did him good. Maybe it was his imagination, but the birds sang louder the closer he got to the pizza shack.

But was he imagining the weight of someone's stare?

He stopped in the middle of the sidewalk and turned around. No one was scurrying into a doorway or doing an about-face, pretending not to see him spotting them.

Early on, his dad had warned him that their line of work could make a guy paranoid. "*When you follow enough people, you begin to wonder if you're the follower or the followed."*

But five steps later, he felt eyes on him again. This time he faced forward and played it cool until he could step inside his destination and look outside the large window as he waited for his heated slices.

Nothing. No one lurked about. *Ladies and gentlemen, now introducing Griffin Whittaker in the most boring film of the year,* The Paranoid Private Eye.

He seriously needed to rest tonight and stop contemplating his mortality from his bed in the dark.

44

FRANCES

SPRING 2022

"I'll get it," Frannie said when her doorbell rang. Both Shane and Art jumped up, but she waved them off. "I need to stretch my legs. I can handle a trip to the foyer."

Besides, Shane was unfazed by her health. He only cared if it was Jean returning from her *hot date*. Art had tried to explain his comment, but to no avail. The green-eyed monster had possessed her son-in-law. Eventually, Art had grown frustrated and said, "I didn't mean it."

No one waited outside the peephole, and as she opened the door, an envelope fluttered to the ground.

Frannie Jerome was scrawled in blue ink on the standard-size white envelope. There wasn't anyone walking, running, or driving away. "Who's there?" she asked, as if someone might leap out from behind a tree and yell, *Surprise!* but there was no answer.

The envelope tore easily as she slid her finger along the seam. A tri-folded piece of white printing paper read, "I AM SORRY."

Unable to ignore the odd sensation that the messenger was watching her, Frannie closed the door and returned to the living room.

"Was it Mommy?" Lexi asked.

Shane's angst was rubbing off on her sweet granddaughter. Since he arrived, he'd texted Jean nonstop, more and more furiously the longer he went without a response. If she thought she could convince him to leave Lexi behind, she'd ask him to take his poor company elsewhere. She realized she spent so little time with Jean and Shane that she didn't know if he was always high-maintenance or, worse, controlling. With the baby steps she and Jean had taken to open up with one another, Frannie might find a way to ask her about her marriage in an inviting manner, rather than a judgmental one. She didn't have a successful marriage to boast of herself, and she understood the challenges.

"No, it wasn't your mother. It was a delivery." She slid the envelope into a drawer to give to Art or Jean for the detective later. There was only one reason someone owed her an apology.

Her phone rang with the song "I Hope You Dance" by Lee Ann Womack. "That's her now."

Art gave her a single nod of respect. "We have ringtones? What's mine?"

"'Happy,'" Frannie answered as she grabbed her phone.

"Pharrell Williams? Cool. That makes me happy," Art said.

Instead of looking relieved, as a worried husband

ought to look, Shane's dark brows collided. "Why is she calling you when I've been trying to reach her all day?"

Angela announced to the room, "Mine for Art is 'Hot in Herre' by Nelly."

"TMI," Art said.

"What? It's on Seth Rogen's Spotify," she said.

"You do know I'm not Seth Rogen, right?" Art laughed and pulled her close.

"Hello, Jean," Frannie answered. "Is everything okay?"

Shane now hovered over her. "Tell her I've been worried."

"Is that Shane? Oh, shit. I stood him up."

"Well done," Frannie replied rather than remind her daughter not to swear, and she moved away from Shane. "She's fine. I'll take my call in my office."

"But . . ." Shane whined.

Once she had privacy, she continued. "Where are you?"

"I'm on my way to check out a preschool—long story. How are you feeling?"

Thinking of Art, and her previous conversation with Jean about Lexi not growing up afraid, Frannie bit her tongue and didn't advise her daughter about the dangers of strangers, even in preschools. Jean loved her daughter. That's what mattered most. She didn't need more of Frannie's scare tactics.

"The nap helped. Where are you?"

"I just met with the investigator. Did you know

Grandpa has sponsored a scholarship at St. Agnes for decades?"

"No, I didn't." It wasn't a stretch that George would support the school she'd once attended. He'd always been committed to helping the community.

"Surely it's irrelevant." She'd almost asked, *What kind of detective did you hire?* But she stuck to her promise to trust Jean.

"Hardly irrelevant. It's called the Imogene Scholarship."

Frannie couldn't blame her weak knees on her cancer as she dropped into the Willowbrook chair. "What?" The single-word question was as much a solicitation for more information as it was a statement of wonder.

"For the past forty-plus years Grandpa helped disadvantaged students with tuition or ancillary costs."

Reeling from the news, Frannie remained quiet. *Why? He never expressed an ounce of regret for letting Imogene disappear into the night.* And when she had sacrificed her own integrity for his, he'd let her.

"I should have waited to tell you in person."

Frannie pushed away the emotions swelling within. "I'm glad you didn't wait. Forty-three years is long enough to find out."

"We need to talk to Grandpa."

"Tell your dad you're looking for me," Dream-Imogene had demanded.

"I will talk to him alone first," Frannie said. She'd face her father about Imogene and her recent diagnosis. A truth for a truth.

"I meant *we* as in me, Art, and the detective. He has questions for Grandpa. He knows how to get people to talk. Trust me."

"He's my dad. I will talk to him first."

"Mom, that's the first time you've ever referred to him as your dad."

The endearment had rolled off her tongue as if she was seven years old again, long before Imogene had vanished. She prayed the scholarship meant something. Possibly atonement and a willingness to talk about what happened. And as far as a tribute could go, a scholarship was a start. What it meant for their relationship, she didn't know; there were too many secrets between them, but her hope for honesty and answers blossomed within.

"When will you talk to him?"

"Once I'm ready. I need to think about what I'll say." When Imogene disappeared, Frannie had learned not to let emotions rush her into a confrontation. She never hesitated to say what she meant, but for a productive discussion that called for expedient solutions and results, she liked to think things through. She couldn't afford to let the much-awaited conversation derail her efforts to find Imogene.

"Promise me you will tell me before you talk to him," Jean said.

"Why?"

"Because I . . . just tell me before you talk to him, please. I'll explain then. Once you do, can the detective, Art, and I meet with him? I mean, once you do, the detective, Art, and I need to meet with him."

Somebody's practicing assertion.

"Mom, it's not just the scholarship. Are you sitting down?"

"Yes."

"They still talk about your friendship at the school."

Frannie released a breath she felt like she'd been holding most of her life. "I thought I was the only one who remembered her."

"No, Mom. You're both unforgettable. You're legends."

45

GRIFFIN

SPRING 2022

Pizza provisions in hand, Griffin walked back to the office, determined to get his work done, drop some flowers off at his father's grave for his mom, and then head home where he would have a five-ounce glass of heart-healthy red wine with Annie before hitting the hay.

He licked the pepperoni grease from his fingertips before he plugged Jean's jump drive into the laptop. Around one hundred digital photos filled his screen. He first sped through them, looking for one Jean might have missed, similar to the single photo that had been in his father's file. She was right. Zip. Nothing.

For the millionth time, he wondered, *Who gave the photo to Dad? What is its significance?*

He took his time and screened the photos again. A picture of the girls in crochet hats tugged so fiercely at his feelers that his heart dropped to his stomach.

He paused on a second photo of the girls together, dressed in matching shirts, the hospital room behind them. The girls' smiles met in the middle. Who could have harmed either one of them? Frannie was a victim too. She'd had to live with her friend's disappearance for decades.

Instinct and experience told him that George Jerome knew something about Imogene Dryker, but what?

He revisited Tony's work on *4/1957*.

The police codes could be significant, especially the number fifty-seven—hit and run—except his dad wouldn't have lumped together the numbers. Police codes were shorthand, and they had used them in notes as needed, especially after reading police reports. His dad would have written *PC 4, 19, 57*.

If Tony weren't ready to quit, Griffin would have him compile a list of addresses and locker locations that might work. He also liked the row, aisle, and seat angle.

He slid his kid's work aside. He still couldn't believe he'd hired Jean and was contributing to her CYA with her friend, but she wanted work and a space of her own. Unlike his concerns about Tony, Griffin didn't care what choices Jean made about her life. If she was destined to enter the PI business, it was no skin off his back.

His phone beeped with a text. Speak of the devil.

Jean had forwarded him a picture:

Someone left this at my mom's door.

He zoomed in on the single line of handwritten words: *I AM SORRY.*

The skin along his spine tingled. Maybe he was being

followed earlier. He peered closer at the writing. It looked familiar.

He'd taken a handwriting analysis course once. He had a decorative certificate of completion to prove it. The analysis came in handy when looking for forged documents, false letters of employment, and more. He wasn't good enough to testify on anyone's behalf, but the tips and tricks helped him recognize anomalies when he looked for clues and leads.

He guessed at the writing pressure, but it looked hard and deep, which meant the person was committed —a sign of true apology. But it could also mean they had a high level of energy or were in a hurry. The writing often needed context. The I was larger than the other letters, which implied arrogance. The pointed, steep, and capped letters indicated intensity. The crowded letters, especially the Rs, were narrow—someone intrusive by nature.

Wait a minute. He grabbed the copy of the redacted report and compared Rodney Schultz's signature. He had printed the first letters of his first and last names while the rest of his name was in cursive. The R and the S in his signature matched the Rs and the S in *SORRY.*

But the drunk and defensive man he'd met seemed incapable of leaving his chair, much less his house, or of summoning the will to find Frances Jerome and leave a note. He needed to see the real deal first and make sure before he questioned Rodney again.

Finally, a possible break in the case. A guilty person desperate to apologize was a guilty person ready to talk.

He texted Jean to bring the envelope and letter with her on Monday. He added:

Your first day of work.

He'd almost asked her to bring it tomorrow, but if Rodney hadn't disappeared after being fired years before, he wasn't going to run away before Monday.

A text and email pinged his phone simultaneously. Damn phone never stopped. Annie wanted to know when he'd be home. And he'd received an email from Nurse Bowman:

I received your message. Below is my phone number. It will be more practical to speak in the mornings, my time.

According to an internet world clock, Haiti was Eastern Standard Time, which made it six p.m. for Nurse Bowman.

He'd call her in the morning, Sunday be damned. In the meantime, he'd learn what he could about her efforts and gain her confidence. He looked up the organization for which she volunteered.

"Let's find out what makes you tick."

She was a bloody saint. The organization's volunteers provided care, immunizations, and education to children and mothers. All the volunteers on the website were smiling, flushed with purpose. He wondered if one of them was Nurse Bowman.

He leaned back and rubbed his chest as if he could exorcise the jealousy. The people looked downright effervescent. What would it take for him to feel such vitality?

Mojo zapped, he closed the website and pushed aside his to-do list, which included calling the woman who'd left a not-so-charming message about going through a divorce with her soon-to-be ex who was "hiding a whore on the side." Until he spoke to her, he wouldn't know if her goal was to gather evidence to use as leverage in the settlement or to let her husband know he hadn't fooled her. Maybe it was time to start turning down potential clients who used shaming and derogatory words.

He took his time as he locked up his office. On the sidewalk, he looked about. If someone had been watching him earlier, he didn't feel their presence now. The chance that Rodney had both found Frannie and stalked him today was slim. Still, he took his time driving to the cemetery and looked in the rearview mirror often.

Sunset wouldn't happen until after eight o'clock, which meant he had plenty of time to visit his dad, leave flowers as his mom had requested, and fire off questions about Imogene at his tombstone. He drove by memory, not relying on the numerical markers that identified each section and row.

He slammed on the brakes, only to hit the gas, violating the cemetery's speed limit by twice the limit—a whopping ten miles an hour. He rolled by his father's section. After a few wrong turns, he finally found the block he wanted.

Four.

He didn't stop until he reached the marker, *1900-1999.*

Leaving his father's lilacs on the passenger seat, Griffin stepped out of the car, his heart beating faster as he counted each plot as he walked across the lawn.

Fifty-Seven.

Water droplets and the green shavings from the freshly mown lawn covered his shoes as he took a deep breath and turned to face the grave.

46

JEAN

SPRING 2022

Jean had no idea what to expect as she walked through her front door. She knew two things. One, Shane had the right to be angry at her for standing him up. Two, Art had called her and apologized for the *hot date* nonsense.

It wouldn't be so bad if she wasn't a tiny bit attracted to Griffin Whittaker and if she hadn't confided more in the detective this morning than she had in her husband in months.

The house was too quiet. She found Shane waiting in the living room with a glass of wine.

She stretched her arms overhead and sighed. "Where's Lexi?"

"Hello to you too. With Art and Angela."

"But I haven't met Angela," Jean said. Yet, she trusted Art with her life, which meant with Lexi too, and now might be a good time to choose her battles with her pouting husband.

"You had a chance today. She's nice. Not what I'd expect for Art, but she's an open book, which was a welcome change."

"Point taken. Shane, I'm sorry I stood you up, but it was for a good reason." She joined him on the sofa and rubbed her palms together. "You're not going to believe this, but—"

"You know what Dr. Pfeiffer says about following an apology with a 'but.'"

"That it's not an apology. Yeah, I get it." He and Dr. Pfeiffer were right—she wasn't apologizing. "I got a part-time job and arranged daycare."

He blinked. "You what?"

"I know!" she said and lifted her hand, but he left her hanging on the high five.

His eyebrows met like two angry caterpillars.

"You got a job and enrolled our daughter in daycare without talking to me? You don't think this should have been a family decision when it involves our daughter?"

Trepidation shadowed her success. "You made her a counseling appointment without talking to me, and you should be jumping up and down and clicking your heels. You've been encouraging me to get a job and arrange daycare since we had Lexi. Now that I have, it's a problem? I know it came about fast, but that's why I didn't want to miss the opportunity. Plus, Griffin handles the school's employee background checks. This is the perfect set up."

"That's what I'm talking about. For years, you've resisted any encouragement to carve out an identity for yourself. But now, after one hot date with a detective, you're no longer a stay-at-home mom?"

Her shoulders dropped. "So that's what this is about. You're jealous."

"Yes," Shane started to yell but then lowered his voice, even though Lexi wasn't home. They'd both grown accustomed to revolving their relationship around parenting, and they couldn't break the habit even now. "Yes, I am jealous. We share nothing. We don't have sex. Now, we don't share family decisions."

Gah. Not the sex talk.

"This decision might help our sex life," she lied.

"Maybe yours and the detective's," Shane said.

"Stop it, please. The detective is older and overweight." She'd once dated a guy who she suspected was cheating, and she'd asked him after one weekend trip with his friends, "Did you cheat on me?" And he'd said, "No. There wasn't anyone attractive there." It had taken her a few minutes to register what he'd said. "But, if someone had been attractive, you would have cheated on me?" She'd broken up with him then and there.

Like that jerk from her past, she had told Shane what she thought might make him feel better, but it wasn't honest.

"Shane, I want a job, and this entire Imogene thing has gotten me curious about investigating." True, but not the entire truth.

"Wait. What? You're working for *him*?" Shane jumped up and down now, but not happily. "Are you fucking kidding me?"

"Too much, too soon?" In her own excitement and tendency to feel defensive, she hadn't chosen her words as carefully. "It's not like that." But at least he'd sworn like an adult.

"What *is* it like?"

"Carla-with-a-C Clarke."

His expression was so sincere, she almost believed she was as insane as his look implied.

"I'm calling Dr. Pfeiffer and asking for an emergency meeting tomorrow," he said, reaching for his phone.

Rather than get sidetracked by telling him that Dr. Pfeiffer wasn't an on-call psychologist, she stayed focused. "This morning, I ran into Carla Clarke. Since you're Instagram pals, you know all about her sublime life and brilliant son."

"Who told you I'm on Instagram?"

That's what you want to focus on? "Carla did. Anyway, Lexi had started stripping in the office supply store, so I didn't have her shoes. Carla had a new car and a bag full of Pottery Barn stuff."

"I don't understand what you're talking about. Do you even know what you're talking about?" Shane ran his hand through his hair and stared at the door like he should make a run for it and get away from his loony wife.

"I have nothing of my own, Shane."

That knocked the wind out of his sails. He sat down and stared at her. "You have Lexi and me."

"I felt like such a nobody standing in the middle of the parking lot, hiding Lexi's bare feet with Blanket, hoping Booby wouldn't make an appearance, and worried that perfect Carla would see my dirty car. She asked me what I was doing at Office Depot, and the lie slipped out. I told her I was working. She asked me what kind of work, and I told her I was a Private Eye."

"You what?!"

It had been a long time since she and Shane had discussed anything but Lexi or their marriage. She couldn't tell if he was incredulous and wanted to put her in a straitjacket or if he was impressed and might applaud.

Regardless, the joy from her interactions with Carla, Tony, and Griffin bubbled to the surface and she giggled. "And she believed me."

He shook his head but smiled.

"I begged for the job, actually a free internship, so I wouldn't be lying, because Carla said she might have a case for me. She said I might get 'most interesting career' at the high school reunion, even though that's years away and I don't give a fig."

A bark of laughter escaped Shane, and he reached for her. "There's the woman I fell in love with."

For a brief second, she recognized the man she'd fallen in love with, too, so she leaned into his embrace.

"Are you still angry?" she asked.

"Is there anything else I need to know? Anything else you're not telling me?"

This wasn't the first time Shane had asked her this question. *Need?* Need was such a complicated word. Did he need to know she didn't want any more children before she could articulate her reasoning for herself? Did he need to know she was attracted to Griffin when it would go nowhere? Did he need to know that her grandfather might be withholding information about a girl's disappearance before she knew the facts?

"No. Nothing else. Now, do you want to hear about the preschool? It's amazing. They have a two-year waiting list, but they are making an exception for us because the owner is the detective's wife."

Shane looked toward the ceiling. "Thank you, God. He's old, overweight, and married."

Jean jumped to her feet. "Let's go pick up Lexi and tell her about school. We should get ice cream to celebrate."

"Or," Shane said, swinging her around theatrically. "We could ask Art if we can pick Lexi up in the morning." He kissed her lips, then her jaw, then her neck.

She tried to relax. She honestly did. But the fear of what could happen long-term won out. She had finally found independence in her life, and she didn't want to lose it.

"Art has already helped a lot today. Let's pick up Lexi and let Art and Angela get back to their regularly scheduled programming."

47

GRIFFIN

SPRING 2022

Griffin's face screwed up, torn between relief and confusion as he read the headstone.

Darlene Moonbeam Dryker
1949 to 1969
The love and light of our lives

Benjamin Dryker's wife and Imogene's mother.

The graves on either side appeared unrelated.

Griffin ran his palm across the stubble on his jaw as he stared at the tiger lilies growing before the headstone. When it occurred to him that the numbers could be a gravesite, he expected to find a game-changing clue, or perhaps even Imogene's grave. After all, the numbers in his father's file implied this spot was fundamental to the case he couldn't solve.

Was that it? Had *4/1957* been a record of a mistake

his dad made? A red heron or rabbit hole he needn't have followed?

He spent his waning energy returning to his dad's plot and replacing the dead flowers with fresh lilacs. "What did you figure out, Dad? Why so cryptic?"

As he left the cemetery more perplexed than ever, he imagined his ideal arrival home. Tony would be practicing the clarinet, and Annie would give him one of her lingering kisses that made him feel like the king of the world for a few seconds.

Instead, they were straight-faced and sitting side by side at the table when he walked in. They weren't glaring at each other but at him.

The walls moved and closed in on him. Which would be scarier, staying or leaving?

"What's going on?" Griffin asked.

"You tell me," Annie said. She slid their son's phone across the table.

"Can I be excused?" Tony asked.

"No," Griffin said, selfishly relieved. His son must be in big trouble, and Griffin was to be the referee. "Wait right there." He set his bag down and leaned over to look at the phone.

It was a picture of Griffin entering the pizza shack.

He reared back, offended and ashamed.

"You followed me?" he barked at his son.

"You've been cheating on me," Annie said.

"What? I have not been cheating on you." He rested his hand on the back of a chair, but his palm had grown sweaty and his hand slid.

"With food," she clarified. "You're killing yourself."

"Not fast enough," he shot back while he took off his jacket to help with the heat.

"Tony, is this what you do when you don't get what you want? Because you haven't earned the right to be in a meeting? You take revenge and follow someone?"

"You treat me like a child," Tony said.

"You are a child, and you're fired." Griffin ignored his escalating heartbeat and a wave of nausea.

"You're the child!" Tony yelled. "You're the one who wants everything his way or no way."

"Oh, poor Tony," Griffin said. "His dad doesn't want him to be like him."

Tony's face turned to stone. "I've said I want to be a Private Eye, but I've never said I want to be like you." His son's footsteps rocked the house as he stormed upstairs to his room.

Griffin's heart thundered in his ears, which seemed impossible since his heart had also dropped to his stomach.

"How dare you, Griffin," his wife continued.

Heat climbed his chest and neck. Sweat beaded his brow.

Tears filled her eyes, and she looked at him with what could only be disappointment.

His chest tightened further. He could handle an angry Annie over a disappointed Annie any day.

Spots swam before his eyes as the room came at him all at once. *Something's wrong.* "Annie."

"Don't you 'Annie' me," she said, swiping at wet

cheeks. "Every day I worry about your health. I've changed my diet to support you. I've read everything I can get my hands on so we can grow old together. And this entire time, you've been running straight toward a heart attack."

He couldn't breathe. His hand trembled as he lifted it to his chest.

"Annie . . ." he tried again, and then everything went dark.

48

FRANCES

SPRING 2022

Last night and this morning, Frannie had imagined seeing her father and had prepared herself to stay focused, march in, demand answers, tell him about her diagnosis, and leave. Who knew if another transplant would work or how much time she had left to live? It was time for George Jerome to tell the truth.

With her car parked curbside outside his house and her window open, her senses overwhelmed her. Freshly cut grass co-mingled with the scent of sagebrush and wild grass on the hillside. Music and the sound of a vacuum carried from a neighbor's open garage. Children laughed as they played with their soccer ball.

She and Imogene had skipped along these very sidewalks on their way home after school, always stepping over the cracks and chanting, "Step on a crack and you'll break your mother's back."

The house's stucco had been painted light blue, hiding all hints of the boring tan, which had once been the uniform color of the suburban neighborhood. There was her bedroom window, the same one she'd peeked out of when Officer Schultz had brought her father home. The steps she climbed now were the exact steps she and Imogene had dashed up, laughing at Frannie's chicken jokes. And here was the door Frannie had run out, eager for her school's open house, unaware that she'd never see Imogene again.

Looking at the well-maintained rambler-style home, no one would guess how she'd lost her innocence inside its walls.

Her teeth chattered. Nerves most likely, since she wasn't chilled. It was strange how time could play tricks on a person. Frannie had climbed out of her car as an adult, ready to confront her father one last time, but now she felt like that same nine-year-old girl, powerless and desperate for answers.

Because after all this time, her father still held the upper hand. It was up to him how much he would divulge.

Cancer was the last hand she could play if her father refused to help. Not that there was any guarantee guilt would work on him. Guilt hadn't worked forty-plus years ago. But the scholarship meant something, didn't it?

Lifting her chin and squaring her shoulders, she knocked on the door.

Naturally, her visit came as quite a surprise.

"Frances, my goodness." He rushed forward and pulled her into his thick arms. His hug was as she remembered. Strong. Solid. When he pulled away, air cooled her cheek where his tears had flowed. For a second, she wondered if he'd somehow found out the cancer had returned.

"Don't mind me," he said as he stood back, his palms gripping her shoulders. "I've missed you. Come in. Come in." He stepped aside. "Ladies first."

Frannie wanted to turn and run. She shouldn't have come, but she'd thought she was prepared to keep her distance. Blame it on her cancer and the flood of memories about her early childhood, but looking at him, she could only see the dad she had idolized during the first nine years of her life.

Oh, how she wished Imogene had never disappeared and that she could have been close to her father these many years. If he'd been honest and tried to help her, she would have been different, maybe more loving, more open with her husband and children. Instead of obsessing about monstrous humans and her children's safety, she might have been Jean's confidant about crushes and dreams. Maybe she could have been Art's comedic and loving mother. If she'd been able to trust her father, perhaps she would have kept her children safe without preaching about danger and making the burden theirs. Perhaps she would have been a comedian, traveling the world, not caring to get married or have children. The possibilities of a life with her dad and Imogene were unlimited. But she would never know who she was meant to be if Imogene had lived; if her dad had been honest.

With his big hand on her upper back, her father steered her toward the small table where he'd been reading. The space was reminiscent of the table that she, her mother, and her father had shared countless times in the kitchen. Dazed by the memories and familiar surroundings, the toe of her shoe caught in the carpet, tripping her.

"Oops, you found that trick stair." Her father laughed, using the same joke he'd always told.

He stacked the medical journals to clear the tabletop. He chuckled as he picked up a glass trophy with a golf ball balanced on top. "Won the recent hospital fundraiser tourney for my age group." He set it aside. "Can I get you anything to drink? Sun tea? Brewed it myself."

Her father couldn't stop talking or moving, and his energy made her more nervous.

"Cat got your tongue?" he asked.

Her mental rehearsals evaporated, and she was as surprised as he was to hear her say, "I have acute myeloid leukemia."

When the doctor had told her, she'd felt numb, resigned. She'd thought, *Okay. It came back. My kids are grown. They are healthy. My estate will take care of them if I die.* She was afraid of being forgotten, afraid of her time being rushed, but she hadn't been afraid of death.

But now, telling her father, she did fear death. She was afraid. So horribly afraid to die.

Her dad did this to her, made her feel vulnerable.

He aged within seconds then, reaching for his chair with an unsteady hand to sit with her. "Who is your doctor? What is the treatment plan?"

"We hope a transplant will work again."

He gripped her hand as if to keep her in this world. "Yes. Yes, a stem cell treatment is right. Thank God we've learned more since the seventies. You no longer need a perfect match, and there are several donor registries. Has your doctor registered you yet?" He reached for his phone as if ready to use his reputation and network to make sure every step was being taken to save her, and her heart melted a bit.

Frannie reached for his phone, encouraging him to set it down. "I'll use my stem cells, like last time, but peripheral rather than bone marrow. I should start the growth factors this week and then prepare for chemo."

He paled, and then outrage, or incredulity, contorted his face. "No. We know much more about transplants now. I'll speak to your doctor immediately. Or, better yet, I'll find you a new one." His grip tightened, forcing her to lean toward him. "Donated cells produce white blood cells that attack any remaining cancer cells in the patient's body. That's most common in a donor transplant."

She pulled her hand away to lean back in her seat, scared by her father's intensity. Shaking her head, she said, "Or my body could reject the donor's cells. My stem cells saved my life in 1977. Not a donor's. I'm not a child anymore. If I trust my doctor, you'll need to as well."

His lips trembled. "We fought it before—you, your mom, me, and the Smurfs."

"And Imogene," she spoke softly.

He stiffened but nodded. "Yes, and Imogene."

Frannie leaned forward. "Tell me what happened to her, Dad."

"You haven't called me Dad in a long time."

"Tell me."

"You've lived a great life, haven't you? You're successful. Have wonderful children and Lexi. All your mother and I hoped you'd have."

"'Great'? I've lived my life with guilt and fear. Guilt for letting Imogene go. A fear that something could happen to my children. How can you imply my life has been normal when you intentionally tried to scrub the memory of Imogene out of my life? Or when we haven't had a good relationship since? You have no idea what my life might have been like with Imogene in it. Now, I might run out of time to redeem myself or to remedy my regrets."

He adjusted his glasses with a quivering hand. "Let's stop this. There's nothing for you to regret. You've done nothing wrong, and you loved Imogene more than anyone. You need to conserve your strength and fight for your life. It's what she would want if she were here with you."

"What she would want is to be with me!" The same frustration she'd felt at nine rushed through her. "You're doing it again. Trying to shut me up, dismiss me. Don't you understand that I'm afraid I might die without knowing what happened to her? If she can't rest in peace, I won't either."

Like a little girl, she wiped her tears on her sleeve despite the tissue sitting before her. "Why won't you tell me? I should have protected her. I loved her. I've missed her my entire life."

"But you moved on. You were popular in school after Imogene."

"You saw what you wanted to see. I wasn't popular. I was a guardian. I was known as the girl whose friend was kidnapped. Those friends? Those calls after school? I made my classmates call me to tell me they got home okay. They felt sorry for me."

He choked, shaking his head in denial. "But you wrote the letters to Ben Dryker and the officer saying sorry . . ."

"Because I overheard you and Mom talking. You said the courts might take me away if I didn't drop my claim. I'd already lost too much. You'd been drinking. Mom was upset. I got scared."

"My god." His frame shuddered. "Your mother and I . . . we didn't know." He rested his elbows on the table and cried.

"You have to tell me what you know."

After a while, he lifted his wet face and stared at the wall, seeing something Frannie could not. "I'm sorry, my love. I wish I was as wise then as I am now."

"What do you mean?" She crossed her arms against her midriff and rocked.

"I was never the strong one. It had always been you. You and Imogene. Imogene was unbeatable. She could make you laugh, smile, and fight for life in your darkest hours. I wanted you to have a normal life, but I didn't know how to give that to you."

Frannie lifted her palms, confused.

"Everything I've ever done for you has been out of

love, and that will never change. No matter what you believe, I have protected you since the second you came into this world, and I'll do so until I leave this world."

"Protected me from what? Honesty? You and the cop covered something up. I know you did. Why else were you worried the court would take me away from you?"

He wiggled his jaw as if undecided, but then he said, "If I could explain, I promise you I would. I have, and will always, put you first. I'd rather you think the worst of me than say anything else. I'm your father. You must trust me; I have reasons for my silence. It's for the best. You must focus and take extra care now."

Tears of frustration poured down her cheeks, dripping on her pants.

"Trust you? Imogene was a part of me. When she disappeared, a part of me did too. That's on you."

The exhale from her father was so deep, it seemed as if it would be his last.

This is it. He won't help me. Even now.

The room was silent except for the clicking of a clock.

Depressed and lost as to what to do next, she asked, "Why the Imogene Scholarship? Guilt?"

He smoothed his palm over his shirt front. "Because no matter what, she deserves to be remembered."

Frannie folded her hands in her lap, closed her eyes, and took a deep breath. "It's all I want, to find Imogene so she won't be forgotten if I die. I don't understand why you refuse to help."

"I don't expect anyone to understand. Even when Jean asked, I didn't explain," he said.

Her eyes popped open. "Jean? When?"

"Last week. She asked me about Imogene."

Frannie's breath caught and the pain of her children's betrayal caused her to sway in her chair. She had opened up to them, let them record her history, read her diary; all in good faith that they wanted to help her find Imogene as her last goal in life, and yet, Jean had broken one of the two promises Frannie had asked of them. And Jean did nothing without Art knowing. Her stomach sank. Had they also dismissed how critical it was to avoid Peter Whittaker? Maybe this entire time they'd been patronizing her, managing her.

What if they were lying and had never taken finding Imogene seriously?

Her core spasmed with the realization her children might be like everyone else, eager to dismiss her fears and Imogene. Her hope that she'd find Imogene this time disappeared, leaving a raw ache inside Frannie that would never heal.

Her father misunderstood her reaction. "Jean said nothing about your cancer." He grabbed her hand. "Focus on getting better and let me help you."

"The only way you can help is with the truth."

He rubbed his eyes, now bloodshot from crying. "That night of your open house—"

"Referring to that night as the night of my open house infuriates me. It's the night Imogene vanished."

"You're right. I lied. I said her dad called and told her to come home, but he didn't. I made her leave, but I won't say more. Fight. Please, consider a donor."

Her father would never help her, but at least he had finally admitted his betrayal. She jumped to her feet, hiking her purse over her shoulder. "You lied to the police over and over," Frannie said. "Your lie misled them. Instead of looking for her that night, they dragged Mr. Dryker in for questioning. You lied again with the forged letter. The truth would have helped them find her. And don't you dare tell me again that she ran away. You and Mom made me bury a piece of her in the cemetery." Her pain took over. She grabbed the crystal trophy on the table and threw it hard across the room. Forty-three-years-late hard. The award shattered, shards flying everywhere.

"That's for Imogene and me."

"Frannie, wait!" her dad called after her as she stormed out.

49

GRIFFIN

SPRING 2022

The only thing worse than not knowing why he was waking up in a bright hospital room, connected to machines that beeped and played back his heart rate, was looking to his left and seeing his ashen-faced mother.

"Mom?"

She bent forward in her chair and squeezed his hand. "You're okay."

He didn't feel okay. He had blurred memories of Annie shouting for help, people leaning over him, shining lights, and sirens.

"What happened?"

"Annie will explain. She and Tony stepped out for some air. We are very worried about you."

Are. Not *were*. It wasn't over.

His mom hit a number on her cell, and soon, Annie's voice carried over the speaker.

"Is he awake?"

"Just now," his mom said before hanging up.

Minutes later, Annie and Tony raced around the corner, but once inside, they walked cautiously toward him as if he would spook easily. He remembered feeling trapped between them and the walls of their home.

The argument came back to him and the monitor beside him echoed his distress.

"Let's not crowd him," Annie said, as if he was a fox about to gnaw off a paw to escape.

"Marnie," his wife addressed his mom, "now that he's awake, let's get you home where you can rest. Tony, help your grandmother get into a cab and call the house to let them know she's on her way."

His mom didn't argue as Tony helped her rise to her feet, making Griffin feel worse.

Once they were alone, he said, "I knew I needed a vacation, but this is a bit much."

"Don't joke," Annie said, sitting next to him on the bed. Her cool palm felt good against his forehead.

"My heart?" he asked. Of course it was his heart. He had his dad's heart. The doctor had warned him, but he hadn't cared.

"No, you lucky jerk. An anxiety attack."

"Lucky is winning the lottery." He'd never had an anxiety attack, but now he was afraid he could have another, which was enough for him to feel like he was that fox who'd better start gnawing.

"How long have I been out?" He should go back to sleep. Life was nice in la-la land. He vaguely remembered running through grass fields, jumping over streams, and floating on music-note clouds.

"Sixteen hours," she said and sniffled. "I told them how you grabbed your chest, and with your history, they admitted you for cardiac observation. They had a hard time keeping you awake."

Maybe he should sleep through the next several years until his retirement.

"The doctor said he'd check on you by eleven a.m. Hopefully, we can go home afterward."

Back to the same life that had caused his attack.

"Annie," he began. "I can't."

She clutched his hand. "Let's wait till you're better."

She didn't get it. She didn't get him. Maybe that was his fault, he wasn't sure, but not talking about it was killing him. Tears filled his eyes. "That's the problem. I can't get better if I can't talk about it. I've been depressed for a while now. I eat because sometimes it's the only thing that stops the pain."

"Pain? Oh, Griff. You never told me you were in pain."

Hadn't he?

"The pain of failure. The pain of hating my job day in and day out. The pain of facing my mortality and feeling like I have nothing to show for my life."

Annie put one hand on her heart and one on his.

"You know what pushed me to eat pizza yesterday? I looked at my life, and, besides you and Tony, I wondered what the point has been?"

Annie nodded; he wasn't sure at what, but the fact that she wasn't telling him to be quiet or treating him like a repetitious drama queen was enough. He was on a roll, and it felt good to spill his guts.

"I lay awake half the night feeling guilty that I've wasted my life. Every Monday, I start counting the hours to Saturday. I wish away forty-plus hours of my life every week."

She wiped the tears from her face.

"You don't agree, but I hate how Tony wants to follow in my footsteps. I want our son to be happy. I don't want him to throw away his life for a bunch of cheaters and frauds. I don't want to be the one to hand this shitty life to him. I don't want my legacy to be this depressing business." The aching truth tightened the muscles in his chest. "I'd rather die first."

There. He'd said it. Out loud.

Her tears flowed unchecked, and so did his.

There was a noise from the hall, and Tony walked into the room. "Grandma's on the road."

Griffin hurried to wipe his cheeks; relieved Tony hadn't returned two seconds sooner. "Got any pizza with you?"

"Don't do that, Dad. You're funny, but not that funny."

"Come here." Griffin lifted his arms, ignoring the discomfort from the IV.

His son buried his face into Griffin's shoulder. "I didn't mean what I said last night. You scared the crap out of me, Dad. Please stop killing yourself with food. I need you."

There went any hope of Griffin not blubbering in front of his son.

A solid clap to Tony's back and Griffin gently pushed him away. "Annie, I need a towel for all these tears."

"Your blankets should suffice," she teased.

Once his face was mopped, Griffin said, "Annie. Tony. I love you more than life. But this was my wake-up call. Something's got to give, and I think I know where to start."

GRIFFIN SENT Annie and Tony home to get some rest while he stretched his legs. The doctor wanted to check his heart rate and blood pressure before giving him a new lease on life, so Griffin wandered the hospital in a pair of scrub pants and a hospital gown, racking his brain to comprehend the significance of Darlene Dryker's grave. Despite his health, he couldn't shake this case. Or maybe the case wouldn't shake him. It wasn't long before he stood at the entrance to the children's ward.

The hallway to the double doors was painted in rainbow colors and covered with photos of families, smiling children, and stenciled words of encouragement: *Cancer Can't Stop Us; Unbeatable Spirits; Laughter is the Best Medicine.*

The little faces gave Griffin pause. *Look at them.* What did he have to complain about? He was determined to get his head on straight and his life in order.

He dedicated time to each person who'd earned a spot on the wall, keeping an eye out for Frannie and Imogene but not finding them. As he made his way through the pictures, he witnessed not only love and resilience but the passage of time captured in film by changes in hairstyles, clothing, furniture, and more. This hospital and ward had impacted many lives over many years.

On the opposite wall were acrylic posters with hospital patient success stories and accomplishments, including one of George and Frannie Jerome holding a five-foot check for a million dollars in 1978. The headline was *Hospital Administrator and Patient's Father Raise $1 Million for Cancer Research.*

"Are you lost?" A white-haired female doctor moved past him and rested her hand on the door handle. "Do you need help?"

Her concern confused him, but then he remembered his trendy outfit. "On a walkabout. Doctor's orders." Smiling to reassure her, he said, "I couldn't help but come here. I know someone who was a patient in the seventies." At the risk of his visit getting back to George Jerome, who was still actively involved with the hospital, he didn't mention any names.

She removed her hand from the door and turned to face him with a serene expression, ready to give him all the time he needed to share his experience.

"I was an intern in the mid-seventies. When was your friend here?"

Griffin wasn't gonna look a gift horse in the mouth. "1977. Bone marrow transplant."

"A successful one since she's still a friend." The doctor smiled.

"It was."

"It's good to be reminded that lives were saved in 1977 too."

"'Too?'" Griffin asked.

"That's the same year the vicious flu swept through the ward, and we couldn't save all of the children. It was devastating."

Griffin frowned. While recording her answers, Frannie had mentioned the flu but nothing about losing any of her fellow kiddie patients.

"How tragic. I had no idea. My friend never mentioned the losses." His words made him cringe. *Losses*—as if they were tournaments or favorite toys. Why was it so difficult to address the death of another?

She put her hands inside the pockets of her white coat. "We did as much as possible to shield the other children from the truth. It was bad enough they were fighting cancer, much less to tell them the flu was a threat too."

His fingers tingled in that telling way. "But didn't some of them wonder where their friends went? What were they told?"

She wrinkled her nose. "We handle everything differently now, learning what we have about child psychology and development. We were advised to keep everything positive for their sake. We told them the flu victims went home. Going home is every child's goal in this ward."

How many adults believed they were shielding children from bad news when it also saved the adults from having to tell them?

"And what about when a child died from cancer? How was that explained?"

She frowned. "In those days? In some cases, the same way."

Griffin raised his hands and said, "I'm not judging." But he was. He was reminded of Rodney's diatribe about being judged for what people knew in 1994, not 1979. Now, here he stood, five decades later, measuring parents, doctors, and nurses for what they told children in the 1970s.

At the same time, the past attitude aligned with his previous idea—what if Imogene's cancer returned in 1979 and George and Sally Jerome opted to protect their vulnerable daughter from the harsh reality of relapses?

What was the right balance in adulting and parenting? Filtering information, or spelling out the dangers as Frances had for Jean and Art? He prayed he was striking the sweet spot with Tony.

"Doctor," Griffin asked, "did the hospital fall under scrutiny for the lives lost to the flu?"

Her chin jutted forward, and she frowned.

Lifting his hands apologetically, he said, "Full disclosure, I'm a private investigator with a curious mind. That's all it is, curiosity. Or an occupational hazard." He pointed at his hospital gown.

Smiling forgivingly, she shook her head. "There was

no negligence or malpractice on the hospital's part. It was a fast-moving virus. We took every precaution we could."

After he thanked the doctor for her time and happily excused her to repair lives, he dropped his smile. Another harsh reality was that doing your best wasn't enough sometimes.

50

JEAN

SPRING 2022

Today is the first day of our new life, Lexi. We are both going to have the best time," Jean said as she tried to make eye contact with her daughter in the rearview mirror.

Unfazed that she was about to get dropped off in an unknown world, Lexi bounced Smurfette across her unicorn T-shirt.

Clearly, the coaching was for herself and not her daughter. If Griffin had replied to her text this morning, confirming her start time and his commitment to their arrangement, she'd be more confident about her first separation.

She was simultaneously excited to work and terrified to leave her daughter at preschool.

Could she handle the reality of being apart from Lexi? Everything could go wrong. What if none of the other kids played with her? Were there bullies in preschool? What would happen when Lexi talked to Booby or Dandelion in front of others?

When she and Lexi arrived, a young teacher was holding a decorated poster that read, "Welcome, Lexi!"

Would it be rude for Jean to take a picture of the woman's—Mel's—ID? Her mom's past warning rang in her head. "*It's more important to be alive than polite.*"

"Why can't you let me be a kid?" Jean had railed when she was twelve. "When I have children, I will not teach them to be afraid of everyone."

Now that it was time to let Lexi fly, Jean wished she had ingrained some safety tips in her daughter's tiny, innocent head.

"Can I say hello to Annie first?" Jean asked, clutching Lexi's hand as her daughter tugged. When Lexi put her right hand into the woman's, it almost tempted Jean to cry, "*No! She's mine!*"

"Unfortunately, Annie had a family emergency. Here's her number. She's expecting your call."

Memories of Tony devouring lunch and Griffin nodding with understanding as she dumped her feelings on him flashed through her mind. "I hope everyone is okay."

Lexi took advantage of Jean's distraction to escape. Away the pixie skipped, right into the fold of laughing children.

"Bye, honey. I'll be back this afternoon," she said to Lexi's back.

Her baby didn't turn around, not for a nanosecond.

"I guess I'm having a harder time letting go than my three-year-old."

"You're not alone. You're welcome to stay, but I promise you, she's safe in our care."

Jean walked backward out of the center in case Lexi realized her favorite person in the whole wide world was no longer beside her.

Nothing. Lexi had no second thoughts.

Jean called Annie from the car.

"How did your first drop-off go?" Annie asked.

"She's already forgotten I'm her mother. Is everyone okay? Mel said you've had a family emergency."

"Yes. Griffin asked me to update you. He's unwell and taking today off work. Your case will not suffer. That's a promise—his words."

"Okay. I'm sorry. I hope he's better soon." Since every day counted, her mom would get anxious about the delay, but what she didn't know wouldn't hurt her.

Once her mother was ready to speak to her father, Jean would admit she'd spoken to Grandpa and tell her that she and the detective needed to talk to him officially. If Griffin was unavailable once the opportunity arose, Jean and Art would do so alone. Except, what were the boundaries between client and intern? She didn't want to cross the lines of either.

Thankfully, Annie had more to share. "Your internship is still a go. In fact, he stressed he wanted to make that clear. He knows how much it means to you."

"What a relief. I'm sorry. I don't mean that he's

unwell"—what did *unwell* mean, anyway?—"but that he hasn't changed his mind."

"There will be changes," Annie said with a definitive voice, "but none that will affect you. Jean?"

"Yes?"

"I'm glad that you'll be working with Griffin."

"Thank you. I am too."

"He'll be in touch."

Her phone rang as soon as she hung up. The number was not familiar, but she had nothing else to do.

"Hello?"

"Jean? It's me, Carla Clarke. You know, Carla with a—"

"C, of course. Hi, Carla."

"Listen, remember that friend I told you about?"

"Yes, I remember."

"Can you meet her on Friday at Bob's Coffee Bean? Say noon? She's found the nerve to get help."

Oh, goodness. She was really doing this. "Friday at noon works well for me. Should I wear a carnation in my hair so she'll recognize me?" It was a lame joke, but it was too late to take it back now.

"No worries. She'll know who you are. Ta-ta."

"Ta-ta."

Now that she had an unexpected day to herself, she could meet with Art and then unpack some of her house.

Her phone rang again.

"Art," Jean said. "I was just going to call you."

"I bet you were," he said.

"You sound annoyed."

"I am annoyed."

"About?"

"You talked to Grandpa about Imogene without talking to me first."

"I meant to tell you, but I got busy. I didn't mention a detective to him . . . Wait. How do you know?"

Art's silence said it all.

"Nooooooooooo!" Jean wailed. "I was going to tell Mom before she met with him. She promised to tell me when she was going to see Grandpa. Now, she'll never believe I was going to tell her."

"I don't think you can play the card that she was supposed to tell you first. You weren't supposed to talk to him at all."

"What happened? When did she tell you?"

This round of silence was different, as if he was quiet because he couldn't talk, not because he wouldn't. "Art, what happened?"

"She said we could plan a dinner together. For the family. I've never cooked with her. I was excited. I stopped by on my way to work to see if she wanted to have coffee together and talk about our menu."

Her brother cleared his throat, but it sounded more like a groan.

Oh no. Was he crying? "Art."

"She blames me too. You should have told me."

For the first time she could ever remember, her brother hung up on her.

51

GRIFFIN

SPRING 2022

Two days of no junk food, and thank the Greek gods, no more attacks. Griffin had heard about anxiety attacks, but no one had ever warned him that once you had one you were also plagued with genuine anxiety and fear about having another. All the more reason that he'd stick to the plan he and Annie had developed; he'd hire a team, scale the company, and set it up to sell in five years. And then, goodbye investigating and hello teaching at the community college.

Chuck from his favorite BBQ truck waved him over, but Griffin patted his belly, shook his head, and kept walking. It wasn't easy to pass up a brisket and coleslaw roll, but he'd be able to look Annie in the eye tonight.

His wife returned to her normal routine today, and Griffin was on his way to the office too. For the first time, he was eager to get to work. He had a job to do. He'd been hired to find Imogene, and damn it, he would.

Jean sat on the steps leading to Griffin's office, her phone to her ear. She disconnected when she saw him.

"Good morning. Ready to work?"

"Ready, boss."

That made him smile. Maybe all along, he'd needed a team. As he unlocked the front door, he said, "I'm going to train you to do background checks today."

"Super! How are you feeling?"

"Better than I have in a long time." Honesty and sharing feelings could do that to a guy.

"My mom found out I talked to my grandfather," Jean said after Griffin showed her how to submit the first background check. "She saw him on Sunday, and my visit came up. Now, she won't talk to me. Neither will Art."

"Does she know about me?" Griffin asked. "And I don't mean the attractive part."

She blushed and laughed. "No, but I think it's time to tell her I hired you. She might disown me, but I know I chose the best person for the job."

"Thank you. That means a lot to me. And we're close to answers. I can feel it."

"I'll tell her tonight or tomorrow. This time, I'm talking to Art first. Oh, here's the note." Jean grabbed her purse and handed him the three-word letter.

The *I AM SORRY* letter confirmed his previous analysis; the messenger was committed, intrusive, and arrogant—like a retired cop. He grabbed the file from his office and returned to Jean's side. "Look here." He compared the Rs and S in the letter left at Frannie's and then showed her Rodney Schultz's signature.

"Omigosh," she said, touching her thumb to each fingertip as if counting. "It would have been the same day you visited him, right?"

"I'll call him after I take care of something else." As he headed toward the door to his office, he paused.

"Jean, why don't you sign up for a handwriting analysis course? You can help me with fraud cases in the future."

Her eyes widened. "Thank you! Maybe Tony should sign up for the course with me."

Nope, he wouldn't because, hallelujah, Griffin's plan had worked. The day before, Tony had admitted that being a private eye was no longer his thing.

"Why the change of heart? Anything to do with my health scare?" Griffin had asked his son.

"Nah," Tony said as he opened the fridge to grab one of the Red-not-so-Delicious healthy apples. "It's just not for me."

"Why did you turn away to answer me?" Griffin was too practiced at observing body language to ignore this.

Tony turned and stared him straight in the face. "I'm not one of your boring cases, Dad. Don't analyze my every move. I've figured out it's mostly grunt work. And I've been talking to someone."

In teen talk, that meant his son was attracted to someone. "*Pfft.* Should have led with the last line." While Griffin didn't mean it, he felt victorious, so he offered, "If you ever change your mind and want boredom again, let me know."

"Liar," Tony said as he stared at his phone and sauntered away.

Griffin rocked back on his heels and smiled widely at Jean. "He's decided this work isn't for him."

"Really? Did he actually say that?" Jean asked. She wrinkled her face as if she'd smelled something funny.

He stopped rocking, not liking what her face and tone implied. "You met him once," Griffin said.

"Yes, but we shared a pizza, and you know how talkative I was that day."

"Did he say something to you? Something I need to know about?"

"It's Tony's business. Not mine," she said. "I shouldn't have said anything. I'm overly sensitive because my mom is a control freak."

His eyebrows collided. "Do you think I'm controlling my son?" The walls began to warp and close in on him in an all too scary way.

"I don't know. Ask him. I'm going to start the next background search."

Oh, he'd ask him.

He left the door to his office ajar in case Jean had questions. While his laptop whirred to life, he flipped through his notes. After inserting an earbud, he scrolled through his contacts.

"Public Health. Records," the woman answered in rapid-fire.

"Hi, Mary Jo. Griffin Whittaker."

"Griffin. It's been a while."

"Just doing my part, using the online tool, and not bugging you."

"Which explains why you're calling me now," she said sarcastically.

"I need you to double-check my internet skills."

"What, or who, are you looking for?"

"A death certificate for Imogene Dryker. I searched 1979, which is when she disappeared, and an additional fifteen years later, but nothing came up in the national archives."

"Got it. Do you want to hold while I check the hard files, or should I ring you back?"

"I'll sit tight and save you the callback."

Chuckling, she said, "You still have a knack for making it seem like you're doing me a favor."

As the elevator music played in his ear, he walked to his office door, pausing when the fax machine screeched. He detoured to grab the incoming facsimile. It was from his friend and retired coroner, Joe. He'd sent one page of Frannie's medical file with a portion of the contents circled in bold, and he'd scribbled, *Call me ASAP*.

He handed it to Jean. "While I'm on hold, can you call Joe Purdy? His number is in the Rolodex." He pointed at the relic on the file cabinet.

"Rolodex? Really?" she asked.

He listened as she introduced herself to Joe.

Like his son, she was comfortable using the speaker and broadcasting her convos with the public. As part of her training, he'd have to discourage the habit in the future.

Greetings over, Jean said to Joe, "Griffin is on another line. I have your fax. You have questions about my mom's records?"

"It's about her bone marrow transplant in 1977."

"Okay."

Joe explained, "According to the records, Frances was part of a trial and received an autologous transplant, meaning they collected her bone marrow and returned it to create new stem cells after the chemotherapy."

Jean nodded, though only Griffin could see her.

"Yes, that's correct."

"The thing is, while combing through her file, I noticed her bone marrow DNA altered post-transplant," Joe said excitedly.

Any minute, Mary Jo would start talking in Griffin's ear, and he prayed for more time.

Jean rubbed her palm across her forehead. "I'm sorry. I don't understand what you're telling me."

Joe said, "A possible explanation for the change to her DNA sequencing and her successful childhood transplant is that her bone marrow transplant was allogeneic, not autologous."

She looked like her head might explode, and Griffin thought his brain might join hers. "I still don't understand."

"She had a donor," Joe said simply.

"But that's impossible. I've heard about how her stem cells were damaged in the process and the doctors feared they didn't have enough to save her." Jean gestured maniacally to emphasize her point to the ex-coroner who couldn't see her. "They didn't have time to follow protocol and find her a donor. My grandfather had to make the impossible decision to risk her life. Her survival was a miracle. A miracle! All due to *her* cells. There must be a mistake."

Joe said, "I'm not an oncologist, but DNA . . . DNA I know."

Griffin's heart started to thump wildly, but not in a you're-having-a-panic-attack way. In a holy-shit-hunch way. He leaned forward and interrupted. "Joe, how much time between her transplant and the night she got the flu?"

Jean's expression made it clear she thought he'd lost his mind to change the subject.

"Less than a week," Joe said.

A miracle, Griffin thought. It was a miracle Frannie had survived her transplant in May 1977. It was a miracle she had survived the flu less than one week later, as vulnerable as she was, when others had not.

"Joe, we'll call you back," Griffin said as Jean hung up.

"I'm calling my mom's doctor," Jean said, dialing immediately. But the receptionist said he was in surgery. When Jean expressed her dismay, a nurse got on the call and asked Jean, "Can it wait for the TeleVisit with your mother this afternoon?"

Jean froze as if someone had dumped a bucket of ice-cold water over her head. "My mom has a TeleVisit today?" Pulling herself together, Jean scrolled through her phone to check for a missed text.

The awkward silence crackled across the line as the nurse confirmed. "The doctor asked her to have someone with her."

The telling words caused Griffin to stand closer to Jean in silent support.

Her shoulders slumped in defeat, echoing his assumption—they were running out of time to find Imogene.

"You there, Griffin?" Mary Jo asked.

He squeezed Jean's shoulder, and once his door was closed, he leaned against it. "What did you find?"

"Nothing," she said. "Good news, right?"

Griffin squeezed the bridge of his nose. Just as Frannie's medical file was difficult to explain, Griffin couldn't necessarily explain his subsequent request. "Can you check May 1977 for a death certificate for Imogene Dryker?"

"Thought you said she disappeared in seventy-nine?"

"I did."

While Mary Jo checked manually, Griffin sat behind his desk. "I hope you've lost your marbles, Griffin," he told himself aloud. Any second now, Mary Jo would tell him that no results were found.

"Griffin," Mary Jo said when she returned.

He straightened at her serious tone.

"I found something."

52

GRIFFIN

SPRING 2022

Griffin couldn't believe his eyes as he read the results Mary Jo had scanned and emailed him.

Deceased Name: Imogene Dryker
Date of Death: May 7, 1977
Hospital or Other Institution: Bay Area Hospital, Children's Ward
Immediate Cause:
a) Sepsis, due to or as consequence of
b) Flu, due to or as consequence of
c) Compromised immune system, due to or as consequence of
d) Leukemia

WTF?! If Imogene died in 1977, who in the hell disappeared in 1979?

What he couldn't explain, he wouldn't repeat, so he sailed past Jean, intending to take his stunned mind on a brisk walk. "You okay here alone? Not sure when I'll be back." He hung a spare key on a hook and pointed. "If you need to see your mom, don't worry about this place." He swung his backpack over one shoulder. Frances's file and his notes were secure inside.

"Thanks, but she's ignoring me. I need the space and distraction more than ever." Her smile was crooked and sad, her earlier enthusiasm to work a distant memory.

As Griffin walked, he asked himself five questions: *If Imogene died of the flu, who disappeared in 1979? Who went to school with Frannie for two years? Who was reported missing to the police department? What did the police report say? How did Darlene Dryker's grave come into play?*

The mysteries and questions evolved in his head. He couldn't go down the rabbit hole now, figuring out who Imogene was, or wasn't, in 1979. That time would come, and soon. The real questions he needed to focus on were the three that sat heavy in his gut, telling him he wouldn't stop until he uncovered the truth:

Who had the most to lose if the truth came out?

Who continued to protect the lies?

And how much had Griffin's father known?

As for the first two questions, he'd start with the man who had knowingly destroyed a police report and evidence in 1979 when some little girl vanished. Rodney Schultz.

GRIFFIN INHALED the fresh air and sat on the shady concrete steps of a closed-down community theater. He was relieved when Rodney answered after the first ring.

"What do you want now?" Surprisingly, Rodney sounded sober.

"Who the hell did Frannie report missing in nineteen-frigging-seventy-nine?"

The weight of Rodney's sigh grated across the wire, his breath crackling, as if it was too heavy to contain. "I made a promise to myself and George Jerome. You talk to him yet?"

For a second, Griffin considered lying, but then he'd be as crappy as the rest of them with their shitty secrets. "No, but only out of respect for Frances Jerome's wishes. Come on, Rodney. Fess up."

"I'm trying," Rodney said. "In '79, when Frannie reported the missing girl, I was blown away. I knew the girls because my wife, Penny, was their head nurse when Imogene died in '77, and she'd cried her heart out for the little ones. I volunteered to take the lead on the call and headed over to George's place, hoping to straighten things out and put the report to bed."

Griffin hit record on his phone in case he couldn't take it all in.

"When I arrived at their house, George told me he didn't want Frannie to overhear us, but he'd explain what was going on back at the station with me. I took Frannie's statement in the kitchen, and she gave me a letter she claimed George had forged, pretending to be Imogene. I'll tell you now, it took everything I had not to wear my thoughts on my face when that little girl made it clear that she thought Imogene was still alive when it was all in her head."

Griffin shook his head as if to clear his mental space and make room for what he'd heard. "Wait a minute. What? She imagined her? For two years?" He blew air into his cheeks, wishing he was on Skype with Rodney so he could read his body language. Hell, he wished he could jump in a time machine to August 1979 and watch the discussion unfold. Beg everyone to handle the situation differently.

"George went back to the PD with me. That's when he explained that, when Imogene died, the doctor recommended they let Frannie realize and accept Imogene's death in her own time. Said it was for her own well-being since she was still fighting cancer. No one wanted her broken heart to weaken her spirit. Except, her imagination lasted longer than they counted on.

Griffin rubbed his temples, recalling Jean recounting her grandfather's focus on the medical file.

Had George Jerome been confirming that any notes about Imogene's death from the flu and their decision to keep it from Frannie had been removed? If so, why was the truth still being withheld from a grown woman in her fifties who was desperate for answers?

"You said you kept your oath, that the rest of us didn't understand the resources and knowledge you had to work with in the past—you meant the psychological and mental health resources available to a little girl with an invisible friend, right?"

"Right. Today, no one overreacts about imaginary friends or whatever. In 1994, also pretty much okay. But in 1979, things weren't the same. Back then, how would you explain parents who let their kid pretend for *two* years? Or a parent who wrote a letter pretending to be the dead girl?"

The letter.

Griffin sat up straight and stretched his neck from side to side. "Keep walking me through this mess. It's 1979, and you know Imogene hasn't run away, been kidnapped, or killed. The hospital could confirm the death. Why not update the report and put it to bed as you wanted? Why black it out? Where's the letter?"

There was a long pause, and Griffin was afraid that Rodney had clammed up. After clearing his throat, Rodney said, "I didn't muck it up immediately. I made a bad decision and tried to fix it the next morning."

Griffin's head jerked up, and his eyes widened. One thing he knew for certain after being a PI for decades was that timing is everything.

"I had no choice at the time," Rodney heaved. "I swear to God I had no choice."

You didn't think you had a choice, but you did. Griffin

kept the thought to himself. One wrong reply and Rodney might close his lips and throw away the key. "What happened between the night of August 10, 1979, when you spoke with George Jerome at the station, and the next day when you blacked out the report?"

"The line between personal and professional got the best of me."

Griffin stroked his chin and said dryly, "I'm hooked."

Rodney's sigh was long and heavy. "Do you know what's included in most steps at Alcoholics Anonymous? Honesty."

A tad of hope surfaced above Griffin's growing impatience. "You're giving sobriety a shot?"

"Yeah. One day at a time. This won't be the first time I've tried to quit."

"Then be honest with me, Rodney."

"If I tell you, what are you going to do with the info? I made a promise to George Jerome. I could lose my pension."

Griffin leaned forward. "You'll get no promises from me, man. Now's your chance to relieve your conscience."

"It's a long story," he said.

"The involved ones usually are."

"I guess you'll have to be the judge of time and circumstance."

"You can do this, Rodney."

Rodney exhaled in spurts, sounding like a sputtering engine. "When George and I left the station that night, I was on duty, but I took him for a drink before I took him home. You know, to settle his nerves before he faced his family and decided how he'd move forward with Frannie. At first, George pushed back, said he didn't hold liquor well, but I pressured him, said it would help. To be honest, I needed a drink after all the imaginary business. I know, bad thinking. I should've listened to him, because his second shot in, George crumbled and cried like guilty men do at the station when they're ready to confess."

Griffin began to wonder which was the greater beast in this case: cancer or alcohol?

"Maybe if I hadn't had a second shot myself, I would have been quicker and stopped him from talking. But he spilled his confession all over the bar, no lawyer present, and after I'd read him his Miranda rights earlier."

Dread settled in Griffin's gut, but like roadkill on the side of the highway, he couldn't look away, no matter how horrible it might be. "What did he say?"

"I hope I don't regret telling you this, making all my sacrifices for nothing. Something happened at the hospital that night Imogene died. Something that could get my wife, Penny, in serious trouble. As in ruin-her-life trouble. I couldn't let that happen to her, and the same would go for George after what he'd done. And . . ."

Ah-ha, he was protecting his wife, and still, Jerome.

"And?"

"It would have, could still, destroy Frances Jerome if she knew what truly happened the night Imogene died. It will also harm the hospital, George Jerome, and me. Are you sure you want to know?"

Griffin didn't hesitate. "Tell me everything he told you."

53

GRIFFIN

SPRING 2022

Griffin was tempted to rush to Rodney's house to hear the story in person, but when you have a man ready to talk, it was never a good idea to say, "Hold that thought. I'll be there in twenty." Therefore, the phone, and ready-and-willing Rodney, would have to do. He kept his butt firmly planted on the concrete step outside the abandoned community theater.

"Griffin, as you know, the flu was bad and all over the hospital. This was only a few days after Frannie's risky transplant. George said they'd barely left Frannie's side, but he and Sally left that night to get some sleep because Frannie seemed to be doing better and was asleep herself. But halfway home, George got a bad feeling and turned the car around to check on Frannie again.

"George knew something was wrong the second he stepped into Frannie's room, and when he pulled back the cover to see his little girl, he found a pillow."

Thankful for shade and a low-traffic area, Griffin

leaned his back against the building. This story was going to take a while, and that was fine by him. It was about time he got some answers.

"George and Sally ripped the bed apart as if they'd find Frannie hiding and yelled for the nurse—my wife.

"That's when George noticed Frannie's bedside drawer was wide open, and some present she'd been begging to give to Imogene earlier that day was gone. He figured Frannie had snuck off to Imogene's room. He was pissed, given that she was recovering from the transplant, and the flu was damn destructive.

"On his way to Imogene's room, he found Frannie collapsed in the hallway. You know, when he was telling me this part, aside from the crying, I could see the fear on his face, as if it were happening all over again. I'll tell you, it made me glad I never had kids."

"I can't imagine," Griffin said. Thank God, Tony had always been a healthy child. "What happened next?"

Rodney said. "Fast forward a bit. They had Frannie settled in her room again, but she had a fever. Things weren't looking good. George said my Penny was beside herself, blaming herself for not noticing Frannie had left her room. But George told her what I would have too; none of this was her fault. It was the damn flu's fault for running everyone ragged.

"At some point, George went to check on Imogene. Earlier that day, she'd shown signs of the flu, like many in the hospital, but again, he found an empty bed. I guess he put two and two together that they'd been in cahoots, and he guessed where he might find her."

"And where was that?" Griffin asked.

"In the nurses's closet. Near where he found Frannie."

Griffin sat up. "What?"

"Frannie was fascinated with that lion, witches, and wardrobe book. Can't remember the name. Some book George was reading to her. Anyway, he remembered Frannie had asked him if the nurse's closet might be like the closet in the book."

In all his years, Griffin had never been more confused about where a confession or story might go.

"George raced to the closet, shoved everything aside, and that's where he . . . Damn it, I wish he were the one telling you."

"Come on, Rodney, stay with me. You're doing the right thing, okay? This secret has been held too long and done too much damage."

"She was dead, Griffin. That sweet, little girl had died of the flu alone in that closet."

Griffin covered his face with his free hand. *Hell.* He filled in the gaps. "Frannie had asked her to meet her there, but didn't make it herself because she was sick, and Imogene was sick too. Sicker than anyone realized."

"That's right. Then George snuck Imogene back to her room."

Stunned, Griffin blinked and settled his palm across his eyes.

Rodney's sense of defeat carried across the line. "They pronounced Imogene dead a few minutes later."

"And George said nothing about how and where he

found her? He pretended Imogene was in her room all along?" Griffin closed his eyes, wishing he could ignore the unfairness of it all; Imogene had died alone on a cold floor, and Ben Dryker was none the wiser.

"No. He'd been in a panic and said by the time he calmed down and realized what he'd done, he still couldn't bear the idea that Frannie would blame herself for asking her friend to meet her. Nor did he think it was right for Penny or the hospital to be held liable for something he ultimately thought was his fault, this hidey-hole. He'd read the book to Frannie that gave her the idea."

So much for keeping his cool. Griffin sneered. "Worst of all, George Jerome might have been in serious trouble as the hospital administrator. Rodney, you and I both know it was wrong for you to help cover this up, no matter the consequences. What about Imogene's father? Didn't he deserve the truth? *Doesn't* he deserve the truth?"

But Rodney didn't respond.

"Rodney?" Afraid he was losing him, Griffin said, "I'm coming over."

"No," Rodney said. "Don't. I'm afraid I won't be able to talk if I have to look someone in the eyes. Give me a second."

"Take all the time you need," Griffin said as a door opened nearby, and a woman and two giggling girls ran out to the sidewalk with a bucket of drawing chalk.

The *flick* of a lighter and an exhale assured Griffin that Rodney was still with him.

"What George did also saved my Penny. I'm as guilty as him, for sure. I believe his heart was in the right place. I've thought about his decision many times, and I don't know what I would have done in his shoes, but he was real busted up about it two years after the fact. They were two little kids trying to be normal, having fun in a secret spot. He told me it was his fault they'd been hiding, something to do with not liking their friendship because of Imogene's dad. The girls might have been safe in their beds if not for his contempt. He wanted to keep his family intact. What kind of father would have his little girl live a life of guilt, questioning her role in her best friend's death, and because of a damn flu? And I didn't want my Penny fired or to lose her license and reputation for not watching them closely. Hell, a prosecutor could have twisted George, Penny, and the hospital in knots. A little girl was already dead—what good would it do to hurt more people? What would you have done, Griffin?"

Griffin glanced at the woman and girls playing hopscotch. "I'd like to think I would have given the hospital a chance to set things right, as much as possible, for Imogene's father."

Rodney snorted and his voice was hard. "See? You're a hypocrite. You picked Imogene's dad to look after, who was unavailable by all accounts. Yet, you'd have people like George Jerome and my wife, who would do anything for anyone, get in trouble. Am I proud of what happened? Hell no. But Penny went on to take care of hundreds of sick children, and George Jerome has made it his mission to raise money to fight cancer."

Griffin sighed. "I'm not choosing people, Rodney, I'm choosing the truth."

That let the air out of Rodney's tires. "Maybe you're right. Thing was, I blamed myself that George confided in me. I felt like a complete asshole, having pushed booze on him while I was on duty. If I hadn't, he never would have said a word. But once he did, I couldn't stop worrying about the fallout. So many more lives would have been ruined when enough pain already existed. It had been two years since Imogene died. I couldn't do it. In my book—in anyone's book, for that matter—cancer and a fever killed that sweet, little girl. They were all victims."

"Damn," Griffin said. "Because of that, you made a pact with George Jerome. The next day, you redacted the report and created a blank evidence folder, hoping no one would notice it was empty or wonder what was missing."

The hiss and crackle made by his cigarette filled the airwave. "I wanted to control any questions that might arise about the letter and why George pretended to be Imogene writing from Maryland two years after she died. Child Protective Services might have gotten involved and asked more questions about why they'd let the imaginary stuff go on as long as they did. What if George caved about sparing Frannie the truth about the closet? What if he told everyone that Penny wasn't doing her job? Maybe he could afford a good lawyer if the truth came out. And the hospital would have a team of legal help. But Penny? We would have to take whatever attorney we could afford to protect her and her job. Plus, the report mentioned the forged letter. It already had a case number and was on file.

I wasn't dumb enough to erase the report's existence. I figured I could talk my way out of it if it ever came up again. Truth was, there wasn't a crime attached to that report. Imogene hadn't gone missing in '79, as Frannie believed. The report could be explained. Redactions happen, especially if a case involves children and when a copy is requested, but not how I did it. Not the original and in its entirety. But, damn it, I never thought it would come up again."

"Except, fifteen years later, my dad saw the redaction and alerted someone there had been a letter because Frannie had told him."

"Yeah. What really upset Internal Affairs and HR once Peter poked around was the missing letter."

A loud scratching noise took over. He could imagine Rodney's scruffy cheek rubbing against the phone as he shook his head.

"That letter was the catalyst for the entire shit show that followed. If he'd never written the letter, his daughter wouldn't have thought he'd done more than let her friend leave. Instead, he created a red flag that even a little girl couldn't look past. When she knew she couldn't rely on her own dad for help, Frannie called the police."

"What happened to the letter?"

"George burned it at the bar." His voice faded as the receiver moved away from his mouth temporarily. Another flick, hiss, and crackle made it clear the man was making his way through a pack of cigs.

"I had no business letting him see it again. But by then, George and I were too deep in the mess. I put a couple blank pages in the evidence envelope instead. Maybe if I'd held on to the letter and redacted it, too, I wouldn't have been forced to hand over my badge. I'll never know. Stupid, stupid, stupid. That's what angered the uppers the most—that I couldn't explain the blank pages, and I couldn't admit what had happened."

"That's why you redacted them in '79. But why not tell the truth to IA in '94? Penny had passed away. She wouldn't suffer." Griffin's forceful exhale fluffed his bangs.

"Frannie was pregnant at the time, and no one wanted to jeopardize her chance at motherhood. After that, well, I guess I hoped it was over. That she had moved on and was happy with her kids. Also, I couldn't confess I'd gotten a 'suspect' drunk on duty and destroyed evidence. I would have lost my pension too."

"What made you decide to step up today?"

If Griffin's hearing was right, Rodney had slapped a table or hard surface in finality.

"You did, Griffin. My life is shit. They say the truth sets you free. I've wanted to make amends for a long time. Step eight in AA, but like I said, I've tried to get sober before."

"You going to stick with sobriety this time?" Griffin asked.

"I'm going to try."

"Frannie received your apology note," Griffin said. How Rodney got to Frances's, Griffin didn't care—as long as he hadn't driven drunk.

"Good. That's an apology I've waited a long time to

give," Rodney said. "Course, I can't say much more than sorry."

"What did my father know?" Griffin held his breath.

"Peter had talked to George Jerome who convinced him the secrecy was purely about Frannie's health and a hope that she'd realize on her own that Imogene had become imaginary. That he'd made up the story about Imogene walking home at night because he'd lost patience and wanted Frannie to start the school year at a new school and have a normal life. Only George and I—and now you—know George moved Imogene from the closet."

"I can't believe my dad stopped there though." But his dad had cried, *"What if I missed something?"*

After a snort, the old cop said, "Trust me. George Jerome is damn persuasive. I think between George's words and Frannie's unexpected pregnancy in '94, Peter decided to protect Frannie like the rest of us. What if learning that Imogene had died and wasn't real for those two years sent Frannie into early labor? He wasn't willing to risk that."

A benefit to a phone call was that Rodney couldn't see the tears building in Griffin's eyes. Yeah, that's something his dad would do; safeguard Frannie and her babies. But Frances deserved, and could handle, the truth now. She deserved closure, no matter her health. Hell, because of her health. And he'd give it to her once his gut told him he knew everything.

"What happens now, Griffin?"

"Now, I talk to George Jerome."

"And then?"

"I take the next right step." *Whatever that may be.*

Only time would tell if Griffin was making the right decision. He did have a team to build, and there was something about Rodney's commitment that meant something. He wanted to give Rodney hope or a second chance. "I'll let you know, but Rodney, kick the alcohol, and I might have a job for you. We'll start small. You'll have to earn my trust. Everything must be on the up and up. Call me when you've gone a month clean and sober."

After Griffin hung up, he compiled the facts for Imogene's file but couldn't make the final note: *Solved*.

Supposedly, over forty years ago, Frannie's father had chosen to protect his daughter from the truth at all costs, even at the expense of their relationship. Unease niggled at Griffin.

Who had the most to lose if the truth came out?

Who continued to protect the lies?

How much had his father known?

The answer to the last was clear. Peter Whittaker didn't know that something happened at the hospital. He'd focused on the mishandled record, turned the case over to Internal Affairs, and returned the check to Frannie, unwilling to endanger her pregnancy. Still, what did the picture on file mean? Why was Darlene Dryker's grave important?

As for the first two: not Rodney. He'd lost his career. Depending on what happened next, his pension too.

But George Jerome? He still had a lot to lose. George Jerome was a pillar in the hospital community, if not in his daughter's heart. Frannie could handle the truth now, sick or otherwise—secrets were proving to be the most detrimental. She wasn't a child. She wasn't pregnant. Frannie had blamed herself and her father for years for Imogene's disappearance anyway. Was it pure stubbornness underlying George Jerome's silence, or was there something darker to hide and greater at risk?

Only one person had all the answers.

54

FRANNIE

SPRING 2022

Frannie opened her sliding glass door, much to Bonnie Bell's delight, though the bird preferred to stay within wing's distance to her cage.

Dr. Cochran would call soon.

"He'd like to speak to you as soon as possible," the nurse had said.

"Then a TeleVisit will do. There isn't any news that I'd rather hear in the doctor's office than in the comforts of my home."

Still, the urgency didn't bode well for Frannie and echoed that every area of her life was in utter shambles. She was nowhere closer to discovering what had happened to her dear friend and had learned what a mess of parenthood she'd made.

Tears rolled down her cheeks as she lifted her face to her ceiling and the universe beyond. She was going to die alone and guilty. With her death, no one would ever know about Imogene. In time, both she and Imogene would be forgotten.

"Forgive me," Frannie said aloud.

"Uh-oh," Bonnie Bell said for the first time in a few days.

Frannie wiped her eyes and stepped close to the cage where Bonnie Bell watched. "I'm sorry. It's okay. Don't let me rub off on you, pretty bird."

Bonnie Bell twittered once then said, "Pretty bird."

Frannie caught her breath. At least she'd been a good foster mom. "I hope your new owner loves you as much as I do." Earlier that day, the shelter had called with the good news.

Bonnie Bell squawked when the computer dinged. The Zoom invitation.

Here we go. She sat at the table, the sun warming her through the bay window.

"Hello, Dr. Cochran."

"Hi, Frances. I hope we gave you enough notice to join a friend or family member."

She'd spent her life protecting her children from danger, but now, she'd protect them from herself.

"I assume you have bad news, but I'm okay alone." Once upon a time, this wouldn't have been a lie, but after the past several days with her family in her life and a renewed hope of finding Imogene, she'd changed.

"Frances, the lymphoma has spread to your organs. We can try chemotherapy and a transplant, but with your history and the number of organs diseased, treatment would need to be closely monitored and in-patient. The chemotherapy would be a maintenance, not a cure."

Her empty house mocked her as she looked around.

"I thought I would fix this," she cried, knowing he assumed she meant cancer. "I seriously thought I could fix this."

55

GRIFFIN

SPRING 2022

The three-mile walk to the music store was refreshing and alleviated the anticipation of nearing the truth. Sorting his thoughts and notes at the office wasn't an option right now, not with Rodney's intel hot off the press and Jean there. He wasn't ready to face her. His poker face was good, but not that good. Besides, from the doctor's call earlier, it sounded as if Jean was running out of time with her mom. Which meant Griffin was too. It was time to talk to good old Grandpa.

After this quick errand and mental health reprieve, he'd return to the office and ask Jean to call Art for his buy-in.

Part of his mental health plan to get through the next several years was to follow his son's example—he was going to start playing the clarinet after work. Tony had suggested it had helped him decompress, albeit after one day of intern work. Better yet, his son had asked Griffin to join him. Why he had walked away from his son's invitation back then astounded Griffin. If he'd learned anything over the past few days, it was that his family meant the world to him. And to be his best self, he needed to strike a healthy balance between engaging with them, addressing his personal needs, and dealing with the rigamarole of life. His someday started now.

Which reminded him . . . Jean's ambivalence about Tony's loss of PI interest pestered him. He wasn't a control freak. Hell, he'd even let Tony intern for him. He revisited his conversation with his son.

Had Tony lied to him about not caring about the job anymore? And why?

Ah, damn! He stumbled over his own stupid feet. Had Tony overheard him and Annie at the hospital? Tonight, he was going to have a long talk with his son.

The scent inside the music store was heady and made Griffin feel seventeen again. The key oil and cork grease welcomed him like old friends.

"How can I help you?" the old, thin man behind the counter asked. Griffin was ninety-nine percent sure it was the same guy who had sold him a clarinet when he was a kid.

"I am looking for a new clarinet." His old one in the attic was attached to aged memories. *Time for a fresh start.*

"I've got one in stock. Say, you're the Whittaker boy, aren't you?"

"Yes, I am. I thought I recognized you."

"It's good to have you back."

"It's good to be back."

"Still playing?"

"I took a long break, but my son plays."

"That's too bad."

"He's not *that* bad," Griffin joked.

"I meant you. Your dad was proud of your talent."

The man must have him confused with someone else after all.

"How's the investigation business going?"

Okay, so the store owner did know something. "It's downright criminal," Griffin said. "My dad was proud of my talent, eh?"

"Sure thing. He came in from time to time to ask me about music careers. He was wrapping his head around the idea of you being a musician. We understood each other, growing up in the same era."

Griffin wasn't sure he believed him. The man wanted to sell an instrument. "Well, he got his other wish. I wrapped my head around the family business instead."

"I knew that too. He continued to come in afterward, looking for ideas about how to get you playing again. Here. Complete this form, and we'll get you out the door with a new clarinet." The man tapped the form with a pen.

Griffin paused before taking the pen, equally confused and touched. His dad had never said a word to Griffin.

He'd gotten as far as adding his name, address, and phone number when someone spoke to him from behind.

"Whittaker, right?"

Griffin put on his best warning look. Looking over a person's shoulder while they supplied contact and payment information was one of the first moves in stealing someone's identity. When he turned around, he was surprised to recognize the guy who worked at the storage facility where Benjamin Dryker lived.

"Hey, man. Yes. Good to see you. You play?"

"Mostly the ukulele, when it's quiet at the sheds. Easy to pack around. I gave Benji your card."

Griffin's heart rate increased for the right reason this time. "He's back from rehab?"

"Yesterday. Still sore, but he's getting around pretty good now."

The man must have become one hell of a drinker.

"Is he there now?"

"He was when I left an hour ago."

Griffin dropped the pen and jogged toward the exit. "Thank you. Good luck with the ukulele."

"But your clarinet," the store owner said.

"I'll be back to buy it," Griffin called over his shoulder. He was outside before he remembered he didn't have his car. He buzzed Jean.

"Pick me up at the McDonald's on the corner of Turk and Fillmore." He had just enough time to buy bribery.

"Good luck," Jean said as Griffin stepped out of her car with the McDonald's bag containing a mouthwatering Filet-O-Fish and fries. Griffin was relieved that Jean didn't argue when he told her where they were headed and that she'd have to stay put in the car.

"We have one chance with Benjamin Dryker, and we can't afford to blow it," he had warned her. In his and his dad's experience, it was never a good idea to have two people knock on someone's door unless they were trying to intimidate someone into talking. In this situation, an old man fresh out of rehab would clam up if he saw two strange people on his doorstep. Plus, Jean still didn't know Imogene had died in '77 or that he'd found *4/1957*.

He made plenty of noise walking up the steps and knocked a friendly *rap-a-tap-tap* on the metal door.

"Who's there?"

"Griffin Whittaker. The front office gave you my card."

"I didn't call you."

"I brought a Filet-O-Fish for you."

"Come in then."

Griffin turned to Jean and gave her the thumbs up before turning the knob.

The room was dark, stale, and filled with smoke. An older man, who couldn't weigh more than a buck and a quarter, sat in an aged recliner. The panel walls were bare except for a clock, a mirror, and a dreamcatcher; the willow hoop hung above a small couch and seemed out of place.

"I remember your father," Dryker said.

Griffin liked a man who didn't beat around the bush.

"He kept his promise," the man said, cigarette burning away in the ashtray.

There were too many promises in this case.

"Which promise?"

"About Imogene. If he hadn't kept his word, you wouldn't need to speak to me now." He pointed at the bag and patted his knee. "I'll take that. The hospital had crap for food."

"Agreed, based on my recent experience," Griffin said and gave the man time to unpack his McLunch. "What kind of promise did my dad keep?"

"How'd you know I liked the fish sandwich?"

Clearly, his new friend, Benjamin, wasn't ready to speak freely after all.

"I poked through your garbage when I was here before."

"Glad you did." The man took a big bite.

"Welcome back from rehab. Sorry to hear about your struggle with alcohol."

Benjamin snorted. "Some detective you are. I haven't drank since I last saw your dad. I had hip surgery."

Griffin's assumption made him cringe. He was acting like a rookie. "My mistake. Why when you last saw my dad?"

"Peter Whittaker promised not to tell anyone about Imogene if I promised to stop drinking for good."

"Frances Jerome hired me. What did my dad vow not to tell?"

Griffin received a sharp nod and again, "Why now?"

"Frannie's dying. She deserves to know the truth about your daughter."

The man closed his eyes as if in pain, the rest of the sandwich dropping with his hands to his lap. "Cancer?"

"Yes." He gave the man some time to digest the information. "Mr. Dryker, I know Imogene died when she was seven."

With shaking hands, Benjamin put the remainder of his meal back in the bag. "Put this in the fridge for me."

Griffin put the bag in a refrigerator that looked like it hadn't been cleaned in years.

"She was doing better, you know? Oh, I know it didn't seem like I was around much, but Imogene was in good hands and doing okay until a few days before the flu. Then the flu took her. My little girl didn't live long enough to use her scholarship and start second grade. But she died believing she would. That's something I hold close on my bad days when I think about how I wasn't there in the end to hold her hand or tell her I loved her."

"When was the last time you saw her?"

Benjamin tugged at his ear and then his nose. "The last good day was the same day as Frannie's transplant. Imogene was scared for her buddy and asked me to stay with her. I stayed longer than usual. I like to think I was a better dad that day. I played cards with her, did a puzzle, and even read to her. Only left when George Jerome let us know Frannie was doing okay and resting. He gave me some cash and said he'd keep an eye on Imogene for me. Meant a lot to me. Like even George Jerome thought I did alright that day."

While the recognition meant one thing to Benjamin, Griffin couldn't help but wonder if it meant something else entirely. With the animosity toward Imogene's dad, and on a day George Jerome should have been preoccupied with his daughter's survival, George was worried about Imogene and whether Benjamin Dryker had money? He gave cash to Dryker? A man he called a drunk?

"I'll always be grateful for that day with Imogene, because the next day her health seemed to fade. When I stopped by each day for a few minutes, she was asleep when she'd normally be climbing the walls."

The dusty dreamcatcher meant to protect someone from bad dreams haunted and held Griffin's attention. "Why did my father keep a note that led me to your wife's grave?"

"I don't remember the first few weeks after Imogene died. I was drunk. George Jerome handled the cremation, even paid for it and gave me money to bury her ashes, but I drank it away. There was no money left for a plot. I was going crazy holding on to my Imogene's ashes, knowing her spirit was trapped in a cardboard box in this run-down trailer. Her mom would've hated that too. Finally, I took a tiger lily bulb to Darlene's grave in case anyone asked why I was digging. Imogene's been at rest with her mother ever since."

No wonder Griffin couldn't find a grave marker online. "You buried her illegally."

Benjamin looked down at his skinny lap. "I'm not sure how, but your dad figured out what I'd done. When he came to see me, he told me he'd found Imogene. We called each other's bluff. I was drunk and stupid, so he drove me to the cemetery to prove it."

"Did you know nine-year-old Frannie thought Imogene was still alive?"

Arthritic fingers smoothed his eyebrows. "Nope. Not until Frannie started calling the trailer after two years had gone by. I didn't know what to think or do. I told her not to call anymore, but George Jerome brought Frannie over to my place and paid me to say my daughter had run away. Jerome said he wanted to protect Frannie from more pain. I didn't want his money. That girl was deeply upset and hurting, and I felt like Imogene was dying all over again.

"Things got worse. Firecracker Frannie wouldn't give up on my girl. She called the police. They dragged me in for questioning."

"Rodney Schultz?" Griffin asked.

"Yeah, I think that was his name. I recognized him from the hospital. He put me in the slammer overnight. To sober up, he said."

"Then what?"

"Then the calls from Frannie, everything, stopped. At least until your dad showed up almost fifteen years later."

Griffin tested what he'd sorted out. "And my dad promised not to tell anyone about the illegal burial as long as you promised to stop drinking."

"We both stuck to our word, sounds like."

"Yes, you both did."

"What happens now? Will you tell someone I broke the law?"

An idea percolated inside Griffin's mind, one that would put an end to the secrets Benjamin Dryker couldn't afford to keep. "If I can square things with the cemetery and legitimize Imogene's burial without causing you money, trouble, or pain, would you be okay with that?"

Tears trickled down the man's weathered face. "I'd be grateful to my dying day."

Jean faced him eagerly when he returned to the car. "How did it go?"

A loaded question if there ever was one.

After settling, he turned in his seat and rested his hands on her shoulders.

"We found Imogene."

56

JEAN

SPRING 2022

Jean gasped and tried to read Griffin's face. "Where is she? Is she alive?" She looked over Griffin's shoulder. Would a grown Imogene step outside the trailer at any second? Would her mom be reunited with her long-lost friend?

Oh, please, please, please let a grown Imogene appear.

"No," he said solemnly. "She's not, but Jean, it's complicated."

Gah. Isn't everything? "I can handle it. I have to, for Mom." Her mom still wasn't taking her calls, and there'd been no update after her call with Dr. Cochran. Guilt and fear were tearing Jean apart.

"Imogene died when the girls were seven."

Jean never learned why Griffin was in the hospital, but now she wondered if he might need to return. "I'm calling Annie. You're seriously not okay."

She wasn't kidding, but Griffin chuckled. "Listen, I

know it sounds crazy. I reacted like you when I found out a few days ago."

First, she glanced at the trailer, and then glared at the man beside her. "And you're just telling me now?!"

His hands resting on his knees turned palms up. "I'm sorry. I technically hadn't found her."

She had to give him that. "But you've found her now?" She gasped and pointed toward the trailer. "Is her body in there?"

"Her ashes were buried without interment rights with her mother. Plot 4/1957 at Cedar's Cemetery."

She gasped and covered her lips with her fingertips before repeating, "4/1957." Her heart exploded in her chest as his earlier words caught up to her. "But who went missing in 1979? Who have we been searching for?"

"It's complicated," he said again.

The repetition and his suspicious tone made the hair rise on her arms and the back of her neck.

"What am I supposed to tell my mom?!"

He shook his head vehemently. "Nothing, yet. I will explain everything when I can. When I understand. For now, tell me everything your mom remembers about her bone marrow transplant and when the flu hit the hospital."

Though her brain felt scrambled, and she couldn't remember what she'd already told him, she extracted the random tidbits her mother had shared about the flu and transplant; including the dream about Gargamel coming to her room and the follow-on conversation with the doctor, who assured Frannie that she was a threat to Gargamel and not the other way around.

"Did you touch base with the doctor about the DNA?"

"He explained that a donor's DNA is introduced in a bone marrow transplant and can last in the system for several months, but they wouldn't have known or looked for this back then. Not that they needed to because she didn't have a . . ."

Griffin scribbled in his yellow notepad as she spoke, circling the words and drawing lines between the bubbles.

"Griffin, what aren't you telling me?"

Closing the yellow pad, he turned toward her and stared intently.

"Jean, do you trust me?"

Her answer, inside and out, was immediate. "Yes. Yes, I do."

"Talk to Art. Then text your grandfather and tell him I need to talk to him. Alone."

57

GRIFFIN

SPRING 2022

With long strides, Griffin bounded up the steps to George Jerome's front door, which swung open before he could knock.

George extended his hand with a forced smile and squeezed Griffin's a little too tightly.

A sure sign of defensiveness. Good.

Skipping the introductions, Griffin said, "Thanks for seeing me."

George shut the door and pointed to a leather chair while he took a seat on the couch. "Can I get you something to drink?"

"No thank you," Griffin said. "I'll try not to take up too much of your time." It was time to learn how much George Jerome wanted Griffin to know. For starters, Griffin would let George believe he knew as little as possible.

"Jean didn't say why you wanted to speak with me, but I met Peter Whittaker, presumably your father, in this same spot. It's unsettling that my daughter didn't tell me she was looking for Imogene again. And to involve Jean, who doesn't understand . . . I'm glad you didn't hesitate to contact me."

Griffin pulled out the picture of young Frannie, refusing to verify who had hired him, when he'd been hired, or how much Jean did or did not know. "You are right. I've been hired to find Imogene Dryker, and I know she was reported missing in 1979 by your daughter."

George closed his eyes and patted the area above his heart as if the reminder pained him.

"Why did my dad save this picture of your daughter?" He slid it across the table.

George hesitated, perhaps surprised not to be peppered with questions about Imogene from the start.

Head held high, the retired doctor stood and walked to his roll-top desk. "I gave it to him." He unlocked a drawer and pulled out a thick envelope that reminded Griffin of the days of one-hour photo shops. When he returned to the sofa, he spread the photos on the coffee table.

The man's actions were self-assured. "A picture speaks a thousand words," he said.

Ah-ha. The lost roll of film.

Most of them were of Frannie alone. Oddly enough, there were several pictures of an empty beanbag chair. The rest included one with Frannie's mom and a few from the school's open house.

Frannie's father tapped the pictures of the empty

beanbag, and he pointed at the empty space next to Frannie on Griffin's copy. "And that's Imogene."

Since Jerome didn't know Griffin had learned from Rodney that Imogene had been anything but alive, he went to great lengths to pretend to be shocked.

While Griffin let his eyes pop from his head and his jaw hang to his lap, there was no rush made to regather the photos. Frannie's dad sat back on the couch unconcerned, as if he had had this exact conversation before, and it had worked out to his liking.

And he had, with Griffin's father.

Rodney's advice that George Jerome could be persuasive settled in. Griffin leaned forward, resting his elbows on his knees. He'd work backward. Besides, he couldn't let George Jerome know that he knew about the closet in 1977. Not yet. "What happened in 1979?"

George's eyes narrowed, and his eyebrows pulled down as if he was concentrating. "We thought we were going to lose Frannie that night during the flu, but we ended up losing Imogene. When Frannie came to the next morning, we didn't know how we'd tell her. She insisted Imogene had slept with her the night before. Then, out of nowhere, Imogene was with us. All the time. Everywhere. None of us knew what to do."

"Why didn't you tell her?" Griffin asked.

"That Imogene had died? That Frannie was imagining her? Her potential for relapse terrified us. I can't explain what it's like to be a parent watching my child dying before my eyes. She had such a tremendous fight ahead of her, one that Imogene had helped her fight until that point.

"We asked her doctor what he thought we should do. He said to give her time, that it might be grief, and it would pass, but not to jeopardize her physical recovery. Understand, there wasn't an internet back then that we could turn to for our own research. There weren't counselors and life coaches on every corner offering alternative mental wellness. No WebMD or easy ways to find support groups."

When Frannie's dad paused, Griffin avoided filling the silence. With enough time, George would keep talking.

"Frannie started recovering, as we had hoped. St. Agnes was as supportive as they could be. Believe me when I say, we thought Frannie would move on without Imogene once she was better, once she was in remission."

"Except, she didn't move on," Griffin said. "Until you made her?"

George's remorse was evident as he covered his mouth and shook his head in dismay. "Yes. Until I made her. She was in full remission and had a chance at a normal life with real people. You've got to understand, this had been going on for two years. The longer it continued, Frannie's sanity could be questioned. Every psychologist and psychiatrist we spoke to suggested medication or hospitalization for our little girl simply because her best friend was someone no one else could see."

Griffin took an even breath. Though he knew there was much more to this story, such as what Rodney had divulged, he also knew that, in this moment, George Jerome was telling the truth about his and Frannie's state of mind in '79.

"We thought the new school would make a difference since Frannie couldn't pretend to be with Imogene. Once we'd told Frannie she would change schools, it seemed Imogene appeared less and less over the spring and summer. Our plan was working—or so we thought. I jumped the gun that night of the open house. I was both frustrated and overconfident. I was afraid for her to attend the open house with Imogene and have the teachers or students reject her for being different. Fourth graders aren't as unaware of or as open to oddities as younger kids. I honestly didn't think a few days or weeks would matter. But I was a fool and pushed too hard."

Griffin cringed inwardly as the father's regret was tangible.

"She's thought the worst of you," Griffin said. "Why didn't you tell her the truth when she was older? Why not now?"

He looked away from Griffin and at the floor.

"Dr. Jerome?"

"This is all I will say, and I can't stress it enough. Frannie must never remember the night Imogene died. She would have more questions that must go unanswered. Now more so than ever, the truth of that night would break her. You're going to have to trust me when I say that I know in my heart that I made the right choice not to tell her Imogene died the night Frannie was feverish, and I never will. And now Frannie has cancer again."

The manipulative tone made Griffin's skin crawl. *Won't work on me, mister.*

"Do you have children?"

"A son."

"Then, father to father, you understand why I'd protect my family."

Interesting tactic. Too bad for the man of the year, Griffin had learned years ago that a commonality was often shared to ensure cooperation, and Griffin wasn't in the mood to cooperate with the decades-old deceit. He let his silence fill the room.

Brushing a shaking hand through his thinning hair, George sighed. "I'll continue to protect Frannie, if that's the last thing I'll ever do."

". . . if that's the last thing I'll ever do." The same words from Frannie's post-transplant dream.

Griffin had the oddest sensation his father had sat in this chair and heard this same speech. It had been enough for his father. Perhaps because Frannie had been pregnant at the time, or for another reason he'd never know. But Griffin wasn't his father.

"'Now more so than ever?' Because she has cancer again?"

"Yes."

"And in '94, the reason you didn't tell her was because she was pregnant?"

George paused then said, "You're good. Yes."

"And in '79, the reason not to tell her was because she

was finally healthy and you didn't want her, or anyone else, to question her sanity?"

This time, Griffin didn't wait for a reply. "And in 1977, the reason not to tell her was because she was recovering from her transplant and still fighting leukemia."

Frannie's dad lifted his chin. "You clearly disagree with my parenting."

Griffin's eyebrows furrowed, and he puckered his lips as if confused. Then he said, "It's just that your daughter is stronger than you give her credit for. She wants to know what happened. Has always wanted to know. She's ready for the truth, so I have to ask myself: why are you so afraid to tell it?"

"You have no idea what you're talking about. If your son ever gets cancer, call me, and we can revisit my choices and your opinions." The man began to collect the photos spread across the table.

"I know about Narnia and how you found Imogene."

The photos were dropped back to the table. George Jerome glared, knowing Griffin had set him up.

"You talked to Rodney Schultz," George said. "His loyalty and pension mean nothing anymore, I suppose."

Griffin wasn't going to honor that comment with a confirmation that Rodney was terrified of losing everything and had been most of his life because of George Jerome's secrets.

"If you know about the night Imogene died then I'm surprised you can't put two and two together as to why my daughter would hold herself responsible. You don't have to agree, but I know I did what was best for my child, my wife, Nurse Penny, and the hospital."

And yourself, buddy. You've done what's best for you too. "But not for Benjamin Dryker."

Rolling his shoulders back and turning his head slightly away, Jerome said, "No. That's one of my regrets." The talk-no-walk sentiment echoed Rodney's.

Griffin visualized the details on his yellow notepad. "On the day of Frannie's transplant, you gave Ben Dryker money and told him you'd watch Imogene. Why?"

George started with surprise, looked away, and then stared at Griffin intently. "So?"

"You knew he'd probably use the money on alcohol when Imogene needed him."

"What has this got to do with anything?"

"Honestly?" Griffin shrugged. "I don't know. I just know it does. I think you wanted Ben to leave for some reason on the day of Frannie's transplant. You wanted him to leave badly enough that you left your daughter's side after a life-saving treatment to give him cash, encouraging him to go. But why?"

"Your skepticism is a waste of my time. I'm a doctor. We knew Imogene was worried and that Ben had been there all day. Sally and I had each other while Ben was a single dad. I wanted to give him a break."

A snort escaped Griffin. "You wanted to give a man you considered a horrible dad a break from fatherhood? Not buying it."

George turned red. "Do not presume to know how I felt about Ben Dryker."

Griffin tapped his temple. "It's all up here. Your daughter wrote about him in her diary. As well as your contempt toward him."

The man's lips turned downward. "I remember the diary vaguely. I didn't know she included me." He shook his head. "Let's not be silly; you can't believe everything a child wrote."

George Jerome looked at his watch pointedly.

It was time to move on.

"You paid for and handled Imogene's cremation."

"Of course we did. We cared for her. She was Frannie's friend. I knew Ben Dryker would be useless . . ." He stopped abruptly, as if realizing he'd validated the accusations of his scorn for the man.

"And you wanted to handle it expediently." Griffin hedged his bet there was more to this story. "Why, I wonder?"

George pointed at him. "What are you getting at?"

"Benjamin Dryker said Imogene was getting better and doing well until her health made a drastic turn the day after Frannie's transplant."

"There is little that is fair and predictable about cancer." George Jerome stood and moved to stare out the window. "Their immune systems were always a concern."

Creating distance, Griffin thought. He was on to something.

"After a transplant, would Frannie's immune system be more compromised, or less so?"

The doctor stiffened. "More so."

Fixated on the father's profile, Griffin carried on.

"And what about donors? Do they need to take extra precautions after donating bone marrow or stem cells?"

Wrinkles fanned the corner of George Jerome's narrowing eye before he responded. "Yes. Why?"

"Dr. Jerome, I must tell my client about the night of Imogene's death, Narnia, and how you moved her body. This is your chance to tell me if there is anything else I should know."

He turned to face Griffin. "You're implying there's more to Imogene's death and that it involves me?"

"That's what I'm asking."

Tapping his chest, George said, "Do you know how much money I've raised for the hospital and children like my daughter and Imogene?"

Yes, the entire Bay Area does. You have a lot to lose. "Your efforts have been commendable."

"I've dedicated my life to helping people, to paying forward the care and support the hospital gave my family. I've made doing so my life's purpose."

A persuasion tactic.

Confident he was on track, a calmness settled around Griffin. "Paying it forward, or paying it back out of guilt?"

George rolled his eyes in disbelief. "What do you want from me? You already know, and I haven't denied, that I found Imogene in a hiding spot she shared with Frannie. Yes, I took her body back to her room and let the hospital think she died in her bed to shield my daughter, her dedicated nurse, and the hospital. Imogene's death was tragic, and she didn't deserve to die alone in a dark closet. But the flu was beyond our control, and it happened more than four decades ago. What else could there be?"

As soon as George finished speaking, Griffin jumped in. "Whose bone marrow was donated for Frannie's transplant?"

George froze and whitened. "What? What are you talking about?"

"Frannie's DNA was different after her transplant, and it's my understanding that this happens when a patient receives stem cells from a donor."

"Where are you getting this information?"

"Her medical file, her doctor, and YouTube-iversity." No need to drag Joe into this.

The man laughed derisively. "And now you think you're an oncologist. I want you to leave."

"Listen, Dr. Jerome. I know who you are—a father in a position of authority who would have done 'anything and everything' to save his daughter—that's what you told Jean, right? That you would have done anything and everything?"

"Who do you think you are, detective?"

The shaken man said *detective* like it was a bad word.

"I'm a persistent detective, Dr. Jerome. I trust my instincts about humans. I might not be able to clarify why I think something worse happened to Imogene or why I think you manipulated Ben Dryker and Rodney Schultz, but I do. I know that when something doesn't make sense, it probably isn't the whole truth.

"You're always going to make an excuse not to tell

your daughter what happened to Imogene. Why? You're not protecting Penny anymore. Rodney has nothing left to lose. I keep asking myself: what's George Jerome afraid of? My guess is that you're afraid of the truth. And I get it; that fear is so powerful that you're not going to tell me the answers either. But I will ask the right people the right questions until I figure it out."

While most men in their eighties might not seem threatening, it took all Griffin's pride to stand still as George Jerome stormed toward him, stopping inches from his face. Spittle sprinkled Griffin's face as the man threatened him.

"Go ahead, pry and try to ruin my reputation, but dig too deep, and I'll take your father's legacy and Rodney Schultz with me."

Griffin wasn't dumb enough to laugh in a scared man's face. They both knew he had nothing on Peter Whittaker, and as for Rodney, well, the dude had lost everything but his pension.

The angry man continued, "Your false accusations will ruin your firm, Whittaker. You'll be accusing a philanthropist of wrongdoing. Your paranoia and skepticism will turn you into the type of man who cares more about proving himself right than supporting his community and saving lives."

Yes, Griffin could imagine the headlines and how people might blame Griffin for stopping a man from doing some pretty amazing things, but if he lost his business due to his integrity, he would still be able to look at himself in the mirror.

"My lawyer will be in touch," George said.

The doctor's direct glare was not a threat, it was a bluff.

Storming to his door, George opened it, and Griffin followed his exit cue proudly.

Before stepping over the threshold, Griffin pulled out the picture of Frannie and Imogene, their smiling faces and crochet-covered heads resting against each other, and left it on the door-side table.

"I'm informing my clients about the night of the flu and the closet. You should tell Jean and Art the entire truth before I figure it out and tell them for you. It will be better coming from you."

One glance at the picture and the steam released from George Jerome like a pressure cooker. His eyes filled with tears as he picked up the photo and closed the door in Griffin's face.

58

FRANCES

SPRING 2022

The song, "I Hope You Dance" filled the room. Jean calling again, for the millionth time. Frannie didn't know what to say to her. Or to Art. Some might think it had been selfish to call Douglas and ask him to tell them about the turn with her cancer and that she needed to be alone. Frannie felt wiped out, defeated, and didn't know how to comfort them—she had thought she'd been learning, but now it was too late.

Too bad she couldn't turn her phone off and hide it in a drawer. She needed it. Her deathbed was being delivered today.

When Frannie could no longer care for herself, a hospice worker would help her, and while she wasn't in a rush to die, being prepared gave her a semblance of control—an impression she desperately needed today. She wanted to be the one to decide when her bed was delivered and where it was set up. She knew which of her personal items would bring her the most comfort. If she made the arrangements now, the space would feel like her new bedroom instead of her final one. This she could still do for herself.

Jean tried to call again. Bonnie Bell danced along Frannie's forearm.

After smooching the bird, she encouraged Bonnie Bell to step atop her cage. Standing aside, Frannie surveyed her living room.

She'd tip the delivery men extra to help her rearrange the furniture as necessary. This was her favorite room in the house, and she would situate her bed where she could stare out the windows at her garden and the bay.

Originally, she'd anticipated using the larger space to accommodate her family too. They'd all fit comfortably in the spacious room next to the kitchen and could visit easily. A few short days ago, she'd thought about how much she'd enjoy cooking with Art and how she could watch him move about the kitchen she'd designed with such care. And lately, despite the circumstances, she had fooled herself into believing they enjoyed spending more time with her too.

The voice mail from the twins shredded her heart into a million pieces. Had she felt a helpless pain like this before? Yes, when Imogene vanished.

"Mom?" Jean cried. "Dad told us . . ." Her sobs prevented her from saying more.

Art cleared his throat until he could speak. "We love you, Mom."

The silence, only interrupted by guttural noises, made her ache more, if possible.

"We'll talk to Grandpa." Her daughter was no longer asking for permission.

Would they demand answers about Imogene, or would they tell him she was dying too? Would either make a difference and spur the answers she deserved?

Douglas's booming voice interrupted. "They're going to be okay, Frank. Hugs, my eternal love." And the line went dead.

Was that a knock?

The delivery men said they'd call her a half-hour before their arrival, but perhaps they'd rang her during one of Jean's calls. When she opened the door, there was no one there.

"Who are you?" Frannie called out to thin air. "No letter this time?" She didn't have time for a prankster or a coward with a guilty conscience who couldn't tell the truth or help find Imogene. She was sick to death of those kinds of people. If she wasn't concerned about Bonnie Bell, she'd slam the door for effect.

Two hours later, she put the last pillowcase on and looked over her well-made bed. The seagull-print flannels and duvet disguised the electric bed just as she'd hoped. She pulled the side table closer and added Charles Dickens's *Oliver Twist*. Maybe she should post her ultimate resting place on Facebook. Jean and Art would probably like the post out of guilt.

KNOCK. KNOCK.

The delivery guys were long gone, but Frannie had neglected to follow them out and lock the door—an oversight she'd never made before. Her phone had fallen silent some time ago, thank goodness. The uninvited visitor was probably Jean or another joker—she didn't have the energy for either.

But she was already dying. Feeling brave and reckless, Frannie shouted, "Come on in!"

Bonnie Bell sang, seeming to join her in throwing caution to the wind.

Her interloper was quiet. Frannie felt her presence before she heard her. She looked over her shoulder at the woman standing there, who was about her age with gentle blue eyes and red hair styled like Ginger's from *Gilligan's Island*.

Recognition overwhelmed Frannie as she reached for her bed to steady herself. It couldn't be.

"Oh, honey. I heard you've been looking for me."

"Imogene."

59

GRIFFIN

SPRING 2022

Griffin sat in his quiet office after Jean and Art left. When they'd told him Frannie's cancer was untreatable, he'd said, "You need to tell your grandfather you're out of time and that he needs to confide in you."

How would George react to his daughter's looming expiration date? Not a praying man, Griffin hoped Jean's grandfather would be honest with her so that Griffin didn't have to follow his suspicions, keep digging, and hand the heartbreak to her and her family.

Jean had asked, "What happened with Grandpa? Art and I need to tell him about Mom, and we can't wait any longer to tell her we found Imogene. We will give her the closure and peace she deserves."

After he shared everything he had learned about Imogene's death, he said, "But I think there's more."

The truth was a blow to Jean and Art. He wasn't surprised by their shock. Learning their grandfather had fabricated where Imogene had died and abused his authority and administrative knowledge to make sure her death remained unquestioned, and at Benjamin Dryker's expense, had stirred up unfathomable thoughts and emotions that were difficult to sort out.

"More?" Jean asked.

"How is that possible?" Art rubbed his eyes.

"Let's give him a chance to explain it to you first. I'll be on deck."

"It's bad, isn't it?" she said.

Art closed his eyes tightly. "As if moving a little girl's body from a closet to her bed and lying about it aren't bad enough."

Griffin nodded. "My father used to say, 'Sometimes the only thing more shocking than the lie a person will tell is the truth.'"

The alarm on his phone went off. At last, it was time for his video call with Nurse Bowman. After the last few days, Griffin didn't expect the school nurse to have something mind-blowing to share, but he was selfishly curious to learn if his dad had spoken to her.

Nurse Bowman's energy and love for life oozed across the miles and through the screen.

He'd no sooner introduced himself when she offered, "I remember Peter Whittaker. He contacted me in 1994 after Frannie hired him."

"My father." Something about the nurse encouraged him to tell her, "I didn't know whether he'd met you. He discarded his case notes, except for this photo of young Frannie Jerome." He held up the photo for her to see. It was too soon to share Imogene's resting place.

Her features softened further. "I assume you know about Imogene then. Frannie was such a darling girl. As I told your father, we all sinned for what we believed to be a good reason."

"Meaning?"

"We were excited to have the girls join us for second grade. The staff developed a curriculum that would catch them up with their peers—Imogene especially. Frannie had been homeschooled, but Imogene's education had been interrupted since kindergarten. When Imogene passed away before school could begin, the entire staff was crushed."

Griffin rested his elbows on his desk, his chin in his hand.

"The thought that we almost lost both children was unbearable. Frannie's parents and doctors were concerned the truth about Imogene's death could be detrimental to her recovery. None of us wanted her to suffer further, so we—the Jeromes, Father Kelly, and the staff—met and agreed we wouldn't encourage Imogene's existence in Frannie's mind, but we wouldn't discount that she was real to Frannie while she fought cancer."

"How did you convince the students to go along with it?"

"We didn't have to. They were kids. Frannie wasn't blatant about Imogene's friendship, and she kept to herself. Most of the time, she appeared to be playing alone, nothing remarkable to other kids with imaginations. We thought her subtlety was a sign that she understood, at some subconscious level, that no one else could see Imogene, and we hoped she would let Imogene go when she was ready, perhaps when she no longer feared cancer. Each week, I checked her vitals and talked to her about Imogene."

Griffin waited as the nurse seemed to collect her thoughts.

"Griffin, for thirty-five years I was a nurse at a school where their entire goal was to teach faith in a higher power that many don't believe exists. Believe it or not, I began to believe Imogene did exist. Frannie loved her profoundly, and if love doesn't make someone real, what does? Who was I to say if Imogene was real or not? If she was at Frannie's side or not?"

"I get your point." He recalled his conversation with St. Agnes's receptionist when she'd told him about the scholarship. *"I've heard time and again that she was a real angel."*

The nurse continued, "Once Frannie had gone into partial remission, her parents, Father Kelly, and I met again. We agreed to pretend to separate the girls for a few activities and field trips to see what would happen. But each time, Frannie felt ill. We decided we couldn't force the issue and that Frannie would let go of Imogene when she was healthy and ready.

"In the spring of 1979, the Jeromes decided Frannie would change schools for the fall. I thought this was a good idea and that the switch could be a healthy transition. As Frannie got used to the idea, she spoke less and less of Imogene and began to join group games at recess. She seemed to be letting go, one week at a time."

Frannie's diary and retelling of the night she'd come from the open house played through his mind. "But George Jerome rushed her."

"Yes. I told your father that George Jerome had wiped out years of patience and care, and if they'd waited a few short weeks, Frannie might have said goodbye on her own terms."

"According to Frannie's diary, you visited her after Imogene disappeared but still didn't tell her the truth."

She shook her head. "It wasn't my truth to tell or my right to overstep her parents' decisions. She was nine. It was 1979, and very different from how adults interact with children these days. Frannie was depressed, grieving, and ashamed. I sat with her, as I had in the past, and suggested she write about Imogene in the diary I had given her years before.

"But my conscience suffered. I checked with the Jeromes a few months later, and they assured me Frannie had adjusted well to her new school. In fact, she had many friends who called her every day after school. But when I heard from your father years later that Frannie had hired him, I accepted Frannie had not moved on as we adults had all pretended. It had been careless of us to leave the burden on Frannie's shoulders and to assume her loss had been underwhelming and forgettable with the distraction of youth, a new school, and friends. Your presence confirms my worst fears—she never moved on entirely. May she someday forgive us the grief and pain we've caused."

Oh man, the woman looked as if she was about to cry.

Griffin decided then and there that he would not advise her that Frannie's cancer had returned. But there was something he'd be honored to share.

"I know from Frannie's diary that you made a positive impact on her life, Ms. Bowman. She speaks, or writes, highly of you. You should know that."

"Thank you for telling me, Griffin. Might I say, you've turned out to be an angel yourself for helping Frannie and consoling me. Your father must be very proud of you."

Oof. Caught off guard, Griffin choked up, wishing he weren't on Skype with his emotions on display. "He died a few years ago."

The nurse rested her palm on her chest. "Then it sounds like you have a guardian angel looking over your shoulder too."

The lump in his throat wouldn't be going away anytime soon, so he simply nodded and kept his sign-off short. "Thank you. Take care."

"You too, Griffin. You too."

Standing up, he pushed his father's chair against his desk. Griffin took time turning off the lights and making his way to the exit. At the door, he looked about the space he had shared with his father for many years, the same space Tony hoped to share with Griffin. Finding purpose wasn't about adding one goal to his life. Purpose was a fluid collection of people, dreams, and accomplishments. Leaving a legacy wasn't about money, property, or a business. Legacy was the lasting impression you left on your family and friends. "You aced leaving your stamp on our world, Dad. You aced it."

ANNIE AND TONY had their heads close together, starting when he walked into the kitchen. Oh crap, was he in trouble again?

"Tony," Griffin said. "We need to talk."

"I can't, Dad." His son turned away. "I've got homework to do."

Griffin pulled out a chair for Annie and sat down beside her at the kitchen table. "We found Imogene Dryker," he told his son's back.

Tony's head lifted, his shoulders hitched up, and then they dropped again, deflated.

Damn it. He'd failed his kid. He was like his father in all ways, both good and bad.

Griffin cleared his throat, eager to say what he needed to say before another anxiety attack could sneak up and ruin the critical moment. "Your grandad didn't want me to be a musician. He wanted me to be like him. We fought constantly about the business, so much so that I don't think I really knew my dad. I held on to an idea, a story of who or what I thought he was about."

Annie rested her hand on Griffin's back, her usual method of encouragement.

Tony turned around, crossed his arms, and stared at the floor.

"I'm afraid that we"—he pointed to his son and then tapped his own heart—"are making the same mistake. I'm not the best detective or dad, but I think you overheard me at the hospital. Now, you're trying to ensure my health and happiness at the cost of your own.

"When I was your age, all I wanted was to have choices. I thought to be a good dad, and to love you the best I could, I should give you what my dad never gave me."

Annie patted the empty spot across from Griffin, and their son sat down.

"But I get it now. I wasn't giving you a choice—I was taking one away. You wouldn't be following in my footsteps; you'd be taking your own."

60

FRANCES

SPRING 2022

Frannie came to, her eyelashes fluttering against her new duvet. She blinked rapidly to adjust to the sunlight coming through her bay window. She had passed out, but it couldn't have lasted long, because she was splayed across her new bed, the balls of her feet still on the floor.

Imogene.

Her breath was quick, her mouth open. All she needed to do was lift her head and see if Imogene was really there. Just a simple turn of the head, and yet, it was the most terrifying moment of her life.

"Oh, honey. I scared the Dickens out of you."

Legs shaking, Frannie scooted onto her bed. "Is it really you?"

Imogene rushed to her side.

Too afraid to reach for her, as if touching her would make Imogene disappear, Frannie hugged herself.

"It's really me."

Frannie didn't hesitate any longer to ask Imogene for the answers she'd craved for years.

"Imogene, where have you been?"

"Lay back, Frannie. You're shaking." Imogene moved to sit in the chair facing the bed.

"But Imogene, what happened to you?"

"We were kids. It was a long time ago."

"Not for me," Frannie said. "It's like yesterday."

"We're together now," Imogene said. "That's all that matters."

"But where have you been? Why have you waited so long to find me?"

"I've been . . . away. But I heard you've been looking hard for me and that you're sick. Now I'm here."

"Please tell me what my dad did when we were nine."

Imogene looked away. "Your dad was guilty of being concerned about you. That's all. He wasn't to blame for me leaving."

"Then who was?"

Imogene's silence spoke volumes as she faced Frannie again. "Me?" Frannie asked. "This was all my fault?"

My father. A lifetime of blaming him. Mother . . . Oh god, my children.

"No. No," Imogene said in soothing tones. "Of course not. We were nine, and you didn't need me anymore. Your life was changing. It was time for you to make new friends at your new school."

"You ran away like they said?" Frannie asked, torn between relief that her dad was innocent and the unnerving hurt that Imogene had moved on with her life without a backward glance. "But my dad forged the letter. I know he did. How could you stay away all these years? I assumed the worst. About everything. This has defined my life."

Imogene's eyes filled with tears, and she couldn't hold Frannie's stare. "Oh, honey. Please don't ask me more. Trust me. If I could have stayed, I swear I would never have left your side. The only truth you need to know is your dad wanted to protect you. Isn't that reason enough for his actions? Wouldn't you go to any length to ensure your children's future?"

A gut-wrenching sob exploded from Frannie. "My dad . . . my kids . . . I've ruined their lives because I thought someone killed you. My entire life has been about this."

Imogene began to cry next to her. "If I could have let you know, I would have."

"But I don't understand. Did you try? All these years, I've been so unhappy."

"Have you? Always? If we had stayed friends, maybe you wouldn't have met your husband or had Jean and Art. Life is funny that way. We can either look back at our lives with regret or accept the past doesn't exist and be happy about today and hopeful for tomorrow."

"Will they forgive me? My family?"

"You know where to start, Frannie. Be yourself, as you always were with me. Let's cherish the time we all have together."

They sat in silence, letting the tears flow until acceptance created the only comfort.

"I don't know how many tomorrows I have, do I? I need to make the most of each day. How long can you stay?" Frannie asked, frustrated she'd never know the answers but more frightened to lose Imogene again.

"As long as you need me."

61

JEAN

SPRING 2022

Jean's fingers clutched the pastry box. "Remember, Griffin said to let Grandpa deal with our silence and fill in the gaps, not us."

"Fine. I wouldn't know where to begin anyway. Why the donuts?" Art asked as Jean knocked on the front door.

"I've seen Griffin ply people with food. It softens them up."

Art said, "Remind me to withhold information from you in the future."

"Speaking of which, what's the 'big, good news?'"

"Now?"

"Anything positive would help."

He withdrew a folded paper from his pocket, opened it with a *snap*, and held it up for her to read.

Her eyes glistened. "You adopted Bonnie Bell? Art, next to Imogene, this is the best gift to Mom."

He brought his fists to his chest and flapped his elbows as if he had wings. "I'm a proud Papa Parrot."

When the door remained unanswered, Art jiggled the knob. It was unlocked.

They found Grandpa slouching in a chair on the back porch, contemplating a dandelion.

Perhaps Jean should be concerned why he was still in his pajamas in the afternoon, hair pointing in all directions, but she and Art didn't look much better. She had bags under her eyes from a sleepless night and countless cries.

There were no hugs or use of nicknames. She figured he knew why they were there. At least, he partly knew.

With a fond smile, he slowly twirled the yellow bud.

Jean sat beside him in a wicker chair while Art leaned against the wooden porch rail, arms crossing his chest.

"How much did he tell you?" he asked without looking at them.

When Art leaned forward to speak, Jean shook her head. *Not yet.* Her gut said to hold off a few more minutes.

Art bobbed his head, hands sliding from his armpits to his pockets.

A breeze teased Grandpa's hair as he lifted a heavy hand to the armrest and tapped it slowly. "Your guy, Griffin, is right. The truth is better coming from me, but now is not the time. Let's focus on your mom's recovery and go from there." He looked up with an earnest smile. "Okay?"

He reminded Jean of Lexi when she wanted to do

something one more time. Jean dreaded telling another parent what she needed to say.

Standing to move beside her brother, the twins wrapped supporting arms around each other's waists.

"Grandpa." Her eyes grew moist. "Mom's cancer has spread to her organs."

Jean jumped forward to grip his wrist as he tilted to one side, and Art lunged to keep the chair from tipping over. Once settled, their grandpa's chest collapsed before her eyes, as if his heart had shattered into a million pieces, leaving a void.

The grief was too much. All of it—the truth, deception, Imogene's death, her mom's health. As her strong grandpa wept, his pain coupled with hers, and she was finally able to let go. Hers, Grandpa's, and Art's tears all ran together, soaking each other while they clung to one another.

Standing over him, Jean hugged him as if he were her child. "Grandpa," she spoke into his crown. "It's time for the full truth. Mom's afraid to die without finding closure for Imogene."

After a while, their grandpa pushed gently at them until they moved away.

His voice was soft when he finally spoke. "The summer when Frannie was three, she thought dandelions were her friends. Sally and I couldn't mow the lawn for several months." He smiled through his tears. "It was a relief when she grew out of the phase because, as you know, the weed grows year-round here. What I'd give to go back to that summer and live it all over again." He tucked the petals into his pocket and patted it.

Jean was struck by the significance of Dandelion, her mom's imaginary friend shared with Lexi, and how symbolic dandelions were of life. Some people considered them bothersome weeds to be yanked from the ground. While others thought them resilient blossoms that signified spring and new life. And over time, each floret grew and transitioned to a seed head, its billowy wisps a wish on a stem for children and adults, offering endless aspirations and optimism. Jean would never look at a dandelion again without recognizing the innocence and hope it offered. Each growth, and each wish, would remind her of her mom. Of Imogene.

Neighborhood sounds carried across the backyard: barking dogs, lawn mowers, and cheerful chatter. Each everyday noise belied the overwhelming distress bearing down on Jean and the yard where her mother once played.

Even while seated, Grandpa's arms appeared heavy, pulling his shoulders down.

A sticky maple donut found its way to Jean's lips.

"I can't explain what it's like to be a parent, watching my child dying before my eyes," he said helplessly.

Lexi's sweet face swam before Jean, and she ached to hold her daughter close and never let her go. "What happened, Grandpa?"

He grimaced. "They say hindsight is 20/20, but I've racked my brains for more than four decades asking myself what I could have done differently to save them both."

Art looked down at his feet, rubbed the back of his neck, and then looked at Jean, worried. His eyes said, *There's no turning back if we don't like what he confides.*

She nodded sadly. *I know.*

Art said, "Start with what you did, and we'll do our best to sort out the answers and next steps, whatever they might be."

"I'm afraid to tell you," Grandpa said. "I don't want you to think about me differently. Please remember when I tell you what I did that I didn't know what else to do to save Frannie. I was petrified to lose our baby."

"We'll try," Jean said.

Their grandpa pulled a handkerchief from the pocket of his pajamas and wiped his face.

"You already know some of this, Jean, but Art needs the full story too. The day of her transplant began hopeful. The autologous trial showed positive results with others in the clinical study. Frannie had reached a critical stage and needed to supplement her stem cells with the supply that doctors had taken from her bone marrow months before. But then we learned that her bone marrow had been damaged during the storage process, and her procedure was likely to fail due to the insufficient supply of healthy cells to inject." He twisted the damp handkerchief with his hands.

"I think parts of Sally and me died then and there. We couldn't imagine how we'd survive without Frannie." He retrieved the dandelion from his pocket and contemplated the small petals. "I had to make one of the most difficult decisions of my life that day."

The way he said *one* made Jean's breath catch. A look at Art and she could tell he'd also heard the inflection.

"I told the team to move forward and give her what stem cells they could salvage. It was our only hope *at the time*."

Jean squeezed her eyes closed. *Again with the ominous inflection.*

"Afterward, Frannie's little hand was limp for hours. Your grandma finally fell asleep in the chair, face puffy from crying. Even heavily sedated, tears leaked from her eyes. I remember thinking that if Frannie died, I'd lose Sally too."

Empathetic tears spilled from her and Art's eyes.

"Frannie lay so still that the only indications she was alive were the *whirs* and *beeps* of the machines attached to her."

Only Grandpa would still add sound effects when telling a story, albeit a worrisome one, to his grandkids.

"As a doctor, I understood the advice I would give family members, but as a father, I was stricken with terror. As both, I refused to consider anything other than life-saving options. It had been risky to move forward with the treatment and her transplant, but like I said, it had been our only hope."

He started tapping his foot against the deck. "I couldn't just sit there and wait to see if she'd survive. I was desperate. I called university hospitals conducting trials on donor bone marrow transplants. I asked if they were having success with imperfect HLA tissue matches. Finally, one institution gave me the encouragement I needed. Their preliminary data testing mice supported success from donors with less than six matching tissue markers, but they were far from gaining approval. The trial could take years."

Art rubbed his forehead. "And Mom didn't have years. You were back where you started, waiting to see how Mom would respond. But you didn't give up, did you?"

Grandpa shook his head and looked at his hands instead of Art. "In my position, it wasn't hard to access patient files secretly and find a number of patients who shared at least six HLA markers, but permissions and clinical protocol tied my hands. There was only one patient who matched that I might get away with doing what I was thinking of doing, and she was the last person I'd want to risk, next to my precious Frannie."

Her grandfather's retelling had taken a dark turn suddenly, and Jean thought of his earlier words. She could hear the remorse in his voice. Feel his angst in her gut. Jean looked to Art in panic. *Grandpa's going to say something he can't take back.*

She asked, "You made another difficult decision, right?"

"Yes." He looked at them eagerly. "Don't forget, whatever I say, I'm still your grandpa. The one you've always known. The one who loves you."

Jean nodded, aching again for Lexi.

"I waited until shifts changed and the graveyard

nurses settled in. As expected, I didn't pass a staff member in the dead of night. My heart and conscience felt heavier than the bag carrying the needed equipment, but hope is a powerful motivator and helped me move one foot in front of the other."

Her body started to tremble, scared to death about what he'd say next.

"Imogene awoke as I closed her door."

Her spirit tanked. As did Art's, if his need to sit down beside her was any indication.

"She said to me, 'Mr. Zzzerome? Frannie better? I'm scared. Can't sleep.'"

"I sat beside her and smoothed her hair across her pink forehead. My hands were shaking. I told her I was going to give her something to help her sleep and that when she woke up, Frannie would be okay, and they could have a visit soon."

"Grandpa?" Jean asked, but she wasn't sure what she was asking. Art responded by grabbing her hand and holding it tightly.

"The child, used to pokes and prods, looked at me with trust when she saw the syringe in my hand. Her concern was for Frannie alone."

Syringe. Jean thought she might vomit.

"She asked me, 'Promise Frannie be okey dokey?'" He wiped his eyes.

Jean's chest heaved as she began to sob silently. She leaned into Art to receive and offer what little comfort existed.

Her grandfather cleared his throat several times.

"Then she said, 'I'm glad I got cancer, because I got Frannie too.'"

That did it. Her sorrow for Imogene unleashed, roaring from her core, and she bawled loudly. Art tightened his hold on her, his agony mirroring hers.

His voice rough, her grandpa continued as if unable to stop after decades of silence. "Only Imogene would say something that sweet and loving. Only Imogene would be grateful to have cancer if it meant having Frannie in her life."

Their grandpa looked at them. His eyes dull. "I asked myself if her love and need for Frannie made what I was about to do okay."

No, Grandpa. The answer was no!

"But deep in my heart, I knew it didn't."

"And you continued to do what exactly?" Art asked in a voice that begged for the unexpected.

He looked away. "Once sedated, Imogene couldn't feel the insertion of the needle into her hip bone. I made sure she wouldn't feel pain or discomfort."

The mom in Jean recoiled, and she gasped. "She was a little girl, Grandpa." The mama bear in Jean roused.

He nodded and cried. "She was asleep, but I told her, 'Now, you'll always be a part of Frannie. What do you think of that?' I didn't leave until I felt confident she was all right."

"But she wasn't okay." Art glared. "You violated her."

Their grandpa flinched but didn't disagree.

"Then what? You gave her bone marrow to Mom?"

She turned to Art. "The doctor said Mom's DNA changed after her transplant."

Art gritted his teeth. "Imogene's DNA."

"Yes," their grandpa said sadly. "I didn't know that could happen at the time, but yes, that's proof that Imogene became part of your mom."

"I think Mom remembers you doing something to her that night. She thought you were Gargamel. The enemy."

His face fell. "Frannie stirred as I neared her bed with the supplies. She was too weak to move, and she could barely turn her head. I told her, 'I will always take care of you, if that's the last thing I ever do.'"

"How could you do that to Imogene?" Art asked.

Their grandpa stiffened. "Imogene saved Frannie's life. I couldn't have known about the coming flu. If I had, I wouldn't have taken her stem cells. I thought I could keep her safe and healthy."

Art's voice was quiet. "That's what the people say when they steal a man's kidney and leave him in a bath of ice. You used her. How could you do that to a child? To another human being?"

"I had plans. I watched Imogene closely over the following days to ensure she didn't get a staph infection from the procedure. The flu was unexpected. As soon as her temperature rose, I did everything I could. But then I left that night when I thought they were both stable. I still believe that we could have saved them both if they'd stayed in bed and if Frannie hadn't caused the distraction by fainting in the hall and almost dying from the fever."

Jean felt like a drone hovering above her grandpa's deck, watching the three people digest what had been said and heard. Then, like a meteor, she violently crashed to the porch. She jumped to her feet.

"How dare you blame Mom. How dare you deny responsibility for what you did. You killed Imogene, Grandpa. Not Mom. It was your job to save lives, not take one." She clutched her arms across her stomach.

"I didn't know. I *couldn't* know the flu would come," he said again. "And then, Imogene was there. Everywhere. All the time. Reminding me of what I had done," he whimpered.

Art pointed a finger. "Which is why you killed Imogene again in 1979 by forcing Mom's hand and making her disappear."

"No, not for me. For Frannie. I wanted her to make real friends. Live a normal life."

Art's neck and face turned an angry red. "Normal life? Is that what you truly believe you gave her?"

Jean shook her head back and forth slowly. "You're making more excuses. The flu is irrelevant. You think you had the right to choose who deserved to live. We'll never know if they both might have survived. They *deserved* to grow up together. To go to college and find their dreams. To be at each other's weddings. And to"—she lifted the bottom of her shirt to dry her face—"to help raise each other's families. Your *choice* made that potential outcome impossible."

"Frannie would have died without the bone marrow!" their grandpa shouted. "And the heartbreak would have killed your grandmother. Believe me, I didn't know what else to do."

Standing tall, her brother extended his hand. "Get up. You're getting dressed and coming with us. After you tell Mom the truth she deserves, we'll find you an attorney. To save your own, you stole another man's daughter. You will set this as right as possible for Imogene's father."

Jean barely recognized her grandfather, and a part of her felt as if she were losing him too. She needed to know for sure. "Would you do it again?"

The importance of the question caused her brother's lips to roll between his teeth, and more tears began to run down his cheeks.

If she thought her grandfather looked remorseful before, he looked wrecked now. "I hope I wouldn't, but then I might have lost Frannie."

For all intents and purposes, he had still lost his daughter for most of her life. "Art's right, Grandpa. You owe it to Imogene, her dad, and Mom to tell the truth."

His face scrunched up as he wept. "I'm proud of you Artsy Fartsy and Belly Jeans. And no matter what I've done, I'm proud to be your grandpa."

Art was a tender soul; even as appalled, hurt, and betrayed as he must feel, her brother was gentle as he helped their grandpa stand on shaky legs.

"Please take me to my daughter."

62

JEAN

SPRING 2022

Shane demanded more context before he'd commit to picking up Lexi from daycare, taking her to Douglas's, and meeting her and Art.

"I need you there when we talk to Mom. Art is on his way there now. Grandpa and I will arrive once he's ready."

"What's going on, honey?"

"Grandpa's responsible for Imogene's death, Shane."

She could only imagine what he wanted to say about Lexi being exposed to her grandpa, or the fact that she'd kept key information from him, but what he decided to say instead was perfect. "Jean, I love you forever. We'll get through this together."

On the drive over with her grandfather, who stared out the window solemnly, she racked her brain; what was the most compassionate way to tell her mom? Could her mom die from a broken heart before cancer? Would the truth set her free?

Art's job was to prepare her for their grandpa's arrival.

As Jean and her grandfather walked through her mother's doorway with the weight of the world on their shoulders, she was greeted by her mother's laughter, followed by Art's fake, hearty guffaw and Shane's forced howl, which sounded maniacal to Jean.

Not what she expected. Her grandpa was unfazed, lost in his thoughts. In the last hour, he'd faded and aged a hundred years.

The door resounded as she shut it, and Art said loud enough for her ears, "That must be them. I'll check. Wait here."

Jean patted her cheeks to add color and dug deep for strength. There was a big chance Jean would break down as soon as she saw her twin again.

Except, as Art rushed into the foyer, his eyes were wide, and his lips rolled between his teeth in his you-are-not-going-to-believe-this expression.

Please. Nothing could shock her anymore.

He guided her closer to the front door. For privacy? She'd rather get this over with. Then he put both his large hands on her shoulders. His eyes bored into hers. "I have to tell you something."

"Now?" Jean whispered. Pointing at their grandpa, she said the obvious without saying anything.

"Imogene's here," Art said in a hushed tone.

"What?" Jean stepped back, hands floating in the air.

She glanced at her grandfather to ensure he wouldn't faint at the news. Oddly enough, he looked more alert and calmer than he had all day.

Art grimaced. "You have to see it to believe it."

"What's gotten into you? We don't have time for games. We have to tell our dying mom that her friend died two years before she thinks she did and that Grandpa is to blame."

Art raised his brows then his palms and tilted his head in question. "*Is* she dead?"

Jean rubbed her face, convinced Art had smoked too much pot. "Please focus. How are we going to tell Mom?"

"Well," Art said, shrugging. "She has something to tell you first. Come with me."

Lost in their bizarre discussion, Jean noticed too late that their grandfather was making a move. "This is not going the way we planned." She punched her brother's arm for effect. They jogged after their grandpa, freezing at the entrance.

"Frannie," their grandpa said as he stepped into the room. "Hi, Imogene," he said without prompting, validating Imogene's existence for his daughter in the most loving way possible. "We've missed you so much."

Her mom sobbed like a little girl. "Dad, I'm sorry. I didn't know. I thought you . . . I've missed you so much."

Their grandfather walked to his daughter's side and collapsed into her embrace. "It's okay, baby. It's okay. This was always my fault. I'll be right here. Always right here."

"JEAN." Her mother's tone was welcoming as she waved for Jean to come closer.

The smile on her mom's face and her rosy cheeks made her look healthier and decades younger. She didn't look like a woman needing the mechanical bed set smack dab in the middle of her living room.

They couldn't tell her tonight. They'd wait. She and Art—if he could focus—would plan when and how to do so in the most compassionate way.

"Jean, come here, sweetie. You did it. Thank you." Her mom waved toward the chair to her right. Misunderstanding, Jean headed in that direction to sit beside her mom, only to freeze when her mom pointed at the empty seat and said, "This is Imogene!"

Astounded, a nerve twitched at the corner of Jean's mouth, and her lips curled in an involuntary smile. She looked from the empty chair to her mom, Shane, Art, and her grandpa, then back to the chair.

"See?" Art lifted his eyebrows, pursed his lips, and nodded.

"Jean?" her mom said. "Don't be rude. Say hello. She's surprised, Imogene."

Her mom was making excuses for her to a chair. A chair.

"Art? Shane?" Jean asked.

"I'm sure you have as many questions as the rest of us," Art said.

"I . . . um . . . I don't know what to say," Jean said.

"None of us do." Shane laughed like a nut again.

"Say hello," her mother said.

Aaaaahhhh. What is happening?

"Hello, Imogene. It's nice to meet you. I'm sorry. This is a bit of a shock."

"I'll say," Shane said.

"She came out of nowhere." Her mom paused as if Imogene had interrupted her. "Oh, honey, I'll tell the story."

Was that a bad impersonation of a Southern accent?

"I had just finished reorganizing the room when there was a knock. When I turned around, it was Imogene. Here in my home. I fainted, but thankfully, I fell on the bed. I can still hardly believe you're here, Imogene." Her mom reached toward the chair, sparks of joy filling her eyes.

Jean had lost all control of her facial twitches. "I can't believe this either."

Her mom giggled like a fool at something Imogene said.

"Jean, Art," her mom said. "You brought Imogene back to me."

"Mom," Art said. "I assure you, Imogene found you on her own. Right, Imogene?"

Great. Now her brother was aiding and abetting a figment of their mother's imagination.

Their mom focused on her friend, listening avidly, nodding in agreement with whatever she had said.

"You're right, Imogene. I am lucky to have my children. They are the best things that ever happened to me. Though, I fear I haven't always been the best thing that has happened to them."

"Um, it's a dream come true to meet you, Imogene, but can you please excuse Art, Shane, Grandpa, and me for one second?"

Silence answered her, and then her mom returned to the conversation with the chair.

Art had to tear their grandpa from her bedside.

As the four of them stood in the kitchen and watched who-knew-what-they-were-watching, Shane asked, "What are you guys going to do?"

Her grandfather clutched his hands against his chest, and his voice was earnest. "Kids, I will own up to what I've done. I'll do whatever it takes to convince you, Benjamin Dryker, the hospital, and the law that I'm sorry for what I've done, but not before my girl leaves this world. To confess now, I'd have to kill Imogene a third time. Please, give this old man one chance to prove he's learned what his daughter deserves and needs most—Imogene."

AFTER HAVING a heart-to-heart and making a call to her mom's doctor, Jean, Art, and Grandpa stood in the entrance to the living room, watching Frannie laugh and smile.

"We agree," Jean whispered. "We won't tell Mom. The truth will do her no good now." But the agreement only extended to her mom's well-being and while they could dedicate every iota of their love, time, and energy to their mom. Afterward and when the time was right, they would work together to do the right thing for Imogene and Benjamin Dryker.

Whether Imogene was an imaginary friend, a ghost, or an angel, she was in their lives. Their mom was dying—afraid to die—and her friend was back to bring her comfort. Imogene could love their mother in a way no one else could. Imogene would give their mother closure and peace. That's what they'd learned from their grandfather's mistakes: Imogene's devotion and love made their mother stronger. She completed her.

63

JEAN

SPRING 2022

The house was silent when Jean stirred in her mother's upstairs bed.

As she moved around, she didn't worry about awakening a supposed-Imogene in the bedroom next door.

"Make up the guest bedroom for Imogene," her mother had said last night. "She's staying for a while."

"I'll stay too." Jean pulled her brother, grandfather, and husband aside. "We can't leave her alone."

"But she's not alone," Art said.

"Not funny."

Shane hugged her tight. "Don't worry. I've got everything covered. You do what you have to do."

"I feel guilty about Lexi." She buried her face into his shoulder.

"You saw her on FaceTime—she loves school. I'll take her in the morning. We'll take this one day at a time, babe."

"Love you," she said before kissing him.

"Get a room," Art said. "I'm taking Grandpa home." Shane left with them.

She slipped downstairs for coffee. Her mom had slept in her new bed after having fallen asleep mid-sentence last night. How long did they have? Months? Weeks? Days? Was this why Imogene had reappeared?

Two hot cups of coffee in hand, Jean pulled Imogene's seat from the night before to the side of the bed. First come, first served must be the way it works with imaginary friends. Or, as Art had argued at one point, "What if she's a ghost?"

"Martha looks good on you," her mother said in a sleepy voice.

Jean wiggled in the designer flannel pajamas. "She feels good on me."

"You can have them," her mom said as she yawned and reached for a cup.

The aroma of coffee and a feeling of contentment filled the room.

"I love you, Mom."

"I love you too."

Jean wiped her eyes on her sleeve. "I have a confession, and I owe you an apology."

"Lay it on me. I need all the forgiveness I can get too."

"Okay, here it goes. Peter Whittaker's son is the detective we hired."

Her mom's jaw dropped. "Ah-ha, that's why you were cagey about him."

"Are you mad?"

"I would've been more afraid than mad. But not now. She's here. She's finally here. I've learned much about the stories I've told myself over the years. Destructive ones I believed to be true."

Her mom's chest heaved.

"Are you hurting?"

"Now that Imogene's back, I'm afraid to die. It's not fair. I want to know you better, see Art settle down, and witness Lexi grow up. I want to be with you. I've made many mistakes as a mother and daughter. My father . . . I thought . . . everything has been my fault. I want to stay and be a part of your lives. It's all I ever wanted, but I told myself these stories about what happened, and what could happen, and my beliefs colored everything in my life."

"Oh, Mom." Jean set her cup down, took her mother's to set it aside, scooted onto the side of the bed, and clutched her mother's hands like she would have held Lexi after a nightmare. She spoke softly, reassuringly. "Mom, you did the best you could with what little truth you were given. Nothing is your fault. You were a child when the seeds of your story were planted."

"Will you forget me?"

"I couldn't if I wanted to. And I promise you, really promise you, I never want to."

"I hope she stays with me until I go," her mom said, and Jean's heart stopped.

Did her mother understand on some level?

"Oh, what have I done? What can I say or do now to redeem myself for how I raised you and Art and treated my parents? I thought I needed Imogene's forgiveness, but as it turns out, I need my family's."

"You know what? Someone wise gave me some great advice once." Jean gently rubbed her mother's chilled hands while leaning down to stare into her eyes. "Make the cake you want to eat."

Her mom smiled. "Yes. Make the cake I want to eat."

"You still have time. Bake away." Jean leaned back, wiped her eyes, and reached for their coffees.

"I need to see my dad again."

Dad.

"Art and I will pick him up today. Okay? He will be here as much as you want him to be. I can promise you that."

Sniffling, her mom nodded and smiled. "Thank you. He's one of the many ingredients I need for my life-cake."

They sipped their coffee in silence for a few minutes.

"Last night, I had another nightmare," her mother said.

"Why didn't you call for me?"

"I don't know. I'm not used to having anyone here." Her mother's lower lip quivered like Lexi's did whenever she was scared. "Maybe I was afraid to tell you about them."

"Why?"

"I don't know, but I was. I still am."

"I won't dissect your dreams, Mom. Get them off your chest."

Her mother closed her eyes. "The first was about this boy from St. Agnes. He used to poke at me and call me a weirdo and other names. He never teased Imogene. I forgot all about him until I opened a Facebook account."

It took everything Jean had to school her features. "Go on."

"My mom was in the dream. She didn't say anything, just looked at me as if she was waiting for me to say or do something. Then it jumped to a special meeting spot Imogene and I had at the hospital. She was opening a present I got her. And . . . the present . . . It was a real present. A copy of *Oliver Twist*. But now, I can't remember when she really opened it."

Sadness and confusion filled her mom's eyes as she opened them, and the corners of her lips drooped as she glanced at the chair where Imogene had sat the night before.

"Next, in the dream, Imogene and I were in my bedroom at home, it was time for her to go home, and then, she was gone, just gone. Do you know, I don't know how Imogene ever got home? Or how she got to my house sometimes. After school, we walked together, but how did she get around? I can't remember Mr. Dryker coming to our house. I don't know why I've never thought of this before."

Jean's heart fluttered. "You know dreams. They never make sense," she said. "It was a long time ago. You were a kid and not worried about logistics."

Her mom's eyes were wide with panic as she turned back to Jean. "But Jean, Imogene can't explain it to me either. Please be honest with me. Yesterday, could you see . . ."

This was it; the most important moment of her relationship with her mother. The moment Jean would either celebrate or regret for the rest of her years. She had one chance to get it right and to tell her mom the truth or the truth her mom might need in her final days. Which was it to be?

Just then, her mom's eyes darted toward the stairs, a look of relief flooding her face.

Jean thought she might resent being interrupted by an invisible bestie in this one-off experience with her mother, but she'd have to be blind not to recognize that Imogene was a piece of her mom that had been missing for far too long; Jean loved her for being a part of her mother again.

"Jean?" Her mother looked at her with uncertainty.

This was a test—a gigantic life-changing test.

Thinking of Lexi and Booby, Dr. Pfeiffer had cautioned her and Shane not to interact with Booby, but she'd also told them not to dismiss her. Surely there was some wiggle room when it came to her mom dying of cancer.

And just like that, Jean knew what she needed to do.

She smiled. "Good morning, Imogene." Turning back to her mom, she said, "We have a few hours before Angela and Art arrive to share his good news.' If you're feeling up for it, would you and Imogene like to see my messy house?"

Her mom's eyes lit up. "I thought you'd never ask. We'd love to."

64

GRIFFIN

SPRING 2022

As far as birthdays went, Griffin's had started well. Win some, lose some.

He'd visited his mom and it had cheered her to understand her husband's experience that sad day many years ago.

With some finagling, Griffin had paid out of pocket to legally secure interment rights for Imogene. They'd recorded the burial of Imogene's ashes and handed over a certificate, which Griffin had dropped in the mail to Benjamin Dryker. Now, Imogene only needed a funeral and a headstone, which Rodney Schultz paid for.

And after a mind-blowing update from Jean, Griffin was confident the twins would hold George Jerome accountable.

A true gift was stamping the file *Solved*. "This was for you, Dad."

The only loss to his day was when he'd stopped by the music store to finish purchasing his clarinet.

"Someone came in and snatched it up," the store manager said, snapping his fingers. "I'd intended to hold it for you, but she had a very pretty smile."

"Can't compete with that. I would have sold it to her too."

He left empty-handed but with an assurance that the man would call when one became available. Griffin wouldn't give up. He would pull out the old one in the attic for repairs and maintenance. He'd wanted a clean slate, but he had time. Lots of time to live.

When he got home, he knew his wife and son would be ready to celebrate. The night before, Annie baked a cake with applesauce and Greek yogurt instead of eggs and oil.

He couldn't wait.

The proof was in the pudding, and the aroma of chocolate cake made his mouth water.

Annie kissed him. "Happy birthday, big boy."

Tony's hug followed. "Happy birthday, old man."

"Hey, hey. Not so fast."

"Can Dad open his present before dinner and cake?" Tony asked Annie. "I can't wait."

"More slippers, I hope." *Not.*

"Ha-ha," Annie said. "Tony, you do the honors."

The gift was large and heavy, but the paper gave way to padding underneath.

"No shaking," Tony said as he rubbed his palms together.

"Nice wrapping paper. I get the hint." Griffin pulled off the heart-printed paper and stilled.

“You didn’t,” he said as he unzipped the case and the fresh scent of key oil and cork wax filled the space, better than any cake might. His fingers tingled as he brushed the beautiful, black clarinet and pulled it out, putting it together by memory.

The clerk was right; Annie had a very pretty smile.

Tony leaned over to grab his own instrument that had been hiding in the corner.

“Want to jam together, Dad?”

“Music to my ears, Son,” Griffin said.

65

JEAN

SPRING 2022

As Lexi slept upstairs that night, Jean leaned into Shane's strong chest and asked, "Do we think Booby is gone?"

"I think Dr. Pfeiffer was right—friends and preschool are doing her good."

"She was right about a lot of things."

"Should we cancel our appointment tomorrow so you can be with your mom?" Shane asked.

"No. Let's keep it. We should ask her how to explain my mom's cancer, and Imogene, to Lexi. Not to mention Grandpa, someday." Jean had a new appreciation for how complicated *family-ing* could be and what a luxury it was to have choices with counseling.

"I'm sorry I didn't tell you about Grandpa. More than anything, I wanted to give him the benefit of being innocent until proven guilty."

Shane rested his chin atop her head and remained

silent, proving he knew exactly what she did and didn't need to hear right now.

Her heart hurt wondering what would happen to her grandpa once he confessed. "His reputation will be in tatters, and the hospital will fire him from the board. Will he also end up in prison? And if he does, will we visit him? I refuse to take Lexi to a prison."

"Slow down, babe. One step at a time."

"I don't know how to reconcile the grandpa I've loved all my life and the man I've learned about. He always made me feel special, and I've admired his passion to raise money for the hospital and help others. How can he be the same man who used a child like that?"

Shane held her tight. "Perhaps he's spent his life trying to make up to Imogene through his choices."

"Maybe. I don't know what to think or feel. Shane, I like Dr. Pfeiffer, but I think I need to find a separate counselor to help me work through my feelings about Grandpa and what's to come with my mom. Maybe Art will want to go too."

"Whatever you need, honey."

She turned her face into his chest and inhaled his scent—a combination of cologne and laundry detergent.

He said, "When I picked up Lexi today, I met Griffin's wife. She has a picture of her family on her desk."

Uh-oh.

"You lied. Griffin's a looker."

Jean rubbed her cheek on his chest. "But you're a keeper."

He kissed her crown. "Then why aren't we working?"

Secrets could ruin relationships. Jean understood that now more than ever. "I don't want to lose you. I'm afraid."

"Of what?" he asked, tightening his hold.

She took a deep breath and remained planted against him. "I don't want any more children."

"Is that what you've been afraid to tell me?"

"Yes." She sat up straight to look at him. "You want more children. I know you do."

"You're right. I do. But it takes more than me wanting them. I also want you. I also want Lexi."

"And I want to work," she said. "You were right. I need something for myself. I think I want to get my private investigator license."

"Babe, if it means we can move forward as a family and as a couple, I will support anything you want to do."

"Thank you. I should have given you more credit. I'm sorry, and I love you." She settled back into his embrace and said, tongue-in-cheek, "It's good I have your support, because I have an appointment with Carla-with-a-C Clarke on Friday."

His laughter rumbled through his chest and against her cheek. The vibration wound its way from her head, to her heart, to her breasts, to her stomach, and continued downward. Shane's laughter had always been an aphrodisiac. She sat up and began to unbutton his shirt.

"Yeah? What's this about?" Shane smiled.

Jean winked. "We have much to *discuss*."

66

IMOGENE

SPRING 2022

Imogene stepped next to Frannie's bed. Her friend looked peaceful as she slept.

For twelve days, as Frannie's health had declined and she'd grown frail and ill, Frannie's family had embraced Imogene. Imogene knew they couldn't see her, but she didn't care. She felt their love. She cherished how she'd become a part of their humor out of Frannie's earshot—more than anything they could have said or done, their private jokes had made her feel like one of the family and given her a sense of what it might have been like to have lived and had a family of her own.

"Who ate the last cookie?" Art would ask, complaining. "I wanted it."

"Imogene," Jean would say, her mouth full.

"Who left a Lego on the floor?" George would ask, hopping from one foot to the other, and Lexi would say, "Oh, honey. Imogene did."

On the nights no one wanted to do the dishes after

Art and Douglas had cooked a huge meal, Angela said, "Imogene promised to do them tomorrow."

Even the hospice worker joined in, explaining, "There are many Imogenes in my line of work. Believe me."

And Imogene was convinced Bonnie Bell could see her as the conure stared directly at her and trilled, "Pretty bird."

She knew Frannie's children were sad to lose their mother now—just when they'd finally found her. George was consoled by the knowledge that his daughter had entered this world surrounded by love, and she'd leave it being loved even more.

Frannie's sleeping had grown more frequent and had lasted for longer periods of time until she didn't wake for hours, her family always within arm's reach. Imogene understood why Frannie's children doubted that she knew they were still there, but Imogene knew Frannie was aware of them all.

But now, it was time to go. For both of them.

Last week, Frannie had confided that she didn't want Jean and Art to wish her gone or to say, *It's for the best. She's no longer suffering.* But Imogene understood the truth. For the living, reaching the point where and when they could love someone enough to say, *It's for the best* was the closest they could get to letting go wholeheartedly. In fact, it was a human's only moment of unconditional love, letting go of someone they'd rather never lose.

Imogene leaned down and whispered in Frannie's ear, "Frannie, why did the chicken cross the road?"

Frannie's lip twitched and turned upward on one corner as if smirking.

Jean, who hadn't taken her eyes off her mother for over an hour, jerked forward in the bedside chair and beckoned her brother, who'd been in the kitchen cooking most of the week. "Art, Mom's smiling. Grandpa, can you see her?"

But George couldn't look. To handle his daughter's passing, he read *Oliver Twist* aloud to Frannie and Lexi, who was fast asleep on his lap:

> *"I know that she deserves the best and purest love the heart of man can offer," said Mrs. Maylie. "I know that the devotion and affection of her nature require no ordinary return, but one that shall be deep and lasting."*

"She looks peaceful," Art said as he sat on the other side of the bed, next to where Imogene stood. He took Frannie's free hand and stroked it.

Imogene patted Frannie's arm and whispered, "Oh, honey . . ."

Frannie's head nodded in Art and Imogene's direction.

"She's smiling again. I love you, Mom," Jean said.

"Mom, I'll never forget you," Art said, kissing her hand.

"You'll always be in our hearts and on our minds." Jean sniffled.

"Frannie, how come the chicken crossed the road?" Imogene asked again.

Again, Frannie smiled without awakening.

"To get to the other side," Imogene said. "Come on. We'll cross together."

AUTHOR'S NOTE

First and foremost, thank you to Ryan Green, the bravest father and video game programmer, for creating the game, *The Dragon Cancer*. I learned about Joel while watching his accompanying documentary, *Thank You for Playing*, I think of him often. Friends, watch this documentary for a profoundly gut-wrenching understanding of what it's like to be a parent to a child with cancer.

I turned to the professionals for processes, records, and details: Assistant Sherrif Daniel Gonzales, retired Director, Dept. of Community Response Bridgette Dean, the records teams at the San Francisco Police Department and Sacramento Police Department, the staff of Cypress Cemetery in Daly City, Oakland Children's Hospital, and the National Center for Missing & Exploited Children. Any mistakes or exaggerations are my own.

I read and watched helpful resources: Anton Visser's book, *Private Investigation*, and Martha Stewart's books, *The Martha Rules,* and *Martha Stewart's Organizing: The Manual for Bringing Order to Your Life, Home & Routines.*

I'm not a doctor. Nor have I worked in the medical field in any capacity. When it comes to healthcare, the only thing I'm 100% confident about is my admiration for those who care for others and those who research treatments and cures. Thank you for being you if you are one of these outstanding humans.

I am an optimist. I do not intend to suggest that someone diagnosed with AML will suffer Frannie's fate. They absolutely can survive and thrive.

I am a fiction author. I research and apply what I can without my mind exploding, and then I try to explain it in a way that won't distract my readers.

To learn more about Allogeneic and Autologous stem cell transplants, I watched the below Leukemia & Lymphoma Society videos on Youtube several times, and I visited cancer.gov on a daily basis to learn more.

- Allogeneic Stem Cell Transplants: https://youtu.be/oLMWPgo6jUY
- Autologous Stem Cell Transplants: https://youtu.be/serLxSvHIBg

I adjusted historical dates to work with the story's timeline when necessary. In this case, I adapted the history of bone marrow/stem cell transplants as follows:

1973: First successful perfect-match transplant from an unrelated donor.

1979: Autologous research and trials begin. *(Frannie's trial began in 1976-1977.)*

1979: A bone marrow registry begins, now known as Be the Match https://bethematch.org/become-a-donor. (I didn't adjust this date in the book. I just thought I would share it if you want to be a donor. Let me know if you do!)

1980-1990s: Research and trials for imperfect-match transplants begin. *(Frannie's dad finds a university studying mice in 1977.)*

If you'd like to learn more about the history of bone marrow transplants, this is an easy-to-read account: https://www.bmtinfonet.org/video/history-blood-and-marrow-transplantation

While I have a degree in Psychology, I am not a practicing psychologist. I relied on the following sites and Mary Jo Hazard, M.A., M.F.T., to gain further insight into child psychology & development, as well as the changing perspectives and viewpoints over the years.

- Clevelandclinic.org
- Thrive.psu.edu
- Pediatricianeducation.org

I appreciate your patience with my changes and apologize for any medical inaccuracies.

I wish you health and happiness.

Teri

ACKNOWLEDGMENTS

I had a seed of an idea in 2018, which needed a pot. Authors Maya Rushing Walker and Lisa Manterfield, thank you for a safe place to share all things writing, publishing, and marketing.

A seed needs soil throughout its life. Thank you to my book coach, Lizette Clarke, and beta readers, Ginger Knight and author Elaine Schroller. Each of you gave me the much-needed, otherwise absent, confidence to move forward. Oh, honey, Mary Jo Hazard, you were the first reader. Your response was what I needed to carry on. Your decades-long family counselor experience and historical insight made this story possible. Karsen and Crystal, it was fun to bounce around ideas as Frannie's character evolved. Adam, thanks for encouraging me to stretch and write something new and unfamiliar. Bridgette and Daniel, thanks for fielding my questions about police records. My fellow Irrational Muses, thanks for letting me be irrational daily. Donald, I appreciate your discretion.

Author Cathey Graham Nickell, thanks for watering this plant. You've answered no less than ten million texts about this novel and read three (or four?!) drafts. From April to July 2020, we were writing buddies during unprecedented times. And you answered on December 7,

2020, when I needed to call someone before my family was awake on the West Coast and cry my heart out. Thank you. I met you in an online course several years ago, but have never met you in person (!!), and I can't imagine life without you. Thanks for being my who-says-we-need-to-meet-in-person-to-be-besties friend. You're the bee's knees.

Plants need pruning and, oftentimes, dead-heading. Thanks to my editors at all levels and through multiple versions: Paige Duke, Edna Bay, My Brother's Editor, The Missing Ink, and Fair Crack of the Whip Proofreading & Editing. Author A.J. Banner, I learned more from you in our one-hour conversation about writing and editing than any course I've taken.

A growing plant can outgrow its pot. There is no one I'd rather replant with than the team at Andrea Hurst Literary Agency. Andrea, Katie, and crew, you made *Finding Imogene* blossom. Your guidance, support, and friendship are some of the best outcomes of writing this novel.

This seed needed a lot of inspiration and sunshine, and for those lovely rays, I'm looking with heart-shaped eyes at Maggie & Devvie. And you'll always be in my heart and on my mind, Bonnie Lou & Bonna Lee.

Ted, you're the green thumb, the pollinator. Thank you for being you.

P.S.: Inspiration credit to Charles Dickens, C. S. Lewis, and the creators of *The Smurfs*, and *Oliver!*. Thanks for existing.

ABOUT THE AUTHOR

Teri lives in D.C. with her partner. She is a proud auntie and sister. Her novels are often inspired by characters she meets while traveling. To learn more about Teri, please visit her website www.tericase.com.

You can also follow Teri on Instagram and Threads. Her handle is @terilcase. She will follow you back!

Also by Teri Case

Tiger Drive
In the Doghouse

Made in United States
North Haven, CT
28 June 2024